THE AMNESIA PROJECT
Copyright (c) 2017 Andrew D Williams

The right of Andrew Williams to be identified as the author of the Work has been asserted him in accordance with the Copyright, Designs and Patents Act 1988.

This is a work of fiction. Names, characters, places and incidents are used fictitiously. Any resemblance to actual events or persons, living or dead, is coincidental.

All rights reserved. No part of this publication may be reproduced or transmitted in any form or by any means, electronic or otherwise, without written permission from the author.

First, thanks go to Coenie Hattingh, for his advice regarding semi-feasible ways of causing amnesia. If the end result makes no sense, it's probably my fault rather than his!

But ultimately, this book is for Jon, who's been there throughout the gestation period. I hope it was worth the wait.

Want more? Sign up at the link below to get your FREE book:

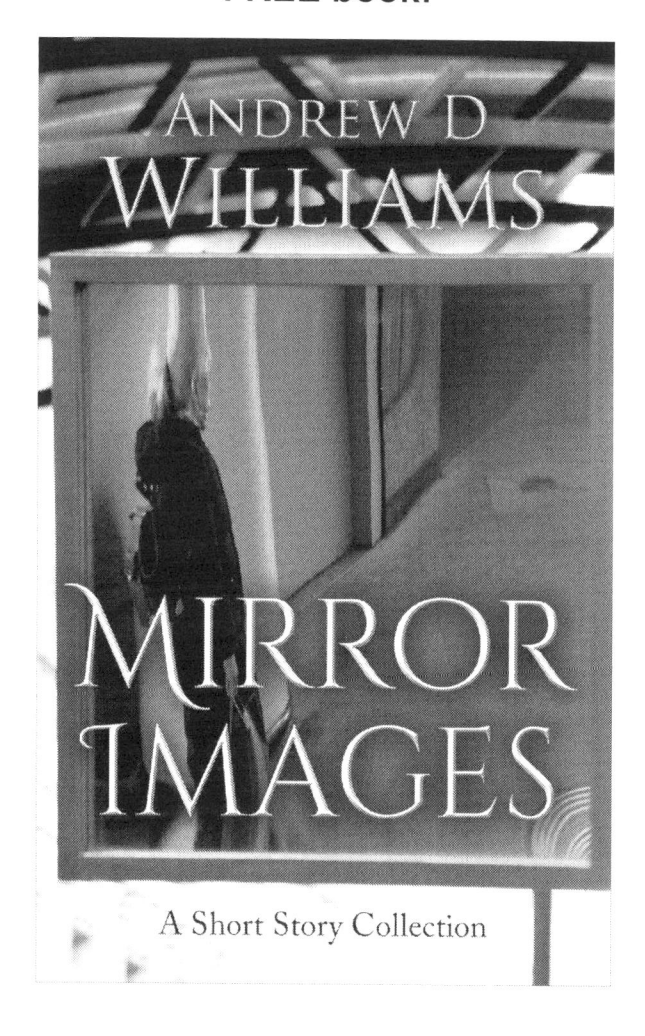

http://andrewdwilliams.co.uk/get-your-free-book/

Contents

The Package	4
TAP 1	7
Jimmy	28
The Story	44
The Message	46
Research	62
The Visitor	76
Detained	87
The Mad Hatter's Tea Party	110
The Investigation Begins	132
Escape	150
Sally	160
The Waiting	178
Evie's Gang	180
Rescue	202
The Bar	212
The Watcher	219
Insomnia	223
The Interrogation	226
Not Quite Right	233
Morning	237
Evidence	242
Raided	248
The Call	261
Lisa's Story	270
The Machine	291
Rob's Story	295
The Deal	310
The Raid	314
One Hour	317
Standoff	321
The Plan	330
Aftermath	341
The End Of The Project	347
Appendix - I Feel I'm Falling	355

The Package

Henry Ford sighed. He knew nothing about cars. Neither had his mother, he often thought, or she would have realised how much bullying she was letting her little boy in for.

The article in front of him, a piece by one of his ever dwindling staff of freelance writers, was about cars. That was about all he could make of it. Henry wondered if he could improve the article by crossing out all the words he didn't understand but felt the result would be something like "there are some new cars out."

Maybe George could have done something with it, but…

"Boss!"

Henry looked up, trying to suppress his irritation. Eddie didn't deserve it, after all.

"Hey, boss! Check this out!"

Eddie ran into the office, panting furiously. He looked like a man in his late twenties but, inside, Eddie remained somewhere about twelve years old. His shirt was buttoned up wrong, one of his shoelaces was undone and his mop of brown hair had gone feral.

"Calm down, Eddie. Deep breaths."

Eddie stood panting for a moment.

He was enthusiastic, you had to give him that. He wasn't cut out to be a journalist and he never would be, but his dream of following in his father's footsteps was unshakable. Henry tried to keep him occupied with general office duties like fetching the mail – though these days the mail was increasingly light.

More than one former staff member had asked why Henry kept him on. He simply couldn't let him go. The magazine was the only workplace Eddie had ever known, and he was only there because he wanted to impress his father.

Not that George was easily impressed.

"Now, what's all the fuss about?"

Eddie grinned. "Something special, boss. We've got a package. Set of tapes. I've been listening to 'em, typing them up. They're... wow!"

Henry raised an eyebrow. The magazine was going through some lean times, and he doubted a mysterious package in the mail was going to turn their luck around, but it was a distraction from an article about the new ninety-seven valve turbo injection hybrid something or other. If the article was sending him to sleep, he dreaded to think what their few remaining readers would make of it.

"What's the story, Eddie?"

"They're from this guy, and he says he's lost his memory – like that film, the one with that man with all the post-it notes..."

Henry made a circular "go on" motion with his hand. Henry sometimes wished Eddie came with a fast forward control.

"...anyway, he's trying to figure out who he is, and there are people trying to find him and..."

"Sounds like a fictional piece."

Eddie looked crushed.

"I might run it anyway, Eddie. We could use something interesting. Do you know what it's called?"

"I don't know," admitted Eddie. "I've done the first tape already. Sorry for any spelling mistakes."

Henry smiled as he took Eddie's papers. It was a slow news day; he quite liked the idea of an entertaining read in the name of work. And why not run the story anyway? He scanned the first page, and then the second - a fictional piece, then. In quite an unusual style.

His eyes caught a date.

"Is this right, Eddie? Is this story really set in 2004?"

Eddie nodded.

"Over a decade ago. Why not today?"

"I don't know," Eddie repeated. "Do you want me to type the rest?"

"Maybe later, Eddie." Henry didn't relish trying to decipher those spelling mistakes yet, knowing that they'd probably outnumber the correct words. "Do you mind if I listen to the tapes myself? You can type them up when I'm done."

Eddie nodded, grinning, before dashing off to fetch them.

Henry gave the car piece a final glance over and moved it to his "ready" pile. Buried somewhere in the back of the magazine, he doubted anyone would see it anyway.

A few moments later, a stack of small tapes sat on Henry's desk. Too small for a regular cassette recorder - and who used those any more anyway? - but just the right size for one of those old dictation recorders, or maybe an ancient answering machine. Either Eddie had found a tape recorder that they would fit, though where he'd dug it up from Henry couldn't begin to guess, or whoever sent the tapes had thoughtfully included something to play them on. But why tapes? Why not a CD or a memory stick?

Each tape was labelled: TAP1, TAP2.

What sort of person couldn't finish writing the word TAPE? Aside from Eddie.

Henry shrugged, put the first tape in the machine and pressed play.

TAP 1

Hello, whoever you are. You don't know me, I'm afraid, but that's okay. I don't really know me either – at least, who I was. But I'm getting ahead of myself. I want to tell you my story, and I don't know whether you'll believe it or not. That's okay too. I'm not sure I believe it either, and I was there. It doesn't matter. What matters is that people hear it – that they learn about Grace Meadows, and Dr Hawkins, and the project. Because if they don't, it could happen again.

I've heard it said that we are the sum of our memories. I think there might be some truth to this. But I think we're more than that – take away the memories, and there's still a lot left. Perhaps the more important part. I prefer to think that our actions and our friends define us more than our memories. But then again, perhaps I'm biased.

Yes, okay. I'm getting there.

I just wanted to give them a bit of an introduction, okay?

Fine, fine. I'll just get on with it. You two have no style, you know that?

I woke up one morning with a start and a sore head. Perhaps I should lay off the late night vodkas, I thought to myself. And could someone please turn down the sun?

As my eyes adjusted to the light I began to take stock of my surroundings. I was in bed, which was a good start. I was alone, which wasn't so good. Getting blind drunk in company is one thing, but getting blind drunk on your own is never a good sign. That suggested I was trying to forget something, but whatever it was I'd been trying to forget, I'd now clean forgotten. I'd probably remember in time, I thought – hopefully after breakfast, and hopefully not along with a load of other stuff I'd done whilst half pickled and would want to forget as well.

I didn't recognise this room. The bed was clean and reasonably soft, the walls a dull and inoffensive magnolia, the carpet brown and hard-wearing. This was not my bedroom. A quick look around (and the discovery of a bible in the bedside cabinet drawer) soon explained things. I was in a hotel room. Not a very expensive one, given the general lack of ostentation and the generous amount of wear on everything. And given the leaflet stating that breakfast was served in a box and contained nothing hot, fresh, or edible. So I was in a cheap hotel room.

It took me just a few minutes to locate my clothes and get dressed. I didn't feel recovered enough yet to experiment with the shower thermostat – even when fully awake, I'd think twice about a cold shower. The "breakfast box" sounded equally unappealing and, after a quick check that I had my wallet and other personal effects, I decided the time had come to check out.

There was just one problem. I had no idea where I was or where I wanted to go. Come to that, who was I?

Amnesia is a frightening thing. It's amazing how much we shape ourselves around our memories. If anything contradicts our memory, even with evidence, we struggle to accept it. Our memories are the thread that we weave through existence, and we remember everything perfectly. Of course we do. Because if we can't rely on our memory, we can't rely on our thoughts, our motivations, our morality, and then we'd have to ask exactly what is the point of anything we do? If we don't remember everything correctly, then maybe nothing we remember is right.

I used to be an expert on memory. At least, I think I was. It would explain my interest in and my obsession with the subject. Problem is, I have no idea who I was. I could remember random little things, like nursery rhymes or pop songs, but not important things like my name, where I lived, or even how old I was. I had no ID in my wallet, just a bundle of cash. No credit cards, no driving licence (could I drive? I didn't even know that). No clues. I have no memory of events before waking up that morning in that hotel room.

There was no-one at the counter when I went down to the front desk. In a way this was good news - I didn't know my own name, so checking out would be difficult, and I didn't know how long I'd stayed there or how much I owed them. Besides, with nowhere else to go, I might want to come back later.

On the other hand, I must have booked the room under some name, and the number on the keycard (128) might give some clue. Then again, I felt a little embarrassed at confessing to not knowing who I was.

Instead, I took a look around the reception area. Apart from the door I had come in by, which led into the back and towards the rooms, there was a nondescript door labelled "Staff Only" and a set of glass double doors that led to the outside world. It was sunny, but a few wisps of cloud in the sky suggested it was not yet the height of summer.

It hit me then that I didn't even know what date it was.

I didn't know who or where I was. I wasn't even sure *what* I was - did I have a job? A wife? A family? No ring on my left hand, but that wasn't compulsory.

All I could remember were odd glimmers. I knew how to walk, talk and dress myself. I knew how to read. I knew that there were a hundred pennies to the pound and three feet to a yard. I didn't know who the Prime Minister was, or remember any being in power. Just odd glimmers, randomly sneaking up on me when I wasn't looking.

"Can I help you, sir?"

I turned around, startled out of my reverie. While I was staring out at the sunshine and staring inwards at the abyss of my mind, a young man had arrived at the reception desk. I needed answers to at least some of my questions so I swallowed my pride and approached the counter.

"Yes, can you tell me who I am?"

"Sir?"

"I woke up this morning in room 128 with no memory. What name do you have on the booking?"

"Sir, I can't give out personal information like that."

"You can't tell me my own name?"

"I can't tell you who booked a room without authorisation."

"But I booked the room!" I paused. "At least, I think I did."

"I'm sorry, sir."

I thought for a moment. "Okay. Then can you tell me where I am?"

"Sir?"

"My location. My point of reference. The place where I am. Where am I?"

"The Travel Hotel reception. Reading, sir."

Reading, Berkshire? I waited for another flash of memory but none came.

"Thanks."

"Are you checking out today, sir?"

"I don't know," I replied. "For now I think I'll go find breakfast."

"You need to order the Breakfast Box the night before…"

"I mean a proper breakfast. Know anywhere good?"

He shook his head. "No, but there's a burger place across the road that sells a breakfast menu until eleven. You'd better hurry, though."

I looked at my wrist. I had no watch, but it was clearly almost eleven. I thanked him and went out into the morning sun.

The burger place was quite busy and I barely made it to the counter before the breakfast menu boards started being replaced with lunchtime menus. I saw little to inspire my appetite on either selection but ordered a coffee and a bacon roll to take away, preferring to eat out in the sunshine rather than sit in the plastic-lined sweatshop.

The roll and coffee went some way to improving my headache, but my memory remained elusive. At least now I knew where I was, but with no idea where I should be or why I was here the information was quite useless. With nothing else to do I began to take stock of what I had.

On me - a faded pair of jeans, a T-shirt and a light jacket. My feet sported a pair of worn trainers. In my jeans pockets I had my wallet (with plenty of cash, but not a vast amount), my room key and a packet of cigarettes, which seemed strange to me as I didn't remember being a smoker. Indeed, I hadn't felt the need for a cigarette since I'd woken up.

In my jacket pocket I found a crumpled piece of paper and a small key. I smoothed out the paper and tried to make sense of it.

"Oh free force heaven hate. Two for one, three for two. Ask for Jimmy."

On the other side, the message was clearer – but alarming.

"They are looking for you. Don't fall asleep."

I returned to the Travel Hotel reception and asked for a pen. Writing the first few words out again underneath the first line, it seemed clear that it was my own handwriting on this note. I suspected as much when I first read it but this really only left more questions than it answered.

"Do you know anyone called Jimmy?" *I asked the young man.*

"No, I don't think so. Is he a friend of yours?"

"I have no idea," I replied. "I left a note for myself and I don't know what I'm talking about."

"Can I see it?" he asked. "I like puzzles."

I felt a strange reluctance to show the message to him, and pulled it away when he reached for it. "Sorry," I replied. "I can't give out personal information like that."

And with that I walked out, my efforts to be suave hampered when I tried to pull the door instead of pushing it.

Oh free force heaven hate…?

Largely because I thought it might trigger a memory, I pulled the cigarette packet out of my pocket. I still felt no desire to smoke or any memory of doing so and realised that I had no lighter or matches. Why was I carrying a pack of cigarettes around when I didn't smoke and had no means to light them?

The seal was broken. I'd obviously opened it already. Feeling a little daft, I opened the packet - and found, not a collection of cancer sticks, but a cassette tape.

Even with my memory broken, I'm pretty sure that's not where I normally keep my cassettes. Hey, did I even have cassettes? Wasn't music all on CD these days?

Puzzling as mysterious tapes and cryptic messages are, I had other questions. It was a short walk into town, and at least there I could answer one of them. What the hell was the date? I didn't even know how old I was. When I looked in the mirror this morning I saw a man of around thirty, still with plenty of dark hair and a slightly pointed nose. Two brown eyes, bright but looking a little lost (or was that just me being poetic?) and a thin face that looked like I'd missed a few too many dinners. No piercings or tattoos, no scars or marks. I was disappointingly normal.

On the plus side, it meant I should have no fear about going into town for such simple pleasures as a newspaper. There was an array of papers in the first newsagents that I encountered and, not remembering which papers I routinely buy (if any), I settled for a local one - if I was in the news, which was unlikely, I'd probably be in a smaller paper.

I was not in the news.

The date - 7th June, 2004 - held little information for me. I could work out how old I was if I knew my date of birth, which I didn't. With no knowledge of recent events I had no idea how long it had been since my loss of memory. How long had I been missing? Days? Weeks? I doubted it could be long - my clothes were worn but not worn out, and I had a supply of cash from somewhere.

Did I have a job? How long had I been absent?

What do you do when you wake up with no memory? Do you go to the police? Do you go to the hospital? I tried them both. Finding Reading's police station, I asked at the counter if they could help. They couldn't help. With no identifying marks or any personal effects of note, and with no missing person reports that matched my description, there was little they could do. They tried a PNC check, but searching computer records requires you to have something to search for. They asked me questions about my general health - had I suffered a head injury? (Not that I knew). Was I epileptic? (How should I know?)

In the end, with nothing more they could do, they told me to go to the hospital for a check up. So I did. Was I an emergency case? No, I just had no memory. Could I fill in some forms and wait until someone was available? Well, I tried. I had no name, no National Insurance number, no medical card reference, no registered doctor. My home address? No idea. Date of birth? No idea. Most of my form remained blank. I explained this to the reception nurse. She told me to fill in what I could. I explained I couldn't fill in any of it, and how long could I expect to wait? She flustered for a moment and then went to answer the telephone. I left the form on the counter and walked out.

No nearer to regaining my memory, I went to a coffee shop to drown my sorrows in caffeine and sugar. I'm not sure whether this was because I don't drink at this time of the day or simply because there wasn't anywhere serving alcohol at this time of the afternoon.

"You okay?"

I looked up and into a pair of blue eyes surrounded by remarkably long lashes.

"You've been sipping that same cup of coffee for half an hour."

"It's fine," I replied. "I'm savouring it."

The owner of the eyes, a girl in her late twenties, sat down on the chair opposite me. Beige trousers and practical flat shoes were matched with a bright top for a flash of colour. A white handbag rested on one shoulder, full of mysterious shapes that suggested she was prepared for anything.

"Can I ask you to do something for me?" she asked. "There's a guy outside that's been following me. I think he might leave me alone if he thinks you're my boyfriend."

I smiled. "Where?" I asked, turning to look.

"No! Don't look!" she hissed. "Pretend I've just told a funny joke and laugh."

I forced a laugh. She frowned for a moment, and then brightened again.

"Good enough," she said. "I'd give it a four out of ten, but it'll do." She smiled. "Just kidding. Thanks for this."

"So do you have a boyfriend?" I asked.

"You don't waste much time," she replied.

"I… uh…"

She laughed. "Are you available or are you just playing with me?"

"Actually, I have no idea."

"Bad break up?"

"No - well, I don't know. I woke up this morning with no idea who I am. I could be married for all I know."

"Good one," she laughed. When I didn't join in, she stopped. "Hey, are you serious?"

"Completely."

"You don't know your name or anything?"

"Nope."

"Not even a credit card?"

"Just some cash in my wallet."

"No mobile phone? Nothing?"

"Not even a wristwatch."

"That's weird."

I wasn't sure why not having a watch made me weird. "Thanks," I said.

"Not the watch," she said. "Everything. It's like one of those science fiction films where they wipe the guy's memory and remove anything that can identify him."

"I wouldn't know," I replied. "I know I've seen films but I couldn't tell you which ones."

"So if we go to the cinema tonight there's a chance you'll remember the ending?"

I laughed at that. "Miss, I could be married."

"I'll take the chance. And my name's Lisa. Lisa Smith."

"I'm…"

"Nearly had it, then, did you?"

"Nearly."

"Until you find out, I'll call you John."

It didn't seem familiar. I was pretty sure my name wasn't John. "Why?"

"That's what they call people they can't identify. John Doe."

It didn't suit me, but it was a name.

"Where do I meet you?"

"How about right here, at seven? Oh, of course. No watch."

"I'll manage. I'll just…"

"…take mine. Bright pink doesn't suit you but I have a spare one at home."

I took it with gratitude.

"No problem. You can buy the popcorn."

"Has your stalker gone?"

"Hmm? Oh… I'm sorry. I made him up. I just wanted to start a conversation with the handsome man drinking coffee on his own and it seemed like a good opener."

That might have been my cue to return her watch and call the whole thing off. If I'd known then what I now know about myself, I might have done. But I was lost and alone, and this was the first person who'd asked me to do more than fill in a form and wait to be seen.

Besides, with hindsight, I doubt Lisa would have taken no for an answer.

"I think you might be my kind of girl," I said.

"I guess we'll both have to wait and see," she replied. I'd like to say a look flashed across her eyes, but if it did, I didn't notice it. She kissed me on the cheek, once, and walked out the door without looking back.

She didn't need to look back. I was intrigued and she knew it.

With nowhere to go and nothing to do until the only thing in my future I had planned, I decided to investigate my condition. A few helpful people directed me to Reading Library, where I began my hunt for information on amnesia.

I, like everyone I suppose, think of libraries in terms of books. Shelves of books on every subject, lined up in a cryptic code they call the Dewey system. Rather like my memory, I suppose - lots of stuff in there, but I can't find anything specific. Occasionally I'll spot something vaguely relevant but my Dewey system is scrambled. Fortunately it seemed I could retain new memories - everything from this morning onwards was clear and easy to recall. I remembered my face in the mirror, the young man at the Travel Hotel, and of course I remembered Lisa. And the strange note in my pocket.

But a modern library is much more than book storage. Reading's library also boasted a number of computers, wired up to the internet, the biggest "library" in the world. I asked for a terminal and as soon as I sat down I felt right at home. I'd obviously used a computer before – I was conducting internet searches without even thinking about it, though that thought didn't occur to me for a little while.

Looking up "amnesia" resulted in hundreds of web pages. Thousands. I looked at a few relevant ones, none of which helped much. I could only hope that my amnesia was temporary and that I'd start remembering things once I was back in familiar surroundings. Wherever the hell they were.

On the plus side, I could be a bit more specific - it seemed I had retrograde amnesia, meaning I could remember everything from this morning onwards, but nothing before. I tried to tell myself this was good news - after all, I'd be able to live a normal life, unlike the guy in that film. I then spent five minutes looking around online to try and find out what film this was, though the internet couldn't tell me if I'd actually seen it or just heard of it.

Next, a vague and hopeless search for myself. I soon hit the same wall the police had - no details, no name, nothing. You can't search for nothing. I looked up missing people in the hope that my face would be there, but it was like finding a needle in a pin factory. So many missing people. Who could notice little me, who actually had money and clothes and a date tonight?

It was about this point that I realised I was using the internet like a pro despite not even remembering my own name. Maybe my memories weren't gone at all - I just couldn't consciously access them. Maybe sleep would help. Sleep was supposed to help restore memories (according to some of the websites I'd visited) and I still had the Travel Hotel - except I kept thinking of the warning on that weird note in my pocket.

In the meantime, what other ways were there to access "lost" memories?

I tried several methods, none of which worked, some which I found online and some which I thought up on the spot - unless I remembered them from somewhere, ha ha. One of these was distraction - the thing you're trying to think of will pop into your head when you're thinking of something else. I tried thinking of the names of famous people - looking at pictures in books or online, putting a name to the face. I could recognise a lot of actors and actresses, though politicians were less effective (this probably says more about my interests than my memory). Quickly - that's the way. See the face, say the name. Think of my face, in the mirror that morning.

Nothing.

Try the same idea backwards. Say the name, think of the face. Kylie Minogue (yep), Elvis Presley (yep), Sean Connery (yep), mum (blank).

Try a different one. Johnny Depp (yep), Bruce Lee (yep), Freddie Mercury (yep), Jimmy (er, no). It seemed mysterious Jimmy was also unknown to me.

I don't think this would have worked anyway. I think we remember "real" people *differently to celebrities.*

Next I tried imagining surreal scenes as a way to "sneak up" on my memories. Curiously, I could imagine simple things like clouds and trees and the famous faces I've already mentioned, but trying to imagine "real" places was much harder unless I'd been there that morning - the burger place, the coffee shop, the police station; all popped into mind easily. A lot of our imagination comes from our memories of similar things, and there was a big hole in my memories.

A number of herbal and homeopathic remedies resulted from my searching. I made a note of a few of them, just in case, but there was nothing to help me right now and I doubted any of them would work. Most of what I found online were things to help me remember stuff I was going to learn. I read about mnemonics, how to remember names and numbers, how to remember appointments. But, as far as I knew, remembering new stuff wasn't my problem - just the old stuff.

My thoughts then turned to the mystery of the tape in my pocket. I felt sure that listening to it might uncover some clues to who I was. Did the library have some means to listen to cassette tapes? Apparently not - CDs and DVDs, yes, but the cassette tape was a piece of technology too archaic, despite the range of "books on tape" that was available.

The key was a complete mystery to me - it looked like a locker key, but to which locker and where it could be, I couldn't say. The only markings on the key were the numbers 097.

I decided to stop thinking for a while and get ready for my date. First I'd need some new clothes - I'd been wearing these ones all day and who knew how long before that?

It is impossible to say what things are new to me, but shopping for clothes seemed instantly familiar. I didn't enjoy it. Especially difficult was shopping for new clothes on a tight budget - I did consider whether it was wise when I had no credit cards and no idea where my next money was coming from. In the end I went for low cost style and avoided labels, coming out with a casual shirt and trousers. At least I knew the sizes to get – they were on my existing clothes. I then headed back to the Travel Hotel for a shower and a shave, realising when I arrived that I didn't have anything to shave with. I decided I couldn't afford to shave and date unless she paid for everything, so stubble it would have to be.

Her watch looked rather silly on my arm, but at least I could tell the time. As it drew near to half past six I did my final check that I had everything and then turned to go. I left the odd items I'd found in my pockets on the bedside cabinet - all except the paper, which I decided to puzzle over some more on the way.

I arrived with five minutes left until seven. Lisa was not there, arriving about quarter past the hour with no sign at all of having hurried. In those intervening twenty minutes I stared at the cryptic paper and stared at nothing in equal measure. Heaven, free forces and Jimmy remained a mystery to me.

"Hey there, stranger. You've changed, I see."

"Hello, Lisa."

"Ah, so you haven't forgotten me. Thought about what you'd like to see?"

I had not. I'd been so caught up in my own thoughts that I'd given none to the evening's entertainment. "They all sound good," I bluffed.

"Okay. Let's go see *Aliens Ate My Car*. *It's meant to be funny."

"Sounds good," I said.

"I made that one up," she replied. "You haven't even looked at the cinema boards."

She was too smart, this one. I confessed that I'd been thinking about other things and hadn't put much thought into what film to watch. I expected her to be annoyed. She surprised me instead.

"I'm sorry," she said. "Of course you've been thinking about other things. If I woke up with no idea who I was, I'd be taking it far less well than you are. Let's forget about the film."

"No, no. I have no idea who I am or how I got here but I do know that you are a very kind and wonderful woman and that tonight I want to enjoy myself. There's no cure for this amnesia - I'll either start remembering things, or I won't. I need normal life, familiar things, not moping around my room at the Travel Hotel."

She smiled. "So I guess you're hoping you've seen this film. Familiar things. Okay, not Aliens Ate My Bus."

"I thought it was a car?"

"Nothing wrong with your memory now. Did you forget you were buying the popcorn?"

I didn't remember the film. Most likely I'd never seen it anyway – it wasn't a brand new release, but it hadn't been out long. Yet I didn't really mind. For a couple of hours I felt normal. Questions of who I was and how I got there just didn't matter.

At the end of the film I briefly excused myself from Lisa and headed for the men's room. Salted popcorn encourages you to drink more cola, with predictable results. Battling my way through the crowd (because everyone suffers the same chain of cause and effect and everyone leaves the screen at the same time) I headed for a vacant cubicle. Though it was hardly pleasant in there, it was good to escape the throng.

While I… you know… my eyes wandered across the mass of graffiti on the walls.

Names and numbers, profanity and surreal gibberish. For all I knew I could have scrawled one of these notes myself, though I think my spelling would be better.

My eye caught a familiar name – "Jimmy". That got my attention, but turned out to be "Jimmy 4 Zoe". Probably nothing to do with my note. But something about that kicked at my head. It wasn't until later that I figured out what it was.

"There you are. I thought you'd fallen in." Lisa's usual wit hadn't deserted her.

"Nah. You're stuck with me," I replied. "Okay, now what?"

"That's up to you," she said. "I chose the film, so it's only fair. What do you want to do now? Go to a club? Back to your place? Or mine?"

"I…"

"Oh, hang on, you don't have a place. Mine, then?"

"I dunno. What would my wife say?"

"You… you're married? You remember?" She must have seen the grin spreading across my face at this point. "Ooh, you…!"

"Nope, still no wife-related memories. You're probably okay."

She laughed, took my hand, and led me out of the cinema. "I'll get us a taxi," she said. "You're a bit too special to risk losing you in a club."

"So, your place then?"

"If my husband is out." She paused. "Damn, doesn't work on you. Perhaps I should lose my memory, but then I wouldn't be able to take you home."

"Then let's get going, in case I'm contagious."

Lisa's place was a one-bedroom flat on the outskirts of the town centre. It was rather more pleasantly decorated than the Travel Hotel but magnolia was still a major factor. The furniture was a mix of feminine style and cheap catalogue stock, the latter I guessed being the original fixtures and fittings.

"It's not much, but it's home. I wish the rent wasn't much."

"It's lovely," I said. "Care to show me round?"

She nodded. "Living room," she said, pointing at the floor. "Kitchen," at the end of the room. "Bathroom," an innocuous door showing tiles beyond it. "Bedroom," another door beside the first. This one was closed.

"A very comprehensive tour."

"It wouldn't take much longer to show you it all. Go and sit down, I'll bring us something to drink."

I did as I was told, sitting on the end of a green and faded sofa that faced an outdated CRT television. It had been left on, currently watching the commercial break by itself with the sound muted.

"Feel free to change the channel," she called over. "If you can find the remote, anyway - I saw it round there somewhere last week."

"It's fine. I'm not really watching it anyway."

She returned to the living room, so far as you can think of the living room and kitchen as separate rooms when the only difference is the flooring, carrying with her two tumblers and a bottle on a tray. "I don't have any wine glasses," she apologised. "Or any decent wine, come to that."

"It'll be fine. I can't remember a finer glass of wine."

"I hope you aren't a Mormon or something."

"I remember hangovers. I must have been drinking at some point in my life."

She seemed satisfied with that, and poured some of her cheap red wine into the tumblers. I noticed that one was chipped, which she quickly picked up herself. "A toast," she said. "May your memory return soon, and with it, no unpleasant surprises."

"I'll drink to that," I said, and we did.

We talked about her. I couldn't really tell her much about myself, so Lisa spoke about her life, the parents she was glad to move away from, her job ("I'm a freelance journalist – take it from me, never work in customer service"), the relationship she'd broken up from a few months ago ("you'd think that guy was allergic to work") and her plan to one day go back to university to study history ("I chose a course to get me into journalism, not because I liked the subject"). I nodded and smiled through it all but many of the details went over my head.

At some point she seemed to notice. "I must be boring you senseless," she said. "Tell me about yourself. What you can, anyway."

"I remember a lot of basic stuff - I can read and write, I know what things are, that sort of thing - just not anything about my life until this morning. I'm educated - I know a lot of big words, I seem to know how to use computers quite well. I remember a lot of famous people, but not any family or friends, and I remember films and music, but not whether I own them or not. I wish I could tell you more. I feel like there's a big hole in my head and I can't see the bottom."

"What about your interests? What do you like doing?"

"At the moment I'm not sure. I think I like the occasional drink, and I don't seem to smoke. I'm not diabetic or epileptic as far as I'm aware. I like coffee, I like bacon. I'm not that interested in sports or clothes. I hate shopping. The film was okay, but I don't think it's my usual choice. Anything else?"

She leaned in closer. "You missed out kind, handsome and generous."

Our lips met, first brushing tenderly together. I pulled away. "What are you doing?" I asked.

Lisa didn't reply. She took the back of my head with one hand and leaned in *again, more forcefully this time. Our lips met once more, but there was no tenderness this time - it was more like an urgent need.*

I struggled free. "Lisa, stop it."

There was a wild look in her eyes now. She leapt for me again, and I rolled aside, feeling her hands clutching at my shirt, pulling me back. I tried to stand. Her hands seemed to be everywhere - pulling at my shirt, tugging at my jeans. As I tried to stand again, she slipped her hands around my waist and undid my belt. I got to my feet as she pulled my jeans down, my first steps forward sending me straight to the floor.

Lisa was immediately on top of me, rolling me over and tearing at my shirt buttons again. I tried to push her away, and finally managed to throw her off. Her head met the coffee table with a nasty thud.

She sat dazed for a moment, and then simply said: "Ouch." Whatever madness had possessed her had vanished now. I took advantage of the opportunity to get dressed again.

"What happened?" she asked.

"I don't know," I said. "Lisa, I like you... but I don't feel that way about you."

For a moment I thought she was angry. She stared at me, wordlessly, as if I'd just told her I was from outer space and she wasn't sure if I was joking. Then her eyes softened. "I'm sorry," she said. "It was wrong to do this so quickly. Is there someone else? Have you remembered something?"

I shook my head. "No. It's just... I'm sorry, Lisa. If you want to…"

"Don't be silly," she said. "I'm not upset. I just got carried away. You're a sweet guy and I took advantage of you. Perhaps you should go."

"Alright. If that's what you want."

"It's what you want - you just can't remember why yet. I'll call you a taxi."

"No, it's okay. It's not far."

She looked at me for a long time, before kissing me once, gently, on the lips. "I'll see you again, John Doe," she said.

Part of me wanted to stay, to set things right, but I knew that tonight was over. I put my jacket back on, said my goodbyes and headed out into the night.

The walk back to the Travel Hotel was a fair bit longer than I had let on, but after a long and confusing day I wanted to walk for a bit, to straighten out my head. I tried to think about my lost memories and what I should do next but all I could think of was Lisa. What had happened? Why had it gone so wrong? Would I really see her again?

I wandered past a local supermarket, now closed for the night, and looked at the darkened displays. Special offers on a number of uninteresting items. I turned to walk on, and something caught my eye. "3 for 2" on baked beans?

I stared at the display for a moment, but the importance of beans was lost on me. I decided that the day had been too long and I was starting to think anything and everything was a key to unlocking my memories. Yet that sign kept kicking at my subconscious mind all the way back to the Travel Hotel.

Three for two on baked beans. 3 for 2. Jimmy 4 Zoe...

A few streets away from the Travel Hotel I froze completely.

Three for two!

I checked my jacket pockets frantically for the piece of paper I'd been carrying with me. That cryptic message was suddenly obvious to me.

"Oh free force heaven hate. Two for one, three for two. Ask for Jimmy."

It didn't make any sense if you read it to yourself. But if you read it out loud...

"Oh three four seven eight..."

It was a telephone number. I ran back to my Travel Hotel room and the telephone *within. It was late, but I gave no thought to the time. I punched in the number.*

Ring ring.

"Come on, come on."

Ring ring.

"Someone answer!"

Ring ring.

"Please let me be right about this!"

Ring ring.

Ring ring.

"Hello? Do you know what time it is?"

"Hello?" I said. "Can I speak to Jimmy please?"

"This is Jimmy. Who… Rob, is that you?"

Jimmy

"Rob? Is that you?"

I didn't know what to say. My mouth carried on without input and uttered something like "Uhhhh..."

"Come on. Who is this?"

"I... I don't know who I am," *I finally managed.* "I woke up this morning with no memory and I found a note in my pocket with your telephone number on."

There was silence for a while.

"Oh man. You don't remember anything?"

"Nothing before this morning. Well, I know how to do things. I can work computers and tie my shoelaces, that sort of thing. I just don't know anything about myself."

"Rob..."

Was that my name? It didn't sound familiar to me, but there was no reason why it should.

"What's my last name?" *I asked.*

"You don't even know that? Didn't you check your wallet?"

"No ID," *I said.*

"You'd better not be kidding me, Rob. If you're serious, we are both in deep trouble. Your name is Robert Walker, and you'll be turning twenty eight on October the twentieth. Where are you?"

"I'm in a Travel Hotel. Reading."

"Reading? Why Reading?"

"You're asking the wrong person."

"Look, I'll come and get you in the morning. I'll meet you at Reading train station at – say, 9am, and I'll see whether I can jog your memory. Oh, and I can't explain this now, but Rob?"

"Yes?"

"Don't fall asleep. Whatever you do tonight, don't sleep."

The note in my pocket had said the same thing.

"Not sure I could anyway, Jimmy. Oh, Jimmy?"

"Yeah?"

"Who are you?"

Jimmy said nothing for a few moments, and then simply said, "tomorrow, Rob. I'll explain everything tomorrow. Don't sleep."

After a long and strange day, sleep was a powerful impulse. Yet something about Jimmy's message stopped me from settling. It seemed absurd to ask that I didn't sleep. Yet I trusted Jimmy, perhaps a little too easily for someone whose name and telephone number were written in code on a scrap of paper in my pocket. I didn't know him at all, and couldn't be sure that he knew me.

I put on the television for some background noise and mused about what I knew, or what I thought I knew. Robert Walker. It was a solid and sensible name (certainly better than John Doe) and now I knew how old I was as well. Even though having a name and date of birth left me no clearer about who I was as a person, I felt better having a hook to hang my hat on, so to speak.

Don't sleep...

I had a horrible thought. Supposing sleep was the cause of my condition? Suppose, somehow, that every time I went to sleep I might be resetting my memory to zero? If that were true, there was no hope for me. A person cannot go without sleep for long.

There are few distractions in a Travel Hotel room. The television is one, but grows less effective after a while, especially late at night. The only channels available were the terrestrial ones - no satellite, no cable. I also had one bible in the bedside cabinet, but I wasn't desperate enough for that yet.

What else did I know from Jimmy's conversation? I felt he knew a lot more than he was letting on. He hadn't asked how I was, or what I'd done. He'd asked where I was, and didn't seem to know how I'd ended up here, but something about his pragmatic approach suggested he'd been expecting it.

If you're serious, we are both in deep trouble.

Trouble? Why? What had I done?

For now there was nothing I could do except keep myself awake and wait until morning. There's not a lot to do at night when you've nowhere to go and no money to spend. My mind just kept going over and over the day's events, and Jimmy's warning. I couldn't relax, didn't dare try to rest. I needed company, and at that time I only knew one other person.

I collected my few possessions, put on my jacket and left the Travel Hotel.

I remembered the way with remarkable ease. Whether having a clean slate for a memory helps things stick or I was just naturally good at remembering routes I had no idea, but a good walk later I found myself back at the door I had left just a few hours before. All the lights were off, and I felt bad about disturbing her, but I rang the bell for Lisa's flat all the same.

There was no answer at first, and I was about to give up when the intercom crackled into life. "Who is this? Do you know what bloody time it is?"

"Lisa! It's me!"

There was a brief pause before she answered. "John? What's up?"

"I'm sorry, Lisa. I… I'm scared."

"You'd better come up," she said, and buzzed the main door open.

She was already waiting at her flat door as I climbed the stairs. I could tell that she'd been asleep and already regretted coming back here. Yet there was a look in her eyes - I felt that, even if she'd rather be asleep, she was still pleased to see me again.

"If you're here to pick up where we left off, you may as well go now," she said. "Otherwise, I'll make us some coffee."

"Coffee sounds good," I said. "Lisa, I know it's late, but I need to talk to someone about all this. I think something's wrong with me."

"It's so late, it's early," she replied from the kitchen (or at least, the end of the room with the kettle in). "You've got no memory. Of course something's wrong with you."

"I don't think this is natural. I did some research on amnesia earlier today and retrograde amnesia is very uncommon. It's normally caused by some sort of trauma, like a head injury, but I don't seem to have any injuries. But the weirdest part is waking up in a strange town with no identification. I mean, doesn't everyone have a credit card these days?"

"Perhaps you've always lived here. You wouldn't know."

"Jimmy knows," I replied.

"Who's Jimmy?"

"He's..." I faltered.

"Perhaps you should start at the beginning," she said.

So I did. I told her how I woke up this morning with a hangover, a cheap hotel room and no memory. I told her about the mysterious contents of my pockets. I showed her the cigarette box with the tape inside, the cryptic note I'd apparently written myself and the small key.

"If I'd just met you right now," she said, "I'd say you were insane. What's on the tape?"

"I have no idea."

"What's the key for?"

"Don't know. Looks like a locker key."

"And what's with this crazy note? It doesn't make any sense to me."

"Read it out loud," I said.

"Oh free force heav… Oh three four seven… oh, I see. That's quite clever. How did you think that one up?"

"Sorry, can't help you there."

"But you called this number?"

"I did."

"And this Jimmy guy answered?"

"He did. He told me my name is Robert Walker and that I'm not far off turning twenty eight."

"Yes, I can see you as a Robert."

"He also said some other things. Like the two of us - me and him - being in some sort of trouble."

"What trouble?"

"I have no idea. He said he'd tell me tomorrow. He's coming to Reading in the morning. Will you go with me?"

"Lucky for you I don't work nine to five." She smiled. "I will. I like you too much to let some strange man kidnap you."

"You think…?"

"Kidding! Wow, we need to work on that." She paused. "What else did he say?"

"That I shouldn't sleep."

She sat up at that. "That's a weird thing to say. What happens if you sleep?"

"I don't know. Perhaps I wake up with no memory again?"

"Best not to risk it until we find out more. Jimmy seems to know a lot about your condition, John. Sorry - Robert."

"I think this tape might explain something to me."

"Maybe. But I don't have a tape player. These days it's all CDs." She waved at a small unit on an end table in the corner of the room. Her music collection was stashed in a cardboard box underneath it.

I drained my coffee cup. She was right. I had the idea now that I'd got the tape and the note just in case I fell asleep and my memory reset. But why a tape and not a notepad or something?

"There is something a bit suspicious about all this," she said.

"Oh?"

"Like I said yesterday afternoon - you wake up with no memory and no identification. It's like you've walked out of Men In Black.*"*

"That's a film, right? Don't know if I've seen that one."

"I'll get you another coffee. It'll help you stay awake. What time is Jimmy arriving?"

"He'll be at Reading train station at nine," I replied. "Look, I know it sounds weird, but this is the only clue I have to who I am."

"I'm not saying you shouldn't go. I'm saying you shouldn't go alone."

We ordered a taxi to the station, arriving there at about half past eight. I felt very tired, having not slept at all - Lisa had stayed up with me after my arrival, for which I was very grateful, but at least she'd had a few hours. We both took advantage of the cafe on the concourse for a strong coffee and a wilted breakfast pastry.

It was also a good position to watch the arrivals as they got off the trains, wondering which of them could be Jimmy. Was he old? Young? Fat? Thin?

I vaguely remember Lisa saying something about checking the concourse. When I looked around a few minutes later, I was alone at our table.

Another train arrived, this one from London. Passengers streamed out of the doors and made their way up the platform to the gates. I watched them pass through, barely aware, until I was eventually startled out of my reverie by a short, plump afro-Caribbean man in a bright yellow T-shirt and faded pink Bermuda shorts. His eyes darted around, never settling on any one thing for long, including me. His hair was short but stubby, refusing to adopt any form of style, rather like the man underneath it.

"Robert!" he grinned. "It's me - it's Jimmy!"

I couldn't help but stare. "Er, hello," I said.

Jimmy's face turned sad. "You really don't remember me," he said. "I was hoping... you really don't remember anything?"

"Sorry."

"We've known each other for nearly ten years now. We were at University together!"

"I went to University?"

"Ah... shit!" Jimmy turned away, swearing to himself and kicking at the wall of the cafe. It all seemed quite absurd - I had hoped the mysterious Jimmy would be some wise figure able to tell me everything, and instead I'd found a short, fat weirdo with no fashion sense and a west highland terrier for a hairstyle. Then he turned back, and I could see he was crying. I felt bad for my rather mean thoughts.

"Hey, calm down," I said.

"You don't remember me at all? None of it?"

"I..."

"Those bastards are gonna pay for this!"

"Who? What's happened to me, Jimmy?"

Jimmy seemed to settle down a little, and looked around a little furtively, perhaps looking out for anyone watching us (which, after his outburst, numbered quite a few people). "Not here," he said. "We'll talk somewhere private." With that he took my arm and ushered me out of the front entrance. I was torn between wanting to go with him and finding out about my past, and with shaking him off as a lunatic. Could I trust anything he said?

Curiosity won over caution. I went with him. I didn't really have any choice - Lisa was gone.

"Somewhere private" turned out to be a bench in a small park, though far too many people were out in the sun for it to be private by my reckoning. In any event, Jimmy was hardly dressed for subtlety.

"How much do you remember?" he asked.

"I remember everything from yesterday morning," I said. "Before that, I don't remember anything. Just odd flashes, like remembering I have a CD collection and knowing what food I like and don't like. Oh, and I can use a computer without thinking about it."

"The not thinking part is right," Jimmy said. "You should know this stuff, Robert. You wrote your thesis on the power of the subconscious mind."

"Thesis? You said we were at the same university."

"That's right. We studied Psychology – that's how we first met. Robert... you don't remember, do you? Oh man... this is going to be hard. I don't want you to freak out. I mean, most of us only have to go through this once..."

"Jimmy, what…?"

"You and me… we've been together for nine years."

I was about to ask him what he meant, and then it hit me.

"We… I…"

"You probably guessed about me the moment you saw me," he said. "I'm not exactly in the closet."

"You should have left the outfit there," I replied, before I could stop myself.

Jimmy grinned. "That's it! That's my Rob!" he said. "I've never known anyone quicker than you with a sarky comment."

"You haven't met Lisa yet."

His face fell. "Lisa?" he parroted. "You mean you…"

I decided not to tell him how close Lisa and I had nearly become. "No. She's just a friend." A conspicuously absent one.

"A friend. Right."

I decided to change the subject. "Jimmy, what's happened to me?"

Jimmy turned silent for a moment and turned away. "I'm sorry, Rob. It's my fault. I got you involved in it all. When you disappeared a week ago, I thought you'd found out about the project and left me."

"The project?"

"The Amnesia Project. I guess you did find out about it."

It was like pulling teeth out. Jimmy seemed reluctant to talk, but I needed answers.

"Talk to me, Jimmy. Tell me about the project. Tell me what happened to me."

"The Amnesia Project… it started out as an experiment into what causes memory loss. Studies into how we remember things, looking into cures for Alzheimer's, stuff like that. We discovered that we could cause memory loss in test animals with a new chemical compound – one simple injection, an electrical current and bam – no memory. So then we thought about reversing the direction of the project, looking into a possible treatment for trauma victims. Imagine being a victim of some terrible tragedy - say, a rape victim or losing a close relative - and not being able to come to terms with it. We could make them forget, let them move on with their lives."

I wasn't sure I liked the sound of all this, but Jimmy was becoming more animated as he warmed to his subject. The thing was, memory or not, I could already see where this was going.

"We had a funding crisis," he continued. "We thought the project was going to fold. Then the military stepped in. They spun us a story about helping to rehabilitate soldiers after the horrors of war, but we know now what they really wanted our research for. Imagine, Rob, letting this compound into the water supply. Imagine an entire city waking up with no memory, no identity. You could just march right in and take over."

"So what happened to me? Lab accident?"

"I don't know," he said. "I got you involved in the project because we'd be working together. You were reluctant at first, and with good reason I suppose. You saw this coming. Then about a week ago you just didn't come home."

"So why do you think we're in trouble?"

"If you'd just had an accident, you might have wandered off, might have even ended up here in Reading, with no idea about what you were doing or who you should contact. But when you said you had no ID on you…"

"No cards, no jewellery, not even a watch," I said.

"…exactly. It sounds like you were deliberately treated. Memory wiped, then dumped in a cheap hotel room in Rochdale, Rotterdam, Reading… some place beginning with R…"

"Pardon?"

Jimmy blinked. "You really don't remember anything, do you?"

"So what now? How do I get my memory back?"

"I don't know."

This was not what I wanted to hear.

"And the thing about not sleeping?"

"Oh, yes," said Jimmy. "I'm not entirely sure about that, but in lab tests, some of the animals seemed to forget things again. They'd learn new behaviours, then the next day they'd have forgotten them again. Not all animals. But some."

"And you're not sure if the same is true for me."

He nodded.

"So now what?"

"I take you home," he said. "I can look after you there. And if you do wake up in the morning with no memory again… well, we'll know. I'll know, anyway."

We couldn't go straight away. I was still hoping that Lisa would appear, but she was nowhere in sight. Certainly when we returned to the station there was no sign of her. I returned to the Travel Hotel, collected my old clothes and settled the bill - it seemed I had only arrived there the night before my memories began. Jimmy paid using his bank card – though the name "D Wright" was stamped across it - as my wallet was too exhausted to cover the cost.

We stopped by Lisa's flat on the way back but there was no answer to the doorbell. I wanted to leave a note for her in case she was looking for us, but we had no pen or paper to hand.

"Come on, Rob. Let's go. We can't wait here all day."

I nodded, and turned to leave. As I did I spotted the communal mailbox and stuffed the note I'd apparently written myself inside. If Lisa checked her mail, she'd remember. And hopefully she'd be able to call me.

"Where are we going?" I asked.

"Home," replied Jimmy, buying me a single ticket. He'd bought a day return ticket for the trip down and had presumably always intended to come back the same day - with or without me, perhaps.

"And where's home?"

"You really don't remember anything, do you?" he replied. "London. We live in London."

"That's a big place. Where in London?"

"Come on, this is our train."

"You know, I might remember things better if you told me about them."

Jimmy fell silent for a while. "I'm sorry, Rob. I'm just worried about you."

"Good, good," I snapped. "I'm worried about me too. Now where are we going?"

"Soho," he snapped back. "Happy now?" He then turned away, then turned back to me, took my face in his hands and planted a kiss square on my lips. I was so surprised I nearly fell over.

"Come on," he said, and I followed. I didn't exactly have a lot of choice.

The journey to London was uneventful. Jimmy seemed content to stare out of the window and didn't take any interest in talking to me. I didn't speak to him either - his behaviour thus far had been erratic at best. Could I really be in a relationship with this man? I had no memory of him (or, indeed, anyone at all, not counting the brief and abortive encounter with Lisa yesterday).

Jimmy didn't look up until we pulled into Paddington. "Come on," he said. "We change here."

I said nothing, and followed his brightly coloured shirt through the crowds to the underground.

Home turned out to be a two-bedroom apartment, in rather better condition than Lisa's flat and with separate rooms for the kitchen and living room. Soft pastels dominated the colour scheme with some darker colours to add contrast. It was completely out of keeping with Jimmy's dress sense.

"Stylish," I said.

Jimmy seemed calmer now we had arrived and smiled at my comment. "I can't take all the credit," he said. "You picked most of the décor. I just chose the soft furnishings. You remember?"

I shook my head. "Sorry, nothing."

"Come sit down," he said. "I'll make us some tea."

I sat down briefly, but my curiosity got the better of me and I followed him into the kitchen. Here the main colour was blue, with light blue walls and slightly darker blue tiles contrasted with navy counters. The cupboards were wooden; proper wood, not some mass produced MDF. It looked expensive.

"Wow," I said. "Impressive."

"Yeah," smiled Jimmy. "It pays to get the professionals in for the kitchen. We raised the value of the place by at least three grand when we fitted this. Can you get the milk for me?"

I looked around but saw no refrigerator.

"The cupboard on your right."

The cupboard turned out to be a false front on a small fitted refrigerator. I quickly found the milk amongst the range of organic yoghurts and fresh produce and fished it out for him.

Jimmy poured the milk into a small jug and added it to a tray of cups, saucers and other items. I had been expecting tea in a mug, not in a pot. I suddenly felt very gauche.

"Go sit down," he repeated. "I've got this."

So I sat down, on one of two pristine white leather sofas. They looked as though they had never been sat on before. Jimmy followed, placing the tray on the real wood coffee table and pouring out two cups for us.

"Milk?" he asked.

"Um, yes," I replied. Milk felt right.

"Sugar?" he asked, holding a pair of metal tongs. I noticed that the sugar bowl contained rough lumps of sugar rather than granulated, and once more felt a little out of place.

"Just one lump, please," I replied. "Shouldn't you know already?"

"Just wanted to make sure you haven't changed your mind," he replied, dropping the sugar into the cup. He even stirred the tea with a silver teaspoon before passing me cup, spoon and saucer.

"And have I?"

Jimmy prepared his own tea, dropping two lumps into his tea and a splash of milk. "No," he said. "That's how you've always had your tea."

I felt a silly urge to take another lump of sugar. Instead I took a sip of my tea. It was the best tea I have ever tasted. Whatever else I say about Jimmy, he made good tea. Of course, having the finest ingredients always helps.

"So," I said. "Tell me about yourself."

"Me? Jimmy Burgess, twenty nine years old. I'm a musician."

"You said earlier that you took a psychology course at University with me."

"I did. Now I write music, though you probably don't remember any of it."

"Sorry."

"Would you like to hear some?"

Faced with trying to hold a conversation with someone who seemed reluctant to tell me anything and unable to add much myself, some background noise could only help. "Okay," I said.

Jimmy headed to a CD unit and pulled out a few discs. They were homemade copies with titles written on in permanent marker. After looking through the small pile he reached a decision and put one into a small but expensive looking CD player. A remote control with far too many buttons was placed in my hand.

"Where's the play button?" I asked.

Jimmy took the remote back, glanced at the remote for half a second and pressed a single button. For a moment I thought nothing had happened, and then the music started.

"We were climbing so high from a misty sunrise morning…"

"Do you remember this one?" asked Jimmy. "We played this at our partnership ceremony."

"Who's that singing?" I asked.

Jimmy nodded. "That's Mac. Great voice. He recorded a lot of stuff with me. Gone now, though – got his own label. Words and Deeds. Doing well for himself."

I took a sip more tea. It was very good tea, though it tasted perhaps a little too sweet. Perhaps that sugar lump was too large.

"I see you in the trees. Are you looking at me?"

"Jimmy," I said. "I feel so tired… what you said before… about sleep…"

"Well, I don't know if you'll forget again," he said. "I'm told that only happened to about a quarter of the lab rats."

"If you're a musician, how come you know so much about this project?"

Jimmy looked hurt. "I love you, Rob," he said. "I want you to know that. I've always loved you and I won't do anything to hurt you."

Everything was starting to grey out. Keeping awake was getting harder. I'd been up all night but surely I couldn't be this tired already?

"The tea… did you… something in…"

"Get some rest, Rob. You'll be fine in a little while. And if you do lose your memory again… well, I'll be here."

I couldn't fight it any longer. My eyes closed and I fell sideways onto the sofa. The last thing I heard before blacking out completely was a snatch of the lyrics on Jimmy's music.

"I feel I'm falling. I feel I'm falling, and when I look up I see you…"

The Story

"Wow."

Henry stopped the tape when it was clear Rob had finished speaking and looked up at Eddie's nervous yet still beaming face.

"You like it, boss?"

"Eddie, I think it's great. Go ahead and type up the rest of the first tape. Remember to run it through the spell checker, though, will you?"

"Y-yes sir!"

"And Eddie... don't type the other tapes. Not yet. Let's serialise it, like Dickens did."

"Who?"

Henry sighed. "Just do the first tape. It'll be better than the crap on my desk at the moment. Then we'll print the next tape in the next edition, and so on."

"What do we call it?"

Henry looked at the tapes again. TAP1 was still in the machine, and now he realised that TAP wasn't a spelling mistake. Jimmy had explained the title just a few minutes ago.

"We'll call it - The Amnesia Project."

Henry mostly forgot about the story, fittingly enough, during the next few weeks. The last of the photographers quit – Henry was barely listening as he waffled something about weddings. No great loss. The man couldn't take a decent picture anyway. A pipe burst in the basement. And his ex-wife went into hospital with an impacted bowel. Henry supposed good news happened to everyone on occasion; even him.

The magazine was struggling. No, that wasn't true. The magazine was dying. He couldn't pay for more staff, so there was no decent content. No content meant no readers. No readers meant no advertisers. No advertisers meant no money. It went round and around.

Perhaps it was time for a new approach. Perhaps fictional pieces were the way to go. It couldn't do any harm.

Every edition, Eddie typed up another tape. Henry read through the drafts, corrected Eddie's errors without comment and put them in the magazine. It was easy. It was also fun.

But he could just hear George complaining about the lack of proper journalism these days.

The Message

I woke up with another sore head. For a moment I didn't know where I was, and I panicked a little. But then memory began to return, though slowly. It took me a moment to remember my own name. Perhaps this isn't so surprising - I'd only learnt it yesterday.

I was in bed - quite a large, plush one. I appeared to be naked. I didn't want to investigate this too much as I was also not alone - I could feel someone behind me with an arm around me. It was quite a hairy arm and this, along with the light snoring sounds coming from behind me, suggested my companion was male.

If I sound rather calm about all of this, perhaps I should also add that my head was remarkably fuzzy. I spent the next few minutes getting my fragmented memory in order, trying to reconstruct the previous night - though, as I eventually recalled, the previous night had in fact gone into morning. I remembered meeting Jimmy, I remembered... what was her name? Lisa, that was it... I remembered that Lisa had disappeared. I remembered coming to London on the train, and seeing the house, and...

The tea. There must have been something in the tea.

I was in bed with a strange man (in more senses than one) who seemed quite happy to drug me, strip me and do who knew what else while I was unconscious. My calm state of mind was fading fast - the after-effects of the drug were probably wearing off. Should I get up, try to escape? I was in a strange house in a strange place with a strange man. I wasn't sure I could get up without alerting him and I had no idea what he'd do if I did wake him.

To make the matter more pressing, I needed to pee.

Several minutes passed without me making a firm decision, when Jimmy made it for me. He woke up, his arm hugging me tighter to him. "Morning, Rob," he said.

"How are you feeling?"

I wasn't sure how to answer that, so went with the truth. "Groggy. My head aches a bit."

"I've got some headache tablets in the bathroom cabinet," he replied. "But I really meant - how much do you remember?"

As it happened, my memories were becoming clearer all the time - since I'd woken up in the Travel Hotel, that is. Before that was still a blank. I also, however, remembered his comment that I might forget things again when I slept - and it appeared I was lucky. I remembered things fine.

But given Jimmy's actions so far, and his variable temperament, I decided not to tell him this.

It was clichéd, but the best I could come up with. "Where am I?"

"Oh, Rob... I was afraid this might happen."

"What?"

"Your amnesia. Something happened to you that's wiped your memory, and when you sleep, it happens again. This is the fifth time now."

"The fifth time?!"

"I thought we were making some progress last time, that maybe the new treatments were working, but apparently not." He hugged me tighter. "Don't worry, Rob. Jimmy's here to look after you."

"What treatments?"

"The new drugs, the psychotherapy... you really don't remember any of it?"

"No."

"The second time was the worst. The pills they gave you after the first attack made you paranoid and you skipped town on me. I found you in Reading. You had no memory of what had happened."

The horrible thing was, it all sounded so plausible. Jimmy mentioned the police finding my credit cards and other identification, hidden in a locker at the railway station, so no-one would be able to identify me. I thought of the locker key I'd found in my pocket. Jimmy talked about my obsession with a nearby psychological research laboratory and my paranoid fantasy that they'd caused my memory loss.

"And then you'd make up false memories to account for the gaps," he continued. "One time you even claimed you'd been abducted by aliens."

I shivered. If my memories of yesterday were real, Jimmy was lying to me and I was in danger. If Jimmy was telling me the truth, I couldn't rely on anything I thought I knew.

Jimmy must have felt me shiver. He pulled me closer to him, wrapped his body around me and whispered in my ear that it would all be alright, that he loved me and he would look after me.

I wanted to believe that.

After a few minutes more I was unable to restrain myself any longer and pulled away. I paused at the bedroom door to ask directions to the bathroom, which turned out to be the next door down the hall. After taking care of my most pressing concern I took the opportunity to take stock.

This was the first time I'd had chance to look around what was apparently my home and I decided to make use of it. The bathroom was a fair size – a laundry hamper in one corner yielded the clothes I last remembered wearing. I wondered briefly how long they'd been there – five days? More? Wouldn't Jimmy have washed them by now? Or maybe he had and I'd worn them since?

I quickly checked the pockets of my trousers and unearthed the small key. The cigarette packet had been in my jacket, which was probably hanging up somewhere. With no pockets to put it in – I was indeed completely naked – I decided to hide the key on the windowsill, behind an ornament of a lady with a big dress. Some time later I discovered this was for holding spare toilet rolls.

Despite Jimmy's assertions that we were lovers, and that he'd already been spooned against my naked body, I felt a little awkward wandering about the apartment in nothing at all and fished out my underwear and a pair of socks for my slightly chilly feet from the laundry basket. Thus prepared, I crept out of the door. Some gentle snoring sounds from the bedroom suggested Jimmy was not a morning person.

Along the hall were two more doors to the left and a door at the end. I opened the first door to find a spare bedroom, neat and evidently not in use at the moment. I could only imagine it was used for visitors. I had briefly considered that Jimmy and I had separate rooms. Apparently not.

The next door along in the hallway turned out to be an airing cupboard filled with towels and bedding and such. A compact vacuum cleaner sat in the bottom corner next to a box of junk. I made a mental note to go through the box at some point in case any clues to my past were inside.

At the end of the small hall I emerged into the living room, with the door to the kitchen on one side. Here I was in familiar territory. The front door was on my right, the kitchen door on my left, everything else as I'd last seen it. I saw my jacket hanging on a row of coat hooks by the front door alongside a ghastly suede affair that had Jimmy's fashion sense written all over it. A quick feel of the pockets revealed that Jimmy hadn't checked them – the cigarette packet with the cassette tape inside it was still there. I wandered over to the CD player that Jimmy had been using before I blacked out but confirmed it was only a CD player – no cassette deck.

I was about to start looking in the various cabinets when I heard Jimmy's voice behind me. "You're up early," he said.

I turned around. Jimmy stood in the door to the hallway, and looked no better naked than he did dressed. A fair covering of body fat did no favours for his lack of height.

"Go back to bed, Rob. I'll make the tea."

I nodded, abandoning my search for the time being. Jimmy had to go out some time.

I was still feeling groggy and returning to bed sounded appealing, though I'd have preferred it without the company. Even so, I tried to look relaxed and comfortable when Jimmy came in a few minutes later with two cups of tea.

"Here we go," he said.

I took a cautious sip, remembering the last cup of tea he'd given me. It tasted fine, though the previous cup had tasted fine too, and look where my sense of taste had got me then. I waited a minute or two until my next sip but nothing untoward happened. At least, not because of the tea.

Jimmy slipped into bed beside me, taking a loud slurp of tea before placing it on his bedside cabinet and wrapping himself around me again. Perhaps a poisoned cup of tea would be preferable.

Jimmy began to stroke my chest, and I felt stubbly kisses as he worked his way down. Exactly what he'd do when he got to my underwear I did not want to know.

Fortunately the telephone picked this exact moment to ring.

Jimmy muttered something about lousy timing and sat up, grabbing the handset from the bedside table. "Hello?"

There was a brief mumble of conversation that I couldn't make out, which seemed to wake him up in a hurry.

"How did you know?" he asked.

More mumbles, quite a bit more. I couldn't even make out if the caller was male or female.

"Leave him alone. He doesn't know anything."

Presumably this was me. I started to speak, to say I'd be alright, but Jimmy quickly waved me into silence.

"Fine, I'll be there in about half an hour."

Angry mumbles.

"Tell that to the London Underground," Jimmy snapped. With that he stabbed at a button on the phone and terminated the call.

"Rob, I didn't want to do this, but I've got to go. I wanted to stay here with you and look after you but... work called. You know what it's like. Well, actually, you probably don't..."

By this time he was already pulling on his clothes, which came as something of a relief until he added the blue Hawaiian shirt.

"...look, just stay in the apartment, don't answer the door and I'll be back as soon as I can. There's plenty of food in the cupboards."

"I'll be alright," I said.

"I love you, Rob," he said, and kissed me briefly on the lips. I realised that he wasn't angry. He was frightened.

I didn't reply, and he didn't seem to expect one. Shortly after he left the room I heard the front door close and lock.

I was trapped here.

I'd like to say that I spent my time attempting escape, that I picked the lock with a paperclip and fled. The truth was a lot more boring. I had a shower, put on some fresh clothes, watched some television and explored the flat. The spare bedroom initially intrigued me – there could be anything hidden in there – but it soon became clear that it only hid spare bedding and assorted junk.

Speaking of junk, I also looked through the box in the cupboard. Amongst numerous souvenirs and knickknacks I unearthed a photograph album, full of pictures of... me. Jimmy appeared in lots of them too, as well as two older people that I suspected might be my parents. They were beautiful. Too beautiful – they looked nothing like me. Hoping for some clue as to who they might be I took a picture out of the album and discovered it was a magazine clipping. The pictures with me in seemed genuine, especially those where I looked quite young.

I was suspicious, though. For a start, Jimmy and I only appeared together in a few photos, all of them fairly recent. Some photos were obvious fakes (such as the magazine clipping, or a bad composite of Jimmy and myself at a wedding).

Despite a lot of searching, a few items did not appear that I was hoping to find. For a start, I couldn't find any identification with my name on it. I could only assume, if it had been here at all, that Jimmy had taken it with him. I found no spare keys for the front door, which wouldn't open from the inside without one (though I couldn't honestly remember if this was unusual or not). I did, however, find a shoebox under the main bed containing a small pile of cash, and took the opportunity to refill my wallet. I also retrieved my small key and slipped my jacket back on.

I was just fixing myself some lunch when the telephone rang.

At first, I wasn't sure whether to answer it. Despite Jimmy's claim that I lived here with him, I felt like a stranger in this house and didn't know how to respond to anyone. Then again, what if it was Jimmy? I picked it up and opened with the only thing I could think of: "Hello?"

"John! I mean, Rob! Is that you?"

"Lisa! How did you...?"

"You posted your slip of paper through my letterbox, remember?"

Ah yes, of course.

"Rob, where are you? What happened?"

"I could ask you the same thing," I said. "Where did you vanish to?"

"I'm sorry, Rob. I didn't want him to see me. I didn't know you knew Damian."

"Who?"

"The guy with no fashion sense? The one you left with? My ex? Shit, Rob, you couldn't miss the guy."

"You mean Jimmy?"

"Rob, listen to me. You're not safe with him. He's... not entirely stable."

"I noticed," I replied. "But your ex? Can't be. I woke up this morning with him spooned up behind me. He was... enjoying it."

"Damian always liked to play with boys as well as girls," she replied. "Were you enjoying it?"

"It wasn't how I'd wanted to wake up."

She laughed, but then turned serious again. "Don't believe anything he tells you. Where are you?"

"London. Soho. Two bedroom apartment."

"Swanky. Doesn't sound like his style to me. Who'd he kill to get it?"

"I think it's supposed to be mine. Or ours."

"You're answering the phone, so I take it he isn't there," she said.

"Well deduced. You really are a journalist."

"We haven't time to be clever," she said. "Get out of there while he's gone. Don't hang around waiting for him."

"I can't. The door's locked."

"Check around for a key," she sighed. "If you can't find one, try the window – but I remember Jimmy always liked to keep a spare key above the door. I was coming down to London anyway – catching up with some old friends – so I'll meet you at... let's say four."

"Where?"

"There's a café I visit in Soho occasionally – it's run by an old school friend of mine." She gave me some details and I jotted them down on a pad by the telephone. "Four o'clock. Okay?"

"Okay."

"And remember – don't trust Damian. Or Jimmy, or whatever he's calling himself." With that, she hung up, leaving me with a maelstrom of thoughts. At least now I had a place to head for.

I quickly gathered together my few possessions, stuffing the directions to Lisa's café into my jacket pocket along with the cassette tape, and returned my attentions to the front door. I felt rather foolish when I realised that there was indeed a spare key hidden on the top of the door frame. It was the obvious place to look, really. I let myself out, then carefully locked the door behind me.

I thought at the time that Jimmy was trying to keep me in, but I've since decided that he'd simply locked the door out of habit. I know now what a mess his mind was in and don't believe that he was thinking clearly. Or maybe he had locked me in, and simply forgotten about the spare key? He'd left in a hurry, after all. I never got the chance to ask him, but I doubt I could have trusted any answer anyway.

Halfway down the corridor that led to the stairs I heard voices. I couldn't make out what they were saying but I could make out two men. The hairs on the back of my neck stood up. With no memory, I was relying on my instincts, and they were *screaming at me to get out of there.*

There was a fire escape just along the corridor from the flat. It didn't look alarmed; I would have to risk it.

The voices grew louder.

"Why'd it have to be the top floor?" panted one.

"I've told you before about all those kebabs," laughed the second.

Heavy footsteps on the stairs. I pushed open the fire escape door as quietly as I could and slipped outside, pushing it closed behind me. It was not alarmed. Behind the door, the voices continued.

"Who is this guy, anyway?"

"I dunno. Damian picked him up. The boss thinks he's important, though, so don't be too rough with him."

"But who is he? I mean, is he gonna cause any trouble?"

"Naah. He's one of Damian's boyfriends."

There was a nasty sounding chuckle.

I heard the footsteps round the stairs and head towards Jimmy's (my?) flat. Then I heard the sound of a key in the lock and the door open, and I headed down the fire escape stairs before they realised I'd gone. I crept down the first flight but practically ran down the rest. They emerged into a communal back garden for the block, which was largely given over to low maintenance shrubbery. A low gate at the end led back to the road.

Now I was outside I felt a little more relaxed, and quickly hailed a passing taxi. I could only imagine what might be going on upstairs, and tried not to.

It was only half past three when I entered the café. There was no sign yet of Lisa - just a young lady with long dark hair and a name badge on her apron that said

"Anne". She leaned forward on the counter as I approached her.

"Black coffee, please."

Anne poured out a cup and looked at me carefully. "Are you looking for Lisa?" she asked. "She said to look out for a handsome man in a leather jacket. Are you going out with her?"

"Uh... no..."

She licked her lips. They were a particularly vibrant red. "Her loss. What are you doing tonight?"

I heard the door open behind me.

"Calm down, Anne, before I get a bucket of water. What would your Gareth say?"

I turned to see Lisa in the doorway.

"No harm in a bit of window shopping," said Anne.

Lisa tutted. "You haven't changed since we were at school. Any man with a pulse. Am I late, Rob? Or are you early?"

"I'm early," I said. "I had to leave rather sooner than I expected."

She frowned. "Did Damian... Jimmy come back?"

"No. Two men called by. I managed to sneak past them but they were definitely looking for me."

"This is bad, Rob. It sounds serious, and I didn't think Damian was anything more than small-time. I think we'd better get you out of London."

"Can I finish my coffee first?"

We sat in the corner, away from the window at Lisa's insistence, and I told her about my experiences. Lisa nodded. "Yes, that's Damian alright. Come to think of it, he used to call himself Jim when he was looking for boys rather than girls. I dated him briefly, but I got out of there pretty quick when I realised how unstable he was.

But this... he's even worse than when I knew him. He always was a bit weird, but he never acted like that. Especially not in public."

"So what do we do now?" I asked. "I still have nowhere to go and my only lead is a psycho."

"You can't rely on Damian," she said. "He's already drugged you and lied to you."

"Has he? Or did I make that up?"

"What was the date when we met?" she asked me. Before I could respond she handed me a newspaper from the next table. "What's the date today?"

She was right. Two days had passed. Not five or six.

"Jimmy is lying to you, Rob. He lies to everyone. Did he tell you he's a musician?"

I thought back. "Yes, he did. He played me some music he said he'd written."

"More lies. He stole it, like he stole the apartment – perhaps from you. He's a cheat, a thief and a liar, Rob. But it sounds like he's in even deeper trouble now than when I knew him. What were these two men like?"

"I didn't see them. I didn't want to risk them seeing me. One likes kebabs."

She gave me a look. "Yes, that'll narrow it down."

"I've got two other leads," I said. "I've got this key, and I've got a tape. I don't know where the key fits, but maybe this tape will tell me."

"Okay," she said. "Let's go. I realised on the way here – I don't have one at home because it's all CDs these days, but my car is older than God. It's still got a tape player installed."

Lisa's car was an ancient Ford Escort, which appeared to largely be made of rust held together by a few patches of light blue paint. It took a few attempts to start it up, but we were soon on our way out of London, battling the traffic.

"I rarely drive nowadays," Lisa said, grinding gears as she forced the vehicle into third. "It's just impossible to get anywhere in London by car, and the congestion charge..."

I nodded in agreement, even though I had no idea what the congestion charge was. I did have a vague sense that London and cars were not the best of friends.

"Okay, get the tape in. I'll switch the thing on."

There was a brief blast of Radio 1 as the radio turned on, and I rapidly adjusted the volume down from ear-piercing to comfortable. I fished the cigarette packet out of my pocket, pulled out the cassette and figured out how to fit it in the machine in two goes. The radio silenced and the tape began to whirr. There were several seconds of silence.

A moment later, we heard a woman singing something about midnight on pavements.

"Hey, I know this one. It's from Cats," said Lisa. "Elaine Page – oh, of course. It's called Memory."

"Someone has a twisted sense of humour," I commented.

After just a few more seconds of Elaine Page the music changed. Another woman, this time singing about someone called Jimmy, or maybe "Jimmy-Mac".

Song three began straight after this - a song about sweet little lies.

"Fleetwood Mac?" she hazarded. I nodded, though I really had no idea.

A fourth song began, this time a male voice.

"Now that's the Pet Shop Boys," commented Lisa. "I don't know it, though."

"Do you have a pen and paper handy?" I asked.

"Sure, in the glovebox. Why?"

I stopped the tape and rewound it a little. Several pens and a number of envelopes and scraps of paper spilled out of the glovebox when I opened it. I restarted the tape and jotted down the more promising of the lyrics.

"I can look them up later," I said.

"Sure, but why? It's a mix tape."

"I think it's a message."

"I think you're nuts."

"Really? Memory, Jimmy, lies?"

"That is a bit weird." Lisa shivered. "Hang on, it's changed again."

Dolly Parton was singing. She got to the chorus and I recognised the song as 'Nine To Five' – except the chorus cut out after "nine". Another song started straight away.

"What's this one?"

"Oh, I remember this one," said Lisa. "I think it's called '7 Seconds'."

Several more songs follows. Later research identified Aswad singing 'Don't Turn Around', a brief burst of 'They're Coming To Take Me Away, Ha Ha' and then, at the end, a song I recognised but could not name.

"I don't know this one," commented Lisa, "though it sounds familiar."

"I've heard it," I said. "I mean, recently."

"I feel I'm falling. I feel I'm falling, and when I look up I see you…"

With that, the tape fell silent.

"Well, that was weird," said Lisa. "What is it with you and cryptic messages?"

"Perhaps someone is trying to tell me something and doesn't want anyone else to know?" I sighed. "I wish I knew what those other songs are. It might make the rest clearer."

Indeed, the tape had given me more questions than answers. I looked at my notes in bafflement and then jumped when I heard my own voice. I'd forgotten that the tape was still playing.

"Hello, Rob. If you're listening to this tape, you've probably woken up with no memory. I'm sorry to have to tell you this, but it's probably not the first time."

"Hah!" said Lisa. "Here's your message, Sherlock."

"You should also have a piece of paper on you, and it may not make a lot of sense to you – it's a telephone number, Rob. Give Jimmy a call and he'll get you safely home. When you've finished listening to this message, rewind the tape and put it back where you found it – in case it happens again."

Lisa stopped the tape. "Hang on. This doesn't make any sense at all. Why a tape? Why not just write the telephone number down sensibly? What about the key? Why are you telling yourself to call Jimmy of all people? And why the music?"

"Perhaps I'll tell me," I said, continuing the tape.

"In case you can't speak to Jimmy, get yourself to the Grace Meadows Psychological Research Centre in north London. They know about your condition and they will be able to help. Tell them your name is Rob Walker and ask for Doctor Hawkins. He's in charge of your case. Good luck, Rob."

The tape went silent again for a few seconds, and then started to play more music. This time it was classical, and neither Lisa nor myself made any attempt to identify it. In any event, the music didn't change as it had before – it simply played through. Any message, if there was one to start with, had now finished. We let the tape play on as we drove, just in case, but it continued to merely play soothing classical music until the end of the tape.

"Well," I said. "At least we have a destination now."

Lisa nodded. "But where in the heck is this Grace Whatsit clinic? North London is a big place."

Once we got back to Lisa's flat in Reading she made it clear she had no intention of letting me anywhere near London again for a little while. She instead told me to stay where I was and that she would "check if the coast was clear". In the meantime, I had free run of her flat, but there would be no excursions tonight.

When she got home again, satisfied that we hadn't been followed, she made up the sofa for me and we ordered a takeaway pizza for our supper. When we'd eaten, I asked for pen and paper.

"There's a pen by the phone," said Lisa, "but good luck finding something to write on. I can't find a single one of my notebooks in this flat lately. What do you want to write, anyway?"

"A note to myself," I explained, "in case I woke up in the morning with no memory."

She nodded. "Good idea. Here, use the pizza box."

I turned the box lid towards me and wrote a few lines. They would have to do.

"Goodnight, Rob," she said.

"Goodnight, Lisa."

She switched off the light as she left. I stared into the darkness for a while, and eventually I did drift off to sleep.

I dreamed, but of my dreams I have no memory.

Research

I woke up with a clear head for the first time the next morning, helped perhaps by a lack of drugged beverages the night before. My memory was also fine, though I still felt a moment of panic as I wondered where I was. Then I saw my note on the pizza box.

You are Rob Walker. This is Lisa. Trust her.

Everything from the last few days came back to me. I remembered Jimmy, and my escape, and the tape we'd listened to in the car.

The note with Jimmy's (my?) phone number on it was on the table. As one of my last links with my past, I was rather glad to get it back – however weird it was. I folded it up and returned it to my pocket.

Lisa snored gently in the bedroom. I walked across into the kitchen area and hunted down mugs, milk and tea. Lisa was stepping sleepily out of the bedroom as I finished making it.

"I must stop sleeping in so late," she said. "I've got myself into bad habits."

Over cups of tea, we discussed what had happened.

"I'll go back to London, check out what's happening," she said. "You stay here."

I shook my head. "It's not safe. What if someone's looking for me?"

"They're looking for you, not me. They won't even know who I am. Besides, I'll be careful."

There was no arguing with her.

"Here, take this." *She handed me a key.* "I'm not going to lock you in here like Jimmy. Just don't go too far."

"Thanks."

"Do you have any money?"

"I'm okay," *I said.* "I picked up some of Jimmy's before I left."

"Great. Give me some. Look, I've already driven to hell and back for you and I'm about to do it again. The least you could do is pay for the petrol."

I fished out a bundle of notes from my wallet. She was right, of course. She usually was.

I spent the first hour or so after she left exploring her flat. It didn't take very long to cover all the rooms and there seemed to be a distinct lack of clutter. Indeed, there were only a few basics in the fridge and virtually no food in the kitchen as a whole (a trip out for lunch was therefore called for). Odder was the general lack of stuff in the living room - a few empty DVD cases, for instance, but no DVDs. The DVD collection on the shelves that Jimmy (Damian?) had declared ours numbered in the dozens – not that I could be sure this was typical.

I looked in the box under the CD player. Despite Lisa's comments about everything being CDs, she didn't seem to have any. She did have a number of cassettes, some very old and most home recorded, but nothing to play them on. This struck me as odd, but I thought perhaps they were old tapes that she just didn't want to throw away.

The bedroom was the weirdest, though. It boasted a wardrobe and a chest of drawers, neither of them particularly high quality, filled with a range of clothes. But there was nothing in the bedside cabinet and a distinct absence of books – and no computer. If she was really a journalist, surely a computer would be essential? There was a cable plugged into a phone line in the bedroom, but it lay unused on the floor.

I decided to shelve my suspicions for a while. Lisa may not be all she seemed, but she was the nearest I had to a friend at the moment. Jimmy was not an attractive alternative. I decided to head into town for some lunch and to mull it over, and do some research while I was at it.

After a sandwich and a packet of crisps in town, I returned to Reading Library and flashed a winsome smile at the librarian on duty. She utterly ignored it but informed me that there was a computer free. I hopped online, this time armed with some more concrete search terms.

First, I looked up Grace Meadows. I was surprised to find relatively few hits – just their rather simple website, and a few published papers. They seemed very quiet for a research facility. Looking for Dr Hawkins and Grace Meadows in the same search got me results from the same site – he kept an online blog about his work there, referring to patients by their initials. I scanned quickly for any mention of RW but there was nothing in his recent postings.

I then looked up the two songs I didn't recognise from my "mix tape" message to myself. The last song, the one Jimmy had played, I could find no trace of – those lyrics seemed utterly unknown – but the Pet Shop Boys one was much easier. I quickly discovered it was called *Kings Cross*.

I remembered Jimmy telling me I'd once run off, leaving my identification in a luggage locker at a railway station.

I looked at my notes again. Dolly Parton singing "nine to five", but it cut into the next song after the "nine". Neneh Cherry singing about seven seconds. Nine... seven... I pulled the key out of my pocket.

097.

Was it as simple as that?

But then why be so cryptic? Why not just say what the key was for in my message to myself?

I decided to do one last search before I left the library. I had a name now – could I find myself online?

"Robert Walker" turned up thousands upon thousands of results. My name was just too common.

I tried "Robert Walker" and "amnesia" in the same search. Nothing relevant was obvious in the first few pages.

"Robert Walker" and "Jimmy". Thousands of results, nothing relevant.

"Robert Walker" and "Soho". Thousands of results, nothing relevant.

In desperation, I tried "Robert Walker" and "Grace Meadows".

The third link went straight to my picture.

It was an old page, last updated a few years ago, but there I was, looking slightly younger and rather more cheerful than I had in the mirror that morning. It related to a research grant I'd been awarded, and the page was an article for the University of Reading's alumni newsletter. I'd thanked the university for their help and resources in getting my thesis published. It was about the causes of memory loss.

I wasn't a test subject, but a researcher, based at the Grace Meadows Clinic in London. I worked there.

I printed out the article, wanting to study it later, as well as the main website pages for Grace Meadows. I then headed back to the flat.

As I came in, I heard the telephone ringing. I picked it up without thinking, started to panic, then relaxed when I heard Lisa's voice. But not for long.

"Where the hell have you been?" she said. "I've tried calling you four times now."

"I've been doing some research," I replied. "I've found out... hell, I don't know how to start. When are you getting back?"

"Oh God... Oh, Rob..." Lisa started to sob, great heaving cries of grief and loss.

"Rob... it's Damian. He's dead, Rob. They killed him."

There was nothing on the news about him. I'd expected a murder in central London to be a big story, but the BBC remained utterly silent about it. Perhaps the police didn't want false leads or something like that. Once again I regretted the lack of a computer in Lisa's house.

It was some time later that Lisa came home.

"Lisa! What happened?"

She shook her head. "He's dead, Rob. Someone killed him. Shot him in the back and dumped him in an alley."

"Shot? Why?"

"You tell me, Rob. Those men were after you."

It made a horrible sort of sense, if you lived in a crime thriller. Those men came looking for me, found I wasn't there, and then must have assumed Jimmy had smuggled me out. When he wouldn't tell them where I was - because he didn't know - they murdered him.

"Why wasn't it on the news?"

"The police spiked the story," she said. "They suspect it's connected with organised crime. I know Damian was involved with some shady stuff but still…"

"Lisa, I need to go back to London."

"Why? You're safe here. Do you want to report in to the Godfather or something? Do you even care that someone's been killed for you?"

"I didn't know about any of this!"

"Really? You're up to your neck in whatever this is about, Rob. You tell me you've got amnesia. Well, that's pretty damned convenient. Who are you, Rob?"

I had no reply.

"Look, I'm exhausted. I'm going to try to get some sleep. Just leave me alone for a bit, will you?"

"Alright. I'll go. I need to clear my head anyway."

So I went for a walk. Walking often helps me think, or so I believe – it certainly had in the last few days, and sometimes it still does. At the moment, all I had were questions.

For a start, who was Jimmy? I didn't know anything about him. All I knew was that he'd lied to me, and more than that – those faked photographs came to mind. Was he trying to convince me we were lovers?

What was this key for? Was there really a message made up of songs on that tape? Why? And why wasn't the key mentioned in the proper message that came after it? A message which had said Jimmy was someone I could trust - so I couldn't trust the message either.

And what about the Grace Meadows centre? The centre which I was supposedly working at, not a patient of? Who was Dr Hawkins? Was I really researching memory loss there? That seemed far too ironic to be true.

Then there was Lisa. Something was itching in the back of my head about her. It was rather a coincidence that I happened to meet the ex-girlfriend of the outright nutcase trying to convince me I was his lover. And her flat – it was spartan, but absurdly so. She had virtually no electronics, as though she'd had to scrounge for what cheap old things she could get. She didn't even have a washing machine. She had no real job – she said she was a journalist, but there was no evidence of it.

Could I trust her?

My walking route came full circle, and as I approached the main entrance to the flats I saw the pale blue Escort parked outside. I wanted to listen to the tape again, to hear my message to myself once more. Maybe things would make more sense this time.

First I needed the car keys. I headed back up to the flat.

I could hear Lisa in the bathroom as I entered. I found her car keys and the paperwork I'd printed out at the library earlier and went down to the car.

After a quick burst of late night radio, I shoved the tape into the player and waited for the music to start, the envelope with my rough notes on it in front of me. I waited longer, but there was nothing. Just the background hiss of the tape. Had it taken this long last time to start playing?

Just as I realised that I had not rewound the tape, and this was side B, the tape revealed there was some noise on it after all. It was muffled, confusing. There were bangs and thuds, and in the background a whirring noise. Voices spoke, too indistinct to make out who they were or what they were saying. All except one, calling out to the others that it would only be a moment, it was just getting some coffee.

It was my voice.

The whirring continued for a moment, then suddenly stopped, and I realised it was the sound of a vending machine. I was indeed getting coffee. I heard myself take a sip, then there were more background noises, and footsteps. They didn't get any louder or quieter, and I realised they were probably mine.

So I was carrying a tape recorder, and recording myself.

"Hey, Rob."

"Hi, Max. Just getting some coffee. How's it going?"

"Not too bad. We're getting some results from the new compounds, but it's still early days. How about you?"

"Not much going on. Same old routine, you know. I can't stay, Max, I'm already running late."

"Hawkins, right?"

My ears pricked at that name.

"Yeah, old Hawkish. He's been telling me off for fraternising."

"You mean Lisa?"

I jumped at that. Lisa! Surely this couldn't be the same Lisa?

"Yeah. Well, either her or Jimmy. I think he's keen on me."

Laughter. "You're in there, Rob."

"Oh, shut up!"

"See you later, Rob."

"Bye."

More walking. Another sip of coffee. Bangs, probably doors.

"Dr Hawkins, sir."

"You're late."

"Sorry, sir. Just getting some coffee."

"I'll keep this short, then. Can't have you falling asleep on me."

"Sorry, sir."

My tape-self gave in almost immediately. Was Dr Hawkins more frightening than I was giving him credit?

"I've called you in here because I'm... concerned. I'm aware that you've been taking a particularly special interest in other aspects of the project."

"I'm always willing to discuss things with my colleagues, sir."

"Talking to your colleagues is one thing. Some of our research data has been leaking out, and that I cannot tolerate. I gather that you've been talking to a certain young lady outside of office hours."

"Are you saying I can't have a social life?"

"Not at all. But you should choose your companions more carefully."

"Is that all, sir?"

A pause. "Get back to work. I don't want to have to speak to you again, do you understand me?"

"Yes, sir."

The sound of a door opening and closing, and my footsteps. Then the click of a tape recorder being turned off, followed by just background hiss. I stopped the tape.

"You can probably guess what was going on."

I looked up, startled, to see Lisa standing beside the car door. She opened it and climbed inside.

"I'm sorry, Rob."

"You knew me before my amnesia?"

"Yes," she said. "You were working at a research centre, involved with some rather dubious projects. We were meeting up outside of work and you were providing me with the details of what you were finding out."

"So what happened?"

"I don't know. We'd started recording your discussions with colleagues on a small tape recorder – that was one of the tapes you've just heard. I've never heard that one before, though. The last tape you sent me said that you thought they were getting suspicious, and that we shouldn't meet for a while."

"Why didn't you say anything when we met a few days ago?"

"You didn't respond to the code phrase."

Code phrase? "You mean the bit about the guy following you?"

"Yeah. If it was safe to talk, you'd have said something about him being a friend of yours. Then you told me your memory was gone, and I thought you were up to something, testing me... I didn't realise that your memory was really gone until... well, that evening."

"What do you..."

"Rob... you told me yourself when we first met. You're gay. How can you forget something like that?"

I thought about my reaction that evening. "I think at least part of me hadn't."

"There's so much more I need to tell you, Rob. And so much I need you to tell me. What happened to you, Rob? What did they do to you?"

I didn't need to tell her that, whatever had been done to me, I had no idea. All I had were cryptic clues that made no sense when combined together.

"But why didn't you tell me this earlier? All this time I've been looking for answers, and you've had them all along!"

Her eyes didn't meet mine. "I... The time wasn't right," she said, staring at her hands in her lap. "I wasn't sure what you really knew, what you were doing... and I didn't..."

She looked up, slowly. "I think you're catching," she smiled, weakly. "To be honest, I just didn't think of it until I heard that tape." She looked away again. "That sounds stupid, I know."

It was some time before I figured out why she hadn't told me before. I believe her now. I didn't then.

"So tell me now. Tell me... tell me about Damian, Lisa. You said you'd dated him. Or was that a lie too?"

This was clearly a difficult topic for her, but she made a clear effort to compose herself. "It's true," she said. "I met him many years ago and we spent a few months together. It wasn't a happy time. You've met him – you know how... unstable he is. The guy had problems and I wasn't willing to deal with them. But still – he could be sweet."

"He didn't seem the type to be interested in girls," I said, remembering waking up *in bed with "Jimmy".*

"I don't know whether he knew he was bi when we were together, or whether he's always batted for both teams," she replied. "He certainly took a shine to you, Rob."

"How did you and I meet?" I asked.

"Outside the research centre. They threw me out for asking too many awkward questions, and you came by in the pouring rain after leaving work and gave me a lift. It was very sweet of you. You were the perfect gentleman, to my great dismay. The other night, when we... I took advantage of you. I'm sorry, Rob. I shouldn't have done that. I told myself I was testing you, but that's not true. I wanted to. I can't explain it. I don't even know why I did it."

"And now?"

"I don't feel that way any more. It's like I was possessed or something. Bad wine, perhaps."

She paused, getting back to her story.

"We started talking, and I said I was concerned about some of the projects taking place in there. You were concerned too – you were working for someone else, I think, but you offered to see what you could find out. Between us we thought we could put a stop to it."

"What is going on?"

"I don't know. They have a number of projects going on that I don't know much about – but they aren't following normal procedures. I think there's some military funding involved as well, but that will be near impossible to prove. Most of the projects seem to involve ways to affect behaviour, but then there's what most of the people there call the Amnesia Project."

"Is that what's happened to me?"

"I honestly don't know. I didn't find out much about it before Hawkins noticed you were digging. And then you disappeared for a few days."

We sat in silence for a few minutes.

"They killed him, Rob. I think whatever you were working on with him has something to do with it."

"Lisa..." I said. "I've been doing some research. I've found out a bit about who I am, but I also think I know what this key is for."

"It's a locker key, right?"

"I think I know which locker."

We did no more that night. Lisa and I returned to bed and sofa respectively, and while Lisa quickly fell asleep (aided, I had no doubt, by the tranquilisers she thought I didn't see her swallow) I lay awake for a while. My mind was too full of ideas to settle down. There was so much I needed to know, so much I wanted to find out, but for now I could do nothing. I read through the papers I'd printed out earlier in the library, catching up on my recent history and the cover story for Grace Meadows. Research was part of their role, with the diagnosis and treatment of mental disorders the main thrust of their website. Amnesia was, as I expected, listed as one of the fields they specialised in.

There were so many other questions. I hadn't given much thought to whether I had a family or a partner (Lisa's earlier bombshell made children unlikely, which gave me mixed feelings). I didn't really believe that Jimmy and I had ever been an item. But was someone else wondering where I was?

I turned the locker key over in my hand. 097. What was in locker 097 at King's Cross station? Would it answer any of my questions, or leave me with more? Was there anything there at all? All I had to go on was a cryptic message made from fragments of song.

I slept badly that night, grateful for the arrival of the morning sun.

"London again. I hope the car can take it."

I nodded. Poor Lisa was becoming a regular commuter. "King's Cross, first of all," I said. "I want to know what's in that locker."

"If anything. You've not got much to go on."

"Then I want to know what's going on at Grace Meadows."

"Rob, I'm not sure that's a good idea. They won't let me into the place and, if we're right, they've already done something to you."

"I need to see Dr Hawkins. I left a message on that tape and I want to know why."

"It's a trap, Rob."

"Maybe." The thought had occurred to me. It was my own voice on the tape, that was plain, but what it said made no sense. Was there something else about this I wasn't considering?

"One more thing," I said. "I know it's dangerous, but I want to go back to Soho. I want to show you the apartment."

Lisa nodded. "Alright," she said. "But we'll need to be careful. Damian's killers were after you, Rob. They might be watching the place."

The drive to London was quiet – we headed out after the rush hour had died down. Lisa picked up a few of her mix tapes at random from the box in her living room, "for the journey". In the end we gave up on all of them - they didn't look that old, but the music on every tape seemed distorted, overlaid with a low droning sound.

"I should throw these things out," she said. "Get a CD player."

"And some CDs," I replied. She ignored me.

I left my own tape in the car, still inside the cigarette packet – I had no idea why I still kept it in there, but something about it seemed right. Lisa kept in her handbag a variety of knick-knacks but, in particular, a rape alarm. She said she hadn't carried one in years, but it was about time she did. We were heading into dangerous waters.

King's Cross Station was busy, but then I imagine it usually is. Crowds of people rushed in all directions, occasionally bumping into me but few even looking round. Garbled announcements fought to be heard over the general hubbub and the smells of coffee and breakfast pastries fought valiantly against the grimy undertones left by an endless stream of thousands of travellers passing through. It took me a while to find out where the luggage lockers were, and even longer to locate the particular locker I was after.

093... 095... 097.

I put the key into the lock, felt it slide home, took a deep breath and turned it. The lock clicked. As I pulled the door open I felt a hand upon my shoulder. I turned my head towards the face of a burly policeman.

"Excuse me, sir," he said. "I must ask you to come with me."

I looked back at the locker. It was empty.

"Now, please, sir."

"Alright," I said. "Can I just..."

I looked around, but Lisa had once again disappeared.

"...never mind."

The policeman took hold of my upper arm and, with a brisk pace I struggled to match, marched me towards the security offices. I looked back at the open locker door, swinging gently closed onto empty air.

The Visitor

When Henry came into the office that Friday, he was surprised to find someone waiting for him.

"Mr Patfield?"

"No, I'm Mr Ford," Henry replied. "George Patfield died several years ago, I'm afraid. Look, whatever bill I've forgotten, I can't pay. Have a chat with Phil when he comes in next. As bailiffs go, he's a nice guy."

"I'm not looking for money. I'm here about your serial piece."

"Pardon?"

The man showed him a copy of the latest edition. "This piece, Mr Ford. The one you're calling *The Amnesia Project*."

Henry looked at it. "Oh, yes. It's proving a small hit, that one. Well, for us, anyway. It's a bit... out there, but I thought... why not?"

"Where did you get this story, Mr Ford?"

Henry sensed trouble. "I'm afraid I can't reveal our sources, Mr...?"

"Doctor. Dr Edmunds." He slid a business card across the desk.

"A doctor, huh? I don't suppose you could fill in for the *Ask Dr Monroe* column, could you?"

"I'm not that sort of doctor."

"Oh well. Worth a try."

"Mr Ford, I want you to stop running this story."

Henry laughed. "Really? Why?"

"The author of this tale, the one writing as Rob Walker, was... is a patient of mine. He has some... issues. I can't go into details – patient confidentiality – but suffice to say he is something of a fantasist."

"It's a good read so far," Henry said. "But I don't see why a fiction piece should be a problem."

"Mr Walker has cast me in a rather bad light. I'm sure you can guess who I am supposed to be."

"You're the sinister Dr Hawkins?"

"Quite so. It's just a science fiction piece, obviously, but some people take these things quite seriously. Especially when they are based on real people and places. My concern is purely for my reputation."

"Your reputation? Not your patients?" Something about his visitor was giving Henry a sour stomach. "This is the first decent break the magazine has had for months. I'm not stopping the story."

"Mr Ford. Neither of us want to get involved in a libel case, do we?"

Henry frowned. "Excuse me?"

"I would rather not go through a lengthy court case, Mr Ford, for a number of reasons. But if you force me to take this route, I will see your little magazine go bankrupt through the legal fees. I will see you and your dimwitted assistant cast out on the streets. Is that understood?"

Henry bristled - more at the comment about Eddie than the threat of losing the magazine.

"Well, Mr Ford? Will you stop printing this nonsense, or do I need to call my lawyers?"

The more this Dr Edmunds pushed him, the more he wanted to run the story anyway, and to hell with the consequences. But the magazine couldn't even afford a regular columnist - it certainly wouldn't survive a legal battle.

"Fine," he sighed, defeated. "It's too late to stop the latest edition, but we'll make this the last one."

"Thank you, Mr Ford. And… one more thing." Dr Edmunds placed an envelope on the desk. "I would very much like to track down the author of this story. Anything you can tell me about his whereabouts would be greatly appreciated."

"I don't know anything," Henry snapped. "Even if I did, why would I want to tell you?"

"A shame. Still, if you do find out anything... should you change your mind... I hope this goes some way to compensating you."

"I've already told you I'll stop printing the story. You'll have to find your patient yourself."

"Consider this a gift, then. But if this next instalment is not the last, I will make sure this magazine never runs another issue."

Henry waited until the doctor was gone before opening the envelope. He wasn't entirely surprised to find a quantity of bank notes inside.

Something stirred in Henry's gut; something he hadn't felt for a long time. There was a story here. A proper mystery. He didn't quite know what it was yet, but he could smell it.

Stop the story? Sure. But maybe Rob had a better story to tell, if he could track him down. The truth behind the fiction.

And maybe he could give Dr Edmunds something to *really* complain about.

Eddie returned a short time later with two coffees and a couple of baguettes, using the lid from a box of photocopier paper as a makeshift tray.

"Lunch, boss."

"Thanks, Eddie. Take it out of the petty cash."

Eddie shook his head. "No money in there, boss. It's on me."

Henry chuckled. "Take another look," he replied. "I've just topped it up. We're about to turn things around, Eddie. Someone's bailed us out."

Eddie's face fell. "You've sold the magazine?"

Henry put a reassuring hand on Eddie's shoulder. He'd forgotten about Eddie's biggest concern – that they'd be taken over, and silly Eddie with his learning difficulties would be out of a job. Henry couldn't imagine the office without Eddie.

"No, we're not selling. Some guy's paid us to stop running that story. Paid a lot, actually."

"Oh, okay." Eddie, no longer worried, began to eat.

"When you're done with lunch, Eddie, I'd like you to do two things for me. First, find out where those tapes came from. There should be a postmark on the envelope – ask the post office about it. And second, look up some plumbers. I think we can start by sorting out the basement."

Eddie may not have been that smart, but he tried to be organised. With his tendency to forget things, he put them in particular places so he'd be able to find them again. He wrote lists and notes – not just one or two, but dozens – so that his desk was barely visible under a sea of scraps. Of course, this often meant he missed things because he couldn't find the right scrap, but the system worked more often than it didn't. Occasionally the boss would gently ask him to sort them out before they got out of hand and he'd spend an hour carefully reading them one at a time and throwing away the ones he didn't need any more (or couldn't remember what they were for).

In one of the desk drawers he kept the tapes, still inside the envelope they'd arrived in. They were only tiny tapes, the ones you got for those Dictaphones. Eddie had always wanted one. He'd seen them in old films and TV programmes, with high powered businessmen recording their thoughts on them. No-one used them any more.

Except for whoever had sent the package. Eddie hoped the boss would let him keep the machine after he was done with it.

The envelope was a large, padded, manila packet. The address was hand written in block capitals and a hand written warning read "magnetic media – do not x-ray". Eddie thought Magnetic Media would make a cool name for the magazine, but the boss had laughed when he'd suggested it.

The postmark was a slightly smudged stamp in one corner. Eddie peered a little closer, trying to make it out, then looked up the details for the post office and gave them a call on the telephone.

"Boss!"

Henry looked up. "What is it, Eddie?"

"The package, boss. It came from Brighton!"

Perhaps it hadn't, thought Henry. If he was trying to hide from someone, he probably wouldn't post it from where he lived. But it was the only lead they had, and maybe the poster of the package hadn't thought that far ahead.

"Good job, Eddie. Have you sorted that plumber out yet?"

"Just about to, boss."

"Go on, then. I have to make a call."

Eddie grinned and left him alone.

Time for a little investigative journalism, then. Henry had two mysteries to clear up - the mystery author, and the mystery doctor. It was probably best to keep Eddie out of the second one, so he'd have to call on some additional help. He picked up the telephone and dialled a number he thought he'd forgotten long ago.

"Hello, Mike."

"Henry! Good to hear from you, man. Is that little magazine of yours still going?"

"We've had a bit of luck, Mike. Someone's paying us a small fortune *not* to run a story."

"That's a new one."

"First he threatened libel, then he paid us off. Weird."

"Is that why you've called?"

Straight to the point. That was Mike. "Yeah. It's got me suspicious. Look, I know it's probably nothing, and I can't afford to hire anyone…"

"Anything you need, Henry. You saved my life that time. I'm not going to forget that."

"All we did was run the story, jog the memories of a few witnesses. The police did the rest."

"Only after that editorial shamed them into it."

Henry sighed. Those had been good times, back when the magazine had made a difference.

"Henry? You there?"

"Sorry, getting nostalgic in my old age. It's like this, Mike. Someone sent us a bunch of cassette tapes in the mail. No idea who, but it's a work of fiction and I decided to run it. What the hell, right?"

"*The Amnesia Project*? Yeah, I've been reading it. It's pretty good, Henry. Weird, but good. Did you know that there actually was a clinic called Grace Meadows? It burned down back in 2004."

"You're kidding!"

"I'm not. This guy's done his research, Henry. He's good. Hire him full time."

"Actually, Mike, that's the thing. I have no idea who sent those tapes."

"You want me to track down the writer?"

"No, Eddie and I can handle that. But I don't trust the guy that's paid us to stop running it. I want you to look into him for me."

"I see. Just a gut feeling?"

"Just a gut feeling," agreed Henry. "But you're the one that's always telling me to listen to my gut."

"Damn right. Your gut knows more than your brain, Henry. It's starting to get big enough."

Henry chuckled. "Mike, we should meet up some time. Get some drinks. Talk about old times."

"I'd like that." Mike paused. "So what can you tell me about this guy?"

"He calls himself Dr Edmunds. He left me a business card." Henry reeled off the telephone number on the card. "Be careful, Mike. My gut's really grumbling on this one."

"I'll be careful. But you watch yourself too, Henry. If this Dr Edmunds really is trouble, you don't want to cross him. At best, you might get sued. You can't afford that. But I don't think he's the type to sue."

"Because he paid me?"

"Exactly. If you're being libelled, you don't start by giving cash to your libellers. You just sue them. If he thinks you're going to run that story anyway, he might decide to send some guys over with baseball bats. Or worse. You don't want anything to happen to Eddie, do you?"

Henry hadn't considered that.

"Good luck, Henry. I hope you haven't got yourself into too much trouble."

"Me too, Mike. Me too. Call me soon, right? I'm serious about that drink."

"That's good. I'm a serious drinker."

Henry laughed as he put the phone down, but without feeling.

"Henry," he said to himself, "what have you gotten yourself into?"

There was one more telephone call to make before they carried on with their investigation. Henry looked up a number he largely had on hand for emergencies.

"Hello, Maggie."

"Henry! Is Eddie okay?"

"He's fine. He's a good boy."

"I know," she sighed, clearly relieved. "I just worry so much. You never call me these days. Not since George... well, you know."

"I know. It's just... hard. I'd known him since we were at school. When I think about you, I keep thinking about him."

"It was one drunken night many years ago, Henry. And it didn't have anything to do with his accident. You have to let go of him some time."

Like it was that easy.

"How's the magazine going?" she said. "Eddie's been worried lately. He's been hearing stories that you're closing down. You know that job's everything to him. It's not true, is it?"

"We're not doing too great, Maggie, but you know I'll do everything I can to keep things going. For George's sake. And if we do go under, I'll see that Eddie gets a job somewhere else."

"Not just anywhere. You know he's... special."

"I know. That's why I'm calling, Maggie. I wanted to ask..."

"He's been through a lot, that boy. Both of us have. The number of times I've had to stand up for him... I'm not blaming you, Henry, you know that. You've always been good to Eddie. You've always made him feel normal."

"Maggie..."

"I'm always worried someone will call me to say he's been arrested or something.

And what happens when I'm gone, Henry? Who'll look after him then? Of course, you'll look after him, won't you Henry?"

Henry looked at his watch. Ten minutes, tops – Maggie Patfield was almost religious with her television viewing schedule.

"Anyway, listen to me wittering on again. What did you ring up for?"

"Maggie, I'd like to take Eddie away for a few days. Get him some proper experience in journalism."

"Not too far, I hope? You know he doesn't like to travel."

Actually, Henry had never found Eddie unhappy with travelling. He found it quite an adventure. Henry suspected that it wasn't Eddie that didn't like Eddie travelling.

"We don't be going that far." That was perfectly true, if you felt the south coast was not "that far". It was closer than Mars, for example. Besides, Eddie needed to get a bit further afield.

"And you'll be with him all the time?"

"Yes, I'll be with him." Mostly true, anyway. There might be a few places he'd be better leaving Eddie behind.

"I'll pack a bag for him, then. Have you told him yet?"

"No. I thought it best to clear it with you first."

"If he doesn't want to go, he stays home. You understand?"

"I understand."

"Thanks for calling, Henry. Goodbye, now."

"Goodbye, Maggie."

Henry put down the phone and breathed a sigh of relief. Dr Edmunds was a little frightening. What Mike had said made him even more frightening. Mrs Maggie Patfield, however, was exhausting. He felt a little bad about lying to her – he might potentially be putting Eddie in danger. It didn't seem likely, but his gut was still gurgling and looked likely to do so all night.

Henry went to find Eddie, who was carefully sorting through the paper scraps at his desk, making sure he hadn't forgotten something important.

"Hey, Eddie. How would you like to come with me and try your hand at some real journalism?"

Eddie's face lit up and his grin threatened to split his head in two. "Boss! You mean it?"

"I mean it. We need to do some digging, and I can't do it alone."

"Not like the regular stuff?"

The regular stuff, as Eddie put it, was the journalism-light copy he was usually asked to put together – he didn't even really need to write it, just put together puff pieces submitted by companies out for some free advertising. Still, they helped to fill up the magazine. Or they used to. Even the people writing the filler were steadily leaving the magazine.

"Not the regular stuff, no. We're going to find out about those tapes."

Eddie bounced in his chair with excitement.

"But boss... didn't they get sent from Brighton?"

"That's right. That's where we need to go."

Eddie stopped. "That's a long way, boss. My mum won't like that."

"I've spoken to your mother, Eddie. She's agreed. She's packing a bag for you - we can go tomorrow morning."

"No way!" Eddie bounced a little more. "Why do I need a bag?"

"We're going to be there a few days, Eddie. These stories take a while sometimes. Do you still want to come?"

Eddie's face was difficult to read. On the one hand, this was a big thrill. This was a chance to do something grown up and real, something his mother was always saying he wasn't ready for. And to be a proper journalist! He'd always wanted to do that. On the other hand, he'd not travelled more than a few miles from home in years.

"I'll be with you, Eddie. Your mother insisted I stay with you."

Eddie nodded. "Okay, boss. I'll come with you. I won't let you down!"

Henry smiled. "You'd never do that, Eddie."

Henry packed his laptop ready for the trip. It still contained all the transcripts they'd published so far, along with a few more they would now never publish. Henry also packed the tapes into the side pocket, in case he wanted to listen to them again.

As he emptied the envelope, he spotted something in the corner – another address, a return address, crossed out but still readable.

It was a company called "JKR Electronics". A London address.

Henry had no idea where in Brighton this envelope had been sent from, but it looked like Rob Walker (or whatever name he was using) had reused the envelope to send his final tapes.

It wasn't much of a lead, but it was worth a try.

Henry made a note to look up JKR Electronics, then sealed up the laptop bag and closed the office for the night. They had a big day coming up.

Detained

I'd like to say that this was the first time I'd seen the inside of a cell, but in truth I really wouldn't know. I can tell you that this was the first time in the last few days, since waking up in the almost as bleak atmosphere of the Travel Hotel, but that's hardly a record worthy of mention.

All in all, the police were rather gentle with me. I was handcuffed, stripped to my underwear, searched, given my clothing back (but not my shoes), placed in a holding cell and then promptly left alone for the next hour or so. Not that I knew how long it really was, as they'd taken Lisa's watch, but it seemed a long time. I spent the time reflecting on what had happened – an empty locker, Lisa disappearing (she had a knack for doing that, I mused) and now my arrest. Well, I called it an arrest. I was pretty sure the police were supposed to tell you what they were arresting you for.

Of all the things I'd expected to find in the locker – some identification, perhaps, or a message to myself, or even in my more fanciful daydreams a handgun and directions to assassinate Dr Hawkins – the last thing I'd been expecting was nothing at all. It was rather a disappointment. Not to mention a tad silly – what was the point in locking up nothing and giving myself a treasure hunt to find it?

I was just thinking that the locker made a perfect metaphor for my memory when a police officer came to the cell. He opened up and motioned for me to come with him without saying a word. I considered asking for my one phone call, but who did I have to call? I didn't even have Lisa's number. Instead I was handcuffed again, marched down the corridor to an interview room and brought inside, where I was introduced to an uncomfortable chair in front of a cheap but sturdy looking desk. A tape recorder sat to one side – more tapes, I thought to myself – and a thin man with a receding hairline and a greying moustache sat opposite me. He started the tape recorder.

"This interview is being conducted by myself, Inspector Jeffries, with PC 4508 Johnson in attendance. Please state your name and date of birth for the tape, please."

There was a moment's pause, after which Inspector Jeffries looked at me pointedly, and I realised he meant me. "Robert Walker, born... uh..." It was no good. The date Jimmy had given me had completely gone out of my head.

"Come on, sir," sighed the Inspector.

"It's a long story," I replied. "I honestly don't know. But I'm about twenty eight."

"Right, we'll worry about that later. Mr Walker, do you know why you are here?"

"No."

"Did you or did you not attempt to access locker number 097 at King's Cross station earlier today?"

"I did, yes."

"What did you expect to find in there?"

"I have no idea."

"Who gave you the key to this locker?"

"I don't know."

"You don't know." Inspector Jeffries drummed his fingers on the desk a few times, clearly irritated. "You know, you'd do much better to co-operate, Mr Walker. Who told you to collect the contents of this locker?"

"I think it was me."

"You're not making any sense."

"I think I'm doing very well, considering," I snapped back. "Are you going to keep asking me questions I don't know the answers to, or are you going to tell me what the hell is going on?"

"Alright, Mr Walker, we'll go over the basics. At about eleven this morning you came to King's Cross station. We've seen the CCTV footage. You then came to the storage lockers, spent some time looking for the right number and attempted to open locker 097, at which point you were apprehended. Are you denying any of these events?"

"No. That's all correct."

"What were you intending to do with the contents of the locker?"

"Find out what they were, for one thing. You're asking me questions again. Would you like me to tell you what's been going on?"

The Inspector sat back. "Alright then."

"I woke up… four days ago with no memory," I said. "I had no identification, no idea who I was, no idea where I was. All I had on me was a small amount of cash, a cassette tape in a cigarette packet, a weird scrap of paper and a locker key."

"Amnesia. I see."

"I'm guessing you don't believe me."

He didn't answer this, but instead took a plastic bag from underneath the desk. "I am about to show Mr Walker exhibit PJ2, a piece of scrap paper. Is this the paper you state you woke up with?"

I looked at the paper in the bag. It was indeed the scrap with Jimmy's – Damian's – telephone number on it.

"Yes, that's the one."

"Can you tell me what it means?"

"It's a telephone number. If you read it aloud, you'll see what I mean."

"We know it's a telephone number, Mr Walker. I wanted to know whether you did. Did you call this number?"

"Yes, around half past midnight a few days ago. I was hoping Jimmy would be able to tell me who I am. He did."

"Did you know this number belongs to a Mr Damian Wright?"

"I've since heard his name is Damian. He called himself Jimmy when I spoke to him. Jimmy Burgess."

"Did you know he was murdered last night?"

I blinked. Though I knew this through Lisa, some part of me was warning me not to admit it. I felt the police were not trying to help me but to simply finish off the paperwork and get me neatly pigeonholed for both the murder and whatever was going on with the locker.

"No," I replied. "What happened?"

"We were hoping you might tell us." He fell silent, until it was clear I wasn't going to add anything to this. "You called this number. What happened next?"

"When I called Jimmy – Damian, I mean – he came to Reading to collect me and..."

"Reading?"

"Where I woke up. A Travel Hotel in Reading."

Inspector Jeffries made some notes, presumably to follow up later.

"Carry on."

"He came to collect me and brought me back to his apartment. He said it was ours, and that we were a couple."

The Inspector raised an eyebrow and made another note.

"I took the spare key when I left the next morning."

"To collect the bag – the contents of the locker?"

Bag? I ferreted that snippet of information away.

"No. I didn't know what the locker key was for at this point. I went to meet Lisa."

"This would be the young lady you were travelling with today?"

"Yes."

"What's her involvement in all this?"

Now, that was a complicated issue. I didn't know where to start with that one, and that part of me was warning me once again to watch what I said.

"None. She helped me out in Reading before I knew who I was, and she wanted to check I was alright now that Jimmy had collected me."

"I see." More notes on his pad. "We'll be questioning her separately, of course."

"So she's here?"

"Tell me about Damian. What was your relationship like?"

Were they trying to get me to admit to killing him?

"I didn't really know him. I had no memory of him and he was a stranger to me. I found him to be a little... odd."

"Odd in what way?"

"He got rather... emotional when he met me in Reading. His clothes were a little strange. And he told me two different stories about my amnesia that day and the next. I don't think he was entirely stable."

"Did he do anything to hurt or threaten you?"

Well, I thought, he drugged me and locked me in the apartment, but I'm not giving you any ammunition to pin a murder charge on me. "No. He was weird, but he was never violent."

"Do you know anyone that might have a grievance with Damian?"

I thought about the two heavies that came to visit that day, and who probably killed him, but I had not seen them and didn't know them. It felt like the plot of a spy thriller, me narrowly escaping capture, but I didn't think it sounded very likely now. I shook my head.

"For the tape?"

"No, I don't know anyone."

"Getting back to the locker. When did you realise what the locker key was for?"

"When I listened to the tape. There was a message on there from myself."

"What did this message say?"

"Well, actually, it was a bit cryptic. It was a series of bits of songs."

"Songs."

"Yes. One was by the Pet Shop Boys, called King's Cross. Then there was Dolly Parton and Neneh Cherry, and they gave me the nine and the seven..."

"I have no idea what you're talking about."

"I'm sorry, I didn't bring the tape with me."

Inspector Jeffries made another note. I felt it might be the word "mad" double underlined and with several exclamation marks. "Would you care to provide us with it?"

I wasn't overly keen. The rest of the tape was rather too strange to disclose at the moment, especially given that I wasn't sure what most of it meant.

"Does that mean you're letting me go?"

"That depends."

"I see." I tried to hide my disappointment. "It's in Lisa's car, anyway. I haven't got it."

"We'll ask Lisa to fetch it for us."

Again, not giving anything away. Did they have Lisa in custody too? Or were they bluffing?

"What's your connection with Maxwell Nicholson?"

"Who's he?"

"You deny all knowledge of Maxwell Nicholson?"

"Yep. Never heard of him."

"Even though you have a key to his apartment?"

What?!

The Inspector sighed. "This is getting nowhere. Interview concluded at one thirty-three. Okay, Johnson, take him back to the cells."

I reluctantly returned to my cell. I had more questions than ever now, but the Inspector wasn't going to be able to answer them.

It was another unknown but long time before anyone returned to my cell. PC Johnson unlocked the door, motioned me out and marched me out once more, this time without the handcuffs.

"You don't say much, do you?" *I said.*

PC Johnson didn't reply.

I was taken this time to a somewhat better furnished room, where I saw a lady of about fifty years, maybe a few more, sitting on one of a row of seats.

"Robert?" *she asked.* "Are you okay?"

"I'm fine," *I said, trying to figure out who this was.*

Inspector Jeffries entered the room. "He's all yours, Mrs Walker. Keep an eye on him and stay in touch – we may want to call him in for further questions."

I blinked. "Mum?"

"Shush, Robert," *she said.* "Not now. Thank you, Inspector. I hope he hasn't been any trouble."

"He claims to be suffering amnesia, Mrs Walker. You might want to take him to a doctor."

"So what's going on?" *I asked.* "You're just letting me go?"

"We're releasing you for the time being while we continue our investigation," *said Inspector Jeffries.* "We'll be keeping an eye on you, Mr Walker. We may want to speak to you again. And if you, ah, remember anything, do let us know."

He handed a paper bag to me, and I looked inside to find all my personal effects - minus the locker key and the scrap of paper. I was glad to see they'd given me the flat key back, or a return visit might have been difficult. My shoes were beside the seats and I quickly laced them up before I put my stuff back in my pockets, leaving the empty bag on the seat.

"Goodbye, Inspector," I said. I held out a hand to shake, but the offer was not taken up.

My mother walked with me out of the station, and soon we were standing on the pavements of London. I was bubbling with questions, but knew now was not the time to answer them.

"Come on, Robert, let's get you home."

Home turned out to be a small terraced house in Walthamstow. The paint on the front door and the window frames was peeling and the small square of weeds and grass between the house and the road could barely be considered a garden, but someone had installed a bird table that seemed popular with the local sparrows. I could see curtains in the windows with flower patterns and a fraying but clean welcome mat was on the doorstep. It didn't seem at all familiar, but it felt safe and comforting.

"I'm sure you've got a lot of questions, Robert. Come on inside and I'll make us all some tea."

"Thanks, mum."

We entered the house, and turned into the living room. Every spare surface, aside from the coffee table, was covered in porcelain. Children playing, animals, little cottages... I moved carefully, worried I might bump into a shelf and upset a dozen ornaments at once.

"Robert! You're safe!"

"Lisa?"

Lisa stood up from a low fabric sofa. "Thank you, Evie. You've been a great help."

"After all you've done for me, dear, I'm happy to help." Evie went into the kitchen and I heard the clattering of mugs.

"Rob, this is Evie. She's an old friend."

"She's not my mother." It wasn't really a question.

Lisa's face fell. "Of course... I'm sorry, Rob, I didn't think. I asked Evie to pretend to be your mother to get you out of there. I couldn't really go myself."

"Why not?"

"I'm not exactly well liked by the police."

I decided not to press the issue further.

"So what was in the locker?"

"Nothing," I said. "The police got there first, and pounced when I opened it. They let something slip in the interview, though – it's a bag, and it's connected with someone called Maxwell Nicholson."

"Max? What do they want with him?"

"You know him?"

"He... works at Grace Meadows. He's... one of the people we were checking on." Lisa pinched her nose, thinking for a moment. "Sorry, I was going to say something else. It's gone completely out of my head."

I remembered listening to the tape in Lisa's car, and speaking to a Max before the meeting with Dr Hawkins. Having exhausted all other leads, all I had left to go on was Grace Meadows and Dr Hawkins.

"Lisa, I have to go to the clinic."

"You can't, Rob. It's too dangerous."

"It's the only place I'll get any answers. If I'm right, they'll think they've got away with it, that I think the message is genuine."

"Then I'm coming too."

I shook my head. "I can't risk it – they know you. If they see us together they'll know you've been talking to me."

"Evie can take you..."

"They'll know she's not my mother. They might even know who my mother is. I'm not planning on staying, just a brief visit. Some reconnaissance. But I have to go alone."

Evie came in with two mugs of tea. "I'll just go and get mine," she said. "Would you like a biscuit?"

"Yes, please," I said. My stomach was grumbling after several hours or so at the police station.

"I'm not happy about this," Lisa said, "but I've got an idea. I want you to wear a wire."

"You mean like the police do when going undercover?"

"That's it," she said. "Though I'm not quite that well equipped. I was thinking of this." She handed me her mobile phone. "Give me a call on this before you go in, and hide it in your jacket. I'll hear everything that happens while you're in there. If you get in trouble, just yell."

"And you and Evie will come charging in?"

"I'm a lot tougher than I look," chided Evie, coming in with a plate of biscuits and a third mug of tea.

Lisa laughed. "We have some friends we can call on," she said. "We'll get you out of there if it comes to it."

"Alright then." I helped myself to a Jammie Dodger. "Get them together, just in case. I'm going to Grace Meadows tonight."

"Take this as well," said Lisa. "If you get in trouble, this might help you break out." She took a device from her handbag – the rape alarm she'd taken along with her to King's Cross.

"Thanks," I said. I slipped it into my jacket. It looked simple enough to operate.

It should have been dark and ominous when the taxi pulled up outside Grace Meadows, not a mellow evening with the last rays of sunset giving the clouds a rosy glow. I handed the taxi driver a twenty, thanked him and got out. Lisa had preloaded the telephone number for Evie's house into the mobile phone she had given me and it was a simple task to call it up.

"Okay, I'm going in," I said.

"Good luck," said Lisa.

I left the call running, slipped the phone into my jacket pocket and stepped through the main entrance into the reception area, which continued to confound my expectations by being spacious, well lit and filled with potted plants and a water feature.

The receptionist also went against type. Rather than a blond haired young girl with a winsome smile, he was a dark haired young man with glasses and an arty goatee. "Hello there, sir," he said as I approached. "How can I...?" He stopped. "Oh, hey Rob. Sorry, went into automatic there."

Of course. I'd been working at the clinic, though I still didn't know in what capacity. A lot of people here would know me, and I didn't really know which of them I could trust. If any.

"Is Dr Hawkins available?" I asked. I was keen to avoid small talk.

"Take a seat. I'll check for you."

I sat down on a comfortable sofa beside a large yucca plant and watched the young man tap an extension into his telephone. "Dr Hawkins? It's Pete on reception. Rob Walker is here and wants to see you." He paused, listening to some response I couldn't hear. Pete put the telephone down and turned back to me. "Dr Hawkins will be here directly."

"Thank you," I said, idly flicking through the magazines on the coffee table. Editions of Psychology Today *were a little more highbrow than the magazines I'd seen in the hospital waiting room. I was in no mood to read, however; I was too busy trying to keep my hands from shaking. The mysterious Dr Hawkins was about to appear.*

When he did, I didn't even realise it was him. He was a short, balding man with a brown suit and a hideous tie. It was not until he walked over that I even looked up.

"Mr Walker! I'm so pleased to see you here. I have been worried about you."

I somehow doubted that, though the smile seemed sincere enough.

"Dr Hawkins, thank you for seeing me at such short notice."

"What seems to be the problem, hmm?"

I had to wonder if this was even the same man. The voice sounded the same as the one on the tape, but the personality was utterly different - charming, friendly, warm. I felt safe with him, and I started to doubt my own convictions. Maybe all of this was just a weird dream, and coming back here was the first step towards waking up.

"Amnesia," I said. "I woke up several days ago with no idea who I was or what had happened to me. I remember nothing before then."

He nodded. "So, it's happened again," he said. "I take it you found the tape in your jacket?"

"I did. It took me a while to listen to it. No-one uses tapes these days."

Dr Hawkins motioned for me to get up and we set off for his office. "Indeed not. A shame – a tape is so much easier to record and to slip into a pocket. It would be far more difficult to do that with a CD. Perhaps we should provide you with a walkman next time? I'm sure we can find an old one somewhere. Though I hope there will not be a next time, of course."

"You said again? This has happened before?" I remembered Jimmy saying the same thing that morning.

"Four times now. The first time, your mother was in hysterics. Her little boy woke up with no idea who he was or who she was. Very distressing, I do not doubt. Your memory before that time never fully came back. Second time, you would have been at university. That was when you came to my attention. And then again, about three years ago. That was what inspired the Project... but I digress."

He led me to a door into the main complex, flashed his ID badge at a panel beside it and paused. Then he muttered something – it sounded like "yellow" – and entered a code on a numeric keypad. The door clicked open and we headed inside.

"What causes it?" I asked.

"We're not sure. Your condition is almost unique, Robert – only a handful of people that we know of suffer this recurring memory loss. We're glad to have you back with us – we've learned a lot from studying you."

"So what can you do for me?"

"Sometimes the patient's memory comes back on its own, or at least partly. Sometimes it seems permanent. But strangely it is only the conscious memory that seems affected – the patient remembers everything they've learned, like how to speak or how to dress, or even how to play music. We have a very talented musician here who knows how to play every song he's ever written - but he doesn't remember writing them."

"I think I know what you mean – I found this place by looking online. So I know how to use computers."

"Exactly. You can still function – but I imagine it must be quite distressing."

We came to Dr Hawkins' office, and he opened the door for me. I stepped inside, looking around at the collection of books, the motivational posters, the modern art. It was a warm and friendly office, and I felt safe there, but some part of me wondered if this was the office I'd been in when I'd been warned about my interest in other projects. For one thing, I remembered the echo of footsteps on the tape. Here the floor was lushly carpeted.

Was this a different Dr Hawkins?

"Robert, I have to tell you that there's not a lot we can do apart from monitor your condition for a few days and help you catch up on what memories you're missing. I'm sure you have lots of questions."

"I don't know where to start," I admitted. "Who am I, Dr Hawkins? What do I do?"

"Why, Robert! Is none of this familiar?" Dr Hawkins smiled. "You work for me, my dear boy. What better employer could you have? Who else would be so understanding if you disappeared without warning for a while?"

Dr Hawkins suggested I stay at the centre for a few days, and arranged a room for me in the eastern wing. I was mindful of my urge to perform a quick reconnaissance and then escape, but somehow I found it impossible to say no to that smile. Questions could wait until tomorrow, when Dr Hawkins promised to give me his full attention.

"We have a special visitor coming next week," he smiled. "I'm afraid preparations for this have taken up a lot of my time. But you are important to us, Robert - to me - and I will make a point of checking in on you."

It was not until I was left alone in my room and rapidly acquainting myself with the bed, en-suite shower and toilet facilities and the television in the corner that my enthusiasm to stay waned and I realised I'd cheerfully wandered into a prison cell. There were bars on the window and a lock on the outside of the door. A security camera in the corner of the room surveyed everything I did, though I couldn't see one in the bathroom. I was beginning to wonder whether I should be panicking when the mobile phone in my pocket began to mutter at me.

I entered the bathroom before I fished it out.

"...you still there? Rob! Speak to me!"

"Hey, Lisa. I'm still here."

"Finally! What the hell are you up to?"

"I'm staying over," I replied. *"Dr Hawkins talked me into it."*

"I didn't realise you were so easy to convince," she said. *"Otherwise I'd have got you to redecorate my flat. Have you gone mad?"*

"I don't know," I said. *"Perhaps I have. But I think this is for the best."*

"Robert...!"

"Stay calm, Lisa. I'm in the best place to find out more, aren't I? I'll call you back when I have some news." Before she could protest, I ended the call and switched off the mobile phone.

I put the phone back into my jacket for a moment, then thought again. I didn't want to risk the staff finding it. I looked around the bathroom for a suitable hiding place, quickly spotting a loose ventilation panel. It was only about a foot wide, but there was plenty of room in there for the mobile phone and, feeling its weight in my jacket, the rape alarm too.

I loosely fitted the panel back on, then returned to the main room.

The door was locked, though whether intentionally or just automatically when I was brought in I couldn't say for sure. It didn't seem like the Dr Hawkins I'd encountered would do such a thing. I whiled away some time watching television and once or twice I waved at the security camera.

Some time later the door opened and a burly attendant in a white jumpsuit came in with a tray. "Supper," he simply said, putting the tray on the bed. I nodded in thanks, then asked when I would be allowed out.

"That's up to Dr Hawkins," he replied. "He'll be back in the morning."

"I see." I looked at supper. "What is this?"

"Beef stew." The attendant turned and left, locking the door behind him.

The stew was actually rather nice, but I felt very sleepy not long after finishing it. This was the second time in mere days that I'd been drugged. Still, when sleep finally took me, I was quite happy to go.

When I woke up, I was not alone.

"Good morning, Robert."

"Hello, Dr Hawkins."

Dr Hawkins smiled warmly. "I trust you slept well?"

"Very. You run a lovely hotel."

The smile flickered. "Do you remember where you are?"

I grinned. "I'm joking," I explained. "This is the Grace Meadows clinic."

The smile returned. "Let's go for a walk," he said.

Back in my old clothes - next time I had the opportunity, I simply had to either buy new ones or wash these - I followed Dr Hawkins out into the clinic. A number of other rooms surrounded mine, but they were either empty or their occupants still asleep. I paid them little heed, instead following hastily after the doctor, whose pace was remarkably brisk.

"So what do you think of our clinic so far?" he asked.

"It's wonderful," I said. I meant it, too. Whatever images I'd had of the clinic (some dark, dank asylum with the inmates howling and rattling chains, perhaps) were entirely unfounded. The rooms were clean and decorated in soft pastel shades. The walls were lined with neatly spaced prints of abstract artworks and photographs of the natural world. The corridors were filled with cosy and inviting furniture and the soft lighting gave everything a warm and soothing feel. In the distance I could hear classical music.

"We try to give our patients as relaxing an atmosphere as possible. Nothing is quite so distressing as the feeling one is losing one's mind, and we hardly want to add to that distress."

"So where are we heading?"

"A brief tour, first," Dr Hawkins said. "Then I'll show you where you work. Hopefully you'll feel better when you're back in familiar surroundings."

"Ah yes. What did you say I do here?"

"Come on. The sooner we're away, the sooner we'll be settled."

I didn't press the issue. I felt sure Dr Hawkins would tell me in his own time. Instead we moved on to the first of our tour destinations.

"This," announced Dr Hawkins, "is the communal area. Not many people about at this time of the morning, though."

I took a good look about the room. A number of chairs, bean bags and a long sofa provided seating for up to twenty people, but for now the room contained just two. One was an elderly woman sat in a chair and knitting what looked like a scarf, which was already several feet long and looked likely to get ever longer. She didn't *look up as we entered the room, her eyes intent on an old television showing even older editions of* Wheel of Fortune. *Her hands moved rapidly, the wool on her knitting needles endlessly looped and tied and twisted and added to the growing garment that hung from them. It was mesmerising to watch.*

"That's Mrs Griffin," explained Dr Hawkins. "She's been here for a few months now. The poor dear doesn't go out any more - senile dementia, you understand. She remembers every detail of fifty years ago but has no idea who or where she is now. She doesn't even recognise her own daughter."

The exact opposite of my own condition, I thought.

"And over there is Roger." I tore my eyes from the knitting needles and followed Dr Hawkins' gaze to the man rocking back and forth on a beanbag in the corner. His baggy overalls made him look a little too thin, and a crop of short and messy ginger hair was accompanied by several days of stubble on his chin. He seemed confused by his surroundings, whereas Mrs Griffin was merely unaware. "Roger has a condition rather like your own, only far worse. He's utterly unaware of who he is or where he is, and he cannot retain short term memories. He lives in a state of constant confusion."

"Hey, Roger," I called out.

"Who's Roger?" he asked. "Where am I?"

"Calm down, Roger," said Dr Hawkins. "We're just visiting. Do you know who I am?"

"No."

"I'm Dr Hawkins. You're in Grace Meadows, do you remember?"

"No, I don't, doctor. Why am I here?"

"Because of your memory problems, Roger."

"Who's he?"

"This is Robert. He's here with memory problems too."

"Robert... Robert... do I know you?"

"I don't know," I replied.

"Do you know who Roger is? People keep asking for him."

"You're Roger," explained Dr Hawkins.

"Who are you?"

Dr Hawkins turned back to me. "You see? He forgets everything we tell him. He cannot remember anything from his past and he cannot form a new life in the present."

"He's like me?"

"A little. You have no recollection of your past either, but you have much longer periods before you forget again. And here, we can help you catch up on the things you've forgotten. We have everything on record."

"Like a library of my life?" I had images of a large room filled with dusty books - or maybe more tapes.

"Quite! Wonderfully put." Dr Hawkins smiled.

"If my life was a book, you would be on every page..."

I turned to see Roger rocking back and forth on his beanbag, singing softly to himself.

"What was that, Roger?" I asked.

"What was what?"

"It happens sometimes," said Dr Hawkins. "He remembers random snippets when he doesn't think about them. Songs are a particularly common thing for him to pick up on."

I shuddered. "Let's move on," I said. "This is starting to spook me."

The second stop was a decent sized room with yellow padded walls. The floor, however, was ordinary carpet and any padded cell vibe was spoiled by the complicated electronic equipment at one end of the room. A set of beanbags were scattered over the floor.

"This is the music therapy room," explained Dr Hawkins. "The brainwave of one of our more musically minded staff. Sadly he no longer runs it, and we've found little use for it aside from the occasional party for our more... settled patients."

"Seems a bit complicated for music therapy," I said. *I wasn't sure how music therapy would work, but I thought you could probably do well enough with a CD player and a varied playlist.*

"It was used for research as well as therapy. He was trying to combine music together, use editing tricks, that sort of thing. He used to say that you could put all kinds of messages into music if you knew what you were doing."

I maintained my poker face. I didn't want to mention my own musical message. If Hawkins knew anything, he was keeping his own face just as impassive.

"Alas, none of us really know how to work it any more. We can play music on it and some of the younger staff can even create... mix tapes, I think they call them. I believe you recorded your own tape with this equipment. At least it wasn't too expensive to install. Our researcher was able to source a lot of old equipment. No-one uses cassette tapes any more. Let's move on."

"This is where we crack open the skulls of our victims and peer at their brains," said Dr Hawkins. He smiled at my expression. "A joke," he explained.

The bulk of this otherwise bare room was occupied by a large, round machine with what looked like a bed inside. "Is this an MRI scanner?" I asked.

"Yes," he replied, clearly impressed. "You remember this?"

"No," I said. "I mean, I remember them generally, but not seeing one. I just took a guess."

"Oh. Ah well. This, as you correctly... guessed, is the brain imaging area. Here we take scans of our patients to determine if there are any physical reasons for their mental conditions. We also use it in our experiments to find out how our treatments affect the brain."

"This must have cost a fair bit."

"More than you probably think. And we don't get much in the way of government funding. Most of our work is financed by private clients with vested interests."

"Can I have a go?" I joked.

He frowned at me. "It's not a toy, Robert. Come, let me show you the rest of the research labs."

The animal labs were next. The first thing that struck me as I entered the lab was the smell – though every effort was clearly made to keep the animals clean and healthy, the collective smell was still a shock after the faintly fragranced air of the rest of the clinic.

The second thing that struck me was the quiet. Monkeys and dogs occupied row upon row of cages against one wall, with smaller cages containing rats lining another. I expected a cacophony of barks and screams, but the room was almost silent.

"Are they asleep?" I asked.

"Hmm?"

"The animals. They're so very quiet."

"Oh, not asleep, no. I suppose some might be. Sedatives affect their thinking too much - we try not to drug them unless necessary. No, they are quiet because they *have no vocal chords."*

"They... what?"

"It's a simple procedure. Can you imagine the noise if we didn't?"

"But that's..."

"You've not joined one of those animal rights groups, have you?" he smiled. "We get them outside sometimes with their placards. We aren't needlessly cruel, Robert. The animals are well fed and well looked after. And they provide very important research data. We try to use human test subjects as much as possible but people would complain far more if we tested our new compounds and surgeries on them."

I looked into his face, and I felt a... the best word might be "doubling". At the same time, I trusted him completely - he was right, this was necessary and useful research, and if he said the animals didn't suffer then they did not - but I also felt a glimmer of the other Dr Hawkins, the one on the tape. He would see no problem in using animals in this way.

Or humans.

We try to use human test subjects as much as possible...

Some rather unpleasant thoughts were starting to surface in my mind. I pushed them to one side and tried to focus on Dr Hawkins as he continued to speak.

"...I can see this is upsetting you. Let's look at something else."

We moved on.

The next lab was filled with benches, industrious technicians and lots of bizarre equipment and mysterious bottles.

"This is our chemistry set," he said. "Here we experiment with different drugs, different compounds. We've come up with several new treatments here for depression, schizophrenia, attention deficit disorders..."

"Anything for amnesia?"

He chuckled. "Not yet, though of course that is one of our fields of study. This is where some of our funding comes from, Robert - the development of new treatments. We have very few philanthropists helping us out. Most of our backers are in it for the profits."

That brought to mind my own stay. "Who's paying for me?" I asked.

"Don't worry about that, Robert. Employees are given free treatment, when it occasionally becomes necessary. It's part of the health plan."

"What do I do here?" I asked. "I don't recognise anything in this lab."

Again, no answer. I started to suspect he was avoiding the question, and more dark thoughts bubbled into my forebrain. Did I work here at all? I was beginning to doubt it.

More rooms followed. The treatment rooms, some little more than a bed and a chair and some more like operating theatres. The courtyard, where patients could get some sunshine and air without leaving the clinic itself. The kitchens. The laundry. We flew through these last rooms, heading back towards the front of the building and the reception area.

"And here we find my office," said Dr Hawkins. "You've seen this one already, of course."

"Of course," I echoed. "Yesterday. Very impressive, too."

"Let me show you to the admin section."

"How much longer is this tour?" I asked.

"This will be the final stop of the tour," he replied. "This is where you work."

The Mad Hatter's Tea Party

Admin comprised of three offices - one dealing with technical support, one with public relations (including, I suspect, keeping the financial backers happy) and one with general duties such as correspondence, filing and database records management. I had the feeling I'd be in the latter of these offices, and I was quickly proven right.

"Here you go, Robert. Your desk is in the corner. Get yourself settled in; the others will soon make you feel right at home. Frank, you know what to do - tell him what he does, help him settle back in."

A balding middle-aged man in a brown suit nodded back to him. "Yes, sir. We'll have him back to work in no time."

Frank walked me over to the desk and talked me through logging on. "Dr Hawkins told me about your amnesia," he said, "so I took the liberty of having your password reset. It's now 'password'. Oh - username. You're 'rwalker' - letter R, then Walker, all one word."

I tapped in all this as instructed.

"You'll need to change your password when you next log in. It needs to be between six and ten characters, and it needs to have at least one uppercase letter, at least one lowercase, a number, some non-alphanumeric characters and be different to your last ten passwords."

"Er..."

I ended up having to write my new password down, which rather defeated the point in my view. Frank shrugged and said he did the same thing, but the IT department set the rules.

"So what is it I do?" I asked.

"You're the office boy," he replied. "Your task is to sort the emails, fetch the post, make the tea, do the filing and get on with any other work we hand you. Don't fret, it's not that bad. Most of the time we do bugger all around here."

And so it went for the next few days. I'd be woken up in the morning by one of the attendants, brought to my little office space and spend the day sorting through emails, opening the mail and filing random paperwork. I didn't really understand any of it - I just did as I was told. It was work, whatever the point of it was. Occasionally I made coffee and tea, and at lunchtime an attendant came by with a sandwich trolley. We ate at our desks. I only ever left the office for toilet breaks, and the facilities were just along the corridor.

Three days went by without me ever leaving the clinic.

My colleagues were all a little strange. My boss, Frank, seemed to be the least odd of them, which wasn't saying much. He had a habit of muttering to himself and apparently not being aware of it. I thought he had Tourette's until I realised he was reciting his multiplication tables. I stopped trying to check them when he got to thirty-seven.

The others, as I discovered when I tried chatting with them, were all patients at the clinic. These included Gerald, a man of about forty that everyone called Fred. If I called him Gerald, he ignored me. I was told that Gerald had a multiple personality disorder, of which Fred was one of his personas. He apparently preferred Fred over the original persona and was trying to eliminate Gerald instead. This explanation came from Derek, however, and Gerald/Fred warned me that Derek was a compulsive liar. Derek also told me that he was really in charge of the clinic and that Dr Hawkins had put him out of the way while he plotted to take over the world. This startling revelation became less convincing when later he told me he'd walked on the moon with Neil Armstrong.

James was a little alarming. He rarely spoke, and when he did it was seldom more than a few words. His desk was covered in stuffed toys, and he would twist or tear at these with his hands when he was distracted from work, which was rather too often for my liking. I noticed one stuffed bear with several straightened paperclips pierced through its chest, and a cuddly panda hung by the neck with a hangman's noose made out of string. Frank assured me that James was harmless, and that this was all part of his "treatment" for his taxidermiphobia - his fear of stuffed animals. Every week he would receive a new stuffed animal and he would "kill" it in some fashion.

Naomi was the only girl in the office, though she was large enough to make three. I assumed at first she was in the clinic for an eating disorder of some kind but apparently not - instead, she was convinced that she and everyone around her was dead. I queried this with interest and learned that she did not believe she was in heaven or hell but a form of purgatory, and she was waiting for her sentence to pass so she could move on to the next life. God was watching her, she said, and He would give her salvation when she had served her penance. I might have accepted this as a slightly weird religious viewpoint rather than downright insanity if she hadn't been convinced that God was the water cooler. I soon learned not to get water from it while she was watching.

I tended not to speak to my colleagues too much. None of them were what I could call chatty in any event. Most of my conversations were with Dr Hawkins, who came to see me each evening to check up on how I was getting on. If there was any form of therapy involved, I don't know what it was - perhaps my condition could not be treated and I was simply being looked after. I enjoyed his visits - we'd often walk around the courtyard, sit in the communal room or his office, or even my room, and we'd talk about what had happened, or if there was anything on my mind. Whatever worries I had would evaporate by the time we finished. He would then take me back to my room, where I would sometimes watch some television and sometimes just fall asleep. I always noticed the sound of the door locking behind him, however often I asked him not to, but for some reason it didn't bother me. For a while, at least.

It was not until the third evening that I woke up from this strange yet comforting spell. That evening Dr Hawkins didn't come to see me - an orderly came by to tell me that he had attended a press conference somewhere and was delayed getting back. I waited in the communal area, with only Mrs Griffin and Roger for company. Mrs Griffin sat knitting, as if she hadn't moved an inch since the last time I saw her there, but Roger was now on a chair close to the television, which was showing one of the shopping channels with the sound down low.

"Hello, dear," said Mrs Griffin. "Haven't I seen you before?"

"Yes," I replied. "You saw me a few days ago. Don't you remember?"

She looked blank. "No, that's not it," she said. "You're that young doctor... oh, what's his name...?"

"I'm Robert Walker, Mrs Griffin."

"Yes, that's it. Dr Walker!"

"I'm not a doctor, Mrs Griffin..." I started.

"Sure you are," she snapped. "I remember it very well. Don't speak to me like I've gone soft, young man." She turned back to her knitting, humming an old tune I didn't recognise. Roger picked up the melody and sang along quietly to himself as he watched the pictures that, for him, were always new.

"You were always nice to me," she said suddenly. "Not like that other fellow. That doctor... oh, what's his name...?" There was a brief silence, only punctuated by the clicking of her needles and the low murmur of the television. "Hawkins! That's him.

What was I talking about again?"

"Dr Hawkins?" I asked. "He seems nice to me."

"That's not what you used to say," she frowned. "You used to say he was a mean old grump, only in less polite words. You used to call him Hawkish."

I remembered the tape. I'd called him that when I was speaking with Max. Max...?

"Mrs Griffin," I asked, "do you know someone working here called Max?"

She looked at me blankly, and I realised that she'd gone again, back several decades into the past. I left her to her knitting and moved on. In the background I could hear Roger singing to himself.

"We were climbing so high from a misty sunrise morning..."

Left to my own devices, I went for a walk around the clinic. I could not get out through reception - the doors to the outside world, and many others, required a keycard. Only the medical staff had these, so I merely explored the areas I could reach. This didn't take long. Many of the research areas were also out of bounds to me - if I was to explore the clinic properly, I'd need to obtain one of those keycards. I wasn't at all sure how I'd manage that.

Soon frustrated, I headed back to my room and sat on my bed, watching television and trying to relax. I felt so tense - normally I'd be chatting to Dr Hawkins by now and any tension would just drain away. Now I felt anxious and irritable and trapped. I wanted to get out into the world again, to see Lisa again, to speak to her...

The telephone!

I glanced briefly at the security camera in the corner of the room before I headed for the bathroom. Could they hear me? I didn't know, so I started the shower just in case before I took off the ventilation panel.

I switched on the mobile phone. As soon as a signal was available the phone chirped angrily at me. Several messages had been left for me.

I dialled the number Lisa had programmed in.

The phone rang three times and then Lisa answered.

"Where the bloody hell have you been?"

"Hello, Lisa," *I replied, stumped for a witty response.*

"It's been three days," *she said.* "I've been organising a raid on the place because I thought you'd been abducted or killed or something. And then suddenly you just think to pick up the phone!"

"I..."

"What have you been doing that's stopped you even giving me a brief call to let me know you're still there? And don't tell me you just forgot, like your amnesia is a convenient excuse!"

"I've..."

"I've been worried sick back here, thinking you were dead or brainwashed or worse - though I think you'd need a brain in the first place to be brainwashed. And then suddenly you just decide to call!"

I waited a moment to make sure she had finished, rather than just pausing for breath.

"I don't know how to explain it," *I said.* "I just... didn't think of it."

"Didn't think of it?!" *I half expected the telephone to explode.* "You've gone back into the place that may well have caused your amnesia, chatted with a doctor so iffy I'd sooner spend time with Hermann Göring - and who may well have had something to do with Damian's murder, I might add - and you didn't think to stay in touch?!"

"Well, I..."

This time she was pausing for breath. "I thought this was a bad idea from the outset, Rob, and the least you could do would be to give me a call to let me know how you're getting on. Or had you forgotten me?"

"Are you finished?" I snapped.

There was silence for a while, and I wondered whether I'd gone too far. "I'm sorry. There's something about this place that messes with my head, Lisa. I've been half asleep a lot of the time, and I suspect they may be slipping something into my food."

"So what's happened tonight that's so different?" *she asked.*

"Dr Hawkins isn't here," *I replied.* "And for some reason, that makes a difference. He's been taking a close interest in me since I've been here, checking up on me and asking how I'm doing, and he seems a really nice man. I find it almost impossible to think he's the same man on the tape, but he must be. I'm thinking we've got him all wrong."

"Remember why you're there, Rob," *she said.* "That really nice man is up to some really nasty things. You're supposed to be looking into that."

I thought back to the tour I'd been given when I first arrived. Removing an animal's vocal chords just to keep them quiet wasn't something a really nice man would do.

"They lock the door," *I said.* "I'm a prisoner in here. During the day I'm stuck in the office, and in the evening..."

"Office? You have a job?"

"Yeah. General office dogsbody, that's me."

"That's great. What do you work on?"

"I don't know."

There was a pause. "You don't know what your job is for."

"No. I sometimes think it's just to keep us busy."

"Have you spoken to any of the staff?"

"The others in my office are all nuts. I mean, really nuts. There's a guy that murders teddy bears, Lisa. This place is crazy."

"You only just realised that?" she said, her voice dripping scorn. "Your office sounds as normal and rational as the Mad Hatter's tea party."

"Let's all move one place on," I muttered to myself.

"What?"

"Nothing. Lisa, I think I need some help. I can't get out of here without a keycard. I can't access anything without a keycard. Can you find a way to slip me one?"

"Not likely," she said. "Security in that place is tight. We might be able to bust you out, but I think we can forget about subtle espionage. But there is something – have you still got that rape alarm?"

"Yeah," I said.

"It's not much, but it might give you a shot at escape. Rob, be careful. Forget about the Project - just get out of there. And remember to call me!"

"I will," I promised. With that, she ended the call and I returned the telephone to its hiding place. The bathroom was starting to steam up so I took advantage of the shower, returned to the main room in a towel and got into bed. I put the television on for a while but my mind was elsewhere.

I was planning my escape.

The next morning I got changed into some fresh clothes – I had asked Dr Hawkins about these on my second evening (after my first day of work) and he had seemed surprised I had not been given any. Since then, a fresh set of clothes were folded on my bed every time I returned from work and the previous ones taken away (presumably to be washed). My jacket was still folded in one corner. I was up a little earlier than normal – my breakfast and my escort to work would not arrive for at least ten minutes, if breakfast television was accurate – and I spent this time in the bathroom, secreting the rape alarm in my underwear and the mobile phone in my jacket pocket. I contemplated the security camera. If I did anything in my room, security would know. Any attempt to break out here would be futile.

I thought about the day ahead. My route to work was not promising, offering few opportunities to nab myself a keycard and make my escape, and so I decided it was better to wait. At work itself I knew none of my colleagues had keycards – surely it was hopeless trying anything there. I decided to make my break in the common room this evening, when I had a modest level of freedom – but, in the end, an opportunity arose much earlier.

After breakfast, I took my usual short walk to the office and settled down to another day of work. This time, however, I approached my "job" with a little more interest in what I was doing, trying to work out what the emails were about and what the paperwork entailed. The mail was equally baffling, and it was the mail that first made me realise that my job was an utter sham.

Up until now, sorting the mail had been straightforward enough because I'd never thought much about what I was doing. I just put the right envelopes in the right pigeonholes. About one in ten items were addressed to particular doctors at the clinic, and these were placed in a tray for later collection. I never did find out who picked them up. A fair proportion of the other mail was just addressed to departments, and I'd look up the addressee on our database, write their name on the envelope and put it in the tray with the others. The remainder was largely junk mail, usually selling medical or office supplies, and these were binned. Today I decided to *break the routine, and I opened a letter.*

This letter was addressed to a Dr Venables. I didn't recognise the name from my recent memories. If I looked him up on the database I could determine which team he was assigned to, but I was more interested in the contents. Making sure my colleagues weren't watching, I quietly tore the envelope open and peeked inside.

The contents, it turned out, were sheets cut out of newspapers. Not whole sheets, not clippings of articles, but random squares of newsprint. I couldn't see any dates on the sections I leafed through but the paper looked quite old.

I opened another one, addressed to the Neuroparapsychology department (I didn't notice the phony department name for a while, either). It too was filled with newspaper and magazine cuttings. None of them made any sense.

My mind was whirling at this point, so I abandoned the paper mail and checked the electronic mail. These were more sensible - I'd looked at a few of these when I first started out and they largely consisted of spam (which I was to identify and delete) and case details. Emails of this type contained information on test cases in clinical trials, some of which were being given new drugs and some placebos. They generally consisted of some candidate details such as name and date of birth, a list of findings about their progress and sometimes a photograph. I'd normally forward them on to the relevant researcher for that trial.

Today I looked closer. I'd spotted on my first day that the findings for each case were constantly repeated - that made sense, as they were only one-line descriptions of symptoms and observations and they were bound to turn up in lots of candidates. I hadn't noticed before how generic they were, or that they didn't make much sense in themselves.

I also noticed that one email this morning mentioned a Mr Craig Harman suffering from increased menstrual pains, and a Miss Rita Jennings complaining that she felt hot and cold in two separate comments. After the shock of the newspaper mail, I decided to look at more of these.

The photos gave it away in the end.

Not all emails had photographs attached, as I've said, but about half did. I think this was their biggest mistake - names were easy to make up, needing just random first and last names thrown together, but there were only a limited number of photographs and it wasn't long before I found the same ones being reused. Unlike the comments, they'd taken care to keep men and women separate here (I didn't see any gender mix-ups), but seeing the same face four times convinced me. The emails were fake. The mail was fake. My job was a fake. I did wonder what happened to the mail, but most likely there was another "office" like mine sending the things to us.

I was being held prisoner, and I hadn't even noticed. If I hadn't spoken to Lisa, maybe I'd still be there now, filing scrap paper like it meant something. But maybe not – Dr Hawkins had his plans, and one way or another I would no doubt have been part of them.

It was going to be a long day doing nothing, made even longer now I realised that it really was nothing. So when the attendant came with the lunchtime sandwich trolley, I made my bid for freedom. The poor lad – he was only about nineteen, and quite possibly another patient at the clinic rather than a member of staff – didn't really deserve it. While everyone else gathered round the trolley to check out the sandwiches, I held Lisa's rape alarm deliberately close to his ear before I set it off.

It was LOUD. Shockingly loud in such a confined space, even to me, and I was expecting it. My ears were still ringing for several minutes afterwards.

The effect on the group was immediate. Frank howled in pain, clutching his fists to his ears, and began reciting: "fifty-nine, one hundred and eighteen, one hundred *and seventy-seven..."* Gerald/Fred ran across the room and started hitting himself over the head with a computer keyboard. The attendant fell over his own trolley, colliding with Derek, who started wrestling with him on the ground. James backed away, slipped on a fallen baguette (salmon and cream cheese, I think) and hit his own desk on the way down. A collection of mutilated and hanged stuffed toys fell upon him and he added his own screams of panic to the din. Naomi knelt before the water cooler, making a good attempt at speaking in tongues, in the hope that God would intervene and silence the noise.

I took advantage of the panic and fled, leaving the alarm sounding somewhere in the chaos.

Outside the "office" I encountered two burly male "nurses" - security, really. I doubt they had anything more than a rudimentary medical background. "In there!" I yelled. "They've all gone crazy!" I didn't appreciate the comedy value of this line until much later but, in any event, my authoritative tone worked - they left me alone and set off to bring order to the chaos. My last sight of the office before I ran for my freedom was of James being restrained from behind by one of the nurses and stamping on his stuffed toys.

They took a surprisingly long time to switch off the rape alarm.

Once back into the main corridor, I stopped running and started walking. It looked less suspicious. But where could I go? I needed a keycard to access so much as a cupboard. I briefly considered tackling one of the nurses but I'd be unlikely to come out of the battle well. I walked on, trying the occasional door but finding them all locked. My escape was not going well.

I heard footsteps approaching from behind me. Running footsteps, and several sets of them. I looked around, but there was nowhere to hide.

"Get off me!" The voice was shrill and angry, but I recognised it as James.

"Get the tranqs!" yelled another voice (one of the nurses, probably).

There were scuffling sounds, and then more running feet. James tore into view, a thin trickle of blood running down his chin from a split lip. A security nurse rugby-tackled him to the ground and was followed by a doctor in horn-rimmed glasses. The doctor held a syringe up to the light and tapped it with his finger.

"Hold him!" he demanded. The nurse attempted to pin James against the wall, but James was putting up a hell of a fight. As the doctor moved in with the syringe, James lashed out with a backwards kick that struck him hard on the knee. The doctor went down.

I watched all of this, entirely unnoticed. The nurse decided to bring James under control by more direct means, slamming his head against the wall several times. James went limp.

"Get him to his room," muttered the doctor. "I'll deal with him later."

The nurse began dragging the unconscious James backwards along the corridor. The doctor staggered slightly as he got to his feet, and then fell against the wall. He swore under his breath.

I then saw the syringe on the floor, half empty, and realised what must have happened.

I went over to him. "Are you okay?" I asked.

"Damned syringe. Caught my arm when he lashed out." He slipped against the wall, and I grabbed him before he could fall.

"Let me help," I said. "I'll get you to the infirmary."

He nodded, but he was already half gone. I looped his arm around my neck and half walked, half carried him down the corridor.

Thanks to my tour with Dr Hawkins a few days ago, I had a fair idea of where the infirmary was. I'd never had to visit it before (at least, not during this stay) but there were plenty of helpful signs on the wall. By now my companion was almost completely out of it and I was getting quite exhausted under his weight. I began to wonder whether I was doing the right thing - I didn't want to leave him there, but this delay was reducing my chances for escape by the minute.

The infirmary door was locked.

My companion, though half asleep, was clearly so used to the doors that he acted on automatic - he took his ID badge from his belt (it was on an extending string, which retracted back into the clip when he let go of the badge) and waved it vaguely towards a black panel to the side of the door. I had to guide his hand. There was a click, and then I could push the infirmary door open easily.

"Hello, what's...?"

I didn't recognise the woman in the infirmary, but she regarded me with a curious look as I brought my companion in. "He's had an accident," I said. "I think a syringe slipped..."

Her face became one of concern, though I think some trace of suspicion lingered. "Get him on the bed," she said. "What happened?"

"Violent patient," I said. "Security are handling him."

I heaved the now unconscious man onto the bed, and the woman helped to ensure his arms and legs weren't trapped beneath him.

"What's his name?" she asked. When I didn't respond, she continued, "check his ID. I need to look up his medical notes."

I took the ID card from his belt. "Doctor Richard Bradshaw," I read out. As the woman turned to her computer screen, I slipped the badge into my jeans pocket - it seemed my good deed wasn't going to be unrewarded after all.

"It's okay, Rob," she said. "I'll handle it from here."

"Uh... thanks." It hit me like a sledgehammer. Like the receptionist a few days ago, she knew me. Virtually no-one else had acknowledged me since I'd been here.

"Such a shame about Max, though. Have you heard anything more?"

"Uh... no."

I had the horrible feeling I'd walked into a play but hadn't read the script. Could I talk openly to this woman? Could I trust her? Presumably I'd been friends with many of the staff before, but I had no idea which, or which of them knew about my condition. Hell, I didn't even know her name!

"I'd, er, I'd best be off..." I stammered.

"Sure," she replied. "Pop by again when you can, Rob. I miss our little chats. Where have you been for the last few weeks?"

"I'll try," I said, pulling at the door. It wouldn't open. I spotted the black panel to the side and pulled Dr Bradshaw's ID card out of my pocket. The door clicked open and I headed out into the clinic.

I knew I didn't have long - so far I'd been lucky to avoid being located but I knew it would only be a matter of time before security realised I was missing and began the search. But I couldn't leave just yet - I had questions, and I didn't think Dr Hawkins would willingly give me the answers.

I tried to retrace my steps from three days ago, finding my way back to his office, and after a few false starts I managed it. With my stolen keycard I easily opened the lock and stepped inside.

Dr Hawkins' office was a spartan affair, lit by the gentle glow of a desk lamp and in pristine condition. Aside from a fake rubber plant in the corner and a set of book shelves against one wall, the only furniture of note was a large desk in the centre of *the room and two chairs, one either side of it. A small door led into a tiny stationery cupboard.*

I quickly checked there was no-one about and then began my search. I didn't know what I was looking for, but I found nothing - a lot of nothing, and none of it reassuring.

The shelves of books, for example, were covered in dust - and, apart from the dust, the books were as new. It was clear to me they had never been opened, much less read. I was unable to open the desk drawers - they were both locked, with no sign of a key - but both were too shallow to hold much anyway. Indeed, the entire office seemed remarkably unused.

I thought back to the tape, and the sound of footsteps on the floor. I walked across the carpet in the office. No footsteps to be heard. This wasn't his office. Except it clearly was - it had his name on the door and everything.

So why would the door open to anyone's keycard?

"It's a fake office," I said to myself, then realised I'd spoken aloud. Quite why a fake rubber plant, clean desk and beige carpet should freak me out remained a mystery to me.

Think it through, I told myself. If this is a fake office, doesn't that mean there's a real one? Where would that be?

Then I heard a noise outside. Voices! I quickly looked about for somewhere to hide, and dived into the stationery cupboard. Inside I was plunged into darkness - the only light coming from the crack in the doors that I pressed my eye against.

The door clicked open and Dr Hawkins stepped inside. Fake or not, he did use the office, at least occasionally. Seeing the man I instantly felt calmer and had the absurd desire to step out and give myself up. I resisted it, though the desire persisted like an itch at the back of my head.

Dr Hawkins was not alone. Two other figures entered after him. One I did not recognise, but wore the white overalls that were common to all the security staff. Beside him walked Roger, looking bewildered as ever and with no idea what was happening to him.

"He was just wandering about," reported security. "Said he had to do something but couldn't remember what it was. He mentioned your name so I thought I should bring him to you."

"You did right," reassured Dr Hawkins. "You can leave him here - he's quite harmless. Have you dealt with the... unpleasantness earlier on?"

"Most of the patients are back in their cells," replied security. "We had to sedate a few of them. Sorry, sir. I know how you feel about that."

Dr Hawkins waved a hand. "It's alright. It couldn't be helped. Any injuries?"

"Stevens got a bit knocked about, sir. He's going to get checked out at the infirmary after he's secured one of the patients. Oh, and there was an accident with a syringe - Dr Bradshaw is in the infirmary now. He should be okay in a few hours."

Dr Hawkins sighed. "What a mess. What caused it?"

"One of the patients had this." He put an object on the desk. I didn't need to see it to know what it was. "Goodness knows how it got in the clinic. With your permission, I'd like to talk to the patients later on..."

"Leave that to me. You may go."

"Yes, sir."

The security officer opened the door and left. Dr Hawkins gestured for Roger to sit down.

"Now them, Roger. What can I do for you?"

"Something I have to do. Something..."

"It's alright, Roger. Relax. You're safe here. There's nothing you need to do."

"Something... the project...?"

"Don't worry about the project, Roger."

"Not my name."

"Hush, hush."

"My name is... is... what's my name?"

"Your name is Roger."

"No! My name is... is..."

Roger seemed to sag in defeat. Dr Hawkins regarded him for a moment - I was unable to see his expression from my vantage - and then he picked up the telephone on his desk.

"Hello, Jackson? I'm afraid Roger's relapsing. Get the machine ready."

"I'm not Roger!"

"Tell security to come up to my reception office. He may not come quietly."

"I'm not Roger!" He was shouting now.

"Don't worry, Roger. In a little while, you'll have forgotten all this."

The security guard returned, along with a second, and they dragged Roger away between them. Dr Hawkins walked along behind. As they took him away, I heard one more shout that made the hairs on my neck stand up:

"I'm not Roger! My name is Max!"

It took a great deal of courage to leave that cupboard and follow the four men out of the office. I quickly lost sight of them, which was probably a good thing - I hardly wanted to be spotted - but it was clear where they'd gone. I saw the elevator doors close in the distance and the LED number above them tick down from 1 (where I was now) to 0 and then to B. They were headed for the basement.

Until now, I hadn't even realised the clinic had a basement.

I quickly called the second elevator, hoping that no-one would arrive with it. To my relief, it was empty. I quickly stepped inside. There was indeed a "B" button for the basement, but nothing happened when I pressed it - I needed to do something more, and spotted a familiar black panel beside the buttons. Another flash with Dr Bradshaw's card saw the doors close and the elevator start to sink.

When the doors opened again, there was no sign of Dr Hawkins or his entourage. Ahead of me lay a corridor decorated by whitewashed brick and a mass of pipework along the ceiling. It angled off to the right at the end. The main clinic was a modern medical environment, all minimalism and soothing pastels. The basement looked like a nuclear bunker.

I could hear shouting in the distance, though I couldn't make out any words, and crept down the corridor to find the source. I passed a number of doors, featureless except for stencilled numbers upon each of them. Each began with a B and they counted up as I headed away from the elevator.

"I said hold him!" That was Dr Hawkins' voice. "Get the restraints on!"

Roger/Max yelled out in response, a cry of fear, pain and anger all in one go. I walked faster, no longer worried about my footsteps being heard, and slowed as I approached the last room on the left before the bend – B12. The voices came from there.

"Don't struggle, Roger. It'll be much easier if you don't."

"My name's Max," he replied. "Not Roger. Max!"

"In a few minutes, your name will be whatever we want it to be."

I risked a peek round the door. Fortunately everyone was focused on Roger, or Max, and didn't look in my direction. Dr Hawkins stood by a table laden with surgical instruments. Roger was being forced into restraints on what looked unpleasantly like a dentist's chair, and he was fighting it with everything he had.

"Get the skull cap on him!" ordered Dr Hawkins. The orderlies managed to force one arm into a restraint and then the other, with Roger/Max still kicking out as much as he could. Even when they locked down all four limbs, he still thrashed his head about and tried to bite anyone putting their hands near him. It did no good – what looked like a bathing cap with electrodes attached to it was pulled down and fastened to his head.

Dr Hawkins took a syringe from the instrument tray, shooting a tiny amount of the contents into the air. He returned to Max, now firmly restrained by the machine, and though he had his back to me I could guess what he was doing. The syringe was half empty when he returned it to the tray.

"Stand clear," said Dr Hawkins, and the orderlies stepped back. He quickly checked the skull cap was properly affixed and then returned to the table, where he picked up a small black device. "Subject now restrained and skull cap fitted. Applying initial voltage."

I realised he was talking to a tape recorder.

Dr Hawkins headed across the room, out of my view. I heard him flick a switch of some kind, and Roger/Max briefly convulsed in his chair.

"Checking for vertebrobasilar ischemia," said Dr Hawkins. A teasing sliver of memory swam out of my subconscious at this – while I couldn't recall much about it at the time, I did remember this medical term. Dr Hawkins was checking for signs of a stroke, though apparently a deliberate and very localised one.

"Negative," he reported. "Increasing voltage."

He headed back across the room and a moment later Roger convulsed again.

"Repeating test." Once again I wished I was in a better position to see what was going on. "Initial diagnosis confirmed – ischemia has occurred. Testing stage two commencing."

Roger/Max groaned in his chair. He looked around himself, though fortunately not toward me, and his expression was one of puzzlement. "My head…" he slurred. "Wha' goin' on?"

"State your name for me, please."

"M' name…" Roger/Max paused for a moment, unable to think.

"Do you know where you are?" asked Dr Hawkins.

Roger/Max looked blank for a moment and then dumbly shook his head.

"Who is the prime minister?"

Another blank look, and another head shake.

Dr Hawkins returned to the tape recorder. "Stage two confirms success. Subject has been reset. Some evidence of palsy, suspected temporary – will place subject under observation. Subject is now ready for conditioning."

He turned back to his "patient".

"Can you tell me your name?"

"Hmm…?"

"Your name is Roger. Can you tell me your name?"

"…R'ger."

"I am Dr Hawkins."

"…Doc Hawk'ns…"

"I am your friend. You are safe when I am near."

"…Fr'nd…"

"You have no memory of your past. You will not attempt to recall it."

"…No m'mry…"

Dr Hawkins returned to the tape recorder. "Conditioning complete. The subject will be interviewed in a few hours to verify success." He switched off the recorder *and turned back to the orderlies. "Take him back to his room and let him recover. And send the data for processing immediately - we're already behind schedule."*

"Yes, sir."

I suddenly realised I had waited too long. There was only one way out of that room, and I was standing right by it.

The Investigation Begins

Henry thought about Roger (or was it Max?) and his treatment – in this state, he was almost a child again; innocent and trusting, and easy prey for anyone out to control him. Rather like Eddie... But surely this machine was supposed to treat the patients, not cause these mental conditions? Why would anyone set out to do this to people?

Still, it was just a story. There was no Max, no Roger.

Just a story.

But what if the process could be reversed? What if it could reverse such a condition in those who were born with it?

Would Eddie thank him for that?

He shook his head. This was absurd. There was no machine. Eddie was Eddie, and always would be. And he wouldn't have him any other way.

He called by early the next morning to pick up his young charge, whose mother saw him off at the door with two suitcases and a sports bag. Eddie himself was wearing a sun hat, some wraparound sunglasses, a duffel coat, a pair of shorts and hiking boots. Not sure where he was going, Maggie Patfield had decided to dress him for all eventualities.

"Hello Eddie," Henry smiled. "Let me help you with those cases."

Between the two of them they struggled the suitcases into the boot of Henry's car. They were remarkably heavy - Henry dreaded to think what she'd packed. After several minutes of her fussing over her son, the two men said goodbye and set off.

This, mused Henry, would be the furthest Eddie had been in his entire life – at least, as far as he knew. He looked across at Eddie, who looked ready to explode with excitement.

"Are you ready, Eddie?"

Eddie grinned. "Ready, steady, go, boss!"

It was a long journey, made longer by traffic and several stops. Eddie's excitement (and fondness for fizzy drinks) made the extra stops necessary, though he began to grow restless as they went on. Henry was starting to wonder if he'd have been better going alone.

And then they saw it, up ahead – a big expanse of blue and grey widening between land and sky, sparkling in the sunlight.

"Boss! It's the sea! It's sea, isn't it?"

Henry hadn't been to the coast himself in years, but he'd forgotten how excited he'd been by a trip to the seaside as a child. Eddie was, in many ways, still a child – and quite possibly had never been there at all.

"Boss, I know we've got work to do, but can we go on the beach? Can we?"

Henry laughed. "We certainly can, Eddie."

"Can we make sandcastles?"

Henry chuckled. "That might be tricky, Eddie. Brighton doesn't have sandy beaches – it's all pebbles."

Eddie's face fell.

"Actually, I think there is a sandy bit somewhere along the promenade. We'll have to see. First of all, let's go find where we're staying."

Eddie nodded. His eyes kept being drawn back towards the sea, still distant but growing nearer by the minute.

Even with Dr Edmunds' cash injection, Henry couldn't afford to splash out on the Grand Hotel. Instead he'd arranged a room in a small bed and breakfast in the

Kemptown area.

"Hi there," he announced. "I'm Henry Ford – I've booked a room for a few nights. Two adults."

The lady at the counter was fooling no-one with her blond hair. Even without the grey coming out at the roots, the wrinkles alone put her in her sixties at least. She fumbled for her reading glasses before consulting the reservations book.

"Ah yes, Mr Ford... here we are. You and your young man are in room seven." She handed over a large metal key with an enormous wooden key fob.

"My young..." Henry paused. "Um, thank you."

"They're only single beds," she continued, "but you can push them together if you need to."

Henry was momentarily baffled. He looked across at Eddie, who was enthralled by a framed photograph on the wall featuring a number of colourfully dressed men and women – and some barely dressed – on a Pride march.

Ah, of course.

"Come on, Eddie. Let's go see our room."

"Sure, boss."

Henry took one of Eddie's suitcases along with his own as Eddie struggled with the rest of his luggage, and they headed for the stairs. They creaked gently under the tread of their footsteps. At the top of the stairs and round a corner they found their room. The paint was starting to peel off the door and the carpet was threadbare, but it all seemed comfortable enough.

"What do you think, Eddie?"

Eddie stared, mouth wide open. This was an adventure for him – he'd probably slept in the same room for about twenty years now. Henry noticed the frayed carpet, the missing handle on one of the wardrobe doors, the subtle patch of mould creeping up the wallpaper and the dust under the beds, but Eddie didn't see any of it. It was all amazing to Eddie, who dived onto one of the beds with youthful excitement.

"I'm having this one!" he yelled.

Henry laughed. "So I see."

Eddie bounced up and down excitedly on the bed. "I'm gonna have a sleepover! I've always wanted a sleepover!"

The squeaking of Eddie's ancient bedsprings was surprisingly loud. Henry couldn't help but wonder what the old woman downstairs thought was going on.

At least Eddie remained entirely clueless. "Can we stay up late, boss?"

"Well, we have work to do, but I suppose we can stay up a little past your bedtime. Oh, and Eddie, don't call me boss. While we're in Brighton, call me Henry."

"Okay, boss." Eddie grinned, and Henry suddenly realised he was making a joke. An Eddie joke, but still a joke.

This trip could actually be fun.

First they unpacked, and then Eddie called his mother. She'd been quite insistent that he called her as soon as they arrived. She didn't ask to speak to Henry. With that task completed, Henry helped Eddie to pick out a change of clothes that would attract less attention than the all-weather ensemble his mother had chosen.

There was a lot to do, but Henry had already decided on their first and most important stop.

"Come on, Eddie, let's go hit the beach."

Eddie cheered, then realised he was in public and looked embarrassed. "Sorry, boss. Henry."

Henry laughed. "If you're good, I'll get you an ice cream."

It was vanilla, with strawberry syrup and a chocolate flake in the top.

Henry sat on the pebbled beach, watching the sea and trying to think. In the distance he could see Eddie splashing in the water with a bunch of children. He'd taken his shoes and socks off but his trouser legs were getting very wet. Still, his mother had probably packed another three pairs.

As investigations went, this barely was one. They had a mysterious package which had been posted from here, but no real leads. If he had the time, the resources and the contacts, he could try to break it down – look for people who had recently moved here, looked for work, and so on. It would be a big list. He could then try to narrow it down. It could take months, and there'd be no guarantee it would even work out. The population of Brighton varied enormously throughout the year, especially with the summer crowds and the university students, and the tapes might even have been recorded somewhere else and simply posted here.

Henry rummaged in his bag for his mobile phone and pulled a number of paper scraps out with it. Eddie's filing system seemed to be catching. He also dug out the envelope that had contained the last of the tapes, as well as a possible lead. What was that address again?

Here it was – JKR Electronics. He'd looked up a telephone number last night and jotted it down on the envelope, but they hadn't been open then. They should be now. He punched the number into his mobile, watching Eddie chasing the children in the surf (and being chased in turn) as the phone rang through.

"Hello, JKR Electronics."

"Hello there," he said. "This is Detective Sergeant Ford of the Sussex Constabulary. I'm looking into a potential credit card fraud and wanted to know if you could help me."

"Certainly, officer. What can I do?"

Henry smiled. It was a risky gamble, but pretending to be in authority had worked for him many times before. As long as he didn't push his luck he could usually get away with it. Of course, impersonating a policeman was a criminal offence, which is why he'd wanted to wait until Eddie was out of earshot.

"Can you tell me if you've had any orders from the Brighton area in the last couple of months?"

"I can look into it, but I'll need a few minutes. Can I call you back?"

"That'll be fine," replied Henry. "Let me give you my mobile number – I'm not at my desk at the moment." He recited his mobile number and asked for it to be repeated back.

"I'll call you right back."

"Thank you." The call ended, and Henry laid back on the pebbles. They were a little uncomfortable against his back, but not painfully so.

In the distance, the children all leapt onto Eddie, who fell backwards into the water. They were all laughing. Henry wondered if Eddie's mother had ever let him play with other children like this.

"Is he alright with them?"

Henry looked over towards the voice. It belonged to a woman fast approaching forty – the children's mother, he guessed – sat beside him on the pebbles.

"I'm not sure I like him playing with the children. It's a bit odd, a grown man like that..."

"Eddie's fine," he replied. "He's something of a child himself, you could say. A bit slow, you know what I mean?"

"Even so..."

"It's probably time we were moving on anyway," Henry said. "Got to get back to work."

She nodded, and shouted down the beach. "Martin! James! Sasha! Time to go!"

"Oh, mum!"

"Shut up and do as you're told!"

Eddie came back up the beach, soaking wet.

"You okay, Eddie?"

"That was fun! Can we come here again and play with my friends some more?"

Henry was about to say something non-committal when the telephone rang again.

"Hello," he said. After giving out false names and titles so many times, he'd grown used to not announcing himself until he figured out who the caller thought he was.

"Hello, is that officer Ford?"

"Yes, it is. Did you find anything?" He pulled a notebook out of his pocket. He might need to write these down.

"Just three customers ordered from the Brighton area in the last two months."

"Okay, what are their details?"

The caller gave three names and addresses, and Henry scribbled them down. He promised that an officer would be in touch to arrange a formal statement and hung up.

"Boss?"

"Henry, Eddie. Call me Henry."

"Henry? What was that about statements?"

"Doesn't matter, Eddie. What matters is that I've got us a few leads. You ready to get down to work?"

Eddie's face lit up at the thought of more journalism. "Yeah!"

"This first address is in Hove. Right next door. Let's start there." He paused.

"Actually, let's get you a change of clothes first. You're absolutely soaked."

Henry stopped the car a short walk away from the house. "Now, remember, Eddie. If they ask who I am, I'm going to lie to them. I need you to keep quiet about that. Okay?"

"I don't think I can tell lies, boss. My mother always told me I mustn't."

Henry wondered how he'd ever get anywhere in journalism without knowing how to bend the truth.

"It's okay, Eddie. You don't need to say anything you don't want to. Just don't contradict what I say." He saw Eddie frown. "Just keep quiet."

"Yes, boss."

Henry felt bad about this, but it had to be done. Eddie had to learn how the world worked some day. "Remember, Eddie – we aren't being bad. We're only lying because... the truth is complicated. It would take too long to explain."

Eddie still looked unhappy, but that was probably the best he could do. He got out of the car and waited for Eddie to join him before they headed to the house.

Number 73. Apparently the home of a Mr Brown, though the two brown cars on the driveway suggested there was perhaps a Mrs Brown too. The front door was, unfortunately, not brown but a fading blue. Henry saw a doorbell to one side and pressed it, setting off a muffled series of vaguely musical chimes.

The door was opened a minute later by an old man in old clothes and old slippers. He looked up at Henry with heavily lined but still alert eyes.

"Yes?"

"Mr Brown?" asked Henry.

"That's me. Whatever it is, I'm not interested. Are you a couple of those Jenova nutters? At my age, it's too late to start worrying about what God thinks of me."

Henry stopped Eddie saying something foolish by speaking first. "We're not Jehovah's Witnesses, Mr Brown. I'm a researcher for JKR Electronics. I believe you placed an order with us recently and wanted to ask some questions about it."

"Did I? Oh, well make it quick. My wife's due her medication."

Henry already had a hunch this wasn't the man they wanted, but he had to ask anyway. "Can you confirm what you ordered with us?"

"Oh, I don't remember exactly now. Some of those scarf cables for the television, I think."

Eddie giggled quietly. Henry tried to ignore him.

"You mean SCART cables?"

"Yes, that's them. The signal's still rubbish. Still, I suppose that's not your fault. Those ruddy freeview boxes. Load of rubbish, I tell you, but I ain't paying for one of them satellite dishes."

"Okay then. Uh... are you happy with the service you've received?"

"Don't really remember. It was alright, I suppose. I'd have complained if it wasn't. Did I complain?"

"Um... no, I don't think so. I mean... I have no record of a complaint here."

"Oh, that's alright then. Put me down as saying it was good then."

It was time for the last question.

"Mr Brown, have you ever heard of the Amnesia Project?"

Henry watched the old face carefully, but there was no flicker of recognition. "Can't say I have. Is that a new chat show or something?"

"No, that's fine. Thank you for your time, Mr Brown."

"Oh, is that all? Goodbye, young man."

The door creaked closed – or maybe it was the old man creaking, who knew? – and Henry headed back down the path, Eddie close behind.

"That wasn't so bad, was it, Eddie?"

Eddie shook his head. "I don't like lying, boss."

"But how much harder would that have been if I'd told him the truth?"

"I know, boss." Eddie thought. "Did I do well?"

"Brilliantly. And Eddie... scarf cables?"

Eddie giggled again.

The second customer was a Jason Arnold, and he lived in Moulsecoomb, a little northeast of central Brighton. Henry went through the same routine, parking up a little down the road and reminding Eddie not to blow their cover, though he suspected Eddie was getting used to the idea now.

It started to go wrong when Jason answered the door as Jocelyn. A sequined silver dress hugged an unlikely hourglass figure, helped out by a particularly large amount of padding around the chest, with an enormous blonde wig to complete the ensemble.

"Hello, my dears," purred the heavily glamorised creature, fluttering her fake eyelashes. She ran a tongue over lips the most vibrant shade of red Henry had ever seen. "What can I do you for?"

"Uh... Mr Jason Arnold?"

"Not tonight, my dear. Ask me again in the morning. Today, I'm Jocelyn."

Henry had never met a drag queen before and was momentarily thrown.

Eddie broke his vow of silence. "Why are you dressed like that?"

"I'm rehearsing, dear. Or I was, before you rang the doorbell."

"We're sorry for interrupting," replied Henry.

"Oh, I don't mind. I am so *sick* of Gloria Gaynor. *I Will Survive*? Not if I have to sing that bloody song again, I won't."

"Why are you dressed like that?" asked Eddie.

Henry sighed. "Eddie..."

"I'm a drag queen, dear. I dress up in women's clothes and sing songs on the stage." Jocelyn turned to Henry. "Is he... alright?"

"He's not that quick on the uptake," muttered Henry.

Eddie beamed. "Oh, I get it. It's like at Christmas, with Cinderella."

Jocelyn frowned.

"Pantomime," explained Henry. He leaned in closer and lowered his voice. "Just play along. It'll be easier."

Jocelyn sighed. "Oh alright. Let's get rid of you two so I can get back to Gloria."

"I just wanted to ask..."

"You know what? I've had it. I've been dying to do my own song for months, and maybe tonight's the night. What do you think?"

"I'm sure you'll do fine. Now..."

"Not that I know why I'm asking you two. What did you want again?"

"I'm here from... uh..." Henry pinched the bridge of his nose, having lost his thread entirely. "Sorry. Who are we again?"

"JKR Electronics," said Eddie, helpfully.

"Thank you. Yes. We gather you've ordered from us recently and wanted to ask you about it."

"News to me, dears. I don't know anything about electricals. I can barely work the microphone."

"You haven't ordered anything from us?"

"Hang about." Jocelyn leaned back inside. "Michael! Have you been using my credit card again?"

A boy of about fourteen poked his head into the hallway.

"Michael, be honest now. Have you been using my card again?"

"Sorry, Dad."

"What did you order?" asked Henry.

"Just some stuff. A few chips, some resistors, that sort of thing."

"Michael's always been into this sort of thing," said Jocelyn. "He does all the electrical stuff for me. I've never been any good at that. He's always making these little gizmos, all these circuits and things. I never know what he's up to."

"Sounds exciting," said Henry, who knew as much about electronics as he did about cars, and cared even less. "What are you making?"

"Just stuff. You wouldn't understand."

"Michael, have you ever heard of the Amnesia Project?"

"No. Sounds cool. What does it do?"

"Never mind. Sorry to bother you, Mr – uh..."

Jocelyn sighed theatrically and shut the door.

"Well, that wasn't what I expected," said Henry.

"He didn't even sing the ugly sister song," said Eddie. "Who's Gloria?"

Number three on their list was a Tom Phillips, and the address was a bar in Kemptown. This one felt lucky to Henry. Mostly because it was the only lead they had left and he didn't want it to fail, but he also thought it made sense – if you wanted to order something without giving your name, why not go through a front?

It was a gaudy, over-the-top establishment with the unlikely name of "The Cruise Liner", painted with a heavy emphasis on pink and purple. It was largely empty at this time of day – just a few customers were visible through the glass fronting – but it was open. Henry felt relieved. He'd be able to speak to someone quite easily while it was quiet - and he didn't like the idea of bringing Eddie to a busy pub, especially in a strange town. And few towns were stranger than Brighton could be.

Eddie seemed enraptured by the place. Everything was new to him down here, but Henry wondered if he'd even been in a bar before. He had almost certainly never been in this sort of bar. Pictures of half-naked young men lined the walls, painted an even brighter pink than the outside. Fresh paint. Henry guessed the place had only recently been done up.

Several customers sat at tables around the bar, mostly alone, all of them male. They all watched Henry as he looked at them. He wondered whether any of them might be Rob, or Max. No way to know, he supposed.

He walked up to the bar, Eddie gawping at everything behind him. A young man in a pink shirt and a bowtie ignored Henry for a full minute before finally deciding he was a customer and not just a tourist.

"Can I get you anything?"

"I'm looking for Tom Phillips. Is he in?"

The man paused. "I don't know anyone called Tom Phillips. Sorry."

"He had a package delivered here recently. Electronic parts. I need to speak to him about it."

The young man shook his head. "Sorry, can't help. He doesn't work here, I can tell you that."

"Can you get the manager?"

"Gaz? He's in the back, sorting out the gear for tonight. I'll see if he's available." He smiled. "It's karaoke night. Performers get one drink on the house. Interested?"

Henry shuddered. He preferred his tuneless singing in the shower, where it belonged.

"Just get the manager, please," he said.

The bartender headed into the back, then emerged again a moment later. "Gaz says to go on in, but be quick."

"Oh, alright. Eddie, wait here for me."

Eddie nodded absently. He was staring at the pictures around the bar. Henry left him to it and went through the staff door.

Gaz was a middle aged man with thinning blond hair. He wore a suit that he'd clearly owned for a while - and was a couple of sizes too small, especially around the middle.

"Hi there," he said. "What can I do for you?"

"I'm looking for Tom Phillips," said Henry. "I'm here from JKR - we believe he ordered some electronics from here."

Gaz shook his head. "Sorry. Never heard of him. You must have made a mistake."

"It's very important we get in touch," said Henry. Inspiration struck him. "We've had an urgent recall on certain electrical components – they could be dangerous."

"I told you," said Gaz. "There's no Tom Phillips here."

Henry sighed. "Look, can I leave you my telephone number? If you find out anything, please give me a call."

"Yeah, alright." Gaz handed him a pen and a scrap of paper from the desk. "Anything to get rid of you."

Henry left his name and number. "Thanks," he said. He paused. "I don't suppose you've ever heard of the Amnesia Project?" he asked.

Gaz hesitated for a moment. "No," he said. "Can't say I have."

Henry thanked him and headed back to the bar.

"Eddie?"

There was no reply.

Henry looked around. He'd only been away for a few minutes, but that was enough.

Eddie was gone.

"Eddie?"

Henry told himself not to panic. Maybe Eddie had wandered into another part of the bar. Maybe he was in the toilets. The first thing he did was take a look around the Cruise Liner.

Eddie was not there.

"Hey." Henry returned to the bartender. "Did you see what happened to my friend there? He's disappeared."

"I dunno. I wasn't watching him."

"Anyone?" Henry looked around at the few customers in the bar. None of them wanted to meet his gaze. Those that did merely shook their heads. No, they hadn't seen anything.

Henry gave up and went back outside. Eddie couldn't have gone far, after all. But he wasn't outside the bar. Henry looked up and down the street, but Eddie wasn't in sight.

It wasn't like him to run off. Henry found himself coming to the unpleasant conclusion that someone had taken him. But that was absurd, wasn't it? Unless someone knew why they were here. Someone with an interest in the Amnesia Project.

"Can't start thinking like that. He must have gone off somewhere."

So where to start? Henry wondered if the best thing to do might be to wait at the Cruise Liner. If he wandered off, Eddie might wander back to this spot. Then again,

Eddie's sense of direction was never that good. He could be wandering the streets for hours.

Henry headed for the beach. Eddie might have gone back there – it was a fun place for him, after all, so he might feel better if he went back there.

Eddie was not at the beach.

The other place he might have gone was the bed and breakfast. Henry had made sure he knew the name and address of the place in case they got separated – how easily Eddie would get there, he didn't know, but he hoped someone would stop to help him. He looked in at the Cruise Bar one last time and tried once more to speak with the bartender.

"Look, Gaz has my number. If you see Eddie, get him to stay here and call me right away. If Tom Phillips shows up, call me as well. Got all that?"

"Call you if Tom or Eddie ask for you. Got it."

"No, not if they ask for me. If they come in."

"Might be tricky, that. I don't know who they are."

"He was right here with me a minute ago!" Henry resisted the urge to scream but he did give the door a good slam on the way out.

He got back to the bed and breakfast a few minutes later. Eddie had not returned. The I'm-not-grey-haired landlady hadn't seen Eddie since breakfast, but promised to let Henry know if anyone asked for him.

Henry sat down on the bed, wondering what to do next. It would be evening soon, and he hated the idea of Eddie on his own in the dark. Eddie's mother would kill him for this. And what if he had been snatched? Eddie didn't know anything. They'd hold him to ransom, perhaps. His phone might ring any moment.

His phone rang.

He mostly managed to suppress a scream, producing a startled yelp instead. He fumbled for the pick-up button.

"Hi Henry. How are you doing?"

Henry breathed out. "Mike! I'm glad it's you. Eddie's gone. I'm panicking that someone's kidnapped him. Stupid, I know..."

"Maybe not."

Henry froze. "What is it, Mike?"

"I've been doing some digging on Dr Edmunds. Routine background check, stuff like that – and he doesn't exist. Flew in from South America to attend a conference, or something like that, and never went back."

"It's a fake name?"

"It's a fake identity. The man has a passport, a house, a driver's licence, a credit card... they're real. He's not. Someone's gone to a lot of trouble to set this up. It's the sort of thing I'd normally expect from a witness relocation programme."

"So who is he?"

"I'm not sure. But because of this story he's interested in, I did some research into dates and events. There was a Dr Hawkins at Grace Meadows. He disappeared nearly a decade ago. Six months ago, this guy shows up. I'm not saying they're the same guy, but... well..."

"They could be."

"Yeah."

"That makes a lot of sense."

"Does it?" Mike's voice remained doubtful. *"That story's a work of fiction. Machines that wipe memories? They don't exist. They can't do."*

"I don't know much about how the mind works," said Henry. "I'm just a journalist. I look at the facts and try to figure out the story in them."

"Here's what I think," said Mike. "There's an incident at the clinic. The news reports all say it was a fire, that a boiler blew up in the basement. The official reports all agree on that. But I looked a bit deeper. I spoke to a few people on the investigation who think maybe it was something else – like a bomb. It's just your usual conspiracy theorist nonsense, but it's compelling."

"What do you mean?"

"Say someone has a grudge against Dr Hawkins. A former patient, a rival, maybe there's even some truth in those dodgy funding rumours. There are even rumours about drugs being manufactured at the clinic, but I don't believe a word of that. Whatever. So, someone plants a bomb, tries to kill him, and the whole thing is played down to avoid a panic. Or a scandal. Dr Hawkins gets a new identity and goes into hiding, until you start printing this story and risk bringing the whole thing back up again."

"So you think whoever planted this bomb is trying to discredit him, or get the truth out, or something like that? I don't give a damn about this story any more. I just want Eddie back."

"If he's just wandered off, Eddie will turn up. Have a little faith. If he's not... you'll just have to wait until they contact you. I'm sorry."

"I know." Henry sighed. "Thanks, Mike. I knew that money was too good to be true."

"Isn't it always? Good luck, Henry. I hope we can still do that drink some time. You, me and Eddie."

"Me too, Mike." Henry ended the call, and sat back to wait for news.

With nothing else to do, he slotted the next of Rob's tapes into the recorder and pressed play.

Escape

I fought back the urge to run. They didn't know I was here, after all, and I preferred to keep it that way, so I walked as quickly as I dared back along the corridor, wishing it had something I could hide behind. My treacherous feet tapped against the hard floor with the volume of a brass band, or so it seemed to me. Desperate for a hiding place, I waved Dr Bradshaw's card at random doors and hoped one would open.

At last there was a familiar click and I dashed inside, closing the door as quietly and as quickly as I could behind me. The room itself was utterly dark. Outside I could hear voices – Roger (or Max; I no longer quite knew what to call him) being half dragged back to the elevator by the two orderlies, and Dr Hawkins giving them his instructions – though I was too panicked and the voices too muffled for me to make much out. For a horrible moment I had the idea that Dr Hawkins was going to follow me into this room, but when I heard the click of a door unlocking and the corridor light failed to illuminate my surroundings I realised he had gone somewhere else. Steadily, one at a time, the butterflies in my stomach stopped trying to fly away.

It seemed like an age before I gathered the courage to move, though it was probably just a few minutes. I felt along the wall for a light switch and eventually found one. At first it seemed to do nothing, and then a series of fluorescent strips flickered into life.

The room was full of files.

Aside from a small table by the entrance, which held a few empty filing trays, the room was entirely taken up by several long shelving units. Each contained about five rows of cardboard files on each side, all slight variations of plain manila. Thousands of them. Tens of thousands. Some of the files seemed older than the clinic itself, which was almost certainly impossible. I supposed damp or use had aged those faster than mere time.

I pulled one down at random and looked at the cover.

Patricia Stevens, PS0020347, 1987-1992

I doubted Patricia had only lived for five years, so these were more likely the years she had attended the clinic. I looked inside the file. There I saw a photograph of Patricia, an elderly lady with a lazy eye and a blue rinse, and a number of reports. They looked a lot like the phony ones I'd been dealing with by email in my "job", but I got the impression this one was real.

She had been the patient of a Dr Herbacre, suffering from a form of dementia. Various reports listed a number of treatments, most of which I didn't recognise, though a few sparked in my head and sounded vaguely familiar. There was nothing in Patricia's file of interest to me, so I placed it back on the shelf.

The files appeared to be sorted by date left (or died?) and then by name. These were clearly quite old now, so I headed to the far end, where I thought all the recent stuff should be. I was soon proved right when I found myself.

Robert Walker, RW1045728, 2004-

I took down the file with shaking hands.

It was a little disappointing. It told me that I was the patient of Dr Hawkins (I knew that) and that I was suffering from retrograde amnesia (I knew that too). My picture was a few years old and not entirely flattering. A similar bundle of reports to Patricia's followed, listing treatments and notes. Again, I recognised the occasional word or phrase but couldn't identify them all. There was a pink sheet near the front that referred to a personnel file, though I couldn't see any others filed under my name.

I stuffed my file into my jacket. I had to leave, whether or not I could find any evidence, and the sooner the better. But I wasn't satisfied – having seen the "operation" in the next room, I wanted to know just what had been done and who exactly Roger was. There didn't seem to be any records for a Roger, though without his last name a thorough search would be difficult. There were too many. And what if he was called Max, as he'd claimed when they took him away?

Then I remembered the police interrogation.

What's your connection with Maxwell Nicholson?

Nicholson! I scanned underneath 'N' on the filing cabinets and worked back through the years. Almost straight away I found the file.

Maxwell Nicholson, MN1004587, 2004-

The photograph inside was definitely Roger, though here he was clean shaven and his ginger hair was neatly combed. And he was smiling; a cheeky grin and a sparkle in his eyes. I felt a flicker of recognition at the sight of that smile - and a flash of anger at what had been done to him.

The file suggested a combination of retrograde and anterograde amnesia, for which treatments were considerably more varied (and frequent) than my own had been. Once again, Dr Hawkins was the assigned practitioner. Max too had a personnel file somewhere, which was interesting - I had thought my personnel file related to my fake job, but Max didn't even have that. Again, there was no sign of any personnel records here. They had to be held somewhere else.

I stuffed his file into my jacket as well and made my way back to the door, fishing out the mobile phone. There was no signal. If I wanted to call in, I'd have to get out of the basement level first. I put the phone back in my pocket and headed for the door again.

Then I heard that familiar click, and the door opened.

"Is anyone in here?"

I recognised the voice of Dr Hawkins. He of all people could not find me here! And yet, once again, I felt the absurd desire to step out of hiding and turn myself over. Dr Hawkins would look after me.

Except I knew this wasn't true. I recalled his final comments to Roger: "I am your friend. You are safe when I am near." *Had he said something similar to me in that same chair?*

His footsteps drew closer as he walked down the racks. There was nowhere I could go. I briefly considered hiding on one of the shelves but they were only about a foot deep - even if I could fit, I'd be easily spotted. I looked around desperately for a hiding place, anywhere at all. There was nothing.

Then the footsteps stopped. I heard a soft click before Dr Hawkins spoke again.

"Memo: remind staff about policy regarding leaving lights on."

Another soft click as the tape recorder stopped again. The footsteps then receded, and I heard the door open. The lights went out and the door closed, leaving me in total darkness.

I waited a few minutes before I moved again. I didn't want to risk stepping out of the dark straight into him again, and part of me simply couldn't believe my lucky escape. Had he really come in just to turn the lights off?

I soon found out the answer was 'no' - using Lisa's mobile phone as a makeshift torch I found my way to the door and discovered a bundle of papers had been left in the filing tray. I grabbed the papers as an afterthought and shoved them into my jacket along with the other files.

I waved Dr Bradshaw's card at the slot and the door clicked open again. I stepped out to find the corridor empty.

I turned back to the room with the machine. It was locked, and this was one door that my stolen card would not open. Clearly Hawkins was very careful about who accessed this room.

I turned away and headed for the elevator.

It was time to leave. A nearby meeting room, currently unused, gave me an opportunity to check the mobile phone again. I now had a moderately strong signal and called Lisa.

"Rob! Are you okay?"

"Lisa, I need to get out of here, as soon as possible. When can you pick me up?"

"I'll be right there. I'm in the area already - I thought you might need me. Ten minutes? Maybe fifteen."

"Meet me at the front entrance."

"That's too risky, Rob."

"I don't think I'll be sneaking out. Meet me there in fifteen minutes and keep the engine running."

"Okay. Good luck!"

Fifteen minutes. Plenty of time - perhaps too much time. I couldn't be sure how long I'd need to get to the way out, or whether I'd get there at all.

It started going wrong the moment I left the meeting room.

For a start, I was at the wrong end of the building. One of the clinic's floor plans was just down the corridor and I mentally noted the route to the front entrance. It would take me past Dr Hawkins' office.

A moment later I was spotted.

"Rob! How did you get here?"

"Derek! I could ask you the same thing."

"Oh, I have free run of the place. Those doctors do whatever I say."

I felt a little better having some company but I also knew that Derek was going to slow me down – and was likely to give me away.

"Derek, I have to go."

"What are you up to?"

I weighed up the various options, and decided to tell him the truth. If he repeated it to the staff, they'd probably just think it was Derek being Derek again.

"I'm escaping, Derek. I have to get to the front entrance in the next fifteen minutes."

"How will you get out the doors?"

"I've got a keycard."

"You're lying to me. Everyone's always lying to me!"

I headed off down the corridor, but he followed shortly behind.

"Stop lying to me!" he shouted. I wished he would shut up. "Everyone calls me the liar but it's not! It's everyone else!"

"Derek, please - don't make so much noise!"

"Shut up! Shut up!"

I ran. Derek gave up following me but I could still hear him yelling behind me. I heard voices ahead and ducked into a side office as two orderlies ran past.

"What's he on about now?"

"How'd he get up here anyway?"

"Hawkins gives these loonies too much freedom, if you ask me."

There was a gentle cough behind me.

I turned to see another doctor sat at his desk in the office I'd just entered.

"Hello there. I'm afraid I don't know your name, young man."

"Hello sir," I replied. "I'm sorry, I didn't mean to barge in."

His hand, hovering by the security alert button at the edge of his desk, slowly moved away. I pretended I hadn't noticed. "So what did you come in here for?"

"I, uh... was looking for Dr Bradshaw."

I have no idea what brought this idea into my head, but it seemed to do the trick. The man behind the desk softened. "Oh, are you his patient? I'm afraid there was an... incident earlier and he's currently in the infirmary."

"Oh," I said, trying to look surprised.

"He should be okay in an hour or two. Is there anything I can help with?"

"Uh... no, it's okay," I said. "I'll go wait for him in the common room."

"I'll take you there," he said.

The common room was not on my way but I didn't object. Refusing his escort would only arouse suspicion.

As it transpired, being escorted by the doctor made things a little easier. We passed several other doctors and orderlies on the way who would otherwise have asked questions. Soon we were in the patient's area once again and I took a seat near the television. Mrs Griffin sat in her usual place and clicked rapidly with her knitting needles. Happy that I was safely settled in, the doctor left me to it. The television burbled happily to itself - repeats of The Waltons, I think - and I tried not to think about how much time was passing.

When he'd gone, I checked my phone. Eight minutes to go.

"Leaving already, doctor?" asked Mrs Griffin. "This is a new one, this is." She gestured at the television.

"No, Mrs Griffin, they're all repeats. They haven't made this programme in years."

"Rubbish! I met John-Boy - the actor, I mean; I've not gone soft - just last year. Lovely young lad."

I paused for a moment, wondering which year the old dear thought it currently was. "Do you know anyone called Max?" I asked.

"No, that wasn't his name."

"Not John-Boy. Someone here."

"You mean Dr Nicholson? I've not seen him in ages."

"What about Roger?"

She giggled. "Hee hee! I see what you mean. They look so alike, don't they?"

Seven minutes to go. "Mrs Griffin, I can't stay. When you see Roger - tell him I'll be back for him."

"Certainly, doctor. I'll tell him."

I knew she probably wouldn't, and that Roger wouldn't remember after ten minutes if she did, but it felt like the right thing to do.

Six minutes to go. Dr Bradshaw's card still worked, which was a relief. I knew I was pushing my luck with every door - it was only a matter of time before Dr Bradshaw woke up enough to realise it was missing, and then I had no doubt that I'd be trapped again. Derek's fit earlier on had distracted a number of orderlies and so I was able to make my way to the front of the building remarkably quickly.

Perhaps Lisa was already there - or not. I had little hope of sneaking out through reception so I didn't dare risk running out early. Waiting outside for my lift was not an option, after all. I took my time, avoided everyone wherever possible and checked on floor plans whenever I wasn't sure about the route.

One minute left.

I stood at the final door, the one leading into the reception area and freedom. Reinforced glass panels afforded me a view into the lobby. There were a number of people in there - members of the public, I thought, just visiting. They probably wouldn't try to stop me and might even slow down any pursuit.

I decided to make my run for it. Dr Bradshaw's card swung by the sensor and I pulled at the door.

It didn't budge.

I realised that I hadn't heard a click, and tried again. Still no click. Then I spotted the keypad by the handle.

There was a door code. Without it, I was stuck here.

There was no answer from Lisa's phone. If she was still driving, she might not be able to answer - or what if she'd been caught? I tried not to think about that. In any event, there was no hope of asking her if she knew the code.

I couldn't risk guessing it. A wrong code, or a string of them, might well set off the alarms. I could hardly go back and ask someone. I didn't even know how many digits to enter. It was hard to believe I could be this close to freedom and defeated by the last door.

My mind kept turning back to Dr Hawkins. I was starting to panic – if he found me, I would be finished – placed back in the chair and reset to zero. If I wasn't lobotomised in the process, that was.

"Calm down," I told myself. I tried to think pleasant thoughts, of flowers and sunsets and stuff like that, but all I kept coming back to was Dr Hawkins. I'd be caught, I'd be taken to him, I'd be tortured...

"Yellow," I said to myself, and stopped dead. Why yellow? What did that mean? It was a memory of something.

Dr Hawkins, meeting me in the reception area days ago. Taking me to his office.

The door – this door – had a keypad on the other side.

Yellow... he'd muttered it under his breath.

I looked at the keypad again. The digits here were plain, but they reminded me of the keypads on telephones. I fished Lisa's mobile out of my pocket and looked at the keys – and, as I thought, they had letters on them. Little letters, under the numbers, which you could use for texting but had been around far longer than that.

I remembered the library, looking up memory loss and reading about mnemonics. Letters instead of numbers. Yellow – that would be 935569.

I didn't stop to reconsider. I simply flashed the badge at the sensor, then tapped in those six numbers and pulled at the door.

It opened.

For a moment I simply stood there, door in hand, stunned at the fact it had actually worked. When I got my jaw back off the floor I strode slowly and as casually as I could into the reception area.

I could see Lisa's car out front, and had to fight down my urge to run. I'd made it. I'd actually made it! I walked up to the car door, leant down to the window and smiled.

"Hello, young lady," I said. "Could you give me a lift?"

Lisa's expression was one of bafflement and concern. "Rob? Are you okay?"

I got inside the car. "Fine," I said. "But I'll be much happier when we're as far away as possible."

She smiled, gunned the accelerator and took us back to reality.

Sally

We returned to Walthamstow to discuss my findings over cups of hot tea and a plate of assorted chocolate biscuits. Evie fussed over me while Lisa asked endless questions. The papers I'd smuggled out got even more attention than I did.

"You said you'd seen Max?"

"Yes," I said. "He's a patient there. Only he has no memory at all, and everyone calls him Roger."

"Sound familiar?"

"The thought had crossed my mind," I admitted. "You think they did to me what they did to Max."

"If these files are right, I don't think. I know." Lisa flicked through the file with my name on. "He's even named the procedure after himself - HMAP. Stands for the Hawkins Memory Adjustment Procedure."

"That's some ego."

"Max has been through HMAP a load of times. You've been processed just once, I think."

I munched on a chocolate finger and let her talk.

"These other papers are even more interesting. You just picked them up on the way out, you said?"

I swallowed a mouthful of chocolate biscuit. "Yeah, just after Dr Hawkins dropped them off. I didn't pay much attention to them."

"You should have done. They're about Damian."

If I hadn't swallowed already, I would probably have choked. As it was, I dropped the rest of my biscuit in my lap and got a pained look from Evie as a consequence.

"I can't tell much from these - just some case notes that Dr Hawkins was finishing off, I think - but it looks as though Damian went through the same procedure as you and Max. Only, not quite the same - something was different about it. I can't tell what from these notes."

"I thought Jimmy - Damian was dead," I said.

"Dr Hawkins would agree. The last notes say 'experiment closed: subject deceased'. I'd hoped it wasn't true, that it had been faked somehow, but it looks like he's really dead."

I nodded. I barely knew Damian (who I still think of as Jimmy, even now) and what I'd heard about him was far from good, but some part of me felt bad for his death even so. If I'd not escaped the flat that day, perhaps he would still be alive. Or perhaps we'd both be dead.

"What's our next move?" I asked.

"We need some more concrete evidence about this HMAP thing," said Lisa. "I can't go to press with all this unless I've got something serious."

"Get the police involved?"

"Evidence, Rob. The police won't just burst in and search the place without good cause."

"You want me to go back in?"

"Absolutely not. You barely got out last time. Next time we go in, it'll be on our terms."

"Then there's something I want to do," I said. "I want to go see the flat."

Lisa shook her head. "Too risky. The police will be watching you. And probably others as well. Damian was keeping you there for some reason and I doubt it was for your own good."

"I can't do anything about the clinic. I can't do anything about bringing Dr Hawkins to justice, or Max, or this bag the police are holding. But I need to do something, Lisa. I can't just sit here."

"Rob..."

"That flat has something to do with me. I'm not even sure whose flat it is – the police said it was Max's, but it could be mine for all I know. And there might be some clue about who those two men were..."

Evie put her hand on mine. "I understand, dear. You might find something about yourself there."

"Your memory... of course, I didn't think." Lisa gave me a weak smile. "Of course you should go. But tomorrow, okay?"

I stood up, ready to argue against waiting. Why not now? Standing up was all it took to change my mind – my vision dimmed, my legs buckled under me and I sat back down rather heavily. I hadn't eaten since breakfast – a few biscuits and a cup of tea aside - and it was now fast approaching late afternoon. I'd been running on nothing but adrenaline for hours and now I was paying for it.

"You're right," I said. "Tomorrow."

We spent the evening at home, at Lisa's insistence – she didn't think we'd been followed, but it was safer not to take the chance of being seen. I fell asleep in my chair for an hour or so, or so she told me. We had a light supper – I forget what it was now; Evie's meals were satisfying but she preferred things in tins and packets to real cooking. We put the television on (Evie wanted to catch her soaps) but mostly Lisa and I talked.

"Tell me about Damian," I said. "How did you meet?"

Lisa sighed. "There's not much to tell," she said. "I was looking into a story, following up some leads on a house fire – arson, not accidental. I was interviewing some of the locals, and I happened to get talking to this guy. He said his name was Damian and he asked me out. He was thinner then, and he dressed much better, but mostly I was drawn to his sense of humour. We had an instant connection."

"So what happened?"

"We had a few dates, spent a lot of time together, eventually got a bit more serious. He was fun to be with. But he was also very secretive, and prone to snap at me sometimes. I got suspicious. In all the time we were together, I brought him back to my place every time. I never saw his home. Having a secretive partner doesn't fit too well with being an investigative journalist, as you can probably guess. So I started to investigate him."

I nodded.

"I began to realise he wasn't entirely stable. I checked out his past, his old friends. A lot of it was made up. I even followed him one day without his knowing – that's when I found out about 'Jimmy'. Even now, I'm not sure which of Jimmy and Damian is the real guy. Maybe neither was real."

"What made you end it?"

"Just... everything, I think. I couldn't trust him, and he had moments when he could get... angry. No, he never hit me. But I think that's because he knew I'd give him hell if he tried it. But when he was in his better moods... he could be so wonderful. He really did care about me, I think. I don't know if you can understand that."

I didn't really know Jimmy at all but I remembered that morning, and the look on his face when he'd left. He was terrified, but not just for himself. Perhaps he cared about me a little, too. I'd much rather think that than believe he was completely beyond hope.

"Perhaps I can," I said.

"Right," she said. "Time for bed. Tomorrow we'll go check out that flat." She stood up and then paused. "You know the really crazy thing? For a while, I thought Damian *had something to do with that house fire. That he'd started it, or at least knew who had. I thought that was silly at the time. Now, I'm not so sure. I don't know what he was mixed up with."*

We headed for bed. Evie had prepared a couple of camp beds – she was always prepared in case of unexpected visitors.

"You're a very special lady, Evie," I'd said.

"My dear, you don't know the half of it," she'd replied.

I slept like a log that night. My raid and escape from the clinic had completely drained me. I woke up at half past nine to find Evie bringing me breakfast on a tray.

"Fried eggs, bacon and baked beans. And a cup of tea. I'm afraid the sausages are still in the freezer."

"Thanks, Evie," I said. "You shouldn't have."

"Nonsense," she replied. "You need feeding up, young man."

I ate quickly. I was surprisingly hungry. "Where's Lisa?" I asked, between mouthfuls.

Lisa came in behind Evie. "I'm already up, lazybones. And I helped with cooking breakfast, by the way."

"Yes, dear," nodded Evie. "Turning the bacon over would have been impossible without you."

Lisa stuck out a tongue.

"Right," I said. "I'd best get ready. Time for me to go and look at the flat."

"I'm coming with you," said Lisa. "And we should take precautions."

"Another rape alarm?"

"I only had one of those," replied Lisa. "But Evie has some other toys."

It felt strange walking up the stairs to the flat again. Strange, but not very familiar. I was hoping that I'd have a strong sense of déjà vu and realise this was my home all along. There was nothing, which proved nothing, of course. I could have been living here for years, or only ever been here that one time.

I took the spare key from my pocket and unlocked the door. My hand shook as I did so, not entirely sure what we'd find when Lisa and I stepped inside. The door swung silently open, revealing... a perfectly normal hallway.

I took a long look around the flat. I have no idea what I was expecting to find, so I simply looked for anything. The bedroom was still a mess, covers thrown back and in disarray. A small pile of clothes in the corner were the only reminder of Jimmy's presence.

The spare bedroom was as pristine as ever.

There was no sign of any disturbance. The two men that had come to get me hadn't broken in – they'd used a key. Jimmy's key. Which probably meant they were the ones that killed him. I suddenly felt even more relieved that I'd slipped away when I had.

I went into the living room. The CD player was still switched on, unlike the central heating, and I noticed a CD inside the player. Curious, I hit the play button.

"We were climbing so high from a misty sunrise morning…"

"What's that, Rob?"

"It was in the CD player. Jimmy was playing it last time I was here - I guess he never took it out."

"I feel I'm falling. I feel I'm falling, and when I look up I see you…"

"Stop it, please."

I did. "What's up?"

"I know that song," she said. "Max wrote it for… I can't remember. It was a wedding gift for someone, I think. So romantic. I wish people would write songs for me." She paused. "It was on your tape, wasn't it? Strange that I didn't recognise it then."

"Max wrote it? You make it sound like he's on our side."

She paused. "He was. We were all friends. I thought I told you that."

I shook my head. "Jimmy said he wrote this. But then, nothing he told me was true, was it?"

She shook her head. "Only that he loved you - in his twisted way. And after reading those case notes, I'm not sure he was lying."

"You think he was... programmed?"

"Maybe. Found anything?"

A thought occurred to me. "Come with me," I said. "I'd like to show you something."

A few minutes later I'd spread the photographs I found the other day on the coffee table. "I think these are faked," I said.

"That one, definitely," she said. "Look at the shadow on your face there – the light source is all wrong. The sun should be over there. These ones are better, but they don't look... right to me."

"What about these?"

"That one looks genuine to me," she said. "You were even cuter when you were younger, you know that?"

"Lisa, please. Try to focus."

"These are weird," she said. "Some of them are obvious fakes." She picked up another of the photographs. "They've not even got the proportions right on this one."

"Fake photos of me and Jimmy. I thought maybe Jimmy was trying to make me *think we were a couple."*

"Now you don't?"

"Now I think someone was trying to fool us both."

"False memories? Damian reprogrammed to become Jimmy?"

None of it made sense. Why would someone want to engineer a relationship between us? Why would they want him dead?

As if on cue, there was a knock at the door.

"Don't answer it," said Lisa. "No-one knows we're here."

The knock came again, louder.

"I think they do," I said. "Besides, if it's who I think it is, they'll have Jim… Damian's key. Let's go find out."

"Alright," she replied. "But be ready for trouble." *She put her hand in her bag and pulled out a small object. I guessed it was one of Evie's "toys" and didn't ask any further questions.*

The door opened to three men. Two of them were heavy set men of few words. Each of them wore an off-the-rack suit in an effort to make them look professional, but the fabric strained over their shoulders. They weren't off-the-rack people. Both had shaved heads, one completely smooth and the other close cropped. The smooth headed one bore an old scar on one cheek. They were probably the same men that had come here before, looking for me. I would have been much happier if they hadn't found me this time either.

The man in the middle was shorter and lighter in build. He was clearly the brains of the trio, which wasn't really saying much. His suit was no better tailored than the others, though it fit him a little better. He too liked his hair cut short, but that may have been to hide a receding hairline. I could see the edge of a neck tattoo over his collar.

"Rob, right? Glad to meet you at last."

"Who are you and what do you want?" I asked. I tried to sound vaguely menacing but doubt I was very successful.

"We've been looking for you, Rob," he replied. "Someone is very keen to speak to you. Come with us."

"I'd rather not," I said.

"It wasn't a request," he said. He gestured to the others, who strode into the hallway and took hold of my arms.

"Let him go!" yelled Lisa. She tore into the two men, spraying liberally into the air with the small object in her hand. I had no idea what it was, but the stench was terrible and my eyes started watering immediately.

The effect on the two men was far greater. They cried out in pain and surprise and let go of me. They began wiping at their streaming eyes, but this seemed to make things worse rather than better.

"Run for it, Rob!" she yelled. I hesitated, seeing the nearer of the two thugs make a grab for her, but when I saw the smaller guy pull a knife and start towards me I'm afraid my confidence deserted me and I did as she said.

"Run!" she yelled again. I darted out the door, headed down the stairs three at a time and out into the street. A taxi sat idle outside the flat and I leapt into the back with relief.

"The police station, please," I panted. I knew the police had no liking for me but I had no idea where else I could go.

Then I realised that there were two people in the front of the taxi. The man in the front passenger seat turned around, and I saw him pointing the business end of a small pistol at me.

"No, mate," he said quietly. *"You're coming with us."*

In a way, I would have been happier if I'd been knocked out or blindfolded. It would have meant they didn't want me to see where they were taking me, suggesting they were going to let me go. Instead they simply drove me to an out of town industrial site and parked up outside the rusting iron doors of an old warehouse. We were the only people in sight and the hum of main road traffic was a distant murmur. I could scream all I wanted here, and there'd be no-one to hear me.

It was not a happy thought.

The man with the gun gestured me inside the warehouse. The main iron doors were sealed, the padlock even rustier than the doors themselves, and clearly hadn't been opened in years. Instead I was directed through a small side entrance and down a dingy corridor that led into the main part of the warehouse. The lighting was poor and many of the fluorescent strips flickered or remained dark.

I was locked into a storage cupboard in the basement. It had no windows and only the door I came in by. Empty shelving took up both side walls. A cheap wooden chair and a bare lightbulb were the only concessions I'd been given to comfort. I sat in the dim glow of the bulb and tried to sort out my racing thoughts.

I heard a commotion shortly after my arrival and raised voices. I was pretty sure one of them was Lisa's. The voices died away again and then there was only silence. Just me and my thoughts.

So Lisa was here. Was she safe? Did she know I was here? Did she know what was going on? I resolved to rescue her as soon as I could, though first I'd need rescuing myself.

It was about an hour later when my guard returned to collect me. I was led back upstairs, the big guy saying virtually nothing the whole time. The gun in his hand said everything he needed to say.

I was stopped outside a simple door bearing a STAFF ONLY sign. Given the gun and everything, I decided it was probably okay to ignore this instruction and pushed the door open.

"Ah, Mr Walker. So good of you to join us."

Behind a plain and functional desk sat a woman in a scarlet top. Brunette hair curled down to her neckline, framing a face of stern, functional beauty. She was a business woman – though the business itself was rapidly becoming apparent. The desk itself was clear of all but an anglepoise lamp and a few papers. She was smiling warmly, but the pistol held loosely in her hand detracted from the warmth somewhat.

"Thank you, Greg," she said. "I have him covered now. Please wait outside."

Greg, the man with the pistol that had brought me here, obediently left the room and closed the door behind him. No sooner had he done so, she put her own gun down on the desk and motioned me to sit.

"That's better," she said. "I detest all this gunplay and threat. You will be a good boy, won't you, Mr Walker? I should warn you that any attempt to escape will be most regrettable for you."

My eyes fell on the gun.

"Don't bother," she said. "The gun is not loaded. Like I said, I cannot stand the things. Threatening me with it will get you nowhere. Those of my men, however, are most definitely loaded. I dislike guns, but they have their uses." She motioned again for me to sit, and this time I did so.

"Now, let's get the introductions out of the way. I already know you, of course, but you may not remember me. My name is Sally Kensington."

She held out a hand. I didn't take it.

"I see. Manners cost nothing, Mr Walker, but we clearly have trust issues. I suppose I shouldn't be all that surprised. Do you know why you are here?"

"No," I said.

"Amnesia. Yes, of course. Very convenient. And, I believe, quite genuine. How much have you rediscovered so far?"

"Why don't you start," I suggested, "and I'll join in when I spot the parts I know?"

Sally laughed. "You still have your marvellous sense of humour, I see. I'm so glad. It would be a terrible shame if you'd been... changed by your ordeal."

"Right."

"Do you remember Jimmy?"

"Big guy, no dress sense?"

She laughed again. "Yes, that's our Jimmy. Not his real name, of course."

"Damian."

"You *have been* doing your homework. Yes, Damian. You and he were working together."

"At the clinic?"

"I see. Not quite up to speed, then. No, Mr Walker, you and Damian worked for me."

"I don't understand."

"We were well aware of the work going on at Dr Hawkins' clinic, Mr Walker. Some of my clients fund such projects themselves, though in this case they simply wanted us to steal the data. Damian was already in place, investigating an unrelated matter, and he alerted us to a new development. We pulled some strings to get him involved in them, set him up with an apartment nearby. And then he suggested we get a couple of researchers in there with him. So you joined him."

"As his boyfriend?"

Sally frowned. "No, that was his idea. I'm afraid his obsession with method acting tended to get a bit carried away. You were never keen, but he was worried that people would see you spending an unusual amount of time together and wanted a cover story. He even faked some photographs of the two of you together."

"I saw them."

"Damian invented this bubbly, ghastly persona for 'Jimmy', someone he could pretend to be during his work for us. I always thought he took it too far myself. He invented a whole history for himself, involving you and more besides."

"So what happened?"

"I think you can probably guess."

"Dr Hawkins?"

"This project is being funded by someone far bigger than we realised. They noticed us snooping and didn't like it. Our agents were spotted and neutralised."

"Your agents? You mean me and Damian. They wiped our memories."

"Exactly." Sally shuffled some papers distractedly. "The Amnesia Project. Quite remarkable. Any subject can be treated and have their conscious memory wiped. Something went wrong, however. They can't have the procedure perfected yet."

"Damian seemed okay."

"He wasn't. They got him, Mr Walker. You saw what he was like. That wasn't Damian – that was Jimmy. With his identity gone, Damian became his character – and it was more a caricature. Jimmy sought you out, but he'd been... coerced."

"You sent the goons for me."

"Jimmy still remembered us. He was working for both sides now – not knowing which was which, his memory all in tatters – and when he found you, he contacted us to let us know. He went to find us, and told us you were in the flat. You weren't, of course."

"I had been. I got out before your goons arrived."

Sally's eyes widened. "Poor Damian. We misjudged him, then."

"You killed him."

She sighed. "It wasn't intentional," she said. "He tried to escape, tried to return to his new master. This Amnesia Project is more than just a memory wipe, you know. When the mind is a blank slate, it accepts anything you put in there. Any instructions at all."

"Like hypnosis?"

"A little. I think Damian's instructions were to await contact with our organisation and then to contact them. We never did find out the details. He tried to run and was killed in the attempt."

"And what about me?"

"You were a special case, Mr Walker. You resisted. We wanted to talk to you about this, but you've proved rather difficult to locate. I gather that you'd slipped away from Dr Hawkins somehow – he was very upset. I fear they took this out on Damian when they discovered him."

"You were watching the flat," I said. It wasn't really a question.

"I knew you would return," replied Sally. "Tell me – where were you?"

"I woke up in Reading," I said. "I had a few cryptic clues and a little money, and that was it. What happened?"

"I don't know, Mr Walker. I'm afraid this escape measure was either something you concocted yourself or you had help from elsewhere. If you don't know how it worked, I can't enlighten you – though I am pleased it did, of course. Perhaps your young lady friend could help on that one."

"Lisa!"

"Yes, the lovely Lisa. She is a wonderful girl, Mr Walker. I would very much like to hire her if you think she'd be willing to join us. So resourceful. So bold. My men were most taken by her spirited resistance. Indeed, two are currently being treated for CS gas exposure. I thought only the police had access to that stuff. Well, the police and ourselves."

"If you've harmed her…"

"Please calm down, Mr Walker. Lisa is fine, for the moment at least. I would very much like to keep it that way but it rather depends upon her… and you."

"I want to see her."

"I'm sure you do."

"Take me to her."

"Come now, Mr Walker. We haven't finished our chat yet."

I leaned over the desk, and she pushed herself away. I was terrified, but filled with an anger I hadn't felt since… well, as long as I could remember. Something in my face clearly broke through her unflappable exterior and I felt a horrible thrill that I was able to scare her like that.

"Take me to her," I repeated.

Just then the door opened, and I heard Greg's voice telling me to sit down. For a moment I didn't care – I was ready to launch myself across the desk and attack Sally with my bare hands – but my temper cooled, the blood stopped pounding in my head and I started thinking again. I sat back down.

"I think, perhaps, we should continue our chat a little later," Sally said. Her rich, calm voice was now ruffled and hesitant. "Greg, please show our guest back to his room."

Greg and his pistol showed me to the door.

"Sally?" I asked. "Just one more question. You said Jimmy asked for a couple of researchers. Who was the other one?"

"You don't know?" She seemed surprised by this. "My dear, the two of you were very close – you lived together in that flat, after all. You really don't remember Max Nicholson?"

I was returned to my ad hoc cell.

I thought about Jimmy. All the lies he'd told me, all the fakery. It made a lot of sense to think he'd been playing a part – I already knew he'd been put through the same procedure as I had. But was it true? I didn't have any reason to believe them. Like Sally had said, an empty mind accepts whatever you tell it. I'd already decided that I wouldn't let that happen to me.

What about Max? Had we really been living together? I didn't understand that. It made sense of the music and the decor – none of it seemed like Jimmy's work – but did it make sense of everything else? I couldn't believe Jimmy's "cover story", for instance. We had a spare bedroom, but it hadn't been used for a while. And I couldn't believe Max would be happy for me to kick him out in favour of a pretend boyfriend.

Who were these people? What did they want, and how were we mixed up with them? Every question I tried to answer seemed only to lead to more questions.

I had to get out of here.

I looked up from my lonely seat to the sound of the door being unlocked. Sally stepped into my cell, Greg standing behind her.

"Hello, Mr Walker. I trust you're feeling better disposed now?"

"What do you want?" I asked.

"We've come to let you go," she said. "Isn't that what you wanted?"

"What?"

Sally smiled. "You seem suspicious. Well, alright, there are some strings attached. Do you know what your mission was about?"

"The Amnesia Project?"

She smiled. "That's right," she said. "You, Damian and Max were spying on the project. We wanted three things – what it is, how it works, who is funding it. I suspect you don't recall any of these things now, of course. A pity."

"A pity," I echoed.

"I know you, though. You were always careful. We believe you have notes on your discoveries somewhere, and we're hoping you can find them."

"I'm sorry, I have no idea." I did, though. A small inkling, barely an idea at all. I had recorded some cassette tapes, according to Lisa, and I found myself thinking about a mysterious bag and a left luggage locker.

"Ah, but you're a clever man, Mr Walker. You knew about the project, so I'm guessing you took steps – clues, as it were. You mentioned cryptic clues when you woke up in Reading. I'm guessing you left them to yourself. Do you have any idea what they might mean?"

"They led me to Jimmy," I said. "Then things got weird."

"And how did you find Lisa?"

"I…" I paused. This felt like a trap. "She found me," I said. "A chance meeting. I didn't know who I was, she was curious – and wanted to help."

"So she has no involvement with the project?"

"No."

"Oh dear. I was so hoping for some honesty. Unless, of course, you really don't remember?"

"Remember what?"

"Lisa has been very helpful. She's been working independently on researching *this project, and she tells me you've been supplying her with information for months. I do hope you're not double-crossing us."*

I was astonished. Had Lisa really said that, or was this a trap?

"Lisa will be staying here with us for a little while, Mr Walker. Find me that information and she will be free to go."

Greg gestured with his pistol, and I let him lead me back out.

The journey back to the flat was also without a blindfold, though Greg continued to keep his pistol on me throughout. I was dropped off outside the building, handed Lisa's mobile phone and cautioned to keep it switched on at all times.

"We'll be watching you," Greg warned. "We've got your number, Walker. We'll be in touch."

They drove off.

I headed up to the flat again. I had nowhere else to go.

The Waiting

Henry sighed. Rob wasn't the only one with no clue what to do next. In many ways, their situations were the same. Granted, as far as he knew, Eddie was not being held under armed guard. But the sitting around, waiting for instructions... that was the same.

His phone stubbornly continued not to ring.

Henry had, on many occasions, tried to get Eddie to remember his mobile number. He'd tried writing it down, but Eddie kept losing the number. Several of the scraps of paper on Eddie's desk were probably his boss's telephone number. And this was exactly why he wanted Eddie to learn it – a simple call to say where he was, and Henry could go fetch him.

Assuming he was just lost, of course. Henry already knew that was unlikely. He may not know Henry's number, but Eddie's mother had drilled her own telephone number into her son years ago. If Eddie had called anyone, it would be her – and Maggie would be yelling his ear off already.

Nothing he could do but wait.

Damn it, why had he even brought Eddie along? George wouldn't have done something this stupid. He would have kept Eddie back at the office to file the paperclips or something.

But that's where Henry and his old partner had always differed. George had always viewed his son as no use for anything more than menial work. Henry believed Eddie was capable of more - and an outing like this, which had seemed so safe and simple, was the perfect chance to show Eddie what journalism could be like.

And now Eddie was missing.

First he was losing the magazine. Now he'd lost Eddie. *If George were here now,* thought Henry, *he would be screaming*.

But he wasn't. Not since the accident. And maybe that was his fault, too.

Henry, I think my wife is having an affair. If I hurry, I think I can catch them.

He could have stopped him…

His phone stubbornly continued not to ring.

Hoping for inspiration, or maybe just distraction, Henry loaded the next tape.

Evie's Gang

I hadn't felt this alone since I'd woken up in the Travel Hotel. Everyone I knew was gone now – Lisa was being held prisoner, Max was in trouble, Jimmy was dead. The only person I knew that could possibly help was Evie, and I didn't think a cup of tea and a Wagon Wheel would help much at the moment.

What do you want?

We want information.

You won't get it!

By hook or by crook, we will.

More random gibberish from my unconscious, brought up by some word association. These moments seemed to be becoming more frequent, which brought hope that my memory may one day return – though I wasn't entirely sure I'd enjoy the experience.

But perhaps it wasn't entirely random.

I was supposed to be a student of psychology, and I'd been involved in the Amnesia Project. So presumably I'd been aware of what it could do and I'd planned for it. I'd leave myself some hints, some cryptic message that I'd be able to figure out later.

I'd left myself a note, which led to Jimmy. I'd left myself a locker key, which led to the bag. I'd left myself a tape with the details of where that locker was. The bag had been intercepted, the information I sought was presumably with the police. But why had the police got involved?

And how had I ended up in Reading?

The tape… it was still in Lisa's car, which was parked in the street. I began to wonder about that tape. Perhaps it was more than just a message about the locker. Lisa had the key, though – I thought I might know how to drive but didn't really want to put that to the test just yet. I could break in if it came to that, but I hoped it would not.

All those songs were bound to be in the flat's music collection somewhere. How else could I have recorded them for myself?

I formed a small stack of CDs from what tracks I could remember. One was easy to find – Max's I Feel I'm Falling was still in the stereo, after all. There was no obvious connection between any of them. The cases were all normal. I took out the CDs and the inlays – nothing. I began wondering if there was some complex secret to it all but decided it was a wasted effort – I didn't have time to crack some imaginary super-code, and suspected I wouldn't have made it that complicated in the first place.

I wondered what I'd used to record the tape. There was no tape recorder in the flat. Perhaps I hadn't – perhaps that was itself a clue – but, again, a cryptic message would have to make sense to me. If I'd left a message for myself, I'd have done it here.

I restarted the CD in the player. I Feel I'm Falling *played through, but there were no obvious messages in that. I let the CD continue. There was a second track, and I let that play through too. The CD ended after that second track. I played them both again in case I'd missed something, but all I got was a vague sense that I'd heard them both before.

"I feel I'm falling… and when I look up I see you…" No surprise that one felt familiar. I'd already heard that song a few times now, but any message was lost on me. But the other? Where had I heard that tune before?

"If my life was a book, you would be on every page…"

My eyes scanned the music collection again for any other tracks I may have *missed. Tucked at the end, turned the wrong way around, was a box set CD. I pulled it out with interest – all the other CDs were in alphabetical order and carefully arranged, but this one was different.*

It was a collection of classical music.

I'd forgotten about the classical piece at the end of the tape, the piece I had been unable to look up. My hands shook as I opened the box.

There was a piece of paper inside.

Rob,

If you're reading this, you've obviously figured out that the tape you've been carrying around is lying to you. Do not go to the clinic – Dr Hawkins is not your friend. The note to yourself is a telephone number. It'll get you in touch with Jimmy – he'll help you out, but don't trust him. I think he may have been compromised.

The tape was meant to be a message to yourself, in the event that they realised we were snooping and put you through the process. They discovered it. When they processed you, they made you re-record the message to yourself and forget you'd done it. I'm sorry I couldn't get to you in time. I daren't speak to you directly or they'll know I'm involved. They may already be coming for me.

Good luck,

Max.

I read the note three times, wishing I'd seen it earlier. Max had risked everything to warn me, and I still walked right into Grace Meadows - though in fairness I had known it was a trap. I'd realised the message was wrong from the moment I'd listened to it.

That didn't help me now, though.

Lisa's mobile phone rang within my pocket. I answered it with heavy heart. I had no answers to give.

"Hello," I said, cautiously.

"Robert?" It was Evie. I sighed with relief. "Where's Lisa?"

"Evie... Lisa's in trouble. She's being held captive by... I don't know who they are."

I expected Evie to panic, or cry, or something. I kept forgetting she wasn't your usual old lady.

"Typical Lisa! Right, I'll get the gang together. Where can we meet you?"

"Do you know where the flat Lisa was taking me to is?"

"Yes, she wrote the address down somewhere – I'll dig it out. We'll be there as soon as we can."

"Uh, what gang...?" I asked. I was too late – Evie had already hung up.

Evie arrived about half an hour later.

"That was quick," I said. "Where's the gang?"

"They're on their way," she said. "Lisa told us to clear our schedules in case we had to bust you out. Looks like she needs us after all. Shall we have some tea?" She wandered past me into the flat and found her way straight to the kettle. "Do you have any biscuits?" she called out.

"Uh... I don't know."

"Never mind, dear. I've found them."

"Evie..."

"Did you take milk and sugar, dear?"

"Evie, I'm sorry about Lisa."

She stepped back out of the kitchen. "Don't be, dear. Lisa's a big girl and she can look after herself. She's been in bad scrapes before – it comes with the job sometimes."

"She let herself get caught so I could escape. And I didn't."

"Now stop moping," she chided. "Moping won't do any good, will it? You're here. And we'll get her back. It's not the first time."

"Evie and her army?"

Evie giggled. "In a way. Actually, I'm rather looking forward to this. It's the first time we've all got together in months."

There was a knock at the door.

"Be a love and let them in," called Evie, heading back into the kitchen. "I'll get the tea on."

The first visitor was a tall, heavily built black man dressed in blue, grease-stained overalls. He looked down at me from his immense height without a word.

"Hello," I said. "I'm Rob. Evie's in the back."

At the mention of Evie's name he broke into a broad grin. "Evie, darling!" he called out. I was startled by the high camp in his voice.

"Howard!" Evie called back. "Please come in, make yourself at home."

Howard walked in, ducking his head to avoid the door frame, and made his way to the living room. I closed the door in a state of baffled wonder and followed in his wake.

"Rob, this is Howard," she said. "He's a lovely lad, runs a garage in Barking. His wife works as a prison warden."

"His wife?"

"Oh, she can't make it," Howard lilted. "Late shift tonight. Just me, I'm afraid."

"Poor Jill," cooed Evie. "How's her mother these days?"

"Better since the amputation…"

Another knock sounded at the door. I escaped the chatter about Howard's mother-in-law and went to answer it.

"Hello there. You must be Rob."

I looked down at a short, fairly plump, middle-aged lady in a patterned jumper and a tweed skirt. Her hair was curled with blonde highlights just starting to grow out and her face housed a big beaming grin.

"I'm so glad to see you, Rob, because Evie's told me sooo much about you. Hard to believe you've been here all along – I only live down the road, so to speak, and I can't believe we haven't met! Of course, you wouldn't remember if we had, would you, with the amnesia and all that. Has Evie mentioned me at all? No? I'm Judy, by the way. Are we meeting in here? Tell Evie to put the kettle on – oh, she probably already has, hasn't she…?"

I waved Judy into the flat, unable to get a word in edgeways. She never seemed to need to pause for breath – later I would observe her drinking tea and eating biscuits while likewise talking non-stop. I briefly wondered at some point whether she breathed through her ears.

"Howard!"

"Judy!"

The two chattered at length for some time, simultaneously. I was unable to follow much of their conversation but caught enough references to soap operas to realise I didn't particularly care to.

Evie provided me with a cup of tea and motioned me to sit down. I sipped at it absently and watched the two newcomers talk. Evie picked up her knitting needles and clicked quietly away in the background.

A few minutes later there was another knock at the door. Evie's gang had a more rapid response time than some emergency services. This time I opened the door and briefly thought I was seeing double.

"Hello," I said.

The two young ladies on the threshold were identical, both their facial features and matching clothes. Both wore loose fitting cotton tracksuits in faded pink; on their feet they wore plain white trainers from a generic brand I didn't recognise. Their hair was the biggest difference – one wore hers shoulder length and loose, the other tied back. They introduced themselves as Nicola and Natasha, and their English was slightly clipped with a noticeable accent.

"Please, come in," I said, ushering them inside. "Evie! Is that kettle boiled?"

"Is that the Korovski twins?" called back Evie. "I think I've got some herbal teas in my handbag, loves."

I followed the two into the living room, where seating was becoming something of an issue. Evie headed back into the kitchen, rummaging in her handbag, and I decided this was a good point to ask some questions.

"Evie, please don't think I'm being ungrateful, but we need to help Lisa. Who are all these people? We need a commando squad, not a reading group."

Evie looked over her spectacles at me disapprovingly. "Rob, I'm disappointed in you. Never judge a book by its plain covers. We're not a reading group. We're criminals."

I tried very hard not to laugh.

"Lisa discovered us a few years back. She was writing up a jewel heist and spotted a couple of clues that the police didn't – she had the imagination to believe a harmless old lady could be a criminal mastermind. She could have reported us. She didn't."

"Why not?"

"She was curious, wanted to know why we'd done it. The jewel heist was just one of a series of raids. We were raising money for the orphanage."

I blinked. "You're telling me that you're a criminal gang that robs from the rich to feed the poor? Aren't old ladies supposed to organise bake sales?"

"I do those as well, sometimes," she grinned. "They aren't as exciting."

"I'm finding this hard to believe," I admitted.

"I'll introduce you," she said, leading me back into the living room.

"This is Howard," she started. "He runs a garage, but he's also our techie. Electronics, surveillance cameras, computers, anything like that."

"Just don't ask me about flat-pack furniture," said Howard, and the gang all laughed.

"Judy does volunteer work for the local church," continued Evie. "She's also a black belt in three forms of unarmed combat and trained in a number of weapons. She also talks people to death."

Judy smiled and gave a little wave.

"The twins here are Natasha and Nicola Korovski. They used to be with the Russian Circus until their visas fell through. Now we look after them. They're fantastic acrobats and astonishingly good at fitting in tight places."

"We run yoga class every Thursday," said Nicola. Or possibly Natasha.

"And as for me," finished Evie, "I make the tea and lend an ear to anyone with problems. But I also have some special knitting needles." She reached into her handbag and pulled out a selection of strange tools.

"Evie used to be a locksmith," explained Howard. "She can get through a locked door in thirty seconds."

"Twenty eight," corrected Evie. "I also do safecracking, but there's not so much call for that these days."

I stood in silence for a few moments. It was all too fantastic to take in. Was I really supposed to believe that this assortment of odd people were a gang of master criminals? I actually felt a sense of hope.

"We've got one more on the way," announced Evie. "His name's Sam. You'll like him, Rob. He's a chemist."

"He works in a pharmacy?"

"Not that sort of chemist. He makes things that explode."

There was a knock at the door.

"That'll be him now."

Sam turned out to be a wiry man in his thirties with a large mop of blond hair. The Hawaiian shirt reminded me of Jimmy, though it suited Sam far more than any clothes had suited Jimmy and added to my impression of the newcomer as a Californian surfer. When he spoke, however, he did so with the precise tones of an Oxford graduate.

"Hello," I said. "You must be Sam."

"That's right," he replied. "Tell Evie I'd like a coffee if she's making one."

"Already doing it!" called Evie from the kitchen.

I led Sam into the living room, and he perched himself by the windowsill. Howard had gracefully given up the sofa for the twins and he was at least pretending to listen to Judy as she spoke about… something. I think I caught mention of hair products but, as before, it was easier to just let Judy talk and let the words flow over you.

Evie brought out more drinks for us all and then called for attention. The room hushed, even Judy petering out in mid flow.

"I'm glad you could all make it," Evie said. "I've called us all together because

Lisa is in trouble, and young Rob here needs our help to rescue her. Okay, Rob, tell us what we're up against."

All eyes turned to me.

"Well… I'm afraid I can't tell you all that much… I only know that Lisa's being held captive by a group of men and that they want me to bring them some information before they'll release her. Except I don't have that information. They're armed and they say I used to work for them."

"They say?" asked Sam.

"Rob has amnesia," explained Evie. "Someone has deliberately wiped his memory, and it's the information on this process that these people want."

"That's about all I can tell you," I said.

"Where are they?" asked Howard.

"An industrial estate, just out of town," I replied. "I can show you where."

"How many men have they got?" asked Judy.

"I don't know. At least six, I'd say, and probably more. There's a woman in charge — Sally Kensington, she called herself."

"Can't say I've heard the name," remarked Evie. "Not one of our old friends, then."

"Are they armed?" asked Judy.

"Yes," I said. "They've got guns."

"Right," said Evie. "Let's get cracking. Sam, you and Judy sort out weapons. Kevlar vests would be a good precaution. Rob, show Howard where this place is — Howard, I want building schematics. Nicola, Natasha, let's get the transport sorted out. I want everyone to report back in an hour. And everyone - drink up before the tea gets cold."

"Do you have an internet connection here?" Howard asked me.

I shook my head. "I don't think so," I said. "No computer, anyway."

"No problem," he said. "I've got a laptop in the van. Back in a minute."

He headed downstairs and returned a few moments later with a laptop bag. With practised hands he soon had his laptop running and connected to the apartment's telephone line.

"Okay. Whereabouts was this place?" he asked. He showed me an aerial view of the industrial district, and I followed the route on the screen that we'd taken to the warehouse.

"That one," I said, pointing.

Howard zoomed in. "You sure?"

"Yes," I said. "That building there."

Howard made a quick note of something on a notepad and then started hunting around online for schematics. He typed too quickly for me to follow and I soon gave up trying. I suspected some of the websites he was visiting were not generally open to the public.

"Here we go," he said. "Original building plans. Did you notice any work done to the place, any changes or improvements, that sort of thing?"

"No," I said. "Actually, the main doors were rusted shut. I doubt there's been any work there for years."

"Right," he said. "Let's get these printed out." He paused for a moment. "No printer. Right. No problem. I'll be back in a minute."

It wasn't long before we all reconvened. Evie brought out a plate of biscuits and called on us for reports.

"Transport is ready," confirmed Natasha (or was it Nicola?). "We have three cars standing by." It grew clear to me over a number of occasions that one of the twins had a slightly better grasp of English than the other, but I never did figure out which was which.

"Here are the plans for the warehouse," announced Howard, handing round our printouts. "I've marked the entrances, key positions and probable locations for our prisoner."

"Excellent work," said Evie. "Thank you, Howard."

"Always a pleasure, Evie my dear."

"Sam, have you and Judy sorted out the weapons?"

"Yes, Evie. I've even managed to rustle up a spare vest for Rob, though I'm not sure how snug a fit it'll be. Ever used a taser before, Rob?"

"Uh... no. I don't think so."

"Don't worry, Judy will show you. Hopefully you won't need it."

"Alright, everyone," called out Evie, "here's the plan..."

The telephone call we were expecting came not long after. The gang fell silent while I spoke, but Evie had told me what to say.

"You've got the stuff, Walker?" It was Greg's voice.

"Almost," I lied. "I'll have it ready tonight." Evie had been insistent that we made the exchange when it got dark, pointing out that most military assaults took place at night.

"Bring it to the warehouse. You need the address?"

I didn't, but I took it anyway. I didn't want to seem too confident.

"Come alone, Walker, and no funny business."

"I want to speak to Lisa," I said.

Greg's reply was to simply hang up the phone.

"Well," I said. "No going back now. I hope you know what you're doing, everyone."

Evie smiled. "Robert, my dear, you're in for a treat."

We were ready to go a couple of hours later. Evie and Howard went ahead in one car, to establish surveillance and counter any security systems we might face. The twins went off together in the second car – they were going to sneak in through the ventilation system. Narrow crawlspaces were no problem for them.

Before the last car set off, crewed by Sam and Judy with me in the back, the two of them fixed me up with my bulletproof vest.

"Put this on under your jacket," advised Judy. "It's just a precaution, but it never hurts to have the element of surprise. I should warn you, though – if you do get shot, it'll still hurt like hell."

"I'll try to avoid it," I said.

Judy picked up a pistol, checked the clip, rammed it home and placed it in a shoulder holster. It was the only firearm I'd seen the entire team take.

"They have guns," I said. "Why are we only taking one?"

"Judy's the only one trained to use it," said Sam. "We've all tried a few shots, been taught how to load it and such, but we're no experts. We leave the gunplay to her because she knows what she's doing."

"Don't worry, Rob," Judy smiled. "We've got some other toys you can play with." She handed me a device that looked rather like an electric shaver. "This can usually do the same job, and it doesn't kill."

"Taser?" I asked.

"That's right. Point the business end at someone, push that button, and those electrodes stick 'em. Then you can zap 'em all you like with that button there. Hard to fight back when you've got fifty thousand volts going through you."

"Where'd you get this stuff?" I asked.

"We have our contacts," she said, vaguely. "A lot of this is police issue, real top quality stuff."

I carefully put the taser in my pocket, not wanting to put fifty thousand volts through my own nether regions. "Great," I said. "Anything else?"

"Take one of these too," she said, handing me a small aerosol spray. "Lisa swears by it. The people she uses it on swear at it."

"CS gas? I think she had one when she got caught. I saw what it did to the guys that got her."

"Don't use this stuff unless you have to, Rob. It's nasty. Get this on yourself and you'll regret it."

I slipped the spray can into my other pocket.

"Don't go all Rambo on me, Rob," said Judy. "We get in, we get Lisa, we get out. No heroics. It looks good in the films but it never works that way in real life."

"No heroics," I said. "Don't worry." I didn't feel remotely heroic. I was terrified.

"We're on our way," said Sam, as we headed out into the deepening gloom.

"We'll see you there," replied Evie. The mobile phone had been set on speaker and all three cars were on a conference call.

"I'm not wild about this plan, you know," I said.

"Don't worry, Rob," said Sam. "If all goes well, you'll be out and safe in no time. If it doesn't, Judy here will protect you."

I smiled. Judy was wonderful company and she seemed to know what she was talking about, but I couldn't picture her in a fight.

"You know what you're doing?"

I nodded, looking down at the bulky sports bag onto my lap and wincing whenever the car hit a bump. "I go in alone with this. You and Judy stay out of sight and I make the swap for Lisa. If they don't bring her out, we go in after her."

"I hope it won't come to that," *said Sam.*

"I hope it does," *growled Judy.*

"Hey, Sam." *Evie was on the phone.* "We're in position, and the twins are on the roof. We're just waiting on your signal."

"Just turning in now," *replied Sam.* "We'll drop Rob off and get in cover. Three minutes?"

"Judy?"

Judy didn't reply.

"She's gone into combat mode," *Sam said.* "Remember that mob bust we did in Tottenham?"

"Ouch. That was messy. The sledgehammer was a particularly nasty touch."

I decided I probably didn't want to know.

"Okay, Rob, we'll drop you off here. Take the bag and good luck. We'll be close by, never fear."

"Thanks," *I croaked. My throat had completely dried up.*

Sam smiled, pulled the car up a little before the gate to the compound and waited for me to step out. My hands shook on the door release and the bag strap tangled with the seatbelt as I tried to get out. After what felt like an hour of useless fumbling, both the bag and I were out of the car. I swung the door shut, shouldered the bag and headed for the warehouse.

Once the car engine had died off in the distance, the only sounds I could hear were the whisper of the night breeze and the heavy thudding of my racing heart.

There were no lights to lead my way, so I waved a trembling flashlight in front of me and headed towards the darker shadow that loomed before me.

When the floodlights came on, I screamed.

Once my eyes adjusted to the sudden glare I saw two people standing by the side door, two silhouettes watching me approach. I stepped slowly towards them, half expecting a hail of bullets to take me down.

"That's far enough, Walker," one said. I recognised the voice as Greg's. "Is that it?"

I put the bag down at my feet. "This is it," I said. "Where's Lisa?"

Greg nodded to the other figure, who headed inside. Hopefully to fetch Lisa. "Okay, Walker," he said. "Bring it over here. Slowly."

I picked up the bag, and walked slowly towards him. As I grew closer I stepped out of the immediate glare and could make out Greg a little more clearly. This was no improvement. I could also make out the automatic pistol he was pointing at me.

I thought about the taser in my pocket. It may as well have been a peashooter.

"Put it down there, and back away."

I did as he said, thinking that a little distance between me and the bag was probably no bad thing. After all, I knew what was in it.

"Where's Lisa?" I asked.

"Not so fast, Walker. I want to be sure about what you're delivering."

Greg pulled the zip open on the bag, still covering me with the pistol. I hoped Sam and Judy were watching.

The other man stepped out of the door again. He was alone. He stepped over to Greg and spoke quietly to him.

Greg smiled at me. "It seems the boss wants to keep Lisa with us a little longer," he said. "She thinks it might be a good idea if both of you were to join us while we look over this little lot. Just in case, you understand."

I nodded. I was no longer afraid. I was tense and ready to spring. Some part of me had known all along that these crooks would never keep their word. I couldn't help smiling as Greg bent back over the bag.

He looked up. "What are you grinning at?"

Then the bag went off.

Underneath a layer of shredded newspaper, the sports bag had been filled with a selection of Sam's finest. Some small explosives set off a few gas canisters, possibly with some other ingredients as well, and the effect was immediate. Greg cried out in pain, dropping his pistol and clutching his face with both hands as he staggered back. The effect on his comrade was less marked as he was further away, but he went reeling all the same, coughing fit to burst and doubtless with eyes streaming.

"Get down, Rob!"

I didn't stop to wonder why. I just threw myself to the floor as Judy ran past me. She threw herself at the two heavily coughing men, delivering a series of punches and kicks that I could barely follow, finishing with a particularly hard knee in the groin that made me wince in sympathy. As the second man hit the ground, she pulled some handcuffs from her pocket and soon had both men secured.

"Are you okay?" she asked.

I nodded, unable to speak. The woman I'd first met in the flat, talking without pause about anything and everything, was nowhere to be seen at the moment. This new Judy scared me. I was glad she was on my side.

Sam came up as Judy pulled out her mobile. "Evie, it's Judy. They didn't go for it. Plan B is a go."

"No problem," *replied Evie.* "Howard's on it. Should be any moment now."

Judy hung up. "Be ready, Rob. We're gonna cut the power." As soon as the last word left her lips, the lights went out. I could hear cries of alarm from inside the building.

"Come on, Rob," said Sam. "Let's get out of the way. This may be messy."

It is hard to explain exactly what happened next. I can summarise it easily enough – a group of armed men came out of the building to find out what was going on, and Judy took them all out. It went something like this.

Man A stepped out of the door with Judy stood to one side. She kicked the gun out of his hands, landed three jabs to his face and pushed him over as he staggered backwards. Man B stepped out while this was happening, tried to rush Judy with a shotgun and was astonished when she took the weapon with both hands, twisted and crouched beneath him and sent him hurtling over her head. Now holding the shotgun, she swiftly swung it round and clubbed him on the head with it.

Man C had, in this time, cottoned on that Judy was a serious threat and hung back a little. He tried to fire a pistol at her, but in his panic had left the safety catch on. By the time he realised his mistake, Judy had pulled a taser from her pocket and given him a good, sharp blast with it. He went down twitching.

I didn't even have time to shout a warning to her when Man D, the last of the group, rushed out of the door. She seemed not to notice him running up behind her – not until the last moment, when she twisted and swung out the shotgun she had appropriated right at head height. It must have been like headbutting a wall at speed. There was a horrible cracking sound, and Man D went down like a sack of potatoes.

The whole thing was over in about twenty seconds. It was about then I remembered how to blink.

"Hey! Is everything alright over there?" asked Evie.

"We're fine," answered Judy. She was barely even out of breath.

"They're probably holding Lisa in the basement," *said Howard.* "It's the most secure location. Head down the corridor – the stairs should be the third on the left."

Judy headed down first, her pistol held in front of her in one hand, a flashlight in the other. Sam and I followed behind, tasers drawn. Judy checked doorways and corners as we went, looking for trouble. There was none. I suspected most of Sally's private army were currently groaning in pain and handcuffed out at the front.

"Here they are," *said Judy, gesturing towards the door Howard had mentioned. A set of stairs led into darkness.* "Sam, you stay up here. I don't think there'll be any trouble but I'd like our backs covered. Rob, you're with me. Evie, how are the twins doing?"

"We are in," *whispered Natasha (or Nicola).* "Three men down here, all armed. Two more watching Lisa."

"Thanks, girls," *replied Judy.* "Rob, when we go down, you stay low and head right. I'll head left. Don't fire that taser unless you know what you're pointing at, got it?"

I nodded. "Got it."

Judy switched off the flashlight, held the pistol ready, and crept down the stairs. I followed close behind, hoping my heavily beating heart wouldn't give us away.

The basement was dark, but not totally. Someone had thought to illuminate it as best they could with a pocket torch propped on a table. It meant that two of the three men were in plain sight while we were hidden in shadow. They didn't see us until we stepped into the room proper, and that was when Judy half-shoved me to my right and I only just managed to stay on my feet. I kept my head down as I went, while

Judy's gun roared in the confined space.

I looked round, ears still ringing, to see Judy sweeping the area for the third man. "Girls! Where's the other guy? Girls?" She dropped the phone hurriedly. "Damn. No signal down here. Rob, keep your eyes peeled."

The other two men lay on the floor, blood beginning to spread from their injuries. Judy had plugged them both neatly in the upper arm. The look on her face and the gun in her hand convinced them both that resisting, or even moving, would be a bad idea.

I looked about, taser ready, but couldn't see anyone nearby. And where was Sally?

"Go check the corridor – and be careful!"

I headed down towards the end of the room, where a doorway led into a short corridor. She must have gone down there. I checked my taser, reminded myself where the firing button was and crept towards the doorway. No shots rang out. I stepped into the corridor, and began my search.

Door number one revealed a storage cupboard. Nothing menacing in there, just cleaning supplies. The second door led to a small room with desk and chairs – perhaps an interrogation room? I didn't waste time speculating. The third door led to my cell from my previous visit.

As I stepped out, I felt something cold and metallic pressed against my neck. "Don't move," whispered a familiar, cultured voice. "Don't even speak."

Sally had found me.

"Now, Mr Walker, we are going to leave. Not that way – through here."

In the darkness I couldn't tell where exactly "through here" was but suspected it was a back exit of some kind. I hoped it was on the blueprints for the building –

Howard would have it covered.

"Morris is watching Lisa. You've met him, I believe – a charming man, if prone to fits of temper. If your friends cause any further trouble, he may... get upset."

I was angry, but I was all too aware of the metal pressed against my neck and resisted the urge to say anything. Where was Judy? I felt the weight of the taser in my hand and wondered if I could use it without getting shot. Possibly not.

"I apologise for the gun, Mr Walker. Believe me, I wish there were another way."

Sally led me further down the basement and towards a rusted fire door – one of those doors with the push-bar across it that I remembered from my school days. (The fact I remembered anything from my school days would have been encouraging if I wasn't being led through a darkened basement at gunpoint at the time, though I gain some hope from it now.)

"Open it."

I did so, grimacing at the painful squeak of the bar and the hinges. It had clearly not been used in years.

I hoped Judy had heard the noise.

There was a metallic clang somewhere nearby. We both stopped. Then, suddenly, the lights came back on. I was momentarily dazzled, and as the pressure on my neck eased I realised I was not the only one. I pulled away from Sally and turned to face her.

"Judy!" I shouted.

Sally quickly recovered and raised the pistol towards me again. As she did so she suddenly jerked back, convulsing horribly, and dropped to the floor in pain. I looked down and realised I was holding my taser with both hands, the firing button pressed so hard I thought I might break it.

"Rob! Are you okay?"

Judy came running towards me. I let go of the taser, with some effort. Judy quickly grabbed the pistol from where Sally had dropped it and covered her prone body. She didn't try to move.

"The twins said you'd been caught," Judy said. "Since we've got no phone signals down here, they've been speaking to Evie for me. I asked them to put the power back on. Where did you learn to shoot like that?"

I looked at the taser again. "I... don't know..."

"Who are you, Rob?"

"Sally said I used to work for her. Perhaps this proves it."

"Maybe," she replied, "but I don't think so. Where's Lisa?"

"Down here somewhere," I said. "Someone's guarding her – Morris, I think she said."

"Hey, Rob!" *called another voice. I looked up to see a familiar face at the air vent.* "Is Natasha!"

"Hello, Natasha!" *I replied.* "Are you okay in there?"

"Fine," *she smiled.* "Is very roomy!"

"Natasha, have you seen Lisa?" *asked Judy.*

"She is in room down hall," *Natasha replied.* "Nicola is watching her. One man with her."

"Hmm. Could be tricky." *Judy looked thoughtful.* "We need to split them up. We can't risk going in like that."

I felt in my pockets and touched the small spray can.

"Judy, I have a crazy idea..."

Rescue

Hey, whoever you are. Rob's asked me to tell you about the next part, but I thought I'd start with a brief introduction.

As you've probably guessed, my name is Lisa. I'm a freelance journalist, writing news articles for publications big and small, looking for interesting stories that'll pay my rent. Mostly I like to write about people, put a new spin on their lives, get some attention. When I first met Rob, I found plenty of stories. This has to be the craziest, and I'm a part of it now.

I honestly didn't recognise Rob when I met him in that café. I knew he seemed familiar, but it was the first time I'd seen him outside of Grace Meadows, and he didn't seem to recognise me at all. I'd only ever seen him as a researcher there, not as one of Dr Hawkins' cases. And yes, I admit I did try to... take things further that night – but how was I to know?

It turned out there was a lot I didn't know – about Rob, and Grace Meadows, and Dr Hawkins. All in good time. This is Rob's story, and I'll let him tell it. For my part, I'll start with the kidnap.

Rob certainly makes me sound heroic in his account, like I consciously sacrificed myself so he could escape the flat, but really I didn't think about it at all. Evie and the gang taught me how to use those gas canisters and it was all fairly automatic. It was also very unpleasant. I imagine most of you hearing this have never been affected by CS gas or whatever the police use these days and let me tell you – you don't know how lucky you are. This stuff is nasty. It irritates the skin, it makes your eyes water like crazy and if you rub your eyes or try to wash it off you only make it worse.

So when I told Rob to run, I had no idea whether he had or not. I couldn't see any more. The guys that had tried to grab me were far worse off than I was but that was little consolation. I made a dash for what I thought was the front door, but which turned out to be the living room, and I was quickly caught, tied up and brought down to the car. They must have had two cars, because I didn't see Rob at any point and he didn't see me.

I had no idea where I was taken and no way of knowing how I got there. The effects of the gas started to wear off eventually, and I found myself tied to a chair in a dimly lit basement room. I briefly thought I might be in police custody but, having been arrested a few times before, I soon dismissed the idea. Whoever they were, these guys were not the police.

I wasn't asked as many questions as I expected. Sally asked me about the Amnesia Project, which I knew very little about – only what glimmerings as Rob had been able to find out. I think she knew more than I did. I didn't know where the information she wanted could be.

I'm sorry to say that I did indeed mention working with Rob for months. It was true, after all, and I think they already knew.

Eventually I realised I was mostly there as a hostage.

I'd like to say that they were brutal, cruel thugs. It would sound more dramatic. The truth is, they didn't really know how to treat a hostage. They alternated threats with kindness. One minute they'd be trying to scare me with talk of torture and various nasty ways I could be killed, many of which they'd clearly picked up from films and wouldn't actually work, and the next minute I'd be asked if I wanted food or water and whether I was comfortable. They made a limited effort to reduce the effects of the CS gas on my face. I was even given toilet breaks, though I was never left alone and always tied back up afterwards.

The first I knew about the assault on the warehouse was when the power went out. One of the men was the shaven headed guy with the scar on his cheek that had been at the flat - this was Morris, as I found out later. He kept giving me a nasty look whenever he caught me looking at him - a heavy stare with a leering grin, like he wanted to beat me and rape me. I think he was just trying to scare me; it was working, but there was no way I was letting on.

Morris was on guard duty. The other guys had left the room a few minutes earlier, I think to meet up with Rob outside, so it was just the two of us. Then the lights went out, and in the distance I could hear shouts and a fair bit of swearing. I figured out Evie was involved very quickly.

Morris tried to act tough, telling me how I was trapped in the dark with him and that he could do whatever he liked to me, but there was a tremor in his voice that hadn't been there before. I thought at first that he was worried about the attack (not that he could know what it was yet) and then I figured it out. It was all I could do not to laugh.

Morris was scared of the dark.

I could hear him pacing in the darkness, muttering to himself, so I had a pretty good idea where in the room he was even in the pitch black. At first he sounded angry, muttering about what he'd do to the others if they didn't get those lights back on right now – and a few minutes later he was pounding on the door and screaming for someone to put the lights back on.

I think it fair to say he forgot all about me for a while. If I hadn't been trussed up like a turkey dinner I might have tried to make a run for it.

Morris was sobbing in a corner when I heard the gunshots. They seemed to wake him up a bit and he came back over towards me, perhaps to use me as a shield if anyone came in.

There was a clattering sound. It seemed to be all around us.

"What was that?" Morris whirled around somewhere behind me, and I could imagine him sweeping his gun around the room in an attempt to locate the source of the sounds.

"Sounds like something's in the ventilation ducts," I said. "Probably rats."

"Rats!" he snorted. "I'm not afraid of any rat."

"You should be," I said. "They're a lot bolder in the dark."

More clattering sounds. It was impossible to say where they were coming from, but they had a rhythm: tap tap taptap tap, tap tap taptap tap.

I knew that code. I'd arranged it with the Russian twins for a job we'd done together three years ago.

"They're probably Siberian rats, by the sound of them," I said, raising my voice a little so the twins might hear. "Much bigger, much nastier than the British ones."

"Shut up," snapped Morris. "It's nothing, just the pipes. Just the pipes."

"Rats," I insisted. "They usually avoid crowds, but it's just you and me in here."

"I told you to shut up!" I felt something cold and metal pressed against the back of my neck, and decided not to push him any further.

In the distance, I heard a rusty squeal.

And then, suddenly, there was light. We were both dazzled for a moment, even though the lighting was rather feeble by all accounts. I looked around and straight into his face, right by mine, sweaty and panicked; but even as my eyes adjusted to the light it began to return to his normal scowl.

"Say a word to anyone," he growled, "and I'll kill you slowly."

A number of responses came to mind, but I decided not to antagonise him.

Tap tap taptap tap, tap tap taptap tap.

The twins were still there. What did they want me to do? I glanced around, then saw Nicola's face at the ventilation grill. I carefully didn't look directly at her, but saw her making hand signals. I realised after a moment that she wanted me to keep him talking.

"I won't say a word to anyone," I said. "I'll be as quiet as a rat... I mean, mouse."

"Are you making fun of me?"

I was, though I regretted it straight away, and a hard slap across the face was my reward.

"Anything else to add, Miss Smart Mouth?"

I swallowed, tasting blood – though only a little. I didn't think it was as bad as it felt. "I'm sorry," I said, attempting to sound tearful. This didn't require a huge amount of acting.

In the background, I could see Nicola attempting to quietly pry the vent from the wall.

"It's just that... well, I'm scared too. I don't know what's going on and then everything went dark and I'm still t-tied up a-and..." And then I started to cry. Ladies, if you ever get kidnapped by a group of bumbling amateurs, I recommend a good weep. They have no idea what to do with a crying woman.

I could have been an actress. This is one of my less well-known roles – Woman Crying Loudly. I made sure I put in as much bawling and wailing as I could to give Nicola plenty of cover.

Morris looked helpless. Maybe he was considering whether kind words, threats or another slap would shut me up, and I'd guess he was also wondering what the boss would say if he damaged the goods too much.

The vent fell to the floor with a crash. Morris was instantly alert, but Nicola was already out of sight. On the floor, hissing rather ominously, was a small canister. A moment later a second hissing canister rolled out of the vent, and then a third. I'd be *crying for real all too soon.*

Really, Rob, did you really have to make your rescue so... unpleasant?

My eyes were soon streaming, and I couldn't actually see what happened next – but I heard it all. Morris, choking and screaming, headed for the door and this time managed to get it open. He staggered out in search of air, leaving me on my own.

Outside the door I heard a few sharp thumps, a much briefer scream from Morris, and then Judy's voice – "hey, Lisa, the cavalry's here!"

I felt my bonds being removed and then I was lifted out of my chair and guided to the door.

Judy and Rob carried me outside, where Judy applied some eye wash to ease the symptoms of the CS spray. Rob told me about the rescue, and then Evie was there, offering me a thermos of tea and some macaroons.

"The others are just sweeping the area," she told me. "We don't want to miss any of them and have them come back in force. I think one may have escaped, but it looks like he's long gone."

"Evie, what are you going to do with them all?" asked Rob.

"Oh, we aren't killers, dear," she replied. "Apart from when we have to be, that is. I'm sure the police will want to have a chat with them, and we'll leave them nicely trussed up until they arrive."

"Can we take Sally with us?" he asked.

Evie paused. "We don't do kidnappings, Robert."

"She knows something about all this," Rob replied. "She knows about me. I want to ask her some questions. Please, Evie."

"She'll lie, dear."

"I know. I think I can get through to her, though. I have something she wants, remember."

I remembered. "The bag. Rob, we don't have it."

Rob smiled. "She doesn't know that."

Tied up and gagged, Sally Kensington was unceremoniously bundled into the back of Sam and Howard's car and "enjoyed" a rather bumpy journey back to Rob's flat. I might have felt bad about treating a woman like that, but the look of hatred in her eyes was acid enough to melt through cast iron and I felt a lot less well disposed to her. Besides, she'd left me alone with Morris for an hour or two, which was at least three hours too long. We were all in high spirits, and I was rapidly recovering from the effects of the CS spray. Rob went on ahead with Evie and the twins, to get things set up for our prisoner, while Judy and I took the third vehicle and chatted about what had been happening since I was taken.

"That young man of yours is a crack shot with a taser," she said admiringly. "Is he single?"

"Sorry, Judy. He plays for the other team."

"Typical. All the good ones do!"

We laughed. It might sound strange, but that's what we did – we laughed together, and gossiped, and chatted. If Howard had been with us we might have been talking soaps. After a harrowing period of kidnap, violence and rescue, we needed to get back to normal.

Judy began to shake. I'd seen this before – when the fighting was over, all that adrenaline left her system and she'd fall apart emotionally. We stopped somewhere quiet, she switched off the engine, and Judy cried.

We didn't speak. We didn't need to. I let her cry, and I held her until she was done. It might have been five minutes. It might have been an hour. It didn't matter.

Eventually she pulled away, drying her eyes with a packet of tissues I'd found in the glove box. Evie had probably left them there for us.

"Ready?" I asked.

She nodded, restarted the car, and we were off once again.

Evie had two cups of tea waiting for us when we arrived at Rob's flat. A plate of biscuits was also on the table, though it was already half empty.

"A very successful mission, dear," commented Evie. "Glad to have you back."

"Evie, I can't begin to thank you for this," said Rob. "If you hadn't been here..."

"Oh, hush now," chided Evie. "This is hardly the first time our Lisa has landed herself in hot water. You remember that time in Glasgow?"

Howard chuckled. "Oh, stop. It took me weeks to get the smell of chip fat out of my clothes!"

"I'm sorry," *laughed Sam.* "I didn't realise the bomb would go off that easily in the fryer."

"So where's the champagne?" asked Rob.

"Oh, not for me, dear," said Evie. "It puts my stomach right off. I'll stick with the tea."

I'd met all of Evie's friends before, of course, but it was rare to see them all at once like this. Most of the time they lived their own private lives, only meeting up when they had a job to do. It was safer that way, but it was a lonely life. Who could they talk to so openly apart from each other? Now they had a reason to gather and simply be themselves, and the room was full of laughter and gossip.

And in the middle of it all sat Rob. I was astonished by how quickly the gang had accepted him. He saw me looking at him and smiled.

"I'm glad you're safe, Lisa."

"Takes more than a few brainless thugs to stop me."

"That reminds me," he said. "Shall we go and check on our guest?"

"Just a minute," I said. "I've got something that might be useful. Evie, do you have my stuff?"

"Oh yes, dear; I'd forgotten about that. Your handbag is in the hall. Did you want anything in particular?"

"Is my tape recorder in there?"

Evie disappeared for a moment. "Why, yes it is," she called.

She brought it back in with her, and I handed it to Rob. "I thought you might like to record her," she said. "Like the police do."

Rob smiled. "Good idea," he said. "I have a lot of questions and I don't want to have to write down all the answers."

Sally was seated in one of the kitchen chairs, hands and legs securely tied and the twins watching over her. She was still gagged. Whether out of absent-minded duty or as a subtle form of torture, I don't know, but Evie had left a cup of tea on the table nearby.

"Hello, Ms Kensington," said Rob. "I'm sorry about the circumstances but I thought we might have a little chat. To be fair, this is the welcome you offered us."

Sally made no effort to reply, which was just as well given the gag. I half expected her to make the customary joke about being tied up at the moment.

"Now. Here's the deal – you want those notes on the Amnesia Project. I might be able to offer you something. Not all of it, but perhaps a little. In exchange, I want information."

Sally's eyes gave nothing away.

"Let's start with the basics." Rob carefully hooked a finger into the top of the gag *and pulled it free. "What is the Amnesia Project?"*

The Bar

The tape stopped.

It was ridiculous – a gang of master criminals led by Miss Marple, complete with tea and cakes, on a rescue mission? It didn't seem believable when he'd heard it before, but it was just a story then.

But was it any more ridiculous than Eddie being kidnapped?

Waiting was hard. Henry tried his best to keep occupied – he made a few calls, trying to hold together his crumbling business, always worried that he'd miss something about Eddie. He made a few efforts to sell some advertising space, but no-one was biting (he remembered when he'd had a sales team to do this job, which he'd always hated). He was terrified of receiving a call from Eddie's mother, but fortunately none came.

Aware he needed to eat but lacking any appetite, he found a leaflet from a local takeaway in the reception area and called for a pizza. Most of it went uneaten. He sat looking out of the window, staring at nothing, waiting for a call. Waiting for anyone to call.

Even a gang of master criminals disguised as a reading group.

Eventually he couldn't stand it any more. He grabbed his coat, picked up his phone and headed back out. Perhaps the manager of the Cruise Liner would talk to him this time. He was in the mood for some answers.

Eddie wasn't in the bar when Henry arrived, somewhere just after seven, but it was a little busier than before. Most of the clientele were younger men, and Henry felt a little self-conscious amongst them. Still, he was here for business, not for pleasure.

"Can I help you?"

This time he was greeted by a young lady, sporting a nose stud and an eyebrow piercing. Her hair was cut short and straight, and she had dyed it bright green. It clashed with the pink and black outfit she was forced to wear as part of the bar staff - a token act of rebellion against conformity.

"Hi there," said Henry. "I'm looking for a guy called Eddie. About this tall, dark hair, a bit simple. He hasn't been in has he?"

"I don't think so. Are you meeting him here?"

"Not exactly. We got separated earlier and I'm worried about him. He's not quite... all there, if you know what I mean."

"And you're looking after him?" She smiled. "I'm sure he'll turn up. Can I get you anything while you're waiting?"

"Yes, I'll have a coke please. Is the manager in?"

"He's in the back. There's a karaoke act on this evening and our host is having one of her diva moments." The young lady set to work pouring out a small glass of coke and took a five pound note from him. There wasn't a lot of change. "Says some kid told her she should be in panto this afternoon. I think they're right. She's rubbish."

"I'm sure she'll be fine."

"Terrible name for a drag queen, anyway. 'Jocelyn Elbows'. That's awful. I reckon all the better names were taken."

Henry choked on a swallow of coke.

"Are you alright, mate?"

"Yeah, sorry." Henry coughed a little more. "I think I met him once. Her. You know."

A few people were starting to line up beside Henry at the bar.

"I've taken up enough of your time," he said. "Tell the manager I'm here if you see him – I'll be sitting in that corner over there."

"No problem."

Despite everything, Henry felt a little better for being here. Partly because Eddie might find his way back here, but mostly it was because there were people. It was too quiet in his room. The bar wasn't exactly noisy yet – it was still too early in the evening – but the background music and the murmur of many conversations was quite soothing.

Damn that story! He should have just thrown those tapes out. If he'd done that, he and Eddie would be back in the office, safe and sound. Although, he had to admit, not for long. Even with the story in print, there wasn't much hope of the magazine lasting much longer.

Then Dr Edmunds had turned up with his money and his threats. Henry's old journalist instincts were still intact, and they'd smelt a bigger story. And he'd unwittingly put Eddie in danger.

It couldn't be that simple, could it?

Henry took a look through his wallet, flipping through numerous business cards until he found the one he wanted. It simply read "Dr Edmunds" and gave a telephone number – no company name, no details.

He punched the number into his mobile phone.

"Dr Edmunds speaking."

"Hello, Dr Edmunds. This is Henry Ford."

"Ah, from the magazine. What can I do for you, Mr Ford? It doesn't sound like you're in the office."

"No. I'm following up a story, actually. Yours."

There was a pause. *"Then you must be in Brighton,"* the doctor replied. *"As it* happens, so am I."

"I'll get straight to the point. What have you done with Eddie?"

"Eddie?" The doctor sounded confused. *"Is he the young man working for you on the magazine? I don't think we were formally introduced."*

"All I want is for Eddie to be released, safe and sound. What have you done with him?"

"Nothing. Why would I?"

"The day we turn up here and start looking into that story, the one you paid me not to print, Eddie goes missing. Don't play innocent with me." Henry realised he was raising his voice and more than a few people were starting to watch him. He fought down his anger.

"Again, Eddie is nothing to do with me. But I would strongly advise you to stop investigating the Amnesia Project, Mr Ford. This is my concern, not yours."

"Release Eddie, and I will. We'll go back home and forget all about it. If you don't – I'll print the rest. All of it."

"Please do not do that, Mr Ford. I was entirely serious about a libel case. But as for Eddie, I cannot release him. I do not have him. But I might know who does."

Someone else? Who else would be interested in this story?

"Remember, Mr Ford – you were just sent the story. Someone wanted you to print it. But they didn't want you to know who sent it, or why. You're getting too close."

"You're saying that Rob and his friends have taken Eddie?"

"It is a possibility. Rob was a patient of mine, and could sometimes be a little unstable. He suffered from attacks of paranoia when he stopped his medication, and I haven't seen him for some time."

Henry's stomach grumbled.

"I have to find him," said Henry.

"Stay away, Mr Ford. I have my own business with Mr Walker – don't get in the way. I will do what I can for Eddie, if they have him." Dr Edmunds ended the call.

Stay away? Henry took a long swig from his drink. Whatever was going on, he was going to get to the bottom of it.

"Ladies and gentlemen, welcome to the Cruise Liner."

Henry looked up. He recognised Gaz from his earlier meeting, now in a tight fitting red suit, at the other end of the bar. His voice was slightly muffled by a poorly set up microphone. Henry hadn't realised there was a stage in the bar – when he'd been here earlier it had been covered in tables and chairs.

"I hope you've all warmed up your singing voices, because it's karaoke night!"

There was a slightly drunken cheer from the audience. Henry expected it would get drunker as the evening went on.

"And, ladies, try not to break the glasses."

The audience laughed, a little half-heartedly.

"Now here she is – the one, the only, Jocelyn Elbows!"

The lights dimmed, a few spots focused on the side door to the stage. Henry vaguely recalled it being the "Staff Only" door he'd used earlier in the day. Music started up.

"The lights go down, the moment's here again..."

So this was the new number Jocelyn had been working on. It was mostly in tune.

"It's time for me to step out on the stage..."

The spotlights brightened, revealing a creature dressed largely in orange and feathers. An enormous blonde wig framed a face that Henry now couldn't help but think of as a pantomime dame.

Eddie would have loved to see this.

"To make my mark, to overcome the pain..."

It was cheesy, but Henry found himself starting to enjoy himself. It was hard to think about anything over the noise and the lighting.

"It's time this songbird left her empty cage..."

Jocelyn's eyed scanned the audience as she sang, and eventually met Henry's. She faltered slightly.

"Tonight I... I'll show the world that I'm a star..."

Henry waved.

"Tonight I'll make... uh..."

The crowd started laughing.

"Oh, shut your cakeholes!" Jocelyn gave up, threw the audience the finger and received the most enthusiastic response of the evening so far. The music cut out, her assistant working the equipment wondering when they'd departed from the usual script.

"Well, boys and girls, you know how this works. You put your name in, and you choose your song. If you sing even half decent, the management will give you a free drink. So what are you waiting for, Christmas?"

There was a brief lull as names were put in, filled with cheesy pop music. Henry got himself a pint and sat in his corner, waiting for a chance to grab the manager, who'd disappeared again after Jocelyn's entrance. Several classics were called out and swiftly butchered, though a few singers were actually pretty good. Jocelyn ribbed them all mercilessly, the bad ones on their singing and the good ones on anything she could think of.

It was during a particularly ear-shattering rendition of "Tainted Love" that Henry finally got the chance to corner Gaz, whose suit on closer inspection looked at least as middle-aged as he did.

"Hi there," he shouted over the din.

"If you want to sing, there are some slips on the bar."

"No, I wanted to talk to you."

"I'm busy. Can't it wait?"

Henry shook his head. "I'm looking for Eddie."

Gaz stopped. "Don't know anyone by that name."

"I think he's in trouble."

Gaz nodded. "I'll let you know if I hear anything," he said, before heading back to the bar area, where he had a brief conversation with another man at the bar and then helped out with serving drinks.

Henry sat back down. For a moment, he was sure the guy at the bar was watching him. Then he turned back to the stage.

But he did look vaguely familiar, like Henry had seen him before.

The Watcher

I quickly looked away. Gaz had warned me someone was looking for me, and I didn't want the guy to know that I knew. His friend Eddie was harmless enough, but the Boss was clearly the brains in the operation. I had no way to know who he was working for.

Gaz told me he called himself Henry Ford. Not the most imaginative of fake names.

It was dangerous, coming back here to watch him. But I didn't think it would matter. After all, he didn't know what I looked like. If he'd heard the tapes, he'd know my voice, but I had no reason to speak to him anyway.

Why was he back here? Was he really just looking for his friend?

Henry sat back down, and discovered there was now another man in the next seat. The new guy was thick set and had a nose that looked like it had been broken more than once. He fitted in with the young crowd even less than Henry did. You could smell trouble in the air, almost as pungent as the cheap aftershave Henry's new companion was wearing.

"Hey, Henry."

"Checking up on me, huh?"

The man smiled, one side of the mouth at a time, as though he'd read about smiles in a book and hadn't had much practice. "Just saying hey. Just come to see how you're doing."

They spoke quietly, but I was close enough to hear most of what they said. It was clear they weren't friends.

"Did Edmunds sent you?"

"The doc? No. Actually, I want to check up on him, too. Seen him lately?"

"I spoke to him earlier. On the phone."

"I reckon he'll want to come down soon. I'd like a little chat with the doc."

"I'll tell him you stopped by." Henry started to get up, but a rather heavy hand on his shoulder convinced him otherwise.

"Stay a little longer. We'll go when I'm ready."

Henry thought for a moment. "How about a drink, then?"

"And a quiet word with the manager?" His companion smiled. "I think not."

"Alright, I'll come quietly. Just tell me one thing – where's Eddie?"

Surprise flickered over the big guy's face. "Your young friend? I was hoping you'd tell me."

I didn't trust the big guy one bit. Henry seemed to be on the level. Perhaps he would be willing to help us. But first he had to get away from this troll.

It was Jocelyn who gave him the opportunity.

"Martin Smith, you're up next!"

No-one got up. Jocelyn entered the crowds, hunting down her next victim, but no-one owned up to the name. I guess he was either in the toilet or had already left. When no-one volunteered, Henry stuck up a hand.

"Well, hello there, shy boy. Come on up and give us your best shot."

Henry turned to his captor. "I'm going up there," he said. "If you try to stop me, in front of all these people, there'll be a scene. I don't think you want that."

"I'll be waiting."

"Man trouble?" taunted Jocelyn. "Come on, big guy, don't hog him to yourself."

Henry looked pale as he headed up to the stage. I wondered whether he could even sing.

"Uh... sorry about this," he whispered. "What did I ask for again?"

"He's forgotten his song!" yelled Jocelyn. The crowd roared with laughter. "I think this one's had a few too many already. Well, here's hoping we forget it just as easily."

The music started. Lucky for him it was an old classic, and a television screen on the stage displayed the lyrics. It may sound like I'm making this up, but sometimes coincidences happen – Martin Smith had selected Queen's "I Want To Break Free".

Henry stared across the bar at the single figure sat at his table. The man stared back, watching him closely. Then the intro stopped, and Henry began. He was pretty tone deaf, but he wasn't really any worse than many of the earlier singers. The hulk at the table watched him impassively.

This was clearly Henry's first time on stage. I suspected it would also be the last. He was pretty tuneless, but unlike some people he seemed to realise this. A few of the audience were even joining in. But not the big man. He continued to watch, not a flicker of emotion showing on his face. Not even on the high notes, which were particularly off key.

Jocelyn was hovering nearby. She knew something was up.

I wondered what was going through Henry's mind. Perhaps he was thinking about his missing friend at that point - not in that way. I knew he cared about his young companion, but he didn't seem the type.

The big guy just watched, waiting for Henry to finish.

When he reached the instrumental break, Henry performed some impromptu dance moves that somehow managed to move him across the stage towards Jocelyn. The crowd laughed. They were as off the beat as his singing was.

I couldn't hear what they were saying, but Jocelyn filled me in later.

"Listen. I'm in trouble, and I need your help."

Jocelyn's smile stayed fixed. "The big guy bothering you?" She exchanged a look with Gaz, who nodded. They'd done something like this a few times before.

"Hell, yeah. Is there a back way out?"

Jocelyn nodded towards the screen. Henry realised his break was over and returned to the song.

He didn't look round when Jocelyn disappeared somewhere behind him.

The song was almost over, and I was wondering whether I should do something myself when Jocelyn reappeared behind Henry.

"Door behind you, when the lights go out." It was a hurried whisper.

Henry twirled, a dance step that entirely missed the beat but gave him a quick glance behind him. The stage door that Jocelyn had come in by was slightly ajar.

I Want To Break Free came to a merciful end.

"Please do break free," sniped Jocelyn, "before our ears melt. Give him a big hand, everyone."

The audience began to applaud, rather more enthusiastically than his singing deserved. The lights dimmed and the spotlights swept the crowds. When the lights came back on, Henry was gone. No-one seemed to have noticed, apart from me and Gaz - and the big guy, of course. But by the time he'd fought his way through the crowd to the front door, it was far too late.

There was a brief pause while Jocelyn prepared for the next singer. I quickly spoke to Gaz while I had the chance.

"What do you reckon about him?" I asked.

"He seems on the level. Mostly worried about his mate."

"How did he hear about Tom?" I wondered. "How did he find us?"

Gaz shrugged. "He said something about ordering electronic parts. Perhaps he tracked you down that way. Is he a detective?"

I shook my head. "No. I think he's a journalist. Perhaps it's time we arranged for an interview."

Insomnia

Henry returned to the bed and breakfast, alone. He was still no closer to finding Eddie. Perhaps there really wasn't anything to do other than wait for a call. He wasn't sure he could sleep, though he knew he needed to.

The clock ticked. The phone did not ring. Sleep did not come.

Who had taken Eddie? And why? The story behind the story was even crazier than the story itself.

Henry sighed. "George, I'm in trouble here."

"So what else is new?"

George looked the same as he always had - the same corduroy trousers, the same tattered old waistcoat he'd always like to wear. He sat at the end of the bed as though he'd been there all along.

"I'm serious, George. Eddie's gone missing, the magazine's falling apart and I'm in way over my head on this story."

George nodded "Yeah, it's a mess. What do you want me to do about it? Wave a magic wand?"

"What can I do, George?"

George took a pack of cigarettes from his pocket. He scoffed at the "no smoking" sign on the bedside table as he lit one. He offered the pack to Henry, who ignored it.

"George, Eddie is gone. I was supposed to look after him. I was only gone a few minutes and he…"

"Henry, you worry about that boy too much."

"But what if someone's taken him?"

George took a long drag before answering. "Then they'll be in touch. Can't do much about that now. You should have been paying attention. But think for a moment. This is Eddie we're talking about. That boy doesn't trust strangers - one of the few bits of sense I ever got into his head. If someone had taken him, in a pub in broad daylight, do you really think they'd have just slipped out without a sound?"

"But how...?"

"Isn't it obvious?" George flicked ash onto the half eaten pizza Henry hadn't wanted to finish. "It was Eddie's idea. He's either wandered off by himself, or he's found someone he knows and trusts. Though who in the hell he could know in this dump is beyond me."

"He wanted to be a journalist," said Henry. "Maybe he's following the story."

"Doing a better job of it than you are, then. You know how it works, Henry. Find your leads and keep following them until you get to the truth."

"George... I'm sorry."

"About what?" Another drag, another flick of ash on cold pizza. "Eddie? You've been doing a fine job. You're a better father for him than I ever was."

Henry shook his head.

"The magazine?"

"I'm keeping it running, but I don't think I can keep it going for much longer."

"Henry, you never wanted to run the thing. That was always my dream, not yours. I just let you do what you did best - write the stories. Do you think I still care about that rag? I'm dead, you idiot."

"I thought..."

"You wanted to run it in my memory or some sentimental crap like that? Henry, let it go. There's only one thing I want you to do for me now - so go and find him."

"George..."

"What?"

"I'm sorry for the accident. It was my fault. Your wife... she was with me that night."

"I know." George tossed the end of his cigarette into the pizza box. "Is that why you're doing all this? Guilt? You're trying to make amends?"

"If I'd told you…"

"I'd still be here? Grow up, Henry. Go find Eddie. Then stop trying to live my life. It doesn't suit you."

Henry blinked. The end of the bed was empty, just as it had been all along. The pizza box held nothing but cold pizza. Even so, something had changed - he could feel it in his gut. The magazine was going out of business… and that was okay. He and Eddie would survive without it.

Sleep still seemed impossible, and there was nothing more he could do for Eddie until morning.

"Might as well play the next tape," he said to himself.

Rob's voice started up again. The next thing Henry remembered was daylight and the sound of seagulls.

The Interrogation

I'll be perfectly frank. To the best of my knowledge, I'd never interrogated anyone before. The way Lisa tells it, I was a suave, unflappable professional – really, I was terrified of screwing up. I didn't want to threaten Sally, and I certainly had no stomach for torture. I just took a deep breath and started the tape recorder.

"Let's start with the basics," I said. "What is the Amnesia Project?"

Sally's response was slow and deliberate. "Could you help me with that tea? I'm very thirsty, and it seems a shame to waste it."

I did, too. For all my efforts to be in control and professional, I actually held the mug of tea to her lips while she sipped.

"Thank you," she said. "I am glad to see I'm being questioned by a gentleman."

"I hope to be answered by a lady," I replied.

Sally smiled at that, though it didn't seem very sincere. "We shall see." There was a pause, and I was about to say something more when she continued. "The Amnesia Project is a secret experiment, funded by certain unsavoury groups and at least one government, though I couldn't tell you which country. It aims to control people's minds by selectively wiping their memories and personalities, and replacing them with whatever fictions the user feels best. They're a long way from perfecting it yet, but the results so far are... frighteningly effective."

"I know."

"I'm afraid I don't know much more about how it works or the exact effects. That was where you and your colleagues came in."

I nodded. "Okay. What's your interest in it?"

"I am a concerned private citizen, wanting to expose the operation and prevent it ever being used." She paused. "No, I didn't think you'd believe that. Isn't it obvious, Mr Walker? I wish to obtain these secrets for myself so that I can sell them to the *highest bidder."*

"How did you learn about it?"

"Some of my potential customers did. I suspect they have their spies, just as I do, and they found out through them. Then they requested my services to obtain the information. Spies at Grace Meadows seem to drop off the radar somewhat frequently."

I could believe it.

"Tell me about Dr Hawkins."

"I don't really know that much about him," said Sally. "He puts on a kind and generous face for the public, but he can be somewhat... unpleasant in private. You probably know more about him than I do. But he pays well." She smiled. "Does that surprise you? Dr Hawkins is an intelligent and highly logical man. Whatever came between us before, he knows that I'm his best chance of finding you and the information you stole."

"Looks like he was wrong about that."

Sally smiled. "Perhaps. We'll see. But he has a deadline, Mr Walker, and it's getting a lot closer. One way or another, he will get what he wants."

"Deadline? What deadline?"

Sally shook her head. "I don't know," she said. "All I know is that there's a big day coming, very soon now, and the good doctor wants the machine ready. Without his research data, he has no way to control it properly. The results are... unpredictable."

So Dr Hawkins was running out of time. Still, we couldn't afford to wait - unpredictable or not, the machine worked. Whatever he had planned, we had to stop it.

"What about Max?" I asked.

"Mr Nicholson? I'm surprised you don't remember more about him yourself, Mr

Walker. The two of you were so close. But let's see - Max is a talented musician, a wizard at crosswords and one of the most brilliant cryptographers I've ever worked with."

"A cryptographer?" asked Evie, somewhere behind me.

"He reads, creates and breaks secret codes," I explained.

"Ah, like those young men at Bletchley Park," she said.

"Indeed he is," added Sally. "Or was, anyway. He also had a knack for creating codes that didn't seem like codes. Anything can be broken, given time – but only if you know it's there in the first place."

I braced myself. It was time for the big question, and I had a feeling that I was going to be fed a mixture of truth and lies. But this was the first time I'd met someone who might be able to answer it and I couldn't pass up the opportunity.

"Ms Kensington... Sally..." I swallowed. "Who am I?"

She smiled. There was humour in it, but no warmth.

"I haven't the faintest idea," she said.

Sally told me what she knew, or at least what she claimed to know. I was one of her many agents, a "sleeper" implanted into a company or government agency purely to provide information on their activities. She said Max and I were recruited after we'd left university - I apparently have a degree in psychology, and a rather good one at that, but she either couldn't or wouldn't provide details - and given some basic military-style training. The two of us were both saddled with significant student debts and we were very grateful for a leg-up into our chosen industry, and in the early days we were not asked for a vast amount of information.

That was the honeymoon period.

When she first heard about the project, Sally pulled some strings to get the two of us into Hawkins' employ. Fortunately she had another sleeper agent in place elsewhere in the clinic – Jimmy. For a while we reported on what limited goings on we could but it was some time before we could penetrate what she called the "inner sanctum". Then the real data had started coming in – and then suddenly stopped. Hawkins had spotted us.

One by one, her agents disappeared. First Jimmy dropped off the radar, and then I did likewise. Max was the last to go, though the three of us disappeared within as many days. Lisa was receiving most of the research data by this point, as Sally later discovered. She suggested I'd had an attack of conscience and thought that public knowledge was more important than money, and her tone of voice suggested she found this most distasteful.

"Surprising, really," she said. "I had no idea my hold over you had slipped so much, but then you never were easy to blackmail. Few family ties, mostly lapsed; no steady relationship; little public image to tarnish. It was a while before I realised you had... feelings for Max."

And then, one day, Jimmy reappeared, half lunatic and believing his own convoluted cover story. Max and I were still missing. Then Jimmy called in to say I'd returned, and the rest... well, I knew the rest.

"What happened to Jimmy?" I asked. "You said he was trying to escape."

"It really was an accident. A gun went off at the wrong time – a warning shot turned into a fatal one. A pity – he was our first real clue as to what was going on in there. May I have some more tea, please?"

I helped her sip some more tea.

"Ah, thank you. What else would you like to know?"

I got up. "I've heard enough," I said. "What I really want to know, you can't tell me about – my family, my childhood, where I was born. That's gone."

"I truly am sorry about that, Robert."

"Thank you." I meant it, too. It was the first time I felt she'd been completely honest with me.

"What do you intend to do with me?" she asked.

"For now, I'm going to leave you here. We're going to stop the Amnesia Project, and then we'll part company – forever. Whoever I was, the man I am now doesn't want anything more to do with you."

"Unless I escape first." She smiled. "You won't hold me for long. Dr Hawkins is getting desperate."

I turned to the tape recorder, watching the reels spin a moment longer. My mind was spinning too. Was I really an agent for this woman? It might explain a lot, but I didn't know how much I could trust her.

"This interview is over," I said, hitting the stop button.

My hands were shaking as I held a mug of tea. Sally had been secured once more and was being kept under guard in the kitchen whilst Evie, Lisa and I sat in the living room and assessed how it had gone. I don't understand how Evie was able to make tea with her in the same room.

"You were magnificent," said Lisa. "She tried to rattle you, and you wouldn't let her."

"I'm rattled, alright," I replied. My hands shook a little harder as if to confirm this.

"But you didn't show it, dear," said Evie. "That was one of the best interrogations I've ever seen, and I've been on the receiving end of a fair few."

"Can I believe a word of it?" I asked. "I didn't do anything to make her tell the truth. I couldn't."

Evie patted my hand. "Rob, dear, torture is a very messy business and it rarely works. People will end up telling you what you want to hear, and we rarely want to hear the truth. You did fine."

"So what do we do now?"

"Just as you said. We get the bag back, we find out what Hawkins is up to, we stop the project – and then we let her go. We'll be long gone by the time she finds her way back to her gang. But until then, I'd rather keep her where I can keep an eye on her."

I sipped my tea. A small amount slopped over the edge and fell on the coffee table. Evie extracted a paper napkin from her bag, wiped the table and flicked the napkin into the bin in a single fluid movement.

"I'm scared, Evie," I said. "I'm scared that she's telling the truth – that I'm her lackey, stealing secrets for her. I'm scared that I'm nothing more than a hired crook. Do I even want to remember all that?"

Lisa put her hand on my knee. "I know that's not true, Rob. I've seen enough hired crooks in my line of work – they're cheap scum only out for themselves. None of them would have gone back for me – not unless you paid them."

I like to think she was right.

After a very long day, during which I'd been kidnapped, released, taken part in an almost military assault and interrogated someone, I felt utterly exhausted. I also felt I couldn't possibly sleep, with thoughts going around and around in my head. Evie bullied me to bed, though Lisa needed far less persuading. I let her take the double and I slept in the spare room, which suited me fine – I remembered waking up with Jimmy all too clearly.

"Don't worry about our prisoner," Evie had said. "We'll look after her. She'll still be there in the morning for you."

I didn't trust most of what Sally had said, but I found I could believe her about Jimmy. It all rang so true. Working for both sides, his psyche torn in two – I'd managed to find friends, people I could trust. Jimmy couldn't trust anyone. I wondered who he'd been working for when he drugged me and locked me in the flat – and I remembered his face again from that morning, that brief moment he'd seemed to truly care for me. Perhaps that was all that was left of the real man.

I thought about Max, and his secret codes. He was a prisoner, of course, but in more ways than one. Getting him out of the clinic was just the start – like me, he was trapped in his amnesia. I didn't know if I could do anything about that. I had to find my own way out first.

I'd gathered by now that Max and I had been an item. That technically we still were. But I didn't remember him. Was I supposed to feel something special for him? If we rescued him, could we ever feel that again? I felt a sense of loss, that something more may have been taken from me than my memories.

I still couldn't sleep. My thoughts kept turning back to Lisa. Something was wrong, but I wasn't sure what it could be. I thought about our first meeting, about the things she'd told me. I thought about her empty flat. It all seemed... odd, somehow. I decided to speak to her in the morning.

I quickly fell asleep after that. I think I dreamed, but have no idea what I dreamed of now. They were already evaporating when I woke up, a form of amnesia that affects us all.

Not Quite Right

One of Evie's cups of tea sat on the side when I woke. I took it with me into the living room, where the gang were already putting away a number of blankets. They'd obviously slept wherever they could find space. Someone had put some music on the stereo, though the volume was low and I couldn't make out the song over Judy's gossip.

"Good morning, Robert," said Evie. "I hope you slept well. We have a busy day ahead of us."

"What are you planning?" I asked.

Evie smiled. "Wait and see," she said. "Howard's coming back with a surprise for you."

"I can't wait. Where's Lisa?"

Lisa was still in the bedroom, as it turned out. She'd needed the sleep even more than I had and her tea was in danger of growing cold. She stirred as I entered.

"Good morning," I said.

She groaned sleepily. "Oh no, not morning already. Evie's probably already worked out a plan to steal the crown jewels."

"Could be," I said. "She's up to something, but she won't tell me what it is." I paused. "Lisa, something's been bothering me."

"Just one thing?"

"Be serious a moment," I said. "I've been thinking about you. About your flat. About your computer."

"What, my laptop?"

There was an "aha" moment. "Lisa, where is your laptop?"

"It's in the bedroom back at home..." she stopped. "No, it isn't. It's being repaired. That's right. Of course it is. Otherwise you could have stayed there rather than going to the library."

"Repaired?" I asked. That would make sense of it – but not of everything. "What's wrong with it, Lisa? When are you getting it back?"

"I don't know. Something technical. Should be any day now."

"Why didn't you get Howard to look at it?"

She blinked. "I hadn't thought of that," she said. "Still, I don't want to bother him with stuff like that."

My suspicions grew stronger, but I had to tread carefully. "Perhaps you should give them a call, find out when?"

"Yes," she said. "Good idea."

"I'll look up the number," I offered. "What's the company called?"

She blanked. "I... can't remember."

"I think there's a lot you can't remember," I said. "More than you realise."

"What are you getting at, Rob?"

I felt we were nearly there. She was almost at the tipping point. One more push ought to do it.

"Lisa, you said you don't have a tape recorder. You have a CD player. So why do you have a box of tapes in your living room?"

"Those old things? I..."

"Do you have any CDs?"

"Yes," she said. "A few dozen. Why?"

"There were none in the flat. I had a lot of time to look. Are they being repaired too?"

"Don't be stupid," she said. "My friend wanted to borrow them..."

"All of them at once? Which friend?"

She screwed her eyes up. "Stop it!" she snapped. "Stop all these stupid questions! Do you have to interrogate me as well? Perhaps you think I kidnapped myself?"

I'd pushed her too far, too fast. "I'm sorry, Lisa. I just wanted to show you something I don't think you've realised."

"And what's that?" she asked.

"That your life doesn't actually make sense," I said. "You tell me you're a journalist. You should do some investigating."

The front door opened as I returned to the living room, and Howard stepped in.

"Are we ready, Howard?" asked Evie.

Howard grinned. "We're ready, Evie. I've had to guess at your size, Rob, but I'm usually pretty good at that."

"My size?"

"Come and see."

"I'm not sure about this," I said. "Isn't this illegal?"

Howard smiled. "We do a lot of illegal stuff, Rob. This is small time for us. Besides, I've done this dozens of times. It's all about confidence."

It was very convincing. If it was a fake, it was an excellent job, but I suspected Howard had managed to obtain real uniforms. I didn't know how he could have done that. I decided it was better not to ask.

"But still... impersonating police officers..."

"Leave the talking to me and you'll be fine. Police stations are hard to get into, but once you're in everyone thinks you must be legitimate. No-one asks questions. Now get changed, and we'll go collect that bag."

I dutifully obeyed, swiftly changing out of my usual clothes and slipping into the *crisply ironed police uniform. I was to be a bog standard detective constable, while Howard's uniform marked him out as my sergeant. Howard had to correct a few details when I'd finished but I'd managed to figure out most of it by myself.*

"That's great," I said. "Now all we need is a police car to get there in."

Howard chuckled.

"You mean...?"

"No, we haven't got a police car. It would be a little conspicuous in our line of work! We'll park round the corner and walk in."

Morning

The morning sunlight felt warm on his face. Seagulls called out in the distance, and the sea air was fresh and invigorating. Then Henry caught sight of one of Eddie's cases in the corner of the room, and his good mood evaporated. He was still no closer to finding his charge, and his efforts to find the author of the Amnesia Project story had all led nowhere.

You know how it works, Henry. Find your leads and follow them until you get to the truth.

He went down for breakfast. A fried egg, two sausages, some bacon and half a fried tomato penned in a small lake of baked beans. A radio in the background was playing some old chart hit he couldn't quite place.

Find your leads. Well, he'd done that. An old man who clearly had nothing to do with any of this. A drag queen and her teenage technician son. And the bar where Eddie went missing.

Follow them. He'd done that too. That's how Eddie had gone missing.

Eddie doesn't trust strangers. But there was no-one in Brighton that Eddie knew, was there?

He dipped some toast into the egg and made an effort with one of the sausages, but he couldn't taste anything.

Who was Tom Phillips? Who had actually collected that package at the bar? He could go speak to the manager again, but twice now that had got him nowhere. There was following a lead until you got to the truth and there was following one until you got a restraining order. If the manager was holding something back, Henry would need something to convince him.

The song on the radio finished, and another one started up - Gloria Gaynor's most famous hit.

I Will Survive? Not if I have to sing that bloody song again, I won't.

Henry stopped cutting into his bacon. There was someone else connected with the bar, someone who might know who Tom Phillips was - and might know what had happened to Eddie.

He left the rest of his breakfast and rushed back up to his room.

"Oh, no. Not you again!"

It had taken about twenty minutes to find his way back to the home of Mr Jason Arnold, sometimes known as Jocelyn Elbows, regular karaoke drag act at the Cruise Liner. This time the door was answered by a plain middle-aged man in jeans and T-shirt.

"Jocelyn…"

"I'm not working now, dear. Jason is fine."

"Okay, then. Jason. I'm sorry to disturb you but I need to ask you something. Eddie is missing."

"Your mate from yesterday? I haven't seen him."

Henry shook his head. "That's not why I'm here. I just wanted to know if you've heard of someone working at the bar called Tom Phillips. Maybe they could be a regular, I don't know."

"Tom? He's Gaz's ex - the manager, you know?" laughed Jason. "Not seen him since he ran off to Argentina with some old guy – wealthy with a heart condition, you understand. Can't see him coming back any time soon. What do you want him for?"

"He ordered some electronic parts from JKR. I think he may have taken Eddie."

"Can't be him," said Jason. "He left the country about three years ago. Didn't Gaz tell you?"

Henry frowned. "Thanks, Mr Arnold. You've been very helpful."

The Cruise Liner was closed when Henry arrived, but Henry could see the bar staff cleaning up inside and he banged on the door until someone let him in.

"Get me the manager."

The young girl who'd opened the door wisely decided this was nothing she wanted to get involved with, and she dashed into the back to fetch him.

Gaz came out a moment later. "What do you want?" he muttered. "Look, I haven't seen your friend."

"Tom Phillips," said Henry. "Someone placed an order for electronic parts to be delivered to this bar, under his name."

"And I told you I'd never heard of him."

"You did. But we both know that's not true, don't we? You knew Tom very well, even if you haven't seen him for a while. And that's interesting."

"Really." Gaz stepped back, arms folded. "I've had enough of your nonsense, mister. I'd like you to leave before I call the police."

"I spoke to Jocelyn. Well, Jason. You know who I mean. I know Tom was your ex, and I know he left the country years ago. No reason for you to lie about that to me, is there? So why did you?"

Gaz sighed. "Alright, fine. Yes, he's my ex. I thought we had something special going and then he met his... older gentleman friend, and the next I know he's dumped me and buggered off abroad. Thank you for reminding me about him. Now will you please go?"

Henry sat down. "I'm not leaving until you tell me the truth," he said. "Call the police if you like. If you won't help me, I'll call them myself. I'm worried about Eddie, and all I know is that he disappeared from your bar. I'm sure they'd have some questions for you."

"Look, I didn't want to get involved in all this." Gaz sat down on the seat beside Henry. "An old friend of mine is working on some electronic gizmo. He's trying to keep a low profile, so he asked me whether I'd let him order some components through here. He's a bit paranoid so I didn't think anything of it at first, but you're the third person to ask me about Tom recently and I'm starting to think he really is in some sort of trouble."

"The third? Who else has been asking?"

"There was an older guy a few days ago, said he was a doctor. The other one was a big guy, sounded a little foreign - maybe eastern European, I don't know."

"Gaz, listen to me. I need to speak to your friend, as soon as possible. I think Eddie has been asking about the Amnesia Project - the thing your friend is working on - and someone's taken him because they think he knows about it."

Gaz shuffled on his seat. "I don't know. He said not to tell anyone where to find him."

"Can you get in touch with him? Tell him who I am, give him my number. I'm staying at a bed and breakfast not too far from here."

"Yeah, alright. I'll get you a pen. You go back to your B&B and wait there."

"This really is important, Gaz. If I don't hear from your friend in an hour, I will go to the police."

"Alright! I'll call him!"

Henry jotted down his details and left the bar. Nothing to do now but wait. He didn't really want to involve the police, as no-one involved would want to speak to him about the Project afterwards, but he would if it came to it. Eddie was more important than the story.

Back in the bed and breakfast he picked up the final tape. Rob was dealing with the police in his own way. Perhaps he could tell him something useful.

Evidence

The police station, as I recalled when we arrived, had a reception area with a security door leading to the main station. I had no idea how we were supposed to get in, as Howard's uniform didn't stretch to a keycard for the door, but in the end it was so simple I'm surprised I didn't think of it myself.

"Hi," said Howard to the desk sergeant. His voice was deeper and his usual tone of light camp had almost disappeared. "Here to collect some evidence. Is Jeffries in?"

"Inspector Jeffries? Let me check." He picked up the telephone and spoke briefly to the operator. "Hello Sandra. Is Jeffries on duty at the moment? Right. Thanks." He turned back to Howard. "No, he's not on shift until tomorrow morning now."

"What about... what was the other officer's name?"

I realised that Howard was talking to me. "PC Johnson," I recalled.

"Sandra? What about PC Johnson? Same department." A pause. "No, that's fine. Thanks, Sandra." He put down the phone. "Sorry, he's on call. Should be back in an hour or two."

"That's alright. We'll just head on up – it just needs a form signing. I'll leave a message for them."

Howard then continued chatting to the desk sergeant until someone came out, when he grabbed the door before it closed, wrapped up his patter and gestured me inside with him.

"See," he said, once the door had locked behind us. "Easy!"

"I'd have thought the police would be a little more security conscious," I said.

He laughed. "You'd think so, but they're human beings just like the rest of us. Being security conscious all the time is hard work. And why shouldn't they trust two fellow officers?"

"What if Jeffries had been in?"

Howard shrugged. "At this time in the morning? Next shift starts in twenty minutes. If he was in, he'd be too busy finishing off everything else he has to do to speak to us."

We headed down the corridor to the lifts. I had no idea where we were going, and it soon became clear to me that neither did Howard. I was terrified that we'd be spotted loitering around the place and quickly caught; to my horror, Howard accosted the first person he encountered and asked directions.

"The evidence lockers? Second floor," replied the young lady. I don't think she was a policewoman – she seemed more like office staff. "Do you need me to show you?"

"Second floor... No, I think we're alright. Thanks, love."

She smiled and headed on into the maze of corridors.

"Come along, Officer Walker," grinned Howard. "Second floor! Lift, or stairs?"

We took the lift.

The second floor greeted us with a sign, to my great relief. The thought of Howard asking directions again terrified me, even though I knew what he meant. We simply weren't familiar with this station. Why wouldn't we be asking directions?

The evidence lockers, which I'd somehow envisioned as a gloomy, caged area with drawers more in keeping with a mortuary, turned out to be a fairly cheerful office. A group of middle aged women in one corner sat at computer terminals, gossipping and drinking coffee. A sergeant walked over to them, said something I couldn't hear, and they all laughed. Then one of the women handed him a file and he left.

"Stop lallygagging and come here!"

I turned back to Howard, who was walking over to a set of cupboards and drawers. Each card had a case number on it, and a surname. Howard was heading for the ones labelled W.

"Did you say you were Rob Walker when you were interviewed?"

I thought back. "Yes," I said.

"Good, good. But there's a dozen Walkers here. I need to find out which one it is. When was the interview?"

"Er..." It was no good. Between my stress at the time and my even greater stress now (for at least then I was sure I'd done no wrong), I couldn't get time straightened out in my head. "I don't know. I'm sorry."

"Rob, it's okay. I'll go and ask those helpful ladies what they can tell us. You wait here by the lockers and I'll call out the case number."

With that, he walked away. My legs turned to jelly and I wanted nothing more than to simply disappear. I simply couldn't stop thinking about being in the middle of a police station, wearing a fake or stolen uniform, about to steal criminal evidence.

"Hello, ladies," I heard Howard say. His normal, slightly fruity tone of voice had returned now. He must have felt it more appropriate for the audience.

"Hello," said the nearest lady. "I've not seen you round here before."

Discovery! I felt the urge to scream and run, but I couldn't have done either even if I'd tried. My throat was dry and my legs wouldn't move.

"Just passing through," quipped Howard. "Here to pick up some evidence. Can you look up the reference number for me?"

"Sure," she said. "They're not exactly easy to remember, are they?"

Howard chuckled. "I should have written it down."

"What details do you have?"

"Walker, Robert. I don't have the date of birth, but the interview was in the last week."

There was the sound of tapping. "Is this the one?" she asked. "Suspicion of handling stolen goods, drug trafficking?"

Drug trafficking?! What the hell?

Howard didn't seem surprised. "Yep, that's the one." He turned back to me and called out a sequence of letters and numbers. I turned to the evidence racks and tried to focus my eyes on the labels, and it was no surprise to me to find the one we wanted was a moderate size locker – just big enough for a sports bag. I opened the locker, feeling a flashback to that day in King's Cross when I opened a similar locker, expecting at any moment to hear someone walk up behind me and...

"Found it?"

I managed to avoid screaming, instead giving off a muffled squawk. The sounds of gossip and typing in the background stopped.

"Nerves of steel, this one," Howard called over. There were some giggles and then the sounds of work resumed.

"This is it," I said. I pulled out the bag. It was smaller than I'd expected. I went to open the zip, but Howard stopped me.

"Not here!" he hissed. "That's tampering with evidence! Wait until we're home and dry. Now pull yourself together – you're the worst actor I've ever met! Much more larking about like this and you'll blow our cover!"

I was about to say something back, but there was a fire in his eyes I hadn't seen before. He was angry, seriously angry, and I caught a glimpse of the steel that hid beneath the fluff and the fun. Evie's gang were professionals; sometimes it was easy to forget that.

And yet, somehow, I could move again. It was like they used to do in old films – a slap in the face for someone in hysterics.

Howard smiled. "Let's go," he said.

"Hang on!"

We stopped. One of the ladies was walking over. Panic began to rise in me again, but this time I was able to fight it down.

"You'll have to sign it out," she said, pointing at a nearby book and pen.

Howard smiled. "Oh, of course. I'd forget my head if it wasn't cemented on." He picked up the pen and scribbled down some details. "What was that number again, Mike?"

I took a moment to realise he meant me. "Oh, er..." Of course he couldn't call me Rob – not with my name on the evidence tag.

I read the reference out from the open locker door, and then closed it.

I had a growing feeling of dread as we retraced our steps to the exit, as though something was going to go badly wrong. I was entirely right about that, as it turned out, but our escape from the police station was effortless. We didn't encounter anyone on our way down to the front desk, and the only comment from the desk officer was a half-interested "see ya". We headed back to the car, drove back to the flat and changed back into our regular clothes on the way. Everything had gone without a hitch.

"Evie!" called Howard, as we opened the front door. "We're back! Mission accomplished!"

There was only silence.

"Evie?" I called.

Howard shushed me. "Take the bag, Rob, and wait here. Something's wrong."

I felt the hairs on the back of my neck rise, and I stayed put. Howard crept cautiously into the house, checking the hall, then started looking in the rooms in turn.

"Rob!" he called. "It's Evie!"

I came running in to the living room. Evie was collapsed against the wall, unmoving. There were signs of struggle, and I saw blood on the floor. But worse was the empty chair in the kitchen.

Sally was gone.

Raided

"Hey, Evie! I'm back!"

I turned around to see Judy come back in.

"Hey Rob! Glad you're back. Listen, we had a call to meet Max! He said he'd..." Judy's chattering trailed off as she looked at me. "Oh, no. What's happened?"

"In here," I said. "Evie's been attacked. Sally's gone."

Evie was now sat in the chair, being fussed over by Howard. Her eyes weren't focusing too well and she didn't seem entirely clear where she was, but she was at least semi-conscious now.

"Evie!" called Judy. "What happened?"

Evie couldn't or wouldn't reply.

"Easy now, Judy. Give her some time." Howard dabbed at Evie's head with a wet cloth. I could see blood, but not much. "She's been knocked out – a nasty blow to the head."

"We really ought to have someone on the team that does first aid," muttered Judy. "I don't suppose you do, Rob?"

"Sorry," I said. "I majored in Psychology. Apparently."

"Lisa's good with a band aid," she replied. "Where is she?"

I suddenly realised that I hadn't seen her since I got in, and said so.

"This isn't good," said Judy, suddenly all business. "Right, roll call, everybody!"

Howard, myself, Evie (sort of) and Judy were all accounted for. We checked the house, but there was no sign of Lisa.

"Where are the twins?" I asked.

"They're safe. They've gone to Lisa's place in Reading – she had a job for them to do."

I decided not to pursue that at the moment. We had bigger problems.

"Where's Sam?" Judy asked.

Howard frowned. "Wasn't he with you?"

We found Sam's body in the garden, carelessly hidden in the shrubs at the back; they'd clearly been in a hurry to leave and didn't have time to hide the body properly. Not that there were many places to hide one; the communal garden area was little more than a walled off square of grass and a concrete path; the shrubs growing alongside the walls were the most obvious greenery. A few hopeful flowers poked their heads out of the corners, but they were outnumbered by the crisp packets and beer cans that littered the place.

From outside the garden, you couldn't see him. From inside, you couldn't miss him - or the blood that had pooled around his midriff.

"Stabbed," whispered Judy. "Oh, Sam..."

There was no sign of the knife.

I briefly considered calling the police, but it would have been a bad idea – we were in enough trouble as it was.

I could hear something. Nearby, still whirring faintly, I spotted Lisa's tape recorder. I picked it up carefully.

It was still recording.

"I think we might have a clue," I said, stopping the tape. "Let's get back inside."

Judy and Howard picked up Sam's body between them – it didn't seem right to leave it there – and we headed back in. As we entered, I heard a familiar trilling.

Lisa's mobile phone was prominently displayed on the kitchen table, and it was ringing.

"Mr Walker?"

"Sally," I growled. "Who did this? Who got you out?"

"It doesn't matter. What does matter is that we have Lisa, and you have something we want."

"The Amnesia Project."

I could almost hear her thin, humourless smile. "Exactly. You have it?"

"Yes."

"Excellent. I'll call back in one hour with the details for the drop-off point. Be ready."

She cut the connection.

"Right," I said. "Tell me what happened."

"We got a call," said Judy. "Lisa's mobile – he said he was Max. Lisa recognised the voice. Max said he was in trouble and needed picking up, so Evie sent me along to collect him."

"Did you find him?"

"No. I was at the pickup for ten minutes before I realised it was a hoax. How did they fake his voice so well, Rob? Lisa was convinced it was him."

"It probably was him," I said. "Max was at the clinic last time I saw him. They could have wiped his memory with that machine of theirs and fed him instructions to call Lisa. Go on. What happened next?"

"When I realised he wasn't going to show, I got back here pronto. But I was too late. It was clearly a diversion so they could get Sally, and it looks like they took Lisa with them."

"As a hostage?" I asked.

Judy shook her head. "Probably. I don't know. Perhaps just to find out what we know."

"And what happened to Sam?"

She shook her head. "I've no idea," she said, and started to cry.

"Perhaps this will tell us," I said, looking at Lisa's tape recorder.

It didn't take long to rewind the tape. Whatever had happened, it had happened in the last twenty minutes or so. Howard and I had missed the whole thing by mere moments, and that made me feel worse, somehow.

I pressed the play button.

"...cryptographer?" That was Evie.

"He reads, creates and breaks secret codes." That was me.

"That's too far back," said Judy. *"That was your interrogation."*

I wound the tape on a bit further.

"...happened to Jimmy? You said he was trying to escape."

"It really was an accident..."

I wound on more.

"...whoever I was, the man I am now doesn't want anything more to do with you. This interview is over."

There was a click where I'd stopped the tape. Now it kept on playing.

First we heard Sam's voice, cryptically muttering *"testing, testing."*

Muffled voices. Evie speaking to a man – no, two men.

A thump – the door being shoved open? I couldn't tell. Evie shouting now, the only words I could make out being *"call the police"* (an obvious bluff, but what they'd expect an old lady to say, perhaps).

"Evie!" That was Sam. There was the sound of a door opening and the other voices grew louder and clearer. Sam had clearly entered the room.

"I thought you said they'd all gone?" yelled one of the strange men.

"Never mind that! Do something about this old bitch!" *said the other. He sounded in pain – I suspected Evie was giving him a hard time. The muffled thumping sounds suggested she was hitting him with something.*

There was a crash, and Evie screamed.

Sam cried out: "Get away from her, you bastards!"

I heard a hissing sound, and cries of pain from one of the bruisers. Probably one of Sam's homemade canisters. There was a clunk – I looked down and saw it on the floor, beneath the coffee table, knocked from his hand.

"The bastard! He maced me!"

A lot of noise, a lot of screaming and shouting. It was impossible to make out any more than a struggle taking place, but we could guess how it worked out.

"Evie! Are you okay?" *That was Lisa.* "What's going on?"

"Hello there," *growled one of the intruders.* "Reckon we could have some fun with this one."

"Now, you know what he'd say about that. Touch her and you'll wake up thinking you're a chicken or something."

"Ah, nuts to it. Now, miss, we can do this the easy way or the hard way. Drop the mace."

I heard Sam groaning.

"Drop the mace, or I slit his throat." *This was quite close to the recorder – they were talking about Sam.*

I heard a can hit the floor.

"Good girl. Now, where's Sally Kensington?"

"She's in the kitchen. Just don't hurt them."

The voices grew fainter. I heard muffled conversation, including Sally's voice. A moment later they grew louder as they re-entered the room.

"Thank you for your help." *That was Sally.* "What are you going to do with them?"

"Leave them. They're not important. But the young lady comes with us. Oh, and leave her mobile here."

There was a lot of noise I couldn't make out.

"Down the back stairs. We don't want to attract undue attention."

A moment later there was silence, and then I heard movement again, and Sam groaning. Footsteps as he crossed to the door, then headed for the fire escape. He headed slowly down, gasping on every second stair, but whether he was injured or simply winded I did not know.

"Where are we going?" *Faintly, in the distance.*

"Back to the clinic." *Equally faint.* "Someone wants to meet you. Both of you."

"Hey!"

Sam had been spotted. We could hear running footsteps getting closer. There was a heavy blow, and Sam coughed, clearly winded.

"How much does he know?"

"I don't know."

"We can't take the risk. Kill him."

There was a sound I didn't recognise. Sam gave a horrible choking sound, and then I heard him fall to the ground.

There were a few more sounds after that – car doors, voices, driving away. Then nothing but background noise. I wound on. Background noise. I wound on further. More background, then footsteps.

"I think we might have a clue." *That was me. Then the click. End of the recording.*

"We know where they've taken her, then," said Howard.

We did. The clinic. That damned clinic. I knew I'd have to go back there but I hadn't considered it would be a double rescue.

"I'm sorry, Rob," said Evie. She still sounded weak but she was coming back to us. "We should have known. It's a classic – distract the guards and draw them off before you move in."

"Never mind, Evie," I said. "You did the best you could."

Judy had barely spoken since we'd found Sam. She'd just sat staring at her hands. Now she looked up, and her eyes were cold. Her voice was low and quiet, and her words left the air decidedly chilly.

"We'll do better."

Evie looked over. "Judy, I know you're upset..."

"Upset." Judy bared her teeth. This was the Judy that singlehandedly took out four men in twenty seconds when we'd rescued Lisa at the warehouse – but more so. "I'm not upset, Evie. Because I'm going to find them, and then I'm going to hurt them."

"Judy, that's not how we do things."

"THEY KILLED SAM!" It was the first time I'd heard Judy scream, and it sounded so very wrong. "You're going to let them get away with that?!"

Evie said nothing.

"I won't let them! I won't!"

Evie still said nothing.

"I won't! I..." Judy began to weep. Evie put an arm around her.

"I think we'd better take a look at this damned bag," I said. Half an hour had already passed since the telephone call and, though another half hour was technically still ahead of us, we all expected another call at any moment.

"There's no way we can look through all that in half an hour," said Howard.

"So we should just hand it all over?" I asked. "I'm not saying we need to go through it. Just find out what we've got."

I hefted the sports bag up onto the table. It was surprisingly heavy. Unzipping the top, I peered inside.

It was filled with plastic bags of white powder.

"But..."

"What in the hell?" asked Evie. "I thought this was meant to be research data?"

"The police said it was a drugs bust," I said. "I thought they were making that up. Looks like that's really what it was all along. Unless..."

I started pulling out the packets of powder, piling them up on the table beside the bag. Underneath a few layers of them I found something else, and dug it out with triumph.

It was a wad of banknotes. A large wad.

"Looks like about three grand, I'd say," said Evie. "Maybe more."

"I think there are more in here," I said, and pulled out another two wads.

For a moment, we all stared at the cash, not quite believing it. Then I continued to dig in the bag.

Nothing but drugs. Nothing but those little bags of white powder.

"Maybe there's something inside these bags?" I suggested. I picked up one of the powder packets, ready to tear it open, but Judy put her hand on my arm.

"No, Rob. Don't."

I stopped, confused.

"This whole thing smells like a set-up to me," she said. "Think about it. The police are watching a locker, containing a bag full of drugs. You come along to collect it, and you're caught with enough coke to put you away for years. Anyone with this in their possession is going to look very dodgy – the coke and the cash say 'drug dealer' in twelve feet high neon letters."

"They didn't hold me before," I said.

"They thought you were the go-between before," she said. "Just a small villain in a big organisation. They wanted to get to the boss. Question is, who set this up?"

"But I had a tape! A message, hidden on the tape!"

And then I remembered something Sally had said: "He also had a knack for creating codes that didn't seem like codes. Anything can be broken, given time – but only if you know it's there in the first place."

Max. Max created that song list on the tape. Play it through, and it's just a mix tape – no-one would think it was a code. And why would Max betray me? This time it was my own words I recalled.

They could have wiped his memory with that machine of theirs and fed him instructions...

"Damn, I've been an idiot," I said.

"What? Why?" asked Evie.

"I've been an idiot. I listened to my message to myself on that tape and didn't trust a word of it – but when I listened to Max's musical code, I never stopped to think it might be lying to me as well."

"What do you mean?" asked Howard.

"I was supposed to find that bag. It was never anything to do with the Amnesia Project – it was always just a trap. If I woke up, and started poking around, I'd be caught and arrested. End of problem."

"Then we need to get rid of it," said Judy. "And fast. If they figure out we've got it, we'll have a police raid on this flat before you can say 'entrapment'."

"It's worse than that," I said. "We've got about twenty minutes until that phone rings again, and we don't have anything to trade. We don't have any information on *the Amnesia Project at all."*

It all came back down to me. Of the four of us that had been quietly collecting data, one was dead, one was a hostage, one was practically a vegetable and *a hostage, and I had no memory of it.*

"Okay," I said to myself, "think it through. I'm collecting data on a top secret project and smuggling it out. I know that, if I'm caught, I could be killed or, more likely, have my memory wiped. So what do I do with it?"

"Store it with someone else. Lisa should have a copy," said Evie.

"She should. She doesn't seem to know anything about it, though. She has a lot of tapes... Evie... can you contact the twins? Tell them to look for cassette tapes. They might not be hidden at all. Tell them to bring Lisa's music collection."

Evie smiled. "She figured that out earlier. She sent the twins over to her flat. They know her usual hiding places – if she has anything stashed away, they'll find it."

"You also said that Max was the code-maker," said Howard. "So what were you doing? I get the idea that you gathered the information and he encoded it. How would he do that?"

"I don't know." I thought about Sally's comment – about codes that didn't look like codes. I thought about hiding things in plain sight. And I thought about music. It was hiding in the back of my head. Something I'd heard recently about music...

But it was so hard to think straight. All I could think about was the phone on the desk, and Lisa - taken hostage because of me for the second time.

Natasha called in a few minutes later. She'd found Lisa's collection of cassette tapes and confirmed that Lisa only had a CD player. Most of them seemed to be homemade mix tapes. I asked her to bring them all back. There was a shout in the distance – Nicola had found something.

I sat waiting eagerly while Evie talked. "Really? That's what I thought... hidden at the back? Doesn't sound like it's for entertainment, then..."

"Well?"

Evie grinned as she hung up the phone. "The twins have found a tape player hidden in the bedroom. There's a hidden compartment at the back of the wardrobe... never mind. They're bringing it back."

"Why would she hide it?"

"It's not exactly your typical tape player," she said. "I haven't seen one of these in years, Rob – you can do all kinds of editing tricks with it. I didn't know Lisa still had it."

"They'll never be back with it in time," I said.

"No," she said. She was still grinning. "But suppose Max was preparing these tapes, and she needed this equipment to listen to them. Doesn't it follow that Max would need to have something similar?"

A tape editing suite? Hidden here in the flat? Was that possible?

"Do you have any idea where it could be, Rob?"

I shook my head. "I suppose we could try the wardrobe," I said.

With ten minutes to go until the phone rang, we started a search of the flat. There were no secret panels in the wardrobe that we could see, which would have been wonderfully convenient. Judy, Evie, Howard and I each took a separate room and conducted a search, looking for hollow spaces, loose floorboards, secret nooks and crannies... I had no idea what I was supposed to look for, though Evie told me that a well hidden secret compartment could look like anything and fool anyone. She knew of professional hiding places that were found in minutes and quick, dirty jobs that were missed by police raids. All bets were off.

Given the time available, we made a good effort. Well, the others did. I was just playing along. But we didn't find anything. Evie told me about things to watch for, like "tells" – such as scratches on the floor where heavy furniture was routinely moved – but I didn't spot anything obvious.

Five minutes to go, and we reconvened in the hallway. "Let's swap rooms," said Evie. "One of us might have missed something."

I stepped into the living room, and the first thing to attract my attention was Max's music. Surely, I thought, any tape recording equipment would be round there?

There was nothing behind the CD rack. I pulled the bookcase away from the wall, but there was nothing there but solid plaster. I checked the floor for loose boards, but everything seemed solid. I tapped the walls, and no hollow echoes came back. Always my eyes were drawn back to Max's corner.

"He wrote music," I said to myself. "How did he record it?"

A truly professional musician might compose in his study, I thought to myself, but he'd record in a proper studio. Not here, with all those distractions and background noises. But you couldn't use a proper studio for recording secret messages. Not unless you had it to yourself...

Howard entered.

"I was just wondering. Do you have an attic here?"

I shook my head. "I don't think so."

"Oh well. It was an idea."

"It's a good one," I said.

And then it hit me.

It was used for research as well as therapy. He was trying to combine music together, use editing tricks, that sort of thing.

"Damn," I said. "He showed it to me. The bastard actually showed me it – does he even know himself?"

"Know what?" asked Howard.

"Max's studio. Hidden in plain sight. It's at the clinic. It was there all the time. Hawkins showed me it on his tour – it's supposed to be a music therapy room. It's a lot more than that – it's a complete recording studio."

Howard was about to reply when the telephone rang.

We were so close, but we were out of time.

The Call

And that was it. The last tape. The story ended there. Was he supposed to wait for more tapes, back at the office? He'd hoped to receive more before he printed the last of the story so far, but Dr Hawkins had put an end to that anyway.

But it didn't matter now. All that mattered was finding Eddie. It was time to visit the police, like he should have done in the first place.

As he was heading out of the door, his mobile rang.

"Henry Ford?"

"Yeah," he replied. "Who is this?"

"My name is Max."

"Max? From the story?"

"The Amnesia Project – yes. But that doesn't matter right now. I"ll get right to the point – Eddie is fine."

Henry felt a huge weight fall from his chest. "He's okay? You've got him?"

"We have. He's been staying with us while we checked you both out. I'm sorry for worrying you. I only found him this morning myself, sleeping on our sofa. Rob hadn't mentioned we had a guest, or I'd have been in touch sooner."

"Can I see him? Are you going to let him go?"

"Of course. Go to the Cruise Liner – I'll meet you there in an hour. Gaz will let you in."

"One hour. Thanks. I'll see you soon."

The street was starting to grow busy with tourists and shoppers as Henry arrived at the bar. Gaz opened the door, a little reluctantly.

"Hello again, Henry. Max said you'd be back. Come on in."

"I hope I haven't caused you too much trouble."

"None at all. It's just... Rob and Max are very... careful about who they want to find them."

"But they've decided I'm safe," said Henry. "Is Max here?"

"I'm here." Max raised a pint glass at a corner table – the same one Henry had been sitting at last night – and Henry went over to him.

"Hi there. Nice to meet you at last," said Max. "Sorry about all the cloak and dagger stuff – we needed to check you out."

"Where's Eddie?"

"Eddie's fine. He's back with Rob and Lisa - he was asking some rather direct questions and we wanted to make sure he was on the level."

"Take me to him. Right now, or I call the police."

"Hey, calm down. I was going to do just that. It's just..." Max paused, taking a long swig on his pint. "I wanted to talk you through a few things first. Rob is... well, he's been through a lot. I want you to understand him a little before you meet him."

"If he's hurt Eddie..."

Max's eyes widened. "He never would. Rob's harmless. It's him I'm worried about. I don't want you upsetting things. It's taken a long time for Rob to settle down. And now all this trouble is starting up again..."

Henry sat down. "Fine. Talk. But I don't care what you say - I'm worried about Eddie, and I won't be happy until I see him."

"Eddie is fine, I told you. Lisa's there, and she'll look after him. I called her as soon as I found Eddie this morning. I'll keep this short. Look, you've heard the tapes, right?"

"Yes."

"Well, there's no point me telling it all again. So how about you ask me your questions and I try to answer them?"

Henry nodded. "Alright. How much of it is true?"

Max smiled. "Does it matter? You can confirm some of it for yourself – Grace Meadows, the explosion, and there was plenty of tabloid gossip about the director's alleged drugs and guns. Even Mrs Griffin is real. Nice lady. Hard to talk to. But it's Rob's story, not mine. You'll have to ask him."

"What can you tell me about Rob?"

Max's cheerful expression faltered. "I do love him, you know," he said. "Maybe things would be easier if I didn't. But there it is."

He looked down at the table, one finger tracing the damp ring left by his glass. Henry waited, giving him time to find the words he needed.

"There's a lot I can't tell you," said Max, finally. "But I think I should tell you this. Life has been hard on him. It's been hard on both of us, but worse for him. I met him through the clinic, you know. I think we were both a bit lost, and we found each other. We needed each other. Then I lost him, and it's taken us a while to find each other again. I don't know whether you can understand that."

Henry thought about Eddie. Life had been hard on him, too.

"Henry, I want you to know – Rob's a good man. He might not be quite what you expect, but he'd never want to hurt anyone."

"Not what I expect?"

Max smiled again. "Well... maybe some of his story was a *little* exaggerated. You'll have to decide that for yourself. Or your readers will."

"What about Lisa? How does she fit into all this?"

"The lovely Lisa... Rob met her first," said Max. "She was fishing for a story, and she found Rob, and he introduced her to me. She's been a close friend ever since - we've stayed in touch for all these years, because I don't think anyone else understands our situation like she does. She's an angel, Henry. Rob has... dark days, sometimes. And lately he's had more than usual."

"Why?"

"All this business with the Amnesia Project. Ten years ago, when it was all still quite fresh, Rob was obsessed with discovering the project data. Said he wanted to finish the work, find a way to reverse the effect. It was all he wanted to do for months. Then, after a while, he settled down. We made a new life for each other, just the two of us. I work in a local pharmacy now. Not quite as groundbreaking as working in medical research, but it brings home enough for us to live on. And then, about six months ago, it all kicked off again. He dug out his old notes, started up the project again."

"Something set him off?" asked Henry.

"Yeah. He saw someone he recognised - our old friend, Dr Hawkins. I think he's been looking for Rob. That's why we're hiding out here in the middle of nowhere, so he can't find us."

"If you didn't want anyone to find you," asked Henry, "why did you send the tapes?"

"It was Rob's idea. You might call it insurance." Max paused. "The story was known to virtually no-one. If something were to happen to the three of us, Dr Hawkins and his employers would get away with it all, and probably start up again somewhere else. If it's out there, people will know what happened."

"So why send it to me?"

"Lisa's a journalist too, you know. Freelance. She's got a lot of contacts, knows a lot of press people. She said she could get it picked up." Max sighed. "We tried that early on. If we sent it somewhere big they'd throw it straight out. It's too fantastic. So we looked for somewhere small, somewhere that might print it as fiction - or as a raving conspiracy theory, we didn't care. It would be out there. Someone would see it. We sent it to about sixteen papers and magazines in the end. None of them printed it."

"And this time?"

"We sent it to you. Lisa said you wouldn't be able to resist it. Looks like she was right. Did anyone see it? Why did you stop printing it?"

"Someone saw it, alright. I got a visit from a Dr Edmunds."

Max frowned. "Can't say I know that name. But I can guess who might be using it."

"He said you'd stolen his story, threatened a legal case, then paid me off. I didn't entirely believe him, but the magazine is dying on me. I needed the money. And I wanted to find out the truth." Henry paused. "Nowhere else printed it? Perhaps we're not the only ones he paid off."

"Perhaps not. But none of the others found us. I'm impressed. Or perhaps I should be ashamed. I'm not exactly an expert at this covert stuff. What did we do that led you here?"

"The envelope. You'd received some specialist electronics in it and I asked the company who ordered them. Led me straight to the bar."

"Damn. You sure you're not a detective?"

"No, just a determined journalist." Henry asked his last question. "What are you going to do now?"

"I don't really know. I've told Rob before that we can't keep hiding away with our little experiments. Given how easily you two found us, I dread to think how fast the good doctor would track us down. The project has to end, or we'll never have any peace. Maybe you can convince him."

And, thought Henry, get Eddie away from all this madness.

Max led Henry to his car, a pale grey hatchback parked on a side street a few minutes away. They were soon heading north on the main road, leaving the crowded streets of Brighton behind.

"Welcome to Falmer," said Max. "Not much to say about it, really. The big selling point here is the university, which we've taken advantage of a few times for our experiments."

"Experiments?" asked Henry. "You're building a new machine?"

"Building? We've built it. It's not as big or impressive as the prototype was, but we're working on a budget here. Rob is still trying to get it to restore memories, but I'm not sure that's going to be possible. Still, you never know."

"The university are funding you?" asked Henry.

"No. We're on our own. But nobody misses the odd student."

Henry blinked in horror.

"I'm kidding! There's no way we'd try this stuff on people. Not yet, anyway. No, we take advantage of the facilities. A few people on the inside, blackmail photos of the faculty, that sort of thing."

Henry remained horrified.

"One of us needs a better sense of humour," said Max. "I'm not sure which."

Henry said nothing.

"You don't talk much, do you?"

"Normally I do," said Henry. "When I get the chance."

"Oh, I get it." Max grinned. "You're doing a journalist thing on me. Keeping quiet so I keep blabbing. I know all the tricks. I studied psychology. Or did I?"

Henry laughed.

"That's better! I was starting to worry about you. Lisa's always telling me to shut up. She once said she'd like to put me and Judy in a room together and see whose ears started bleeding first. Anyway, this is it – home sweet home. And lab sweet lab. And sometimes we hold raves for the students. That's how we grab our specimens."

"Uh... you're kidding, right?"

Max grinned again. "You're learning."

Home sweet home was a three-bedroom farmhouse a couple of miles from the university. Trees lined the road, hiding it from view, and the small turn off the main road that was the main drive was barely noticeable unless you were looking for it.

"You really are hiding," commented Henry. "You built a machine out here?"

"No neighbours to complain about the noise," laughed Max. "As for the machine – we designed it and assembled it here, we didn't make it from scratch." He brought the car to a stop at the end of the drive. "Shall we go in?"

They walked up the front path, and Max knocked on the door. A moment later it was opened by a young woman holding a spray can in a menacing fashion.

"Here he is, Lisa. This is Henry Ford."

"Hey, Henry. It must be... what, five years now? How's George?"

Henry shook his head. "George is dead," he said. "About a year ago now. Car accident." He studied Lisa carefully. "I'm sorry, but I don't remember you."

She put the spray can down on a side table. Rather than the can of mace he was expecting, it turned out to be furniture polish. "Best I could find," she shrugged. "Well, it was a long time ago. And I wasn't called Lisa Smith then. We met at a press convention in... was it Sheffield?"

"Birmingham, I think. Did you write that piece for us about the explosion in the chip shop?"

"That's right!" laughed Lisa. "Come on in, Henry. There's someone here who's eager to meet you."

Henry had barely closed the door behind him when Eddie came barrelling out of the living room.

"BOSS!!"

It wasn't so much a hug as a rugby tackle. Henry grabbed the banister to avoid falling over.

"Boss! You're here!"

"Hey, Eddie. Good to see you, too. Could you let go now, please?"

Eddie carefully let go again. "Sorry, boss. But it's, I mean, I'm, it's... wow!"

Now released from Eddie's iron grip, Henry took a deep breath. "Yes, it's definitely wow. So this is Lisa, and Max. Where's Rob?"

"Down in the basement, as usual," replied Lisa. "I'll go tell him you're here. He'll want to meet you, Henry."

"Looks like I'm on tea duty," said Max. "Milk, sugar?"

"Yes, and one spoon," replied Henry.

"One spoon of milk. Sugar, darling?"

Henry paused. "Uh... what?"

Max laughed. "Still not got that sense of humour working, eh? Mine or yours, I'm not sure. One of us is broken, anyway. One sugar and milk. What about you, Eddie? You want in on the tea?"

"Yeah. Four sugars, please."

"Four! That's twelve more than last time!"

Eddie giggled.

"See, Henry? Eddie gets my jokes. Then again, maybe that's not a good sign. Eddie, why did the chicken cross the road? Half past two!"

Eddie's giggles grew deeper.

"That one didn't even make sense! You'll laugh at anything, kiddo. How about this one...?"

"Max!" Lisa's voice echoed out from down below. "Go and make the bloody tea!"

"Oops. The mistress has spoken." Max dashed off to the kitchen. "Make yourselves at home, Henry. Eddie will show you round."

"Thanks, but I'd rather know more about the story. The last tape ended rather suddenly – what happened?"

"Probably best to let Lisa tell you that," said Max.

Lisa returned from the basement. "He's in the middle of tinkering with something at the moment," she said. "Best wait a few minutes. He doesn't like being distracted. He finds it hard to remember where he was."

Henry nodded. "Of course. Lisa, what happened to you after the kidnap? The last tape ended a little suddenly."

"Oh, you mean the part where I was hauled off to the clinic? Yes, we still haven't recorded the rest of the story. Rob's been a bit distracted lately. To be honest, I wasn't sure you'd pay any attention to the ones we did send. Looks like my plan worked."

"Plan?"

"Using tapes. I knew that would be too weird to ignore. If I'd sent you a CD or a memory stick, or just a bunch of paper, would you have paid it any attention?"

Henry shrugged. He decided not to mention that he'd probably have printed a shopping list by this stage. "Maybe. Who else did you try?"

"We sent copies out to several major papers all those years ago, but none of them were interested. This time, it was just you. One last try."

"I'm honoured. So what happened?"

Lisa's Story

I know Rob doesn't mean it that way, but you'd think from all this that I'm rather partial to being kidnapped. I mean, twice in two days! I'm not suggesting I get off on it – the only Stockholm Syndrome I've ever come down with was a cold during a conference in Sweden.

Not all journalists get routinely kidnapped. I'm special like that, given my fondness for Evie's gang's antics. Seriously, that Glasgow chip shop incident was one of the oddest experiences of my life – not that I can tell you much about it. There are so many stories I could tell that would win me the Pulitzer – but that I can never tell anyone, for Evie's sake... or, sometimes, for the sake of those we help.

Even so, two kidnappings in such rapid succession is not normal, even for me.

After Rob and Howard went out to do their *Mission: Impossible* raid on the police station, we were left a bit at a loose end. There were plenty of us to guard Kensington and, in hindsight, if we'd all stayed put then we wouldn't have ended up in the mess we did. And Sam might still be here.

Guard duty is exciting at first. You've got unknown assailants waiting to pounce when you're not looking, so at first everyone's watchful and alert. But after a while, it gets increasingly dull. You're stuck indoors, nothing happens and you can't do anything without someone else covering for you. It's not so bad when there's a group of you as you can entertain each other, but cabin fever sets in eventually.

All we could do was wait, and think. And I kept thinking about what Rob had said. He was right. My life didn't make sense. I was a journalist with no computer, had a CD player and no CDs, and I realised I had no books either. Where were my notebooks? My novels? I had very few electronics. I remembered my rape alarm and the mace, both of which I'd picked up from Evie in the couple of days before I met

Rob. I used to have more in my flat, I know I did, and they were conspicuously absent. Or at least, they were now. Until that moment they'd just been absent – I hadn't missed them at all.

I remembered him saying I should investigate it like a journalist. So I put my own thoughts aside, and looked at my flat like it was a crime scene. What was the story? Virtually no electronics. No books. No discs... it all seemed very familiar. Then I realised – if the police thought you had illegal data, they'd take everything that might hold it. Cameras, MP3 players, computers, CDs, memory sticks. They wouldn't take notebooks, would they? They might.

That was the moment I first started to figure out what had happened – to the flat, and to me. But I had to be sure.

"Natasha, Nicola," I called out. "I have a job for you. I want you to drive up to my flat in Reading…"

For some reason, I didn't want to go myself. I felt I was needed here, though mostly I think I was just worried about Rob. Besides, the twins were much better at searching than I was. They'd spot anything out of place. More than I would, certainly – I'd been living there at least a week without realising anything was even wrong.

My telephone rang some time after they'd gone, and at first I thought it would be Rob. It wasn't – it was a voice I had trouble placing at first.

"*Hello?*" he said. "*Can you help me?*"

"Who is this?" I asked.

"*I'm in trouble. I've escaped, but they're after me. Can you pick me up?*"

"Who is this?" I repeated. But then I realised. "Max?"

Max gave an address, which I scribbled down on the notepad by the phone. "*Please come and get me.*"

He hung up before I could reply.

"Did you say Max?" asked Judy.

"He escaped?" asked Evie.

"It seems a bit... convenient," muttered Sam. "He just happens to escape and get in touch?"

"Rob managed it," I said. "Twice."

Even so, something seemed off about it all. Max had sounded weird, though I couldn't explain how.

"Evie, we can't let Max down," I said. "If it is him, we need to bring him back."

"I agree," said Evie. "But Lisa, you stay here – let Judy go. This sounds like a trap to me."

Judy nodded. "I'll get him, Evie. If he's there, I'll get him. What does he look like? Can you describe him?"

"Better than that," I said. "I can give you a picture." I found the paperwork that Rob had liberated from the clinic and fished out Max's photo.

"Thanks." Judy set off, leaving Evie, Sam and me alone in the flat. Well, alone apart from Sally, still bound to a chair in the kitchen.

"We should set a rota," said Evie. "One of us should keep an eye on our guest at all times."

"I'll go first," I said.

"Fine. Sam, you take over in an hour." Evie smiled. "Now, who wants some more tea? Don't mind me, dear, I'll just work around you."

"What are you going to do with me?"

I'd drifted away into my own thoughts, and jumped to attention a little too quickly.

"I'm sorry," Sally continued. "Did I startle you?" Her voice was entirely calm, as though being tied up and held prisoner was a daily occurrence and she was just passing the time.

"No," I lied. "What did you say?"

"What are you going to do?"

I thought for a moment. What were we going to do? We could hardly let her go – she knew who we were, where we were and what we knew. We couldn't kill her and we couldn't keep her here indefinitely either.

"I thought not. You don't know, do you?"

"Shut up," I hissed. I understood now why Rob had been so nervous about the interrogation. Sally was sly. She knew how to get inside your head and manipulate your thoughts. "That's up to Evie."

"Your fearless leader, yes. She with the knitting and the endless tea."

"You think that's what Evie's like? She's..." I paused. "No, you don't think that at all. You're trying to trip me up."

Sally smiled.

"You're quite right," she said. "It's difficult to trick a trickster. Poor Robert. You tried to take advantage, didn't you? A handsome young man with no memory."

I couldn't see it, but I could feel the blush spreading up my face. Sally chuckled.

"One more word out of you..." I growled.

Sally raised one sardonic eyebrow. She didn't speak, but I could hear her thinking: *Or what?*

"I'm not listening to any more of this – either you shut up, or I gag you again."

Sally said nothing, but there was a smile on her lips and laughter in her eyes.

Sam came in to check on me a few minutes later. He didn't say anything, but I got the impression he wanted to know I was alright. Sally hadn't said a word since I'd threatened the gag, and didn't say another until the raid, but I could feel her thinking up catty one-liners and psychological assaults. It didn't occur to me until later that she was deliberately using the silent treatment to rattle me.

"Hey Lisa," said Sam. "How's the evil mastermind doing?"

"Ugh, don't," I groaned. "I'd rather be babysitting."

"That bad, huh?"

"Sam, could you do me a favour? The batteries have about had it in my Dictaphone. I don't suppose you have any spares in your bag of tricks, have you?" Sam generally kept all kinds of knickknacks amongst his tools — sometimes he'd need to put together something in a hurry. Like, say, a detonator.

"I'll take a look," he said. "Give it here — I'll see if I have anything that'll fit. Planning on another interrogation?"

"Not right now. Planning an article for a magazine. Might as well do something useful while I'm standing guard."

"Try not to murder our prisoner while I'm gone," he said, heading for the door.

I smiled. "No promises."

Sam left, closing the door behind him. A few minutes later, all hell broke loose.

It started with a knock at the door. At first, I thought it was Judy — we only had one key to the flat, and Rob had it; the only other key had been in Jimmy's possession. I heard Evie get up to answer it.

I soon realised it wasn't Judy. I heard two male voices, spinning some tale about checking the gas meter by the sound of it. Evie wasn't convinced. I heard her raised voice telling them to get out or she'd call the police.

I glanced at Sally. She didn't say a word, but she was smiling.

"Evie!" That was Sam, coming to the rescue. With two men up against our chemistry graduate and an old lady, I knew they'd need backup. I fished in my handbag for my spray can. I wasn't going out there unarmed.

"I thought you said they'd all gone?" One of the men.

"Never mind that! Do something about this old bitch!" That was the other one. I heard a lot of scuffling, and what sounded like Evie hitting him with something metallic. When I stepped out later, I discovered it was a tea tray.

Evie screamed.

"Get away from her, you bastards!" Sam leaping to the attack with his own spray can. One of the two men cried out, and there was a thump as Sam was thrown to the floor.

"The bastard! He maced me!"

"Good," I said to myself. I opened the door, but carefully, not wanting them to see our captive. "Evie! Are you okay?" I called out. "What's going on?"

I looked into a thick-set, rather ugly face; one I hope I never see again. "Hello there," he growled. "Reckon we could have some fun with this one."

I held up my spray can and tried not to let my trembling knees give away how scared I was.

"Now, you know what he'd say about that," said his colleague, stood over Evie. She was slumped awkwardly against the wall and she wasn't moving. I hoped she was okay. "Touch her and you'll wake up thinking you're a chicken or something."

That told me who'd sent the goons, at least. I briefly imagined Dr Hawkins telling these uglies to cluck like chickens, as though he were a stage hypnotist. It actually made me feel a little better.

"Ah, nuts to it," Heavy #1 said, kneeling beside Sam. "Now, miss, we can do this the easy way or the hard way. Drop the mace."

He held a vicious blade against Sam's neck.

"Drop the mace, or I slit his throat."

I dropped my unused can.

"Good girl. Now, where's Sally Kensington?"

"She's in the kitchen," I said. "Just don't hurt them."

Heavy #1 left Sam on the floor, still winded, and shoved past me into the kitchen. He used his knife to cut Sally free and then led her back out.

"Thank you for your help," she said. "What are you going to do with them?"

"Leave them," replied the heavy. "They're not important. But the young lady comes with us."

My arms were pulled behind my back and I felt a set of handcuffs click onto my wrists – they'd come prepared.

"Oh, and leave her mobile here. We'll need to call Mr Walker later."

Heavy #2 snatched my handbag from me, rummaging carelessly through in search of my mobile phone. He threw several items onto the floor in his search and then found it tucked into the side pocket.

"I could have got that for you," I commented.

"There's plenty you can do for me later," he smirked.

I considered a swift knee to the groin, but thought better of it.

Heavy #2 went over to the window. "I think we've got company," he said.

"Down the back stairs," replied Heavy #1. "We don't want to attract undue attention."

I was half walked, half dragged out of the flat and down the fire escape stairs, leaving poor Evie and Sam injured and alone. There was nothing I could do. I was led out the back, across a communal garden and towards a black car parked just outside it.

"Where are we going?" asked Sally.

"Back to the clinic," replied Heavy #1. "Someone wants to meet you. Both of you."

Sally was led by Heavy #2 towards a red Ford parked further down, while Heavy #1 took me to the black car. I noticed it had tinted windows. There would be no attracting anyone's attention once I was in there.

"Hey!"

I turned my head to see Sam running towards us. Heavy #2 leapt into action, landing a heavy blow to Sam's stomach. He gasped, sinking to the floor.

"How much does he know?".

"I don't know," Sally replied.

"We can't take the risk," said Heavy #1. "Kill him."

I saw the flash of a knife blade, and then turned away. I couldn't watch. I felt a brief twinge of pity for Sally when I noticed she couldn't watch either. But it was very brief.

I don't remember the journey. I was numb with shock. All that kept playing over and over in my mind was that flashing knife blade. I'd try to think of a way out, try to plan an escape, but every time I tried I just kept thinking that Sam was dead. And Evie – was she dead too? I didn't know. I hadn't liked the way she was slumped over like that.

It wasn't until the car stopped that I realised where they were taking me. I'd been scared before, at the warehouse – a remote location, little chance of rescue – but I'd been able to tell myself that they wouldn't harm me, that they needed me alive and well. Here, that wasn't true at all. Here they could do anything they liked, and with a simple procedure they could make it seem like none of it had ever happened at all.

They'd brought me to Grace Meadows.

"Okay, get out."

They held the door open for me as I climbed out of the back. My legs turned to jelly beneath me and I wobbled on uncertain feet as I stood up. The second man had to support me as we walked to the door.

It was perfect for them. An infirm young lady being brought into the psychiatric unit – I could yell for help and no-one would pay any attention, unless you counted the orderlies and their shots to help calm me down. I could do nothing but wait. Wait and hope.

The reception area was quiet. A couple of outpatients sat waiting for their appointments – despite everything they did, Grace Meadows still had to at least pretend to be a normal clinic – and the man at the front desk barely looked up as we came in.

"Hey, Pete," said one of the heavies. "This is Miss Smith. Dr Hawkins is expecting us."

Pete looked up. "Oh, hi Phil. Sure, I'll just buzz him for you." He pushed a button on the telephone and a moment later I heard his voice... the mad doctor.

"Hello?"

"Dr Hawkins, Miss Smith is here for you."

"Miss Smith?"

"Lisa," whispered Phil. "Lisa Smith."

"Miss Lisa Smith, sir. I'm told you're expecting her?"

"Lisa! Ah yes. I'll send someone to collect her."

And so we waited. It seemed both forever and no time at all. I could only hope that Rob and Evie would be able to rescue me. I'd been in prisons before – on both sides of the bars – and this was much, much worse.

The door opened, and a heavily built man in a slightly off-white orderly outfit stepped out. His nose had been broken at least once and wasn't quite set properly, which gave his voice a slightly bunged up sound on the rare occasions he spoke.

"Here for Lisa," he snorted.

"She's right here," replied Phil.

The orderly simply shrugged and led us all inside.

The door closed behind us, and locked with a solemn click. I tried to recall what Rob had said about his escape, but I couldn't think straight. There was a word, I remembered that much, but in my panic I had no idea what it could be.

We headed into the depths of the clinic, our footsteps swallowed by the softly carpeted floors. I'd half expected the screams of the insane, not this eerie quiet. Screaming would have made me feel better. I felt as though I was the only person here. Our guide, who I mentally named Igor, eventually led us to Dr Hawkins' office. The plush one, not the basement one – I briefly wondered what it said about the man's state of mind that he had two offices in two very different styles.

The door opened, and I saw Dr Hawkins himself sat across the desk.

"Ah, Miss Smith. So nice of you to come."

To my surprise, Dr Hawkins was a polite and charming host. I was offered a drink, asked if I had been harmed and he generally tried to put me at ease. If I didn't already know about the things he'd done, I might have relaxed my guard. As it was I found myself starting to doubt what I knew. How could this man possibly be involved with such inhuman experiments?

The first thing he did was order my handcuffs removed and my escorts outside. "I hardly think she's going to escape," he said. "Please wait outside the door while we have a little chat."

I looked around, and noticed Igor still stood in the corner. Escape was unlikely. I'd have thought twice even if I still had my bag – Sam's chemical spray wasn't the only toy I had to play with – but they'd taken it from me back in the flat.

"Now, my dear lady," said Dr Hawkins. "Please, tell me – how is young Robert getting on?"

"He'll be here to get me soon enough," I replied. I tried to sound brave, but I'm not sure I succeeded. "You can ask him yourself."

Dr Hawkins smiled. "I expect so," he said. The bastard was humouring me!

"He's not alone," I said. "He'll be bringing the police along with him."

"Oh, I doubt that very much." Dr Hawkins continued to smile, as though he'd thought of a very funny joke and was keeping it to himself. I had the nasty thought I was the joke. "I suspect, if Mr Walker attempts to contact the police, they'll be all too glad to see him again. And I doubt they'll be very interested in his stories."

"The police take kidnapping and murder very seriously," I replied.

"They take *evidence* very seriously, Miss Smith, and I've made sure they'll have plenty of that. I had originally intended it for whoever Mr Walker and his colleagues were working for, but your friends will take the fall quite nicely. But I was hoping to discuss a different topic. What is your opinion of our mutual acquaintance, Ms Kensington?"

"Never mind that bitch!"

"Yes, she does tend to leave a bad first impression. Still, she is useful for some things. Such as kidnapping and murder, as you say. That really wouldn't sit well with the head of a high profile research clinic like Grace Meadows, would it?" He chuckled. "But, between you and me, I don't particularly like her either."

"What are you going to do with me?" I asked.

"If Mr Walker does as he's told, nothing," he said. Something about his eyes told me he was lying. "We'll let you go back to your normal life, or as normal as it can be when you're part of a ragtag gang of thieves and bandits. Yes, we know all about them. Ms Kensington was a little reluctant to explain how she lost you the first time, but I am assured it won't happen again."

"Rob escaped," I said. "So can I."

"Robert was... allowed to escape," said Dr Hawkins. "We could have stopped him several times, but we wanted him to leave. It was clear when he was our... guest... that he did not have any information on the Project. I hoped that by letting him go he might find it for us."

"You want information on the Amnesia Project?" I was stunned. "I thought you developed it?"

"I did." Dr Hawkins frowned. "I see no harm in telling you this, Miss Smith, as you will not be able to make use of it. During their employment here, Robert, Max and Damian managed to steal a large quantity of research data. They were subtle at first, taking copies of important papers and so on. Once I realised what was going on, they were rather more... overt. Computers were wrecked, papers shredded or burned, backups destroyed. It will take years of research to regain what we have lost - time we do not have. Ms Kensington told you we have a deadline, I believe?"

"She did."

"But do you know why?"

I shook my head.

"We have a special visitor coming here in a few weeks. Very special. You see, Miss Smith, this clinic doesn't just create mind-altering devices. We really do help sick people. It's all I ever wanted to do, once. Before I discovered how life really works. Do you know why our VIP is coming here? The press will say it is because of our work in researching dementia. In truth, we paid them to come."

A special visitor... a VIP? I started picturing one of the royal family cutting a ribbon, or the Prime Minister, and then being strapped into that chair. "Who's coming?"

"That's not your concern. What matters is that we have a working prototype, but no idea how to fine tune it. We were lucky your friends didn't destroy the machine itself."

"Perhaps they tried," I said.

"Perhaps. In any event, they took some of the original data with them and, as far as I know, it is still out there. They would not reveal the location, even under threat of death. Robert would not talk even after his colleague was driven mad."

"Good for him."

"Not so good for you," said Dr Hawkins. "He simply watched Damian lose his mind, and I suspect he would also have said nothing when we turned Max into a virtual vegetable, had he been here to see it. Why would he now risk surrendering the project for you?"

"You don't know Rob at all."

"We shall see. Ms Kensington is arranging an exchange – the Project data for you. We'll soon see which of us has the clearer diagnosis."

He gestured to Igor. Our session was over. I was still buzzing with questions, and if... when Rob came for me, we'd want all the information we could get.

"Tell me one thing before you chuck me in one of your padded cells," I said. "Why is Sally working for you? Isn't she the one who put Rob and the others in here to spy on you?"

Dr Hawkins chuckled again. It was a chilling sound – as though he'd read about chuckles in books but didn't actually know what they were like. "You're quite right. Ms Kensington and I have... come to an arrangement," he said. "She doesn't care for her agents, just for the information they were sent for. I've offered to share it in exchange for her assistance. Goodbye, my dear."

Before I could respond, Igor took a rough grip of my arms and I was dragged out.

My cell wasn't padded. It was sparsely furnished, and what furnishings it did feature were cheap and not very sturdy. I studied the room for potential weapons, as Judy had taught me, but short of suffocating a guard with the single thin pillow on the bed I was out of options. The furniture was fixed to the floor. The bedding was thin and slightly stained.

It wasn't likely, I suppose. This place was designed to hold potentially dangerous patients; they'd hardly leave anything lethal lying around.

I tried to remember what Judy had taught me about unarmed combat. This didn't take long – her main message had been "avoid it wherever possible". I knew a few moves that could get me out of common holds and I had a better than average chance of avoiding a punch or kick, but I was under no illusions that I'd be able to Bruce Lee my way out of this place. The best thing I could do was wait.

I didn't need to wait long. Igor came for me about twenty minutes after my incarceration – they'd been kind (or forgetful) enough to leave me my watch – and took me back to Dr Hawkins' office.

Dr Hawkins sat behind his desk, his hands folded in front of him, silent and sinister. He was not alone.

"Hello, Lisa. I'm so glad you could join us."

"Sally Kensington. Let me guess - you want to make a deal."

"Something like that," she smiled. "We're just about to call on an old friend."

I was expecting her to use the big telephone on Dr Hawkins' desk, but that would have been foolish. Calls from there would be traceable. Instead, she used a cheap mobile phone that would presumably be destroyed once everything was over. She put it on speaker for our collective benefit.

"*Hello.*" That was Rob.

"Hello, Mr Walker."

"*Sally.*" Rob paused. "*I want to speak to Lisa.*"

"Lisa is fine," said Sally. "I have her right here. Say hello, Lisa."

"*Lisa? Are you okay?*"

"Hello Rob," I said. "I'm fine. I'm at–"

I felt Igor's hand over my mouth. "I'm sorry, Mr Walker," Kensington continued, "but that's all you're getting until we get the Project. Now listen carefully..."

"*No. You'll listen to me for a change.*"

The sudden edge to Rob's voice took me by surprise – in fact, it took everyone by surprise.

"*You see, I've been thinking about this. You've been bluffing me all this time with an empty hand. You want the Project, and only I can get it. You've got Lisa, but it's an empty threat – hurt her, and you've thrown away your only bargaining chip. I have no other family or friends for you to threaten. What I do have is the Project, a can of petrol, and a box of matches.*"

There was only stunned silence in reply.

"*Good. You haven't hung up yet, so you're still listening. Very good. These are my terms. Release Lisa. Give her a phone so she can call me when she's safe.*"

"You can do that one right now," I said, realising Igor's sweaty hoof had been removed from my face.

"*If I don't hear from Lisa in one hour, I'll hand details of your activities to the police, the major newspapers and every television and radio station I can think of. How long do you think you'll last when that investigation kicks off?*"

Sally floundered. "Mr Walker... Robert..."

"*You know I can't let you have the project, Sally. I intend to destroy it. Release*

Lisa, or face the consequences."

Sally fumbled the phone, dropping it on the desk.

"*You have one hour.*"

Without waiting for a response, Rob ended the call.

There was silence for a moment.

Dr Hawkins broke it first. "I am deeply disappointed, Ms Kensington."

"He can't... he won't..."

"He can and very likely will. I know him better than he knows himself." Dr Hawkins picked up his desk telephone. "Hello, Sandra. Please send in a couple of orderlies. Thank you."

"You're going to let her go?" asked Kensington.

Dr Hawkins chuckled. "Good gracious, no," he replied. My heart sank. "I intend our guest to remain with us for a little longer. My dear Miss Smith, I must show you our prototype. I'd be delighted to provide you with a demonstration, but we'll need a little time to set it up."

"Don't hurry on my account," I said.

I was dragged back to my cell, and left to stew a while longer. Elsewhere in the clinic, the machine was being made ready and the chemical cocktail that accompanied it being prepared. I know a lot more about the process now than I did then. At the time, all I knew was the waiting.

Dr Hawkins and the two orderlies from earlier returned a short time later and between the three of them I was bound and helpless in no time.

"I didn't think you used straitjackets here," I said.

Dr Hawkins gave his cold smile again. "Not usually, no," he admitted. "I am, however, a collector of relics from psychiatric history. It is good to know they still work so well today. Now do come along. I'm dying to show you what the Amnesia Project is all about. It's an unforgettable experience. Well, almost."

He led the way, and the orderlies dragged me along behind. I didn't particularly want to see the machine that poor Rob had been subjected to, but I didn't really have much choice.

I was shaking as we entered the basement. A small crowd was waiting for me; a collection of medical staff and orderlies, and a number of Hawkins' guards, all armed. He was clearly taking no chances. Sally Kensington stood beside the machine, studying it with interest and, I think, a slight revulsion.

"The machine itself works," said Dr Hawkins. "We have carried out a number of successful operations on a range of patients. But the results can be… unpredictable. Some subjects are only given temporary amnesia. Some forget too much. Some even go insane, like Damian did."

"So why do you need the project data?" I asked. I already knew the answer but the longer I could keep Dr Hawkins talking about his pet project, the longer I could keep my mind. Rob would come for me. I just had to buy him time.

"The machine is quite simple, but the human brain is not," Hawkins explained. "We are working in the dark. The project includes details of every test we ever carried out, experiments on different parts of the brain, different anaesthesia… enough to improve our success rate enormously."

"And you're on a deadline," I said.

"Yes. Our humble clinic is being visited by a very important person, as I said earlier. I suspect their interest in us is purely for their own publicity, but my employers are keen that they leave with some… new ideas. However, to do so with an uncalibrated machine... no, the risk is too high."

"Rob will never give you the Project," I said.

"I fear you are right. But it doesn't matter either way. We're halfway towards rediscovering what was lost, thanks to repeated experiments on our control subject."

"Control subject...? Max!"

"Correct." Dr Hawkins smiled. "The risk of failure is still rather high, but better than the risk I face by *not* carrying out the procedure. Of course, we can always use more test subjects."

I was prepared to die. I was willing to accept pain. I had faced both pain and death more than once before, and through luck and the help of my friends I'd beaten them both. But this was different. I was terrified of losing my own identity. And, worse, of betraying those same friends.

"Dr Bradshaw," said Hawkins. "Shall we commence?"

From Rob's tale of his escape earlier, I'd felt almost sorry for Dr Bradshaw. I'd felt he was a genuine doctor trying his best to help sick people. Finding him in this torture chamber changed my opinion of him. Perhaps I'm being unfair. Rob and Max were involved in this project too and I never questioned their intentions. But as he nodded and held up the syringe, I hated him. I braced myself for the needle.

But, it turned out, it wasn't for me.

"Secure her," said Hawkins. Two orderlies seized Sally by the arms and placed her in the chair, tying the straps around her wrists and ankles.

"Hawkins! What are you doing?!"

"Following orders, Ms Kensington. You've attempted to steal my research and sabotage my efforts. Your agents have set back the project by years and all your efforts to recover the information have been disastrous. My employers have been in touch, and they are far from happy."

"Give me another chance!" shouted Sally. "I just need more time!"

"Time we don't have. Our best hope now is to get some more experimental data, and that means fresh test subjects." Dr Hawkins smiled. "I'm giving you the project, just as you asked."

Kensington screamed. No, that's not right. As they fitted the cap to her head, she *shrieked*. It was piercing. I saw half the staff flinch, and I certainly did, but not Hawkins. He didn't move a muscle.

"Dr Bradshaw, administer the compound."

Dr Bradshaw stared at the needle in his hands as though he'd forgotten what it was.

"Dr Bradshaw!"

Bradshaw came back to reality. He rolled back Sally's sleeve and injected the contents of the syringe into her arm. I can remember every detail with horrible accuracy. I could almost count the beads of sweat forming on her forehead.

She screamed again, though not as sharply, and Dr Hawkins barked out orders to the staff to start the machine. I didn't understand the medical or technical terms like Rob might, and I still don't. All I know was that the body in the chair convulsed every time they activated that machine. All I could hear were the screams. I still wake up hearing those screams some nights.

"Kensington. Sally Kensington. Can you hear me?"

She looked up slowly, her eyes bleary. "Mm?"

"Listen to me, Sally. I am Dr Hawkins. I am your friend. You will trust me and obey me. Repeat these instructions."

"Doc' Hawkins. Frnd. Trust and obey." Sally's voice was slurred and indistinct, but even by the end of the final sentence it was starting to clear. Her eyes began to regain their focus.

"Right, get her out of there," said Hawkins. "Take the straitjacket off our other guest and get her ready."

I felt the orderlies removing the straps from my restraints. I might have felt relieved if I hadn't known what that meant - they could hardly sit me in the chair with my arms wrapped around me. I put up as much of a struggle as I could, but it was no use.

"Recalibrate the machine," said Hawkins. "And make sure the data from both procedures is copied to my office. We're running out of time."

As I was placed in the machine, I had a horrible sense of déjà vu. It all made sense now.

"To be honest, I just didn't think of it until I heard that tape."

"My laptop is being repaired." "What's the company called?" "I... can't remember."

"Max? ... Sorry, I was going to say something else. It's gone completely out of my head."

I'd been here before. The bastard had already taken my memories, and he was about to do it again. I could feel tears welling up, but I fought them back. Whoever I ended up as later, the woman I was now would go out with as much dignity as I could.

"Last chance, Miss Smith. I cannot guarantee you'll be able to tell me after the procedure. Where is the Project?"

I gritted my teeth. "Go to hell."

Dr Hawkins nodded. He'd expected nothing else from me.

Dr Bradshaw prepared another syringe. I felt his hand on my arm as he looked for a vein. I closed my eyes.

And then the fire alarm went off.

"A fire?" asked Dr Bradshaw. "Now?"

"No," said Hawkins. "It's him. Mr Walker has come to rescue his damsel in distress."

He dismissed the medical staff – if there really was a fire, they needed to get the patients out – and turned to me.

"I'm sorry, my dear," he said. "You'll have to wait a little longer. Please, just... sit tight." He chuckled briefly at his little joke.

It was at that point that my friends arrived at the clinic. And Hawkins had, regrettably for all of us, forgotten all about Sally Kensington.

The Machine

"I'll go and check on Rob again," said Lisa. "He must have finished tinkering by now."

Henry nodded. Eddie led him into the living room, where an old fabric sofa had apparently doubled as his assistant's bed.

"So what happened to you, Eddie?"

"I saw a man in the pub. I asked him about the Amnesia Project. That's what a journalist would do, isn't it? Talk to people?"

"That's right, Eddie. We go and talk to people. That's what a journalist does." While he'd been playing detective all this time instead. "So what happened then?"

"He asked where I'd heard of it. I said I worked for you on the magazine. He asked me to come with him. I was going to tell you but you were talking to the pub manager."

"You shouldn't have gone off by yourself, Eddie. It could have been dangerous."

"Sorry, boss. But he did say I wasn't to tell anyone about it. He said he had to find out who we were first."

"Tea up, boys." Max came back in with three mugs on a tray. There was a small plate of biscuits.

"No posh sugar lumps?" asked Henry.

Max looked blank for a moment. "Oh, you mean like Rob mentioned on the tape? That was pure Jimmy. Rob and I are happy with the cheap stuff. I guess he liked to show off. You ready to see… The Machine?"

He coughed gently. Eddie, remembering his cue, hummed a dramatic "dum dum duuuum."

"Picture that phrase with capital letters. The Machine – a bit ominous, a bit scary. It doesn't look very scary, so every little helps. Of course, Rob doesn't make it any easier. He's been thinking up dull acronyms. His favourite at the moment is ARM – the Amnesia Reversal Machine. I wanted to call it BEMUSE."

"What's that stand for?" asked Eddie, taking a biscuit from the plate.

"Nothing at the moment. I was hoping you might think of something."

Eddie giggled.

"Come on then," said Henry, taking a slurp of tea. "Let's go see this scary Machine."

They headed down into the basement. Henry half expected dark, damp stone, possibly with manacles for securing their victims. Instead it was brightly lit by fluorescent strip lights, with wooden flooring and mirrors along one wall. It was almost a disappointment.

"One of the things I was adamant on when we got this house," said Max. "We can't do mad scientist stuff in a back room. It has to be a basement. I think the previous owners used it as a private gym. They left an exercise bike behind when they moved – Rob used it for parts."

They emerged into the basement. A cluttered workbench occupied one end of the room, covered in tools, components and papers. An ancient desktop computer displayed a screensaver, whatever task it was performing long since completed.

"Um. Hey," said Rob. He was crouched behind a cobbled together collection of random parts surrounding an office chair and didn't look up as he spoke. "Welcome to the lab. This is the ARM – unless Max has thought up another name."

"I'm going with The Machine for now, Rob. Still working on BEMUSE."

Lisa emerged at the top of the basement stairs. "If you boys spent half as much time working on the thing as naming it..."

"I know, I know. We'd have cured world peace or something." Max grinned. "She's a right slave driver, this one. Just wait until you've gone, Eddie. She'll have us chained to the wall before you know it."

Eddie laughed.

"You see what I have to put up with? I wish we could wipe his memory of these terrible jokes at times." She paused. "No, I'm sorry. I don't mean that. I wanted to destroy the thing, not build a new one. But the boys had me outvoted."

"This is the machine?" asked Henry. "It's one of the… oddest things I've ever seen."

"W-well, I admit it's not a patch on the original," said Rob. He picked up a random piece of electronics and passed it distractedly between his hands. "I'm building this one out of scrap for the most part. We don't have private funding and a team of engineers like the first one had. But don't be fooled by its hokey charms. It's still lethal."

"Or it will be, if we ever get it to work," said Max.

"What happened, Rob?" asked Henry. "Max told me you'd abandoned the project. And now, ten years on, we get those tapes in the post and you're working on another amnesia machine."

"Well, at first I wanted to fix our memories. I didn't know whether it was even possible, and then we just got used to it. You know? Max and I had each other, and all the bad stuff just faded away. It didn't seem important any more." Rob looked down at his hands. "Then, about six months ago, I saw him again. Like he was looking for me."

"Dr Hawkins?"

"Yeah." Rob turned quiet, tinkering aimlessly with the settings on the exposed circuit boards of the machine. Henry had no idea what they were for. It all looked like junk to him.

When it became clear Rob wasn't going to say any more, Max took over. "We saw him in the town centre. I don't know whether he saw us; I don't think he did. Maybe it was just a coincidence."

"No." Rob shook his head. "He's looking for us. He wants the project back. That's why I had to start again. I have to find a way to reverse it."

"He saw the story in our magazine," said Henry. "He told us to stop printing it."

Rob glanced briefly over at Henry, then turned back to his work. "Are you going to?"

"I don't know," said Henry. It was probably best, he felt, not to mention his decision to close the magazine down. "But you haven't given us the rest of it yet."

"Please finish it," said Rob. "Whatever Hawkins said to you, please print the rest of the story. It needs to be out there."

Henry nodded. "One way or another, I'll get it in print." He turned to Lisa. "So what happened next? You were saying earlier that you were about to be put through the original machine when Rob turned up. What happened?"

"Well, I didn't know it was Rob at first. All I knew was that the fire alarm had gone off." Lisa smiled. "Rob, why don't you tell Henry what you were doing?"

Rob grinned, his nerves instantly disappearing. "This is the best part, Henry. This is where we rescue the damsel in distress."

Rob's Story

This is the part where the hero straps on his armour, draws his sword and mounts his trusty steed, ready to charge in and save the day. I've never even held a sword, I wouldn't know how to put on a suit of armour and horses make me nervous. I'm not your classical hero. Far from it.

While Lisa was being prepared for the demented creation of Dr Hawkins, I was a gibbering heap. I'd just shouted down a group of kidnappers with little more than bravado and bullshit, and for all I knew condemned Lisa to a slow and painful death, and I wasn't even entirely sure why I'd done it.

Actually, that's not entirely true. I was angry, and I was upset, and something in me just snapped. My closest friend had been forcibly taken, another friend had just been murdered and my only hope of escape from this nightmare could be hidden anywhere – if it existed at all. I have no idea whether the silence I got in response to my speech was from fear or astonishment. Maybe it was both.

"Rob... that was... bold."

Poor Howard was just as stunned as Lisa says her kidnappers were. "Bold"? "Reckless" would have been a better word.

"We have nothing to trade for her," I pointed out. "I think we're onto something here, but it could be nothing. For all I know, it could be Max's secret recipe for ginger biscuits."

"So what now? We wait for her to be released?"

I shook my head. "They won't release her. She's the only bargaining chip they have, and they know it as well as we do. It gives us a little more time, though."

"I hope you're right."

Nicola and Natasha returned about ten minutes later, with Lisa's tape collection and a somewhat complicated tape deck.

We didn't even look it. The news about Sam's death and Lisa's kidnap hit the twins as hard as it had hit the rest of the group – I didn't really know him, but the others had been working alongside him for years.

We all gathered in the living room. Evie made tea, purely to keep her hands busy; none of us really wanted any. It occurred to me that, in all their adventures together, this must be the first time they'd lost someone. For all their forward planning, they hadn't been prepared for it.

There was no time for grief now, however, even though the air was thick with it. Lisa needed them. I needed them.

"We have two things going for us," I said. "We know where Lisa is being held, and we have the element of surprise."

"We're also a man down," said Judy. "Without Sam, we're limited to what supplies we have on us. Don't go expecting me or Evie to knock up a bomb or something."

"I don't have a plan," I confessed. "I just want to go in, get Lisa, and get out."

"And Hawkins." Judy cracked her knuckles, loudly. "I want him. I want to have a little chat with him."

She started to sob. Howard put his hand on her shoulder, and she got herself under control.

"We can't risk a frontal assault," said Evie. "That place is a fortress. True, it's meant to keep people in, not out, but it's still a tall order."

"Then we'll have to be subtle," I said. "Howard, I want you to look into the plans. That place is a maze, and I want to know the fastest way to the cheese."

Howard nodded, and went over to his computer.

"Natasha, Nicola, you and Judy are on weapons. I want us all armed and ready with everything we can use. Don't skimp. We may need to use lethal force."

Evie shook her head. "We don't kill, Rob. Not unless we absolutely have to. Not even after... this."

"I know," I replied. "I hope it's not necessary. But I'd rather be prepared."

Evie nodded, and resumed staring at her unwanted cup of tea.

"Evie, I think I can get us in through the front door, unless they've changed the door codes. I don't think they'll have thought of that yet. But if I'm wrong... are you any good at electronic locks?"

"Not especially," she replied. "All those card scanners and whatnot. But Howard might be able to do something."

A plan was starting to form in the back of my mind. I could see the shape of it forming, but not the details. I had learned to let my ideas grow in the darkness and only emerge when they were ready.

"There are three parts to this rescue," I said. "We need to find a way in. I think I'm starting to see how. Once in, we need to find Lisa. And then we need to get out. That might not be as easy."

It was Judy who spoke next. "You're forgetting something, Rob," she said. "It's not just Lisa we're after. There's Max, and then there's the machine."

Max. Of course. I didn't remember him at all, but everything I'd learned suggested he was once important to me. Then there was the message he'd hidden – a message he'd risked a lot to leave me. I had to save Max too – not just for his sake, but because he might also be a key to recovering my own memory.

And the machine. Judy was right. That machine had to be destroyed. Without the notes from the Project, Hawkins and his team had virtually no idea how it worked, but eventually they'd figure it out. I had to stop that. I didn't want to think what such a device could do in the wrong hands.

"Getting in... Rob, that keycard you stole probably won't work, you know."

"I know that, Evie," I replied. "But it might – and I think I can get another. As long as the door code hasn't changed, I can get us in."

"Once we're in, we find Lisa, Max and the machine," said Judy. "They won't know we're coming. I hope."

"Judy, what do we have that could take out the machine?"

Judy thought for a moment. "Sam was the expert with explosives," she said. "I could probably find something in his stock, but I wouldn't know how much to use or what to do with it."

"Don't worry, dear," said Evie. "I've used a few explosives in my time. Safecracking isn't all finesse, you know. But I admit I've never used them in large amounts."

"There's a first time for everything," said Howard. A faint smile shone through the gloom for a moment.

"Let's get started," I said. "I don't want to think what Lisa's going through in there right now."

Ten minutes later, we were gathered around the living room table again. The atmosphere was still gloomy, but having something to focus on had reenergised the group somewhat.

"Here we are," said Howard, handing out maps. "They're a bit basic, but I didn't have time to put anything special together. I've marked the entrances, the patient lounge and Hawkins' offices. I couldn't be exact with some things, but I've marked the most likely locations from what Rob told me."

"This is excellent," I said. "Thank you. Judy?"

"After our last raid, we're running a little low on the spray. I've been able to rustle up a can for each of us and we have a couple spare. We've got the tasers, of course."

"And the gun."

Judy patted her shoulder harness. "Yes. I have the gun." There was a hard edge to her eyes.

"Okay. Here's the plan." I paused, collecting my thoughts. "Evie, you and Howard will come with me. Once we get the door open, we're in. They won't be expecting us, but we won't have long before they get security together."

"I'm fast, Rob, but I'm not that fast," said Evie. "If we need to break the security code, it'll take me a little time."

"That's why Judy and the twins will be causing a little distraction around the back. Ever set fire to something, Judy?"

Judy smiled. It was the first proper smile I'd seen from her for a while, even if it was brief. "Accidentally or deliberately? Actually, I've done both."

"Good. We'll make our move when you've got that going. Get round to the front as quickly as you can, without being seen if you can help it."

"Of course."

"When we're inside, we'll need to split up. We have three objectives – Lisa, Max and the machine. I suspect Dr Hawkins will be with one of them. Nicola, Natasha, you head for Lisa. Howard, Evie, you find that machine and put it out of action. Permanently. If you're not sure how much explosive to use, go with more. Judy and I will get Max."

They all nodded, and I suddenly wondered where all this take-charge attitude had come from. Was this normal for me? I'd spent my entire life from the moment I'd woken up in that Travel Hotel following other people and doing what I was told. It hadn't done me any good so far.

We set off a few minutes later. Along with our various weapons and our vague hopes of success, I brought the bag. It seemed the best thing I could do with a sports bag full of illegal drugs was take it back to its rightful owner. Mostly I just wanted to be rid of the thing. It had proven to be nothing but a dangerous red herring and I worried that the police could find me with it at any time – just as intended, no doubt.

We parked the car a short distance away from the clinic and went the rest of the way on foot. Judy and the twins went on ahead, heading for the back of the clinic for our distraction. I watched them stride purposefully off.

"Evie, shouldn't they be a bit more... sneaky?" I asked.

Evie laughed. "You've been watching too many movies, Rob. If you see someone sneaking in the shadows, what do you think of them?"

"That they're up to something," I said.

"Right. If they're walking confidently straight towards somewhere, they look like they're meant to be there. People don't tend to question authority."

"You should know," said Howard. "You were doing the exact same thing in the police station earlier. Rather badly, I should add."

"Thanks."

We took our time heading towards reception. Judy had considerately found me a baseball cap to hide my face a little (but not too much – a full disguise would have been more suspicious) but I still worried about being recognised on the way in. Howard was pretty much unknown to them, of course, and Evie had gone to such lengths as changing her clothes. As she put it, old ladies all look the same to most people.

I was ready for security to pounce as soon as we entered the reception area. They didn't, of course. It was surprisingly empty – no patients in the waiting area and only one person on the reception desk. I found this lack of presence slightly unnerving – it was too lucky for my liking. I had the feeling Dr Hawkins was expecting us.

Trying to embody authority and confidence, I strode up to the main door into the clinic and swiped my stolen card over the sensor.

Bzzzt.

A red light came on. The card didn't work. I tried again.

Bzzzt.

I was attracting the attention of the young man on the desk. Rather than let him ask me any awkward questions, I took the initiative.

"Damned card isn't working again," I said. "I keep asking for them to replace it but you know what the IT guys are like here."

"Oh, yeah," he replied, softening slightly. "I know what you mean. I've been waiting for them to fix the email on this machine for three days now."

"I'm sorry to be a pain," I said. "Could you buzz me in?"

He had a conflicted look on his face. "Well, I'm not supposed to do that," he said. "I have to be sure who I'm letting in. Tell you what – why don't you call Dr Hawkins and get him to confirm your identity?"

I hadn't expected this.

"He's out all day," I lied. "Look, I'm only coming in to pick up some urgent papers. I have to get them done by tonight or he'll have me barbecued."

Human empathy battled professional integrity in his face. "Alright," he said, "but I'll have to scan your ID first. Standard procedure. Since that patient tried to break out the other day, they're red hot on standard procedure. I don't want to be barbecued either."

I hesitated. The photograph on Dr Bradshaw's ID card looked nothing like me. I struggled to think of an excuse, and came up a blank. His concern started to turn to suspicion as I flustered. Could I get my taser on him before he hit the alarm?

The air was suddenly filled with an ear-splitting ringing noise.

"Crap, the fire alarm!" He quickly forgot about me and quickly dashed back behind the desk, securing his station and grabbing the visitor sign-in book (for making sure they hadn't burned to death, and all the lawsuits that might entail). He headed for the exit, then stopped. "Come on, you three! Let's go!"

That's when Judy and the twins appeared in the doorway, and Judy gave him the business end of her taser.

Pete the Receptionist – I never did look up his last name, though I vaguely recall him being on duty during my first visit to the clinic – had an ID card on him. He now also had Evie on him, doing her best to secure him with some duct tape from her bag. As she said, "duct tape is such a useful thing to have with you, I'm surprised more girls don't carry some."

We swiftly bundled the muffled lump that was Pete the Receptionist into the shrubs outside the main door and waited out of sight for a scattering of doctors and orderlies to emerge. This took longer than I expected. I realised later that they had to get the patients out, too, and that might be quite complicated – some might need sedating or restraining. A column of smoke was rising from the area behind the clinic and Judy had a nasty grin on her face. I hoped she hadn't gone too far with her distraction. It would be silly to get caught in our own fire.

I couldn't help but grin at the sight of my old "work colleagues" being led out. Frank was first, quite docile and led by an orderly with one hand on his shoulder. I could hear him muttering what sounded like multiples of a number somewhere in the seventies.

Gerald was next, and was almost normal – you just had to discount the odd way he was arguing with his Fred persona. I got the impression Gerald thought it was a real fire but Fred thought it was a cover for the aliens to abduct them all.

Derek was running between orderlies and doctors, gabbling to everyone that he'd started the fire. They all ignored him.

James had a disturbing grin on his face. I could only imagine he was thinking about how easily stuffed animals burned.

Oddest of all was Naomi, who finally emerged with the water cooler in her arms. How she'd been able to carry it out of the building I have no idea. Clearly being crazy makes you strong. She was shouting out that she alone had saved the Almighty, and that she alone would be spared from purgatory unless we all repented.

Once the flow of people had slowed to a trickle, we snuck inside. I'd seen no trace of Sally, Lisa, Max or Dr Hawkins in the evacuation – it was possible they'd gone by another exit, but I didn't think so. More likely Dr Hawkins had a shrewd idea what was going on, and that didn't exactly inspire me with confidence. So much for the element of surprise.

Swiping Pete's card at the door rewarded me with a soft beep, and I punched in the code I'd seen Dr Hawkins use. There was a click, and the door opened. Judy stood ready with gun drawn in case anybody was waiting behind it, surprising a couple of medical staff who were checking the building was clear.

There was a very brief struggle, and then she ushered us all in and closed the door behind us. Two quietly groaning heaps on the floor were stripped of their access cards and Judy handed one each to Howard and Nicola.

"Time to split up," she said. "Good luck, everyone."

I didn't really need the map Howard had provided to find the patient common room, which is where I'd hoped to find Max. He wasn't there. I did find Mrs Griffin, however.

"Hello, Doctor," she said. She seemed completely unaware of the ringing of the fire alarm.

"Hello, Mrs Griffin," I said. "This is Judy."

"Hello, my dear. Are you a doctor?"

Judy blinked. "Uh, no. I'm... security."

"Mrs Griffin," I asked, "why are you here?"

"Oh, I can't leave now. I'm in the middle of my favourite programme."

"Which programme is that?" asked Judy.

"*The Waltons*, of course. Though I don't think much about how this episode is going."

The television was showing something involving Bruce Willis and a car chase, which I don't believe appeared in any episode of *The Waltons*, but I let it pass. We had more important things to worry about.

"But didn't you hear the fire alarm?" asked Judy.

"Oh, that horrible noise? It's very loud, isn't it? I wish they'd stop it. They tried to take me away from my programmes." She turned to the ceiling. "Shut up, you noisy thing!"

As if the alarm had heard her, it suddenly did.

"Ah, that's better. Now I can hear John-Boy again. He's not as handsome as he used to be, is he, dear?"

"Mrs Griffin," I asked, "have you seen Max?"

"Who, dear?"

"Dr. Nicholson," I said.

"Such a handsome chap," she sighed. "He was always happy to spend time with me. Have you met Dr Nicholson, Judy my dear?"

Judy shook her head. "Not yet. I'd like to, though. Where is he?"

Mrs Griffin looked around. "I thought he was here a moment ago," she said.

Judy took my arm. "This is useless," she said. "They've stopped the alarm. That means they'll be coming any minute now. We should go."

"I suppose he might be in his room," said Mrs Griffin.

I looked up. "Which room is that, Mrs Griffin?"

"Which room is what, dear?"

"Dr Nicholson's."

"Oh! That dear Dr Nicholson. Is he coming?"

Judy suppressed a scream. Mrs Griffin didn't seem to notice.

"I was just going to go and fetch him. What's his room number?"

"Oh, I can never remember things like that," she said. She picked up her knitting bag.

Judy grabbed my arm. "Come on, Rob. We haven't time for this."

"Oh, here it is." Mrs Griffin pulled out a battered notebook. "My memory isn't what it was, Dr Walker, so I started writing things in here. I keep forgetting to do that, though." She began to flick through. "What were we looking for, again?"

"Dr Nicholson's room number."

The notebook pages were marked with lettered tabs, so you could find what you wanted straight away. It was an address book, I realised. Arthritic fingers turned to the section marked N.

"Nicholson. Nicholson. Here we are. Room 143."

"Thank you, Mrs Griffin."

"Always a pleasure dear." She beamed happily, then looked at Judy. "Hello, dear. Have we met?"

Judy ignored her, instead glancing quickly at the map. "Upstairs, western side.

Let's go."

"We'll see you later, Mrs Griffin," I promised, though I knew she'd have forgotten we were ever there in the next ten minutes.

Room 143 was entirely nondescript, exactly the same design as my own room on my previous visit here. The door was unlocked, perhaps because of the fire alarm, and opened easily from the outside.

There was very little inside the room to identify the occupant. The same spartan furniture that had occupied my room also occupied this one. Even the bed sheets were the same colour. Sat on the bed, looking faintly puzzled, was Max.

"Hey, Max, we're here to rescue you," I said.

Max looked up at me blankly. "Who's Max?"

I'd expected this might happen. "I'm sorry," I said. "Hello, Roger. Why didn't you leave when the alarm went off?"

"Alarm? Is that what the noise was? I couldn't get out. The door was locked. Who are you two? Where's Dr Hawkins?"

"I'm Dr Walker," I said. "I've come to check on you. It was a false alarm, and a number of patients were a little upset by it."

Max smiled. "Thank you, Doctor. Is there anything else?"

"Yes," I said. "We've come to get you out of here. You and Lisa."

"Lisa..." Max's eyes dilated, as he looked inwards. His memory was far more broken than mine. "I knew a Lisa once. I think I did, anyway. Who is Lisa?"

"You remember her?" I was encouraged.

"Not now, Rob," urged Judy. "We're going to have company any moment. Let's get him out of here and we'll see what we can do for him later."

"Get me out...? But I'm sick. I'm supposed to be here."

"No, Max," I said. "Dr Hawkins is making you sick. We want to make you better."

"My name is Roger," he replied. "Not Max. But... I knew a Max. Why does that name mean so much to me?"

"Come on," I said. "I can explain everything later."

There were voices in the distance.

"Rob!" Judy poked her head out the door and quickly back in. "There are guards coming. We have to go. Now." She pulled the gun from her shoulder holster.

Max's reaction to the gun was immediate. "Security! Help!" he yelled.

I swore.

"Well, that's blown it," said Judy. "I'll hold them off, Rob. You get him out of here. One way or another."

"Max! Please!"

"No way! I don't know who you two are but I'm not going with you!"

"I'm Rob! We've been friends since university!"

"And you can't even get my name right. Security! In here! She's armed!"

Judy started firing. Warning shots, I hoped. The gun was horribly loud in the confined space. A few shots fired back. I hadn't realised that Dr Hawkins hired armed guards for the clinic.

I turned back to Max. "Now look here! You're coming with me. I don't have time to explain just now. You have to trust me."

"Trust you? Why should I trust you?"

From the depths of my memory, a song came to mind.

"We were climbing so high from a misty sunrise morning…"

Max's eyes widened.

"That's…"

"I see you in the trees. Are you looking at me?"

"I remember! I wrote that song! I wrote it for..." he blinked. "I wrote it for you. For you, Rob. I remember you. I remember you!"

He smiled, his eyes lighting up. It was the same smile I'd seen in his photograph, and I remembered him. Not facts and dates; those were still lost to me. But I remembered how I felt about him, and I've never let myself forget it since.

Judy looked over her shoulder. "Time to go, boys. The corridor to your right. When I start shooting, you run like hell. Don't look back. I'll be right behind you."

She fired three shots. I grabbed Max's hand with my right, slung the sports bag over my shoulder with my left, and we ran for the corridor. I didn't look back, but I already knew Judy wasn't following.

I wasn't sure where we were headed. I turned down corridors and through doors almost blindly. I was lost and I was frightened. It was more by chance than by plan that I found myself in the corridor leading to Dr Hawkins' office. I let go of Max's hand and drew my taser. If he was in there, I was taking him out.

I kicked the door open to an empty office.

There was a chair knocked over to one side of the room, and a discarded set of handcuffs. Lisa had been here, I just knew. So where was she now?

There was really only one place she could be.

I realised that I was still carrying the sports bag over my shoulder. Not knowing quite what to do with it, I dropped it under Dr Hawkins' desk. I was sick of the thing, and he was welcome to have it back.

"Max," I said, "I need to find Lisa. Will you come with me?"

"Yes, of course, Rob. I don't want to lose you again."

"Then take this." I handed him my can of Sam's mace. "If we get caught, use it. Be careful. This stuff is nasty."

He nodded.

"I need to get to the basement."

"The machine," he said. "I remember a machine."

"That's right. We have to destroy it."

"I don't like that machine. It hurts."

"Come on, Max."

We left the office, and headed for the elevator.

No security forces got in our way – I suspect Judy had proven a very big distraction. I was still careful when the elevator arrived, not wanting to be surprised by anyone inside, but it was empty.

It all felt too easy.

Max and I headed down to the basement. I had no idea how we'd destroy the machine and no idea what we might find. As it turned out, we found a lot more than I'd bargained for.

The Deal

"And here it is," gestured Rob. "The terrifying machine at the heart of the Amnesia Project." He paused and looked down at his shoes. "Well, the new one."

Henry looked at the machine. The office chair was surrounded by a gantry holding in place a nasty-looking metal bowl that had started out as a colander. Several electronic components were fixed into it and numerous electrodes poked through the holes.

"How does it work?" asked Henry.

"It's all controlled by the computer," explained Rob. "You start by giving the person an injection – it's a cocktail of several anaesthetic compounds and a few more, uh, bizarre things. I don't know exactly how it works. We still don't have all the data."

"Then they sit in this chair," said Henry, "and that helmet thing goes on their head."

"R-right. Controlled electrical impulses to key points of the brain allow you to 'block off' areas of long term memory. It can be temporary, but the right amount of exposure can make it permanent. We're trying to find out if repeating the process can remove those blocks."

"Can it?"

"Tricky to say," said Max. "We can't exactly pull people off the street and give them amnesia. But we've got some rats to try it out on. That is, if Rob can ever bring himself to do it."

Henry looked over at a small cage in the corner. He hadn't noticed the rats until now. Now he couldn't help but hear their gentle squeaks.

"They're like family now," said Rob. "The one on the wheel is Howard. The large one is Judy. That's Evie at the food bowl, and I think Scott's asleep in the straw somewhere."

Max sighed. "You shouldn't have named them, Rob. It's easier to experiment on a nameless rat."

"So what's the plan?" interrupted Henry.

"I think we have to d-destroy the project," said Rob. "Dr Hawkins is still looking for us. I thought perhaps he'd started again, but he must be desperate. He was working for someone, and I think they must be impatient for results by now."

"After ten years, I would be too," quipped Max. "I'm surprised the good doctor hasn't made any progress on his own."

"What makes you think they'll stop if you destroy it?" asked Henry. "I don't think they'll just pack up and go home. Do you?"

Rob and Lisa exchanged glances. "I hadn't thought of that," said Rob. "Doesn't matter what we do, then. We're stuck."

There was a knock at the door.

"Are you expecting someone?" asked Henry.

Lisa shook her head. "No."

"I'll go." Max headed up the stairs. "Lisa, Rob, cover me."

Henry followed the others upstairs, Eddie following close behind.

Max went to the door, while Rob and Lisa waited in rooms to either side of the hallway. He opened it slowly.

"Hello, Dr Nicholson. And hello, Mr Ford."

"Hello, Dr Edmunds," said Henry. "Or is it Dr Hawkins?"

"Hawkins is fine," smiled their visitor. "May I come in?"

Rob stepped out. "So y-you're working for this creep, Henry?"

"Not out of choice. And I didn't tell him where you are."

Dr Hawkins smiled. "It's true. I've known where you are for some time now, Mr

Walker. I simply did not want to alarm you. May I come in?"

"Do I have a choice? A-alright. But don't try anything."

Dr Hawkins stepped into the hallway and closed the door behind him. He kept his hands raised and a smile on his face the whole time. He looked up when Lisa stepped out, and if anything the smile widened.

"It's so nice to see you all again."

Rob frowned, his eyes focused on his shoes. His hands were starting to shake. "Shut up."

"Now that's most uncivil of you, Robert. You know you can trust me."

The shaking in his hands grew more pronounced. "No..."

"Lisa – will you listen to what I have to say?"

Lisa nodded. "Yes," she said. "I'll listen."

"And you, Max?" Dr Hawkins turned to the final member of the trio.

Max nodded. "Of course. But no promises."

Rob took a step backward. "I, I know what you're doing," he said, "but it won't work on me."

"What am I doing?" asked Dr Hawkins. "I simply want to talk."

"It's okay, Rob," said Lisa. "He doesn't mean us any harm."

Rob shook his head. "No! Don't listen to him! He's trying to, to hypnotise us!" He turned towards Henry. "Don't listen to him!"

"Dr Hawkins? What is it you want?"

"I told you that when we first met, Mr Ford. I want the Amnesia Project. I cannot allow Robert and his friends to carry on with it. They could cause a lot of damage." He turned to Rob. "Mr Walker, we should work together. We did before. All I ask is that we do so again."

"So you can make me into a raving lunatic? No way."

"I don't want to do that, Robert. I never did. Please, work with me. You've done so much already. By working together, we can all benefit. If I have to force the issue, we'll both lose out."

"I'll remain in control of the project?" asked Rob, his eyes finally meeting the doctor's.

"Of course." Dr Hawkins held out a hand. "Do we have a deal?"

The Raid

Could it be true? Did Dr Hawkins really only want to help? Perhaps, despite all my efforts, his brainwashing was beginning to take hold of me. Once he had his hands on the project, it couldn't be long before he'd use it on Max and Lisa and me again.

"What do you get out of this, Dr Hawkins?" asked Henry. "Money? Fame? Power?"

Dr Hawkins' smile faltered.

"Mr Ford, I don't have any choice. Not now. My... employers will not stop. Certain powerful agencies have spent a lot of time and money on development of the project. They mean to have it, and they won't give up until they do. They would have killed me after your raid on Grace Meadows if I wasn't the only one that could tell them anything about it. I don't know if they'll be so generous next time."

"Then tell them it was destroyed," I said. "Tell them there is no project."

"And if I do that, they will simply kill me." Dr Hawkins placed his hand in his pocket and pulled out a pistol. "I was hoping it wouldn't come to this. The project data, please, Mr Walker."

I heard a strange noise to my left, and looked over at Eddie. He'd been very quiet since Dr Hawkins had turned up, and the sight of the gun had apparently upset him a great deal. He was rocking back and forth on the floor, hugging his knees to his chest, and seemed to be focused on a spot on the wall.

"Poor guy," said Henry. "Eddie isn't good with stress. He panics whenever something goes wrong in the office." He went over to Eddie, trying to calm him down.

"I'm guessing everything is in the basement," said the doctor. "That's the only place for these mad scientist experiments, isn't it?" He chuckled to himself. None of us joined in. "Let's go," he said, motioning with the pistol. "You too, Mr Ford. And young Eddie."

We didn't have any choice.

As well as housing all the data on the project, and the machine itself of course, the basement had one other notable feature - there was only one way in or out. Dr Hawkins stood on the stairs and covered us with his pistol while we could do nothing but look up at him. All our efforts to stay hidden, and now our refuge had turned into a trap.

"We can't give you the project," I said. "You know that. In the wrong hands... imagine the damage it could do."

"And what's to stop me shooting you all and taking it for myself?"

"It's encrypted," said Max. "All the data is triple locked down. Each of us has a password to unlock part of it. But you'll need all three passwords to access it all."

Dr Hawkins hesitated. "You're bluffing," he said.

"Well, if you're sure." Max grinned. "You know I always liked secret codes. Why wouldn't I put some on the project?"

It was news to me. I'd been thinking about some sort of data security for the project for a while, but I'd never got around to discussing it with the others. It had to be a bluff, and it was actually quite a clever one. If Dr Hawkins tried to use his brainwashing techniques on us, they wouldn't work. We couldn't give him the passwords if he asked for them as there were none to give.

Of course, there was nothing stopping him from just shooting us in the leg. But I wasn't going to suggest that.

Dr Hawkins looked thoughtful. "I see. You leave me little choice—"

There was a loud knock at the door.

Dr Hawkins cast a nervous glance back up the stairs, and held his pistol ready. "Who is that?"

"No idea," said Lisa. "We don't get many visitors."

The knock sounded again, more urgently. A moment later, a series of violent thuds echoed down the hallway.

Max realised first. "They're breaking the door down!"

"Not friends of yours, then," said Henry.

"Not friends of mine, either," remarked Dr Hawkins. He held out the pistol to me. "Take this. It no longer matters whether or not you give me the project. They've already found it."

"Good thing we're prepared." Lisa reached up onto a shelf near the back of the room and took down a second pistol. "There are more guns hidden in the living room and kitchen," she said. "If we can get to them, we'll be able to outflank them."

"Robert, your friends proved themselves rather effective on their raid on the clinic," said Dr Hawkins. "I hope you are just as effective now."

"We may even be better," I replied.

Upstairs, the door crashed open.

One Hour

Lisa and I crouched in the basement doorway at the top of the stairs, guns drawn, the others close behind. Lisa, Max and I had trained for this, never knowing if or when someone would find us, but I was surprised at how quickly Dr Hawkins had fallen in step with us. Minutes before he had been the enemy, and now we were fighting alongside each other.

I fired a couple of warning shots. Whoever was out there quickly scrambled for cover – they'd apparently not expected armed resistance.

"If we can keep them outside, we should be able to get upstairs and into better positions," said Lisa. "We're trapped like rats in here."

"Hey, Henry!" hissed Max. "Have you or Eddie ever used a gun before?"

"No!"

"If this goes badly, you may be learning in a hurry."

I looked back at Eddie. He was rocking again in the corner, and now he was making an eerie keening sound.

"Is he freaking out?" asked Max.

"I think so," said Henry. "Eddie's not good at leaving his comfort zone. This must be hell for him."

"We can't help him now, Henry. He'll be safe down here – if any of us are safe, that is."

Henry nodded. "I know. I'll look after him."

"On three?" asked Rob. Lisa nodded. She fired a shot towards the doorway, and a shadow hastily moved back.

"One. Two. *Three.*"

We half ran, half fell up the last few stairs and round into the side rooms. Shouts from up ahead suggested the invaders were going to try again while the defenders were moving, but Lisa fired a wild shot in their direction as she ran for the kitchen. I leaned back into the hallway from my position at the living room door, gun at the ready, but they were holding back.

There were a couple of pistols taped to the underside of the kitchen table. Lisa pulled them free and threw them back towards the basement, one at a time. Max and Dr Hawkins took one each.

"Hawkins, with me," said Lisa. "I need someone to watch my back. I'm worried they'll try to come through the side door. Max, get to the stairs - we'll cover you."

"Gotcha." Max crawled up the final stairs and awaited his chance.

"Hawkins, look at the end table with the telephone on it. There should be a pistol taped underneath. Slide it over to Henry. I hope he won't need it."

"Me, too," agreed Henry.

Dr Hawkins quickly found the second pistol. Strips of duct tape were still stuck to it. He slid it over towards Henry, who took it as though it might bite him.

"Go!" I hissed.

Max crawled along the hallway to the stairs. Dr Hawkins and I fired a few rounds towards the door as he did. No-one tried to come in. Max reached the stairs, headed about halfway up and sat against the wall there, gun poised.

"What about the windows?" asked Henry.

"Didn't you see the bars when you came in?" said Max. "This place is a fortress, or near enough. Believe it or not, the front door was reinforced."

Then, finally, something crossed the threshold.

"Get back!" yelled Dr Hawkins. "Grenade!"

The grenade began to give off a thick, nasty smelling gas. In a matter of moments the hallway was filled with smoke and we were all coughing heavily.

"What's happening?" spluttered Henry.

"Sm-smoke bomb," coughed Dr Hawkins. "Trying to flush us out. They don't want to risk damaging the goods."

"The project?"

"Or us."

"That's good, right?"

Dr Hawkins coughed some more, producing a nasty rattling sound. "That depends," he wheezed, "on how badly they want us to talk."

There was a sudden rattle of gunfire. Holes appeared in the door frame and in the plaster of the walls around the basement door. Fortunately, everyone had been sensible enough to stay down.

I heard the sound of breaking glass in the kitchen.

"They're trying to outflank us!" coughed Hawkins. He fired off a couple of rounds towards the back door, breaking more glass in the process. Henry heard a clunking sound and more smoke began to drift out of the kitchen doorway. Another smoke bomb.

"We have to fall back!" said Dr Hawkins.

Lisa and Hawkins backed out of the kitchen, spluttering more than ever. It was impossible to organise our defences now – our eyes were streaming and we could barely see what was going on. It would have been impossible to shoot straight, or know who we were shooting at. When two large men cautiously entered the house, thick scarves wrapped around their faces to protect them from the worst of the smoke, we gave no resistance.

"Drop your weapons and step outside with your hands up." The accent was clipped; English was not his first language. "Hey, Mr Ford! You sing like a drowning cat, you know that?"

This was the man I'd seen in the bar with Henry.

"You first, Mr Ford. Come with me."

"I don't know anything about..."

A hard punch to the stomach cut Henry off mid-sentence.

"No talking. Move."

The man was suddenly struck by a yelling blur. It wasn't until they hit the floor that I realised the figure sat on top of the man, hitting out with wildly flailing arms and screaming as loud as he could, was Eddie. I couldn't make out any words in that screaming. It was just a wild cry of rage, panic and fear.

The other man turned to see what was happening and hesitated, not sure whether to risk a shot and hit his friend. Those few seconds were long enough for Max and I to regain our guns; Dr Hawkins was already reaching for his.

The second man backed away to the door, keeping us all covered. I could see other armed figures approaching to join him – men with much bigger, nastier looking weapons. "Let him go, or we will kill you all."

"I wouldn't do that," replied Dr Hawkins. "They've triple-locked their data. You'll need them alive to give you the password."

The man thought for a moment. I couldn't make out what the other men were carrying. They clearly hadn't expected us to be armed at all or they would have come in with the heavy weapons in the first place. There were only two reasons why they didn't come in with them now: our hostage, and the project itself.

"You have one hour to release him. Or we come for him and the project."

The men withdrew.

Standoff

This wasn't the first standoff I'd experienced. I'd been surrounded on all sides by people with guns once before.

It doesn't get any easier.

Hawkins looked up as the elevator doors opened. "Ah, Mr Walker. Welcome."

So much for surprising him.

He was surrounded by three of his security guards, their guns drawn and pointed at Evie and Howard, who had their tasers held ready. Between them stood Sally, an arm around Lisa's neck and a gun held to her head.

On the floor beside Evie, Nicola crouched over her twin sister's body. I could hear her crying. Natasha was hurt badly, if not already dead.

"Rob!" Lisa gasped. "Do something!"

"What the hell is going on?" I asked.

"My dear Mr Walker," said Sally, "this is not exactly how I planned to run the exchange. But the deal is the same. Give me the Amnesia Project and I will give you Lisa."

"Give me one reason why I shouldn't just zap you and take her from you."

"Rob, no," said Evie. "If you fire that taser at her, she'll shoot her. She won't be able to stop herself."

"When someone's given an electric shock, their muscles clench," explained Howard.

I held my fire.

"What about you, Dr Hawkins?"

"Mr Walker, I don't particularly care for Ms Kensington. But I do realise that you and Lisa are the best chance we have of recovering the Project data. Give us what we want and we'll let you all leave unharmed."

"Even Max?"

"Even Max."

A radio crackled. A security guard muttered something into his receiver and then spoke briefly to Dr Hawkins.

"Oh, good," he said. "Bring her down, please."

I froze. Judy!

"Your friend upstairs has caused me a lot of bother. She didn't want to go down without a fight. I'm sorry to say she's a little the worse for wear."

"She's alive?"

"For now, yes. The Amnesia Project, Mr Walker. You really don't have any choice."

"...Alright. I give in."

Dr Hawkins held out a hand. "Please hand it over."

"Not to him!" Sally snarled. "Give it to me!"

"I don't have it with me," I said. "It's not exactly sensible to bring secret information with you when you're busting someone out."

Dr Hawkins chuckled. "I guess not. I suggest you go and get it while I keep your friends here as my guests." His voice turned serious. "You'd better hurry. I fear the young lady here won't last long. Ah, here comes your other friend now."

The elevator doors opened once more, and two guards half walked, half carried Judy towards us. She stumbled as she approached.

"Judy!"

"Hey, Rob." She smiled weakly. "I did my best. Have we won yet?"

She looked down, and saw Natasha. The smile vanished.

"I think we've lost, Judy," I said. "I'll go back and fetch the Project. You look after everyone while I'm gone."

Judy nodded, holding out a hand to me. "Take care, Rob. Don't be too long."

I took her hand. She seemed so frail that I was very surprised by how firm her grip was. Then I looked into her eyes and noticed that cold edge. I somehow knew, as though she'd put the thought straight into my head, that she was faking it. She really was hurt, but not as badly as she was making out.

Evie crouched beside Nicola. "Come on, dear," she said. "We'll be alright. Remember that time in Belfast with the terrorist cell? We got out of that one."

Nicola's eyes widened, and I sensed a change in her posture. Howard was also shifting. I had no idea what had happened in Belfast, but it was clear Evie was doing more than just telling old stories.

I carried on towards the elevator, but I kept my hand on my taser. I was tensed for a signal, and I wasn't disappointed. I heard Evie cry out behind me and couldn't help but turn around. She was knelt on the floor, clutching at her chest.

"It's all right," she said. "It's my heart, that's all. The stress is all a bit much."

With all eyes on Evie, the others acted. Howard and Nicola fired their tasers at the nearest guards. Judy sprung to life, throwing one of her escorts over her shoulder before the other could react, and then throwing some solid looking punches into the second guard's face. She was hurt, yes, but I suddenly remembered Sam talking me through their equipment – including several Kevlar vests. Judy was almost bulletproof.

"Stop them!" yelled Dr Hawkins.

Before the last guard could react, Evie fired her own taser and he fell in a twitching heap. I quickly pointed my own taser at Dr Hawkins but I was too late – he ran further into the basement corridor and round the corner before I could fire a shot.

I turned my attention to Sally, who hadn't moved throughout the entire exchange.

"Let her go, Sally," I said. "Let her go and we let you walk out of here."

"You don't understand, Robert," she replied, and her voice was different now. She was scared. "Or maybe you do. You most of all."

"What do you mean?" I asked.

"The Project. I need it. That machine... I've been in it. The bastard took my memories!"

"It's true," said Lisa. "I don't think it's worked the way it was supposed to, but it's done something."

I could believe it. Max, Lisa, Jimmy and myself had all been... altered by that machine, and none of us had come out quite the same way. Without the research data, Hawkins was largely guessing at the process. I tried to imagine what Sally was feeling, and had to give up.

"Help me, Robert. There are such big holes in my memories. I can't stand it!"

"I don't know if we can get them back," I said. "I'll try, but I don't know."

I decided not to tell her that we intended to destroy the machine. I didn't want her losing her grip on her sanity when she had such a strong grip on the gun at Lisa's head.

"If you don't know," she said, "there's someone who does." She suddenly shoved Lisa towards me, and as I grabbed for her Sally ran off down the corridor after Dr Hawkins.

"Rob! Go after her!" gasped Lisa. "She's gone mad! She's going to kill Dr Hawkins!"

"Good riddance," I muttered.

"Rob, I don't care what you think of Dr Hawkins," said Evie. "There are two reasons why you have to try to save him. One is that Sally may be right – we might need him if we're going to restore anyone's memories."

"And the other?"

"If you let him die, you'll have become the man you're so frightened you might really be."

That one stung.

"Alright," I said. "I'll save him. But he's still going to pay for what he's done."

I hadn't realised how far these corridors stretched on my first visit. I went carefully with taser at the ready, worried that if I ran I'd go right past the two of them in some little side room, but I found nothing on the way. Eventually I was rewarded by the sound of shouting.

"Come out and face me!"

Sally had the not so good doctor cornered. I picked up speed and headed towards the sound.

I found her at the end of the corridor. She was standing on the other side of a set of glass panelled double-doors, which she'd somehow locked behind her. I shoved at the doors and yelled at her to open them, but she seemed completely oblivious to me. Judy's gun could have shot through the glass – one of the disadvantages of the non-lethal taser.

The room was apparently a storage area. Cabinets and boxes were piled fairly haphazardly and the lighting was poor – a good place to hide.

"Hawkins! Come on out! I know you're in here."

Sally continued to sweep the room with her pistol. Dr Hawkins didn't emerge.

"Come out now and I won't hurt you," said Kensington. The crazy edge to her voice had calmed down somewhat. "I think you know that I need you alive. Come out and we'll talk."

To my surprise, I saw a shape stand up in the back of the room. I hadn't expected

Dr Hawkins to give up so easily. He slowly walked towards Sally, hands raised.

"Certainly, Ms Kensington," said the doctor, soothingly. "Let us talk. We can do so much more by working together, yes?"

Sally began to lower the gun. Dr Hawkins had such a lovely voice, so deep and relaxing. I felt like everything was going to be fine. As he spoke, I could almost hear him talking to me, telling me to relax and that everything was under control.

Sally lowered the gun. "Yes, of course. So much more. Dr Hawkins, I want my memories back."

"Of course, of course. And I want to give them to you. But I can't do that without the details of the project. We need to get them back, remember?"

"Yes. I remember."

I felt as though it would be so easy to just shout to them both that I'd be happy to give them what information I knew, that they just had to give me my memories back and they could have it all. And then I realised what Dr Hawkins was doing.

Sally didn't.

"Give me the gun, Sally."

Sally Kensington struggled for a moment, clearly unwilling to give up the pistol. Her hands began to shake.

"Please, Sally."

Her hands shook harder.

"No." Sally raised the pistol again. "You can't make me. I know what you're doing. You can't make me!"

"Sally!"

She raised the shaking pistol to her head.

"You can't make me!" She laughed, though it sounded more like a cackle. There was a single gunshot, and then she fell to the ground.

The strange hypnosis that Dr Hawkins had put over me was instantly broken. I backed away from the door, then turned and ran. I didn't want to meet the good doctor with just my little taser when he was armed with such a powerful means of persuasion.

I returned to the rest of the group. Lisa threw her arms around me with relief. A moment later, Max did the same.

"Sally's dead," I told them. "Dr Hawkins tried to talk her into handing over her own gun and she shot herself."

"Rob, we have to get out of here," said Judy. "The police are on the way. It seems a fire, a load of gunshots and a lot of confused people talking to the emergency services were enough to get them interested."

"Okay. What about the machine?"

"We've packed in all the explosive we had around it, and Howard's rigged a detonator up."

"It's an old mobile phone," he explained. "When we get clear, we call the number and... boom!"

"Will it work?" I asked. "Will it be enough?"

"No idea," he confessed. "Sam was the expert. But it should do some serious damage. Like you said - when in doubt, go with more."

Howard and Max took Natasha between them and Evie helped Judy as we all hobbled to the elevator and to the exit. Nicola dialled a number into a mobile phone when we reached the reception desk, and the ground shook behind us.

I think it worked.

The clinic was in chaos. The explosion had set the fire alarm off again. Security forces were largely trying to help the orderlies contain the patients, and it seemed half were trying to bring them back into the clinic and half were escorting them out. Several ambulances were parked outside and I could see several police officers talking to various people, apparently trying to find out what was going on.

"Rob, this is where we part company," said Evie. "We'd rather not get involved with the police, you understand."

"Of course," I said.

"Take care, Evie," said Lisa. "And thanks for everything. Give me a call when everything calms down and we'll all go out for teacakes at that little café in Soho you like so much."

"I look forward to it, dear," replied Evie. "Robert, do me a favour and distract that paramedic. We need to steal an ambulance."

I blinked. "Do what now?"

"Natasha's in a very bad way, dear, and we can't exactly just take her to hospital. We know a few people that won't ask questions. Now please hurry up about it."

I shrugged, and tried to act normal as I walked up to the paramedic. He was tall and muscular and his head was shaved; I reckon he was a boxer or something like that in his spare time. The last thing I wanted to do was upset him. Still, all I had to do was keep him talking - it was Evie and the others that were taking all the risks.

"Excuse me," I asked, "but could you take a look at us, please? I think my wife is in shock."

Lisa didn't need to act shocked.

Max was surprisingly good in the circumstances. "Please, mister. She's my sister. She's the only family I have."

His name was Jeff, and he was a friendly and helpful man. He made sure Lisa sat down and wrapped up warm and asked her several questions to check she was lucid. When a police officer came up asking for a statement, Jeff waved him away ("not now, man, can't you see she's in shock?") and he even offered us some hot coffee from his thermos flask. It was very hard for me to keep Jeff occupied whilst his ambulance slowly and quietly rolled away up the clinic's driveway.

I hope he didn't get into trouble over that.

The Plan

It was a couple more minutes until the smoke cleared, though it would be a fair bit longer until our lungs did likewise. Bouts of coughing continued to strike all of us for a few hours after the event.

We took up better positions. We barricaded the kitchen door with the dining table and partly blocked the front door with the coffee table from the living room, though we didn't really expect it to help much if our attackers came back in force.

They hadn't expected armed resistance. Next time they'd be ready.

Our prisoner was tied up in the basement, strapped into the ARM (or "The Machine", as Max insisted on calling it – though I admit that did sound scarier when we were threatening to use it).

"Who are you?" I asked. "Who are you working for?"

He replied with some choice words that don't need repeating. When I threatened to switch on The Machine, he was a little more forthcoming. "Dmitri."

"Nice to meet you, Dmitri. Where are you from?"

Silence.

"Eastern Europe, I think," said Dr Hawkins. "Not that it makes any difference. My former employees hired a lot of their mercenaries from the former Soviet bloc."

"And who are they?" I asked.

Dr Hawkins shook his head. "I have no idea. One of the conditions for their funding the Project was that I didn't ask. They could even be the British government for all I know, though it seems unlikely."

"Maybe he might tell us," suggested Lisa. She pointed to the colander hanging about Dmitri's head. "With the right persuasion, I mean."

Dmitri's eyes widened a little, but he remained professional.

"I doubt he knows himself," said Dr Hawkins. "And we all know how erratic the procedure is. We don't want him forgetting everything green, or how to speak English."

I had to admire our prisoner's refusal to talk despite his obvious fear.

"We'd best secure the rear entrance," Dr Hawkins continued. "We'll decide what to do about him later."

"We can't leave him here alone," I said.

"I'll keep an eye on him," said Lisa.

Dr Hawkins and I went to check the back door, while Max and Henry stood guard by the front. Eddie was lying on the sofa in the living room. He'd gone very quiet after his... I suppose "meltdown" is the only word I can think of. Now he was sleeping, or looked like it. I could tell Henry was worried about him, but there was nothing else we could do for him right now.

The back door was still secure, our barricade still in place.

"Robert, I wanted to talk to you alone," Dr Hawkins said. "I don't blame you for not trusting me. But you need to listen to this."

"To what? Just give up and hand over the project?" I shook my head. "We need to destroy it. All of it. While we have the chance. Max was right - I should have done this years ago."

"If you do that now, we're all dead."

"I don't think your friends out there are going to just let us go," I replied.

"Robert, please. I know what these men are like. If you resist, they will kill us. If you destroy the project, they will kill us slowly and painfully."

"And if I give them the project, I've given them the power to rewrite history, control people's minds, who knows what else? Death might be better than living a life they've invented for you."

"We all live invented lives, Robert. You and me, more invented than most."

"They'll kill us anyway."

"Perhaps. But it's our best chance." Dr Hawkins looked round, and spotted Henry in the doorway. "Ah, Mr Ford. How is Eddie?"

"Sleeping. I think. Probably best for him."

"Henry, I'm sorry we got you involved in all this. What do you think we should do?"

Henry looked thoughtful for a moment. "I don't know. Can we hold up until the police arrive?"

Dr Hawkins shook his head. "The police? I don't expect they will come here. Not until it's all over, anyway. I suspect our friends outside have already made sure the police stay out of the way."

"Friends in high places?" asked Henry.

"Exactly."

"I don't know," Henry eventually said. "This is all a bit outside my area. The way I see it, we either stay and fight a losing battle, we try to run, or we give up. If we destroy the project, they'll probably kill us. If we don't, we'll all wake up thinking we're Napoleon, or something."

"Napoleon?" Dr Hawkins chuckled. "More likely we'll end up making public confessions to numerous criminal and terrorist acts. And we'll believe we did them, too."

"There's got to be another option," I said.

"That's what I've been saying," said Dr Hawkins. "I think I have one. Henry, have you ever heard of cold fusion?"

Henry nodded. "Yeah, I read an article on it once, a long time ago. I don't know much about it, though. All that technical stuff is beyond me."

"I'm not an expert in nuclear physics," I said, "but I know a little. It was supposed to be a massive breakthrough that would have changed the entire world. Unlimited free energy. No need for coal and oil. No more pollution."

"It received a lot of attention," continued Dr Hawkins, "until it turned out that the research had been falsified and the published results were fake. Nuclear fusion is real enough, but so far it only works at enormous temperatures, such as inside the sun. The only use for it here on Earth is in bombs."

"After that, cold fusion became something of a joke," I added. "Maybe it's possible, but it's hard to get anyone to take it seriously." I looked at Dr Hawkins. "What are you suggesting?"

Dr Hawkins smiled. "We do the same thing, but in reverse. We give them a fake project. Mess up the stuff that works, fake the results. And when we get out of here, we publish it ourselves."

"We'll be ridiculed in the scientific community," I said.

"And the Amnesia Project along with it. I think, compared to the alternative, that's a price we'd all be happy to pay."

"And our friends out there will drop it like a hot potato," said Henry. "Will that work? Won't they realise we're holding out on them?"

"Not necessarily. They don't know how it works - they only know about the results. The whole project rests on those results, and they won't be able to replicate them. We just need to make sure they believe they are genuine." Dr Hawkins checked his watch. "Gentlemen, we don't have long. We'd better get started."

"I'll need Max," I said. "Henry, can you take over guard duty for him?"

"I've never fired a gun in my life!"

Dr Hawkins put a hand on Henry's shoulder. "Robert, you go and get started. But keep an eye on our prisoner – we don't want him to get wind of what we're doing. I'll show Mr Ford how to use a firearm. I hope for all our sakes he doesn't need it."

I headed for the basement and left them to it.

Lisa was waiting with gun in hand when I entered the basement. She relaxed when she recognised me.

"How's our prisoner?" I asked.

"Behaving, so far," she said. "Anything happening upstairs?"

"Not yet. Henry's getting a crash course in firearms from Dr Hawkins – I need him to take over from Max."

"Wouldn't it be better to let me go?" she said. "If things go bad out there…"

"No, I need you here too." I looked over at Dmitri. Could he hear us talking? "Hawkins has a plan," I said, keeping my voice low. "We're going to pack up all the data on the laptop and try to sneak it out."

"And use the failsafe?"

"Yes. We'll use the failsafe." It was one of Max's clever ideas – sort of a self-destruct device. All the data held on our various computers would be completely scrambled. Anyone trying to use our equipment would be left with a bunch of dead machinery and no way to use it. We just had to enter the command.

I began copying files onto the laptop. I'd need Max before I could make any real changes to the data – I couldn't afford to make them too obvious. Lisa kept an eye on our prisoner while I worked.

Max appeared in the doorway a few minutes later. "Henry said you needed me down here?"

"Yeah, I need your help with this data. Did you speak to Hawkins?"

He nodded. "Yeah. It's a risky plan, Rob. I'm not sure it'll work."

"I know," I said. "But it's the best we've got."

I was checking my watch every few minutes as we worked, conscious that our hour was rapidly running out. Lisa went to join Dr Hawkins in the kitchen. I left Max to finish up and went upstairs to check on Henry. After all, we'd left him alone with a gun that terrified him and just an upturned coffee table between him and a group of armed killers.

I found him sat beside the doorway, sensibly not relying on the coffee table to protect him from any stray rounds. I wondered whether he'd thought of that, or whether one of the others had told him.

"Hey, Henry."

Henry gave a strangled cry, dropped the gun in his panic and fell onto his back. He was totally unprepared for this.

"Hey, easy there." I knelt beside him and offered him a hand up. "How are things?"

"I never knew it was possible to be bored and terrified at the same time."

"Don't worry. It's nearly over. We're just putting the final touches together."

"So what are you doing?" he asked.

"We're giving them the project - the fake one. Max is working on the last changes. Once we're done, we'll sneak out and leave them to it."

"Time to hide again, huh?"

"Just hold tight. It won't be long now."

Max was muttering about needing more time as I returned to the basement, but that it would do for now.

"As long as it's good to go," I said. "We're almost out of time."

"It's good to go. I hope."

I headed back upstairs and into the kitchen, where Lisa and Dr Hawkins were waiting. "Everything okay?" I asked.

"All quiet," said Lisa. "If they're out there, they're not moving."

"They will be soon. If this all goes wrong, what are our chances of getting out that way?"

Dr Hawkins smiled grimly. "Bad. I think we're surrounded. I'm hoping our gambit will prove enough of a distraction to let us slip away."

"What gambit?"

"I'm going down to the basement," said Hawkins. "Max should be about done but he could perhaps use my help."

"Certainly." I settled back against the counter as he left, noticing as I did that one of the knives was missing from the knife block.

I wasn't there to see it, but this is how I imagine it happened.

Max would have been busy at the laptop, finishing off any last minute changes he was considering. Naturally, the real data was safely stored on a memory stick in his pocket, but our prisoner wouldn't know that. He looks up as Dr Hawkins comes down the stairs.

"How's our prisoner?" Dr Hawkins asks. He moves in for a closer look, and whispers in the prisoner's ear – something like "I'm getting you out of here – get the laptop while I deal with him." Then it would be a short job to cut through the ropes and release him.

"Why are you doing this?" Dmitri might ask.

Perhaps Dr Hawkins mentions loyalty, or simply tells him he doesn't want to die. It doesn't really matter.

I heard Max cry out. Dr Hawkins hit him pretty hard, I think. I saw the prisoner run up the stairs with the laptop. I heard Henry shout and I heard his single gunshot. It went harmlessly into the ceiling. By the time Lisa and I emerged from the kitchen, our former captive had already hurdled the coffee table and ran into the street.

I joined Henry at the door.

"He got away. I'm sorry, Rob."

"You were perfect," said Hawkins, returning from the basement. "They wouldn't believe it if he'd just walked right out of here, would they?"

Henry suddenly realised what had happened. "You let him go. You wanted him to escape with it."

"Of course. Much less suspicious if they took it against your will. But who's side am I on?"

"What was on that laptop?" Henry asked. "Nonsense?"

"Pretty much," I said. "Now's our chance, while they're distracted."

Lisa and I pulled our barricade away from the back door and I looked outside, checking both sides and staying near to the ground. The back yard looked empty.

"Henry, you go with Eddie and Lisa. Take Max with you – he took a bit of a beating down there. Run straight for the car and go – don't wait for us."

"What about you?"

"Dr Hawkins and I need to activate the failsafe. We can't risk them finding anything here. Go!"

They set off. As they got to the car, I heard shouts from our attackers. There were a few gunshots, but none hit.

"I hope they make it," I said, as Henry took off as fast as his little car would go. Our attackers scrambled to get back into their vehicle and were soon in pursuit, but Henry had a good lead.

"So do I," said Dr Hawkins. "I have no doubt our visitors will be back here very soon, either way. We need to move quickly."

"If they catch them, they'll find the project. Max has the memory stick on him. It's encrypted, but I don't know how long it would take to break it."

"No, they won't." Dr Hawkins took a memory stick from his pocket. "I took this from Max during our little stage fight."

"What are you doing with that?" I suddenly realised I was alone with him. The gun in my hand seemed very small as I thought about his powers of persuasion. Would I go the same way that Sally had, back in the clinic?

"It's amazing to think it all fits on here. All that data, on one little piece of plastic." He paused. "You know, I could just take this. You wouldn't be in any position to stop me."

I nodded, defeated.

"But I don't want it. I'm done with the project." Dr Hawkins smiled, then handed me the memory stick. "Destroy it, Robert. Take it away from here and burn it, or melt it, or whatever you do with these plastic things."

"Max's program is all set to run," I said. "You won't get anything off those computer hard drives in an hour or so."

"Is that enough time?"

"It has to be. Besides, the first stage only takes a few minutes. You'd need an expert to piece together anything on there just after that. The rest is insurance." I waved over towards the corner. "Grab the cage while you're here. I don't want to leave the rats behind."

"And the machine?"

"We can leave the structure," I said. "For all anyone can tell, it's just modern art. The main components – we'll take them with us. There's a scrap dealer just outside town. He'll be happy to crush them for cash."

I stepped over to the computer.

"Wait," said Dr Hawkins. "Before we destroy the machine – I want to ask you to do something for me."

My hands hovered over the keyboard. "What?"

"I've done so many things in the name of this project. I'm a weak man, Robert. I should have refused. But I was struggling to find financial backing in those days, and research takes so long. They offered me a way to make a real discovery in my own lifetime. Cutting a few corners here and there didn't seem so bad." He sighed. "And then they started threatening me. They wanted results, and you and your friends... I got desperate, Robert. I'm not proud of my actions, and I paid for them dearly."

"You seemed to do okay out of it."

"The clinic was destroyed. My reputation along with it. Years of work, lost. The only reason they did not kill me was so I could start again. When they saw your story, they realised the project was still out there and sent me back here to find it."

I still didn't trust him, not entirely, but I did feel sorry for him. We like to pretend our villains are cruel and unfeeling, because we prefer them that way - if they're just the victims of circumstances, how do we know we wouldn't do the same? I still don't know what I did before my time in the chair, back at the clinic. Maybe back then I was someone else's villain.

"I'm a weak man, Robert," repeated Dr Hawkins. "If our pursuers find me, I *will* tell them everything I know. You need to destroy this project, and that means destroying me, too."

"There's no time," I said. "You know it takes a while to mix up the formula."

Dr Hawkins took a syringe from his pocket. "I found your chemistry set in the kitchen cupboard earlier. You'd already prepared a batch before I arrived."

"That's for the rats, not people."

"It should still work. I remember that much from my own tests. Rats and humans are very much alike in many ways. Though I sometimes think the rats are smarter than we are."

"It could kill you."

"Either way, I won't be a danger any more." He sat in the chair, and lowered the helmet of The Machine over his head. "Please, Robert. It's the only way."

I sighed. "Alright. I don't know if it will work, but alright."

Dr Hawkins rolled up his sleeve ready for the needle.

I activated The Machine for the last time.

Aftermath

You're probably wondering what happened after the explosion at the clinic. I'm afraid it's not as dramatic as you might think.

I did eventually speak to a police officer, though I gave a false name. She was a rather nice lady from a special forces unit, called in to clear the clinic - to be fair, there had been gunshots on the premises. A large explosion had collapsed the basement, and that this had covered a number of bodies. Several of these were security personnel, mostly stunned but largely unharmed, but they also unearthed the body of Sally Kensington.

I wasn't the one who identified her – I read about it a few days later in the newspapers. She left behind a husband and two children. I had no idea.

Dr Hawkins was also trapped in the wreckage of the basement. Initially he was released without charge, but rumours circulated that a large quantity of cocaine had been found in his office and that he was using the clinic to run a drug dealing operation.

I do know that he never went to court. Dr Hawkins had powerful friends. He disappeared entirely a few weeks later.

If there were any VIPs coming to visit the clinic, they quietly cancelled their plans once the whole incident hit the press. We never did find out who the intended victim was.

I gather it was several hours before anyone found Pete the Receptionist.

I only saw Evie and her gang once more, though we keep in touch through indirect means that I won't explain here. Lisa got a message a week after the raid to let us know that Judy was fine and that Natasha was on the way to recovery, and to invite us to Sam's funeral. It was a quiet affair – Sam was laid to rest under a false name and, aside from the gang, Lisa, Max and myself, the only attendees were a *couple I assume were Sam's parents.*

I don't think we'll ever know exactly what happened. Everyone involved is either dead or had their memories wiped. This is what I think happened, and at least it fits the facts rather well.

I think Sally was telling the truth about our involvement, at least for the most part. Jimmy (or Damian) was working in the clinic when Sally heard about the project. She got Max and I in there as well. We worked with Jimmy to steal the data, encode it and smuggle it out to her.

At some point we encountered Lisa. She'd discovered something was going on and convinced us that it was wrong. So we stopped sending the data to Sally, and sent the bulk of the research to Lisa, in order to expose what was going on. And we started to destroy the project from the inside, until Hawkins discovered us. First Jimmy was processed – his true, Damian persona was wiped, and he fell back on his cover story, the only other identity he had.

The papers I picked up at the clinic did not include a full transcript of his processing, but Dr Hawkins made some notes. He wiped Damian's identity, and he either wiped his memory of the Project data too or Damian never actually knew where Max and I hid it. There were the usual imprinted commands to trust and obey, and that was it. There are no notes here about the Jimmy personality. Maybe it took a while for that to come through.

Then they processed me. I have no way to know whether I talked. Perhaps I did, though I'd like to think I resisted. And then I escaped, possibly thanks to Jimmy and certainly thanks to Max. They didn't expect me to end up as far away as Reading. But I suspect that wasn't entirely Jimmy's idea. Hawkins wanted us to escape, to find out where we went back to. They lost track of me but I suspect Hawkins found Sally through Jimmy.

And Lisa – they knew about her. She was brought in and interrogated, but they didn't dare wipe her memory completely as she was the last one to know where the project data was. Or maybe they didn't realise she was the only one who knew at that point. Either way, she didn't tell them. They searched her flat, took everything that they thought might hold the data, but either didn't find or simply didn't think of her cassette tapes. We were lucky.

When Lisa found me, she'd already been processed. She said and did things without knowing why. She rationalised away the parts of her life she was not supposed to think about, like her empty flat, but whether they'd only given her a light dose of the treatment or they'd simply screwed up, I don't know. Her memories, unlike mine or Max's, started to return with the right prompting. We don't know how much more she may have forgotten.

I have no notes on Lisa's processing, but her odd behaviour when we met - and her later attempts to seduce me - suggest that she was given some extra conditioning. I don't know whether she was meant to be a trap for me or whether someone was simply playing a sick joke. Either way, this conditioning didn't stick for her either, and she seemed to shake it off when she became aware of it.

Max – poor Max tried to warn me. He left me a coded message, which was discovered (and I have no idea what it originally was). Hawkins had me record a new message over it, leading to a trap in the luggage locker at Kings Cross. The classical music at the end was probably all that was left of the original message. Max was processed, repeatedly – they used him as a lab animal.

And the rest, well, you've just heard it.

You're probably wondering about the Project itself. That's still undecided – but we found it, hidden in the background of Lisa's cassette collection. Weird droning noises over the music that sound like a bad recording at normal speed became something very different when you sped them up. Some of it is voice recording. Some of it appears to be computer data – unfortunately, it's Max that would know what to do with that and he has no memory of even recording it. But it's all still there, just hidden away, much like my memories - and we can recover it.

Of course, there's no guarantee, even if we do decode it all, that we can reverse the process. I get the occasional flashes of memory, but nothing I can build on. I still have no idea about my life before I woke up in Reading that morning. I'm getting used to the idea that I may always be this way. And it's not so bad – I've heard several different stories about my life before the Project, and I don't particularly care for any of them. I might be better off never knowing which is true, if any of them are. Maybe I'm just an ordinary guy who ended up in the wrong place at the wrong time. I like that story most of all.

I'm tempted, then, to simply burn the tapes and let the Amnesia Project disappear along with my past. But then I think about Dr Hawkins and the data he'd already rediscovered. Only by studying the Project ourselves can we prevent anyone else from developing it.

And what about Max? The three of us have moved on now – it wasn't exactly safe to stay in our flat (if it was ever truly ours). You'll pardon me for not telling you too much about our new home. Max still has no memory of his own life, but he's either remembered or simply accepted his own name now. Now he's no longer under Dr Hawkins' control, his mental state seems stable. He's bright and curious about the world around him, keen to rediscover who he is and his place in it. Like me, he has perfectly normal recall since we rescued him. But no further.

However, Max has an avenue that I don't – his music. We got him a keyboard, and he can happily spend hours playing on it. Sometimes he just practices songs he's learned since we arrived. Sometimes he writes new ones – that talent is still very strong, though I don't always know (and perhaps he doesn't either) whether he's writing them or remembering them. Sometimes he starts playing something and then stops, finding it somehow familiar but unable to identify it. Perhaps music might work for him, might unlock that door between him and his past. Either way, it makes him smile - and I love that smile, and the way my heart jumps every time I see it.

Lisa has made it clear that the future of these tapes is up to me. Whether we destroy them, decode them or simply stash them away, she has told me she will support my decision. Max doesn't know what he wants – he hasn't had as long as me to find his way in the world. He also doesn't know what it's like to wake up alone and frightened with no idea who you can trust. He has a sort of family now. He wants to get his memory back – but not at any price. I'm not sure I would, either.

I simply can't decide what's best.

It's been a week since my last recording, and I've been doing a lot of thinking. I've decided to carry on with my indecision. We're going to break the code and find out what it is, which could still take months. Or years. There's no guarantee that we'll actually use what we learn. But it'll give me time to think. Time, perhaps, for our memories to return. That would be good. In the meantime it keeps Max busy – and me, too.

The tapes – the ones with the encoded messages – have already been destroyed. I burned them as soon as I'd finished extracting their data. I didn't want to risk anyone else finding them. The only tapes that now exist are the ones you have been listening to, and there are no secrets buried in those. Everything else is stored digitally now – easier to hide, easier to work with, and much easier to destroy in turn *should the need arise.*

As for the tapes you are now listening to, that was Lisa's idea: "what happens if you try this thing and it makes you forget everything that's happened to you?" Even if we do get it working, it's always been wildly experimental. I'd hate to end up with a few psychoses for my trouble. I don't even know whether I want to try yet, but I'd like a record of my experiences in case I do. And that's not the only possibility. If someone else figures out a way to build their own machine, they might decide to put me through it again.

Lisa's Dictaphone has given me that record. It's not just insurance - it's helped me to get things straight in my head. I've been living my half life for a matter of months now, but it's going to take a lot longer before things start feeling normal. If they ever do.

I'm not entirely sure what I'll do with these tapes – if my brain gets fried again, I'll need them to learn who I am... or at least, who I have been this time around. Or then again, maybe I should make them public. Hello, public. I don't know whether you'll believe a word of all this and, frankly, I don't care. If it's known, even as a story, it might mean it never happens again. No more Amnesia Project. The people who funded and developed this technology are still out there, and I don't expect they will ever stand trial. Hopefully they'll think it lost for good and abandon the whole idea. Still, we're going to be careful for a while.

This is Rob Walker, signing off. Thanks for listening.

The End Of The Project

"Boss! Boss!"

Henry Ford looked up from the laptop as Eddie came running. He still knew nothing about cars, but he knew about good writing, and the drivel on the screen wasn't it. No-one was going to take this story seriously. Still, this was only the first of a dozen new submissions this morning. At least one of them was bound to be good.

But even reading this tosh was a welcome change from journalism. Henry wondered whether he should have switched to publishing fiction years ago - it was much less hassle, and usually more believable.

"Boss! It's arrived!"

"What's arrived, Eddie?"

"It's a tape! It's the last tape!"

There was also a note. Henry put the tape to one side as he read the short message: *Here you go, guys - a tape in the post, just like old times. Now you can finish the story. R, L and M.*

"So this is it," he said. "The end of the Amnesia Project."

As it was, he'd have to change the names and fudge the descriptions. But at least he wouldn't have to find a publisher for it.

He took the tape player out of his desk drawer. It had been carefully set aside, it felt so long ago now, for this very tape. "Stay and listen with me, Eddie," he said. "Let's hear how our story ends."

He pressed play, and a familiar voice began to speak.

I awoke with a start and a headache. The sunlight hurt my eyes and I could hear music playing in the distance. There were some painkillers and a bottle of water on my bedside table, and I immediately took advantage of them to ease the throbbing in my skull. It wasn't until a little later that I wondered who'd had the foresight to put them there.

I was in bed, in a cheap motel somewhere. I was alone. My watch on the bedside table told me it was just past nine in the morning. But which morning? I'd lost all sense of what day it was. I also had no idea where I was. But, most disconcerting of all, I couldn't remember who I was.

I started off with a shower – the facilities were little more than adequate. Wherever I was, it was cheap and functional. I found a set of clothes – my own, I guessed, as they fit me well – and looked around the room for any clues. It was largely empty. There was a bible in one of the bedside drawers, but I doubted that would tell me anything, and a cardboard advertisement for a "breakfast in a box", which looked decidedly unappetising. I decided to skip breakfast for the time being.

The only items of note were in my trouser pockets. My wallet contained a quantity of cash, but no identification. This struck me as odd. Had I been robbed? But why take the cards and not the cash?

It also contained a scrap of paper. A telephone number was written on it. No name, no details.

I had a mobile phone in my other pocket. It took me a couple of minutes to figure out how to operate it – had I forgotten this along with my identity? I thought this was unlikely. I had worked the shower, tied my shoes and read my wristwatch without even needing to think about it, so my amnesia probably didn't affect my kinaesthetic or my unconscious memory. That suggested the phone was not mine. And that suggested a very strange robbery indeed. What kind of robber would steal your credit cards but leave you cash and a phone?

With nothing else to do, I called the number.

"Hello, Robert speaking."

"Hello, Robert," I said. "This may sound silly, but... do you know who I am?"

"That depends. Where did you get this number?"

"It was on a scrap of paper in my wallet."

"Okay." Robert paused. "Do you remember your name?"

"No."

"We were afraid this might happen. Your name is Dr Charles Johnson. You were visiting me regarding a paper I'm writing."

"A paper? A thesis?"

"You remember?"

I thought for a moment. "No. But it sounds right."

"You've been in an accident, Dr Johnson. Delayed onset amnesia was always possible. Are you otherwise okay?"

"I think so. I don't seem to have any injuries. Robert, where am I?"

"You were going to stop in Reading on your way back to the university. Does that sound familiar?"

"No, but this looks like a hotel room. It could be anywhere."

Robert laughed. "Those places are pretty soulless, aren't they?"

"Wait a moment," I said. I rummaged through some papers on the bedside table and located a booklet of hotel information. "Here we are. I am apparently in a hotel in Reading."

"We're not far away from you – ask at the desk for a taxi. I'll give you the address – have you got a pen handy?"

There was a pen in my shirt pocket. "Yes," I said. There was a notepad marked "suggestions" on the room's desk, and I tore a sheet from there. "Go ahead."

Robert gave me an address in a place called Pangbourne – I didn't recognise the name, though the taxi that took me there had no problem with it – and promised we'd speak more when I arrived.

Charles Johnson. The name didn't feel at all familiar to me. I am Charles Johnson, I thought to myself. Charles Johnson, Charles Johnson. I said it over and over in my mind, wanting to make it stick, wanting something I could hold onto. I still do sometimes, usually when nervous. People tend to find it an endearing quirk, or think of it as some form of mantra. Perhaps they're right.

I left the Travel Hotel – for that's what it was – with a sense of relief. It was a little too grim for my liking. The young man on the front desk arranged for a taxi with considerable disinterest, and I had a short and tedious wait in the reception area until it arrived. I spent the time trying to remember who I was, what I did, how I got here. I had no memory of an accident. I had no memory before that morning.

I asked the young man whether I had booked the room. Apparently I had, paid in cash, checking out this morning. Or at least, someone had booked in my name. My still unfamiliar name.

The taxi was not entirely clean and was in good need of an airing. I tried not to breathe too much during the journey, which was thankfully not too long. I looked out the window and hoped to see something familiar. I did not. I was a stranger to this place, or at least I was now.

It was thus something of a surprise to me when we pulled up at a house and the driver told me we'd arrived. I took a couple of notes out of my wallet and told him to keep the change. Once I'd got out, he turned the car around and drove back the way he'd come. I was alone out here.

I looked at my piece of paper. Number 33. There was nothing else to do but knock on the door and see what Robert could tell me about myself.

The door was opened by a young man in his early thirties. His shirt was untucked and his feet were bare. Beneath a shock of ginger hair, one eye was contused and slightly swollen, but the other was bright and alert. Whatever trouble he'd been in, the grin on his face suggested it was all behind him.

"Are you Robert?" I asked.

The young man shook his head. "No," he said. "I'm Max. Rob's inside. Is he expecting you?"

"I'm Dr Charles Johnson," I said. Those words still didn't feel natural yet.

"Come in," he said. "I'll get the kettle on."

He led me to a slightly sagging black leather sofa in the living room. A television in the corner, the volume muted, showed images of some unknown game show. I sat watching for a few minutes, wondering if I might recognise it, whilst Max headed to the kitchen to make tea and find Robert.

"Dr Johnson?"

I looked up to see Max had returned with another man in tow. This could only be Robert, I assumed, and I was proven correct.

"Dr Johnson, I'm glad you found us okay. How are you feeling?"

"I have a slight headache. Physically I feel fine, but I have no memory of any events before I woke up this morning. This is a little... disconcerting."

"I understand." Rob paused to take one of several mugs from a tray Max had brought in. Max offered me the tray and I took a mug at random. I didn't really want anything to drink but felt it polite.

"You said I'd had an accident?" I asked.

"Yes," said Robert. "You were coming here to see me about a paper I'm writing.

This is going to sound crazy, but I wanted your opinion, as an expert on psychology, on whether it was possible to cause amnesia in a patient."

"And then I develop it myself. Your method clearly works."

Robert laughed. "The car accident did that, Dr Johnson. I can't recommend it as a reliable method, I'm afraid. The seatbelt took most of the force but I think you took a nasty blow to the head."

"That might explain the headache. How did I end up in the hotel room?"

"Delayed reaction," he replied. "You were a little groggy, but you seemed otherwise okay. You said you'd book a room and get the train in the morning. I wasn't really expecting you to call this morning."

"And why do I apparently have no cards or identification on me?"

"We're not sure," said Max. "We came as soon the hospital called us, but we think someone took your things at the scene of the accident. We've arranged for replacements – they should be arriving in the next few days, I'd imagine – but in the meantime we gave you some cash to tide you over and an old mobile phone in case of emergencies. I'm glad we did, now."

"Dr Johnson," asked Robert, "does the Amnesia Project sound familiar to you?"

I thought for a moment. "No, I don't think so. It sounds like a science fiction novel. Why do you ask?"

"It's just something I'm working on. I'm researching amnesia sufferers, looking for common experiences, techniques that help to treat it, that sort of thing. I'd appreciate your input on one particular case."

"Oh? Which case would this be?"

"Yours, of course," said Robert. "Will you stay a few more days, Dr Johnson? We'd like to keep an eye on you, make sure you're okay, and then make sure you get home safely."

"I'd be glad to," I said. And I was – I felt safe here, surrounded by people who seemed to know me. Out there I was lost and alone, with no idea where I should be or what I should be doing.

"That's great," said Robert. "Max, get in touch with Henry when you have a moment. Tell him Dr Johnson is going to help out with the project."

"He'll be glad to hear that," said Max.

"So what do you want me to do?"

All they wanted was an account of everything I could remember since my memory loss, and my thoughts now. I hope my input has given some benefit to Robert's project.

My account, as you have heard, was quite short. I have less than a day's worth of memories – more a journal entry than a full account – and I cannot say I am entirely happy about my state of affairs. I have no way to know as yet whether my memory will return – Robert and Max tell me that every case is different, and I may recover part or all of my identity. Or none. I am prepared for this possibility, in so far as anyone can prepare for such a thing.

My doctorate is apparently genuine, though I cannot recall any details of it. I understand medical terminology, and I agree with Robert's opinion that my amnesia was probably caused by cerebral ischaemia, though neither of us can come up with a course of treatment. I have taken up a new research position at the nearby university and I find the work comfortably familiar.

I have no past. My future is uncertain. Yet, somehow, I feel at peace. I feel as though some great weight has been lifted from my heart, yet I have no idea what this could be. Meanwhile, I've come to a simple conclusion – I may not know who I was, but what counts is who you are here and now.

I'm sorry, that last part sounded terribly trite. Should I start again?

THE END

Appendix - I Feel I'm Falling

This song, referenced several times in the above text, is actually the work of musician, artist and long time friend, Mark Sheeky. Aside from a gift for music, there is very little resemblance between him and Max. No tune exists for this song at the time of writing, but the lyrics are reproduced below. Thank you, Mark, for letting me use them.

I Feel I'm Falling

(Copyright Mark Sheeky, 2007)

We were climbing so high

from a misty sunrise morning,

and together we lie

like the fog on this day dawning.

I see you in the trees.

Are you looking at me?

I feel I'm falling.

I feel I'm falling.

I feel I'm falling,

and when I look up I see you.

I see you from afar

where the air is clear as water.

Tiny people and cars

friends and visions of our daughter.

All are dots in the grass.

Safe and warm in the past.

I feel I'm falling.

I feel I'm falling.

I feel I'm falling,

and when I look up I see you.

Now I'm swimming alone

in a lake of cold reflection.

I see you in our home.

I see me and see a question.

When I sleep will I drown?

Should I stay or dive down?

I feel I'm falling.

I feel I'm falling.

I feel I'm falling,

and when I look up I see you.

Want more? Sign up at the link below to get your FREE book:

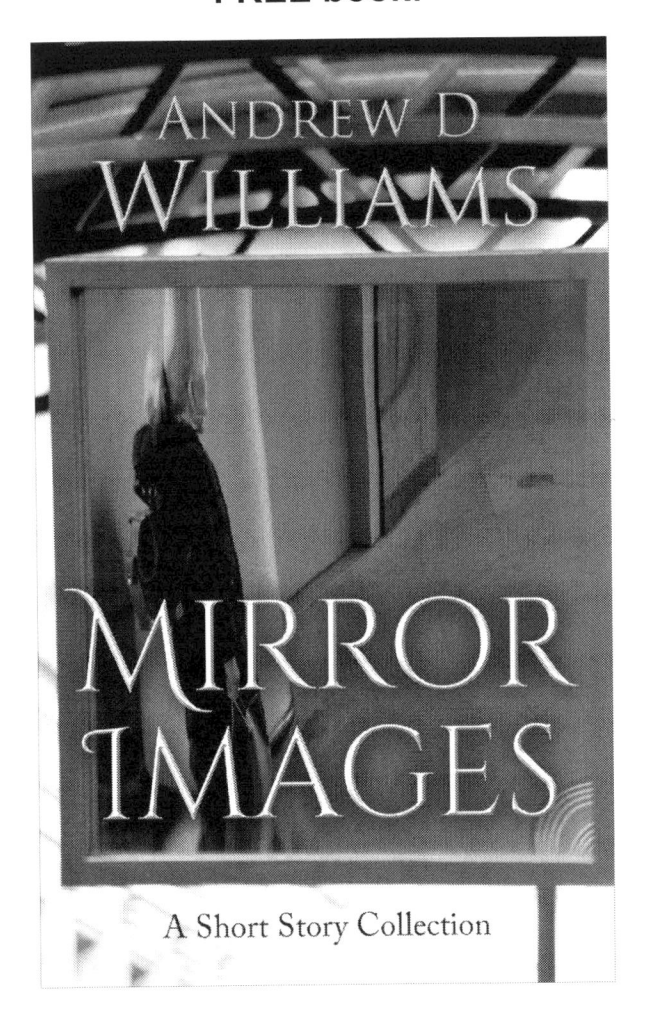

http://andrewdwilliams.co.uk/get-your-free-book/

About the Author

Andrew D Williams was born in Bedfordshire, England. He writes psychological thrillers with a tinge of science fiction to them. Writer, proofreader, computer technician and part time philosopher, he is now convinced that the meaning of life probably revolves around chocolate, cats, or both.

Andrew's writings are intended primarily to entertain - what else are stories for? Along the way, they seek to explore and question those things we take for granted - who we are, why we do the things we do, whether there really is such a concept as good and evil, or even the nature of reality itself. Aiming to excite, amuse and make you think in equal measure, you might want to read them again straight away.

For the latest news and promotions, sign up here:

Author website: www.andrewdwilliams.co.uk

Printed in Poland
by Amazon Fulfillment
Poland Sp. z o.o., Wrocław